A REDISCOVERED FAITH

BOOK 2 • FAITH REIMAGINED SERIES

J. A. BOUMA

EmmausWay
PRESS

To "Calvin"
For helping me rediscover my faith

CHAPTER 1

"WHOEVER SAID '*The road to Hell is paved with good inten-tions*' should be shot," Peter Daniel Young mumbled, trying to focus on the yellow center lines of the highway taking him back home.

Because thanks to his genius insight, I'm screwed.

Peter scowled as sheets of blurry rain cascaded down his windshield.

"Seminary, pretty good intention," he continued ruminating. "Returning back to my fundamentalist roots, definitely Hell on Earth!"

A bolt of lightning flashed in the far-too-close foreground followed by a deafening clap of thunder, eliciting a domino effect of brake lights up ahead. Peter slowed on cue, his past-due brake pads grinding in response.

"Training to be a pastor," Peter continued, "good intention. Doing so under the watchful eye of my conservative, fundie, backwater parents...Hell!"

Peter's twentysomething angst continued to mount as traffic returned back to its original crawling pace.

"Reimagining the Christian faith to win souls for Jesus in a culture that's said 'Thanks, but no thanks!'—the best intentions possible!" Peter crescendoed in sync with his accelerator. "Doing so while being accused of going 'liberal,' of compromising the faith by said conservative, fundie, backwater parents...Sheol. Gehenna. Hades!"

The rain was angry that afternoon, perhaps only outmatched by Peter's own irritation. As he weaved his way north along highway 23 through Ann Arbor, he wondered if his car would survive the barrage. Already one of the windshield wipers quit working. Thankfully, it was on the passenger side.

"Of course it's raining," Peter murmured. "How fitting."

He wiped a bead of sweat weaving its way down his forehead across his right temple. His hatchback was born in an era when air-conditioning was considered a luxury add-on. And because of the onslaught, the windows were rolled tight, creating conditions far more suitable for his mother's petunias than his current expedition back home. He took the shirt he shed at the start of the deluge and tried to wipe the fog away, managing to clear a hole in his perspiring windshield.

By now he had lost his parents, Danny and Maggie, several miles back. He hoped they were managing alright in this deluge, especially since they were carting every one of his earthly possessions. The drive was going relatively well up until they crossed the Michigan border, which was when the universe decided to unleash what seemed like a summer's worth of rain.

Again, fitting.

The past few days had been a churning cauldron of emotions and activity, filled with packing, and saying his goodbyes—to friends, to mentors, to the students he spent two years pouring himself into in his campus ministry, even the ministry coworkers who abandoned him when he needed them most. After five years working and living in one of the most powerful cities in the world it had been an emotional roller-coaster severing ties to a place he had planted firm, deep roots. It had become home.

Now Peter was that much closer to the place he fled years ago, a place he vowed he would never again return. The place he had once called home.

And yet here he was. Going back home again.

"Is that what I'm calling it now? Is that what it is, home?" Peter stared ahead, trying to make out a path between the raindrops and fogging windshield.

Home had always been an interesting word for Peter. While he had a generally pleasant upbringing, he had long ago disconnected from those people, that place. In fact, Peter found it difficult to attach to any people or place. Although for the first time he'd finally let himself become attached to DC, which made the cross-country move that more unbearable. Yes, he loved his mom, dad, and two brothers. But West Michigan wasn't exactly attachable. Especially, Coopersville—good old "Salad Bowl City" as he used to call it. It represented everything Peter had worked so hard to progress beyond: from rural rut to high-brow urban living; conservative politics to progressive social action; even more conservative Christianity to a far more progressive faith. And every wiper blade swish ticked by the moments when he was that much closer to the abyss that would become his home once more for his three-year journey preparing to personally lift the American Church from the edge of cultural irrelevance.

Burr Burr blasted the horn of the semi Peter nearly sideswiped.

"Are you kidding me?" Peter blasted back. He swerved back into his lane, but overcorrected. His wheel barely found purchase on the slick, puddled shoulder, the rumble-strips telling him to focus as he brought his car back to his lane.

"Focus, Peter." He slapped both cheeks, raked a hand through his sweaty thick hair, then turned on the radio.

Some new rocker chick was performing a newfangled power ballad on a local top-40 station. He was more of a bottom-40 kind of guy, preferring indie post-rock numbers, so he kept searching before settling on the local NPR station.

"In Michigan news, the state unemployment rate hit another historic high at the close of July, cresting over 14%. Over 600,000 people are now unemployed in the State of Michigan, marking a significant milestone in the so-called Great Recession."

"Just great," Peter sighed as state highway 23 connected with west I-96. "Remind me why I'm moving back to this Godforsaken state?"

Regret returned as he reminded himself why he was doing what he was doing: the Church.

Moving back home to train to be a pastor was a long time coming, actually. As a child Peter would play pastor like most boys played any number of childhood heroes: firefighter, police officer, teacher. Not Peter. He was more content preaching to his stuffed-animal congregation than chasing backyard bad guys. This early interest in God's work blossomed into a full-grown field of flowers in high school when he joined his church's jail ministry at Coopersville Baptist Church. At sixteen he could preach a mighty fierce sermon, strong enough to set a few convicts down the straight and narrow. This wasn't fire and brimstone, mind you. But it was the type of preaching that could only come from Christian fundamentalism.

His wasn't the fundamentalism of the 1920's or 30's. This was a milder, more respectable variety. Going to movies, playing cards, and dancing were tolerated. Though swearing was a big no-no, his parents must have missed that part of the handbook— both Danny and Maggie had quite the potty mouth. In fact, euphemisms were as big a no-no, like shoot, darn, crap, and heck. Guitars and jeans on Sunday? Not so much. And anything outside of hymns or the occasional praise chorus from a careful selection of 1970's and 80's praise songs was strictly prohibited. While the preaching was interesting, it was nothing less than a hour-long gold-mining operation in search of the 'nugget of truth' from the only version of the Bible that God ever blessed, anointed, ordained: the King James Version.

It's no small wonder that Peter felt compelled, beckoned, wooed to preach some day. Boys were bred that way. Yet Peter chose a different path, one almost as opposite as preaching, yet on the same spectrum of societal indifference: Politics.

They say there are two things in life you should never talk about, politics and religion. He was never all that popular at parties; Peter broke that rule with abandon. Though he disappointed his parents by not majoring in Bible, Peter chose the next best thing. He majored in Government with all of the passion and gusto of an eighteen-year-old right-wing political activist. He was going to place his Jesus-shaped mark on culture and storm the gates of the White House to take back America for Christ. And what better place to study than at one of the prime Christian institutions of White House gate-stormers, Freedom University.

Freedom is a college plucked straight from one of those campy Thomas Kinkade print paintings. It's as if a perpetual shimmery glow hovers just above the picturesque, quaint town of York, Pennsylvania, precisely because of the well-behaved, well-bred—and well-heeled—college students plucked from legions of mostly homeschooled children. Girls glide gracefully across the quad in dresses and skirts; this is a no-slacks zone. Boys, with close-cropped hair and noose-like ties, dutifully open the doors for said girls. While most of the girls will eventually play second-fiddle to the Freedom boys they eventually marry, everybody studies to prepare as if the future of America depends on it. They're bred that way.

Though he was only homeschooled in elementary—he and

his brothers strained their mother's patience to the breaking point —Peter found himself a home at Freedom. The school's founder and president even took him under his wing, treating him like the son he never had. Under his mentorship, Peter was encouraged to abandon his pursuit of the pulpit in favor of the political bullpen; he came in a pastor and left a politician.

After graduating, Peter did the only thing anyone with a B.A. in Government could do: he up and moved to Washington, DC. His parents couldn't have been more thrilled. "Little Petey is going to peck his way through the wall of separation between church and state and take back America for Jesus!" they would say to their friends.

Peter had always hated his nickname, a play off of his initials P. D. for Peter Daniel. But he liked the idea of taking back America for Christ. And if he was honest, he liked the idea of pecking his way to the top—power and position had always been a weakness of his.

So with a thousand bucks in his pocket, ambition in his belly, and a U-Haul trailer filled with every one of his earthly possessions, he and his parents set off four years ago in their family's aging, sagging Plymouth Voyager to the Promised Land. Within months he landed a gig on the staff of the majority leader in the House of Representatives.

It was Peter's dream job. He had plenty of influence on policy, gained exposure to lots of interest groups, and worked for a Christian Member of Congress. He had power, position, and a clear opportunity to peck, as his mother would say.

Yet here he was—a pocket full of brilliant intensions heralding his way back home again.

A book full of plot points had been sketched between that first trip nearly five years ago and this rain-soaked one now. Those memories were a mixture of vinegar and honey—sweet and sour memories, for sure.

Interrupting his trance back in time, the low-fuel light begged for his attention, and so did his bladder. Thankfully, the next exit would relieve both, and just as this dreadful storm began to wane.

PETER PULLED into a local gas station along I-96. It was a mom-and-pop joint with only two pumps: one for diesel, one for unleaded. An anti-corporate streak still lingered from his days in DC, so he pulled into the small-town pump over the national one next door. He got out and put his shirt back on to refuel his car and relieve his bladder. Afterwards he picked up a packet of sunflower seeds and a bottle of mineral water, two longtime obsessions. When he stepped outside, Peter was surprised to see that his parents had just pulled up behind his Honda. He rushed through the convenience door as his dad began pouring diesel into his Chevy Silverado.

"Hey, I thought I lost you," quipped Peter as he strolled up to his mother's window. "What happened?"

"You know your father. Never one to actually go the speed limit," replied Maggie in that tone familiar since childhood, her blond curls bouncing with emphasis.

"Maggie, it was like the days of Noah out there!" bellowed Pete's dad from behind the truck in a rough, grainy voice with a harsh Midwestern accent, a tough man with an equally tough gut extending over his belt. "I thought the Ark itself was gonna go rolling right down 23. So, Pete, how did that Honda of yours hold up under all that rain?"

"Well, Dad, it's not a GM, so it held up pretty darn well," Pete replied.

"What, your dad's company ain't no good for you?" Danny shot back with a scowl that had etched his leathery face with years of harsh labor on the assembly line.

"Well, I'm pretty sure it's not your company anymore—"

"Oh, would you boys stop!" Maggie interrupted, shaking her fist out of her window. "We've got another hour to go, so get your gas and get a move on!"

Danny huffed off to go pay, looking dejected. Maggie leaned out of her window to address Peter. "Why'd you have to go there? GM. Why'd you have to go there?" She didn't wait for a reply, rolling up her window and putting her seatbelt back on as Peter stood outside.

He slinked back to his car, his ears burning and stomach turning. In the past few years his dad had begun to disapprove of Peter's choices. And for Peter's dad, his car seemed to symbolize how far gone he'd gotten. He also felt like a royal jerk. A year ago, GM announced the closing of Dad's stamping plant, the Grand Rapids Metal Center. After two decades on the line, he was sacked along with over 1,200 others. It was supposed to have taken until the end of next year to finalize the closure. It didn't, and Danny was laid off at the start of the year. Since then, he'd been out of work nearly ten months. Peter knew it, too. He used his dad's pain to strike a blow. And it worked, driving the wedge that much deeper between them.

Peter slammed his car door, letting a curse slip as he hit his steering wheel with both palms. He didn't bother waiting for his parents. He rolled down his window and sped out of the mom-and-pop joint, spitting gravel and dirt in his wake.

CHAPTER 2

"HOW DOES HE DO IT?" Peter huffed in frustration. "How does he get into my head? Why do I *let* him get inside my head?"

As he merged back onto I-96 the angry hornets returned in kamikaze sheets, as if he'd disturbed the universe with his bitter swipe at his father.

"Just great," he moaned as he rolled his window back up.

For most of his life, Peter had a great relationship with his father. A fantastic relationship, actually. He had always felt his dad was interested in his life. Dad and Mom both gave him tremendous support and lots of freedom to try a number of different things. Though his three-week stint as a tuba player in sixth grade was short lived, his dad paid the one-month rent with glee. Though he favored drama, rather than sports like his father, his parents faithfully occupied row 3, seats A and B, camera in tow. Unlike most of his guy friends, he had been close to his dad. Until the last few years, that is.

Two years ago, Peter had what experts have begun to call a 'quarter-life crisis,' that angsty stretch of self-doubt, self-discovery, and self-reimagination—much like a fortysomething might experience in the middle of a ho-hum marriage and stalled career, just twenty years early. But this was slightly different in that, just a year out of college, Peter already was contemplating his existence and doubting his purpose in life.

At twenty-three, he started work for a campus ministry after his year on Capitol Hill as a congressional staffer. Washington jaded him more than he could have imagined, and it tested him like the furnace fires of a power plant. He came in with high, idealistic hopes of putting his mark on government—all for Jesus, of course. Only, after a year of working as a legislative assistant, Peter thought that wall his parents expected him to peck through should be buttressed, guarded, and preserved at all cost. From his perch in politics, he saw the seedy underbelly of the intersection of Church and State, how the government uses the Church like a two-bit whore for its own powerful ends, and how the Church willingly whores herself to both political parties for a place at table. Democrats and Republicans alike skipped with adulterous abandon, nearly tripping over each other to prove how talented they were in bed. So Peter the Idealist danced the dance of the caterpillar, slowly emerging into Peter the Cynic.

After a particularly painful episode, he bailed and found himself journeying back, full circle, into ministry, working as a campus minister at Georgetown University. Each day, he met with students for Bible study and discipleship, and prayed with struggling students. It was a welcome relief from the frenetic pace and freak-show carnival of Capitol Hill. But it also brought with it an entirely new set of problems, ones almost worse than the whoring he witnessed between Church and State.

As a campus minister, he dove deep into the life journeys of his students, especially their spiritual journeys. The only problem was, the Christian fundamentalism of his childhood that was supposed to have equipped him for ministry was itself ill equipped to deal with people's journeys. He loved the privilege of walking with people, but was often stumped by how to best serve and care for that stuff. Along the way, he began to face the fact that his own faith was massively out of step with the rest of the world. And that led Peter to question his own journey and beliefs.

Of his theology and spirituality, beliefs and practice, Peter questioned it all. Nothing was off limits. And this concerned more than a few people, particularly his parents. He made his mom cry after she put two and two together that he voted for a Democrat for president. His father accused him of being a liberal backslider, the single highest insult in his neck of the Christian woods. Not only was Peter a *backslider*—someone who had slid backward from someone else's list of dos and don'ts—he was a *liberal* one at that. It was as if Peter had transformed into the seven-headed dragon from the book of Revelation. Somehow voting for a Democrat, drinking beer, smoking a pipe, and questioning six-day creationism revoked his Christian creds. In their minds, he was suspect. Still their son, but a suspected son, which was no good place to be.

It all started with an organization called Prosurgent, which launched what had become known as Prosurgence Christianity, a group of disaffected evangelical pastors dreaming of an alternative movement to connect the Christian faith to the changes taking place in the twenty-first century. They were revolutionaries as much as missionaries, seeking to help believers rise from the ashes of post-Christendom. Hence the name Prosurgent, a mash-up of two Latin words, *pro-* for "forward" and the verb *surgere*, meaning "to rise." Provoking the traditional Church to rise for the sake of the faith was their mission.

They took for themselves the emblem of the ancient phoenix, the mythic desert bird that cyclically regenerates itself from the ashes of its predecessors every five hundred years. It was a tangible icon to represent this rising Church movement. For them, this symbol best represented their hopes and dreams for a reimagined Church. Not only because of the cyclical nature of the Church itself—which regenerated itself every five hundred years—but because early Christianity embraced the phoenix to represent the resurrection, the bringing of new life.

The phoenix symbolized the prophetic, almost revolutionary mantel Prosurgent leaders adopted, believing they were joining the ranks of other Church leaders over the past two millennia who shifted the Christian faith forward. Every five hundred years or so, the Western Church and culture had gone through a time of rebirth, a period of ecclesiastical renaissance. There was the collapse of the Roman Empire during the fifth century, which had wide-ranging implications for all of the Western world, including the end of the classical era of Christianity and the transition to monasticism and medievalism. Five hundred years later saw a bitter division between the Eastern and Western churches, known as the Great Schism. And then, of course, the Great Reformation in the 1500s gave rise to Protestant Christianity and all of its variations apart from Rome.

It was under the inspiration of these protestors that Prosurgent arose at the dawn of the twenty-first century, rising out of the ashes of a disintegrated Western Church and postmodern, post-Christian culture. Its pioneers were three evangelical pastors, Bryan McLaughlin, Dale Pagels, and Trevor Bohls.

Bryan pastored an innovative so-called "postmodern church" just outside of Washington, DC. He had become something of a grandfather figure to the Prosurgent movement after his first book *A Reimagined Christian* catalyzed a broader conversation about Christianity at the turn of the millennium. The book followed the journey of one fictional pastor out of fundamentalism and into the lonely, uncharted territory Prosurgents themselves were exploring. It gave a new generation the permission to question the faith that had been handed to them, while charting a course forward into new Christian territory. He sought to better connect the Christian faith to the twenty-first-century world by reimagining and redefining what it meant to be a Christian in the first place.

Dale Pagels, a pastor in Minneapolis, followed up this watershed moment with another book of his own, *A Christian Faith Worth Believing*. Where Bryan fictionalized a tale of reimagining, Dale personalized it by describing his own journey and the questions he'd been asking for years, yet was too afraid to voice. He also offered alternative answers to traditional questions traditional Christianity had given for centuries.

Both Dale's book and Bryan's drew heavy criticism from the standardbearers of the Christian faith, which drew people like Peter all the more closely to the movement. He figured if crusty, traditional Christian voices whom he felt were out of touch with the changing world had issues with Prosurgent, then it was definitely the place for him. So he devoured their books and attended their conferences. He even joined the local DC chapter of the organization with the desire to connect this movement to his work with college students, while also helping him reconnect to a faith that began to flicker and fade in his own life.

But one evening Peter made a crucial mistake: he mentioned the group to his father over Christmas break. He had hesitated bringing it up, given that his parents and childhood church members were precisely the kinds of people to whom Prosurgent was reacting. His father erupted in a holy panic. Weeks later, he broached the subject again in another heated phone call, saying just that Sunday a traveling preacher had spoken on the heretics and heresy of Prosurgence Christianity. The call ended when Peter abruptly slammed his flip-phone shut, cracking and sending it flying across his bedroom in two pieces. Their relationship had never been the same since.

Peter's painful trip down the overgrown, bramble-strewn path of memory lane was interrupted by the welcome sight of the Grand Rapids skyline, if you can call it that. Grand Rapids isn't like other trendy cities, but it had come into its own over the past decade, transforming from a sleepy Midwestern rust bucket to an emerging, hip metropolis. The sight quickened his pulse. It was a big, fat neon sign that announced his arrival back home.

PETER STARTED POPPING sunflower seeds and took a swig of his mineral water.

They have good coffee here. And beer.

Peter sidestepped the normal I-96 bypass around Grand Rapids toward Coopersville in favor of a view-soaking experience of his new home.

Construction cranes hovered over a city that was once known as the furniture capital of America. Over time, and with the help of several benefactors, those former furniture manufacturing plants, warehouses, and shops had given way to loft apartments and condos, a number of coffee shops and restaurants, banks and business, and a surprising art scene that had begun to rival other more established metropolitans. Medical Mile, the stretch of medical facilities and research institutions that breathed new life into the city, emerged on his left. In the distance, DeVos Place towered above the city as an ode to one of Grand Rapids's main benefactors, Richard DeVos, the same guy who made billions through his Amway corporation. Peter found himself smiling as he drove farther into his new city's heart, wondering what surprises and opportunities it held for him.

As Peter breathed in the sights of his new home, he followed the serpentine Grand River north onto highway 131 to make the final leg to where he'd be living for the next few years, his parent's house. Making his way out of the city, he flipped the radio to one of his DC presets, which happened to connect to a West Michigan Christian radio station.

"...listening to family-friendly 91.5 WXAN. If you're just joining us, you're in for a real treat. Today we have with us one of the leading Christian thinkers on the issue of faith and science, Dr. Alfred Morris."

Peter's heart faltered, nearly tripping over the next beat. "Freddy Morris? Are you kidding me?" Peter bellowed at the radio announcer, turning up the volume. "Leading Christian thinker, my butt."

The announcement smarted a still-fresh memory, like a squirt of peroxide on an open wound. Last November his ministry had invited Freddy to debate a well-known local DC progressive evangelical on the topic of science and faith, particularly creation. Let's just say the fallout in Peter's life was widespread. Not only did it affect his students, it was the inciting incident that later led to his journey back home again.

"...and is the president of *Creation Studies Institute* and the *Creation Museum*. Thanks for being with us this afternoon, Dr. Morris."

"Thanks for having me," replied the well-known creationist in a polished Aussie accent.

Peter jammed another preset to escape the Christian station, landing midway through a weekend top-40 countdown. After listening to the latest angsty boy band drone on about the dilemmas of young adulthood, Peter's interest in the Christian radio station was piqued.

"Let's see what I've been missing for few years," he murmured, turning back to WXAN.

"...absolutely absurd. And what's clear is that the real agenda of the scientific establishment is to replace God with the idol of scientific certainty."

"Mmm. Interesting, Dr. Morris," the radio announcer said approvingly. "What do you mean by that?"

"What I mean is that from the dawn of Darwin until now, the scientific community has been hellbent on destroying belief in God itself. And what better way to do that than by dismantling the very foundation of that belief in creation?"

"You've often used the illustration of a canon that's aimed directly at the foundation of a city—seeking to blow holes in the foundation. And that foundation is the reality of a Creator who fashioned the universe, particularly in six literal days."

"Exactly!" Freddy Morris responded. "The foundation of biblical Christianity is Genesis 1 and 2. That there is a Creator who created the universe—a Creator we're responsible to, that we've sinned against, and that Christ came to save us from. By undermining belief in a Creator, scientists are undermining the cross itself. And what's worse is that Christian leaders are doing the very same thing! They are undermining the cross by challenging six-day creation that is clear biblical truth."

"Give me a break," Peter moaned, rolling his eyes.

"Now what do you mean by that? That Christian leaders are undermining the cross?" the radio announcer prodded.

"The majority of Christians in churches probably aren't sure whether God really created everything in six literal days. Many believe it doesn't matter whether it took six days or six million years. However, it is vital to believe in six literal days for many reasons. Foremost is that allowing these days to be long periods of time undermines the foundations of Scripture, which calls into question the message of the cross itself."

"Nice to see you're still riding the same rhetorical pony you trotted out at Georgetown, Freddy," Peter complained.

"So your argument, Dr. Morris, is that someone who doesn't believe in a six-day, literal creation of the universe, and teaches this, is undermining the cross of Christ itself?"

"Absolutely. The whole message of the gospel falls apart if one allows millions of years for the creation of the world. You cannot be a Christian unless you believe in six-day creationism."

And with that, Peter jammed the CD button on his stereo, summoning musical escape.

Shaking his head, Peter sneered, "Yep. Definitely back home." He rolled down his window to help him breathe, spending the next several miles jamming out to the latest Passion Pit album.

It was as if Peter had borrowed Dr. Emmett Brown's DeLorean from *Back to the Future* and taken it for a spin back a few generations. Since fleeing his childhood version of Christianity, Peter had forgotten that such wings of conservative Christianity still existed, even in mainstream venues like Christian radio stations. How exactly such venues continued to survive was beyond him.

As he reflected over Freddy Morris's comment, *You cannot be a Christian unless you believe in six-day creationism*, his gut tightened with apprehension. He remembered the same line from that fateful debate in DC, and now it was following him home. In the days leading up to the decision to move back home to pursue seminary, he was petrified of the fundamentalism that awaited him. Not merely from his family, but from his surrounding culture. DC was a free-range experience that permitted Peter to explore the boundaries of his faith, to truly own his beliefs in a way he had never before explored or owned. All without the debilitating pushback that often comes from conservative cultures. Like West Michigan.

That was about to change. And it freaked Peter out. And his serendipitous encounter with Freddy Morris wasn't helping his anxiety levels.

He began tapping nervously on the steering wheel in sync with the song "Little Secrets," working out his surging emotions.

Intuitively, he knew the creeping sense of dread had nothing to do with the blockhead he'd just dismissed. It was deeper than that. It was family deep. More specifically *parents* deep.

As a homeschooled kid, *Creation Studies Institute* formed the foundation to his elementary science education. And while he attended public middle and high schools when his mother had had enough and had to work, the version of the scientific story drilled into Peter carried him through the onslaught of an evolutionary scientific worldview. Danny and Maggie often proudly credited 'the fundamentals of the faith' with safeguarding Peter's faith through the typically taut teenage years. Those fundamentals were the bread and butter of Peter's Christian experience.

Little did they know that it was those same fundamentals—or rather the worldview and posture of *fundamentalism*—that carted Peter off the reservation of respectable Christianity, leading to his crisis of faith, near-abandonment of the Church, and quest to reimagine the Christian faith. Not to mention the continental rift in their relationship.

Peter cursed WXAN for dredging those feelings to the surface after having reconciled most of them before he had left for home.

Speaking of which, Peter thought as the strong, pungent smell of rotting garbage wafted into his car. He breathed deep his hometown air.

"Home sweet home," he exhaled as he passed the Ottawa County Farms Landfill, situated on the south side of Coopersville.

After exiting the highway, Peter made his way through the quaint downtown. Main Street bore witness to a simpler era, when neighbors whiled away the morning hours over grits and coffee; when family farmers raked in a sizable wage from an honest week's work; when church and faith sat squarely at the center of the small town's orbit. While small diners still existed, they struggled. While farmers sill farmed, they existed as consolidated corporate conglomerates. While churches still existed, they did so at the periphery. While Coopersville still existed, it did so as an also-ran, quaint cliché.

Peter's palms grew moist as he drew closer to home. Though he vowed he would never return, there was a piece of him that was just a bit happy to call this place home again. Lots of Young family memories stained the soil of this small town, though Peter couldn't decide if he was ready to unearth them.

Peter pulled into the only neighborhood he ever knew outside of Adam's Morgan in DC and slowly made his way to his parents' elaborate turn-of-the-century, restored Victorian home. It once belonged to the founder of Coopersville, Benjamin Cooper, a regional sawmill titan who harvested precious timber for the hungry furniture mills of Grand Rapids. Over a few decades, 640 acres of forests were reduced to farmland, one of the main industries of the four thousand-person town.

The house came into his parents' possession through random means. Three decades ago, Coopersville was on the verge of bankruptcy after being ravaged by the recession of the seventies, so city fathers sold one of the only things of value that they thought would plug the gap: their founder's house. The city council thought they'd be able to raise well into the six figures, but they didn't count on their own citizens being ravaged by the same recession that ravaged their town. Come auction day, twelve people showed up: the auctioneer, eight city council members, and Peter's parents holding newly born Petey. One of the council members tried to goose the sale by bidding along with Peter's parents to increase the sale price. Not only was this ethically shady, the councilman realized he might be stuck with the house himself. So he quickly abandoned his goosing mission. For $64,650, Peter's parents were proud owners of founder Cooper's home, leaving another half-million gap on town's ledgers.

Peter drove up to his parents' home, slowed to a stop, and sat in his idling car, like an apprehensive teenage boy mustering up the courage to walk up to his date's front door. Cooper Manor, as it was called, sat up on a hill on a modest plot of land overlooking the town's historic district, if you can call it that. Surrounded by a cluster of massive sycamore and maple trees, leftovers spared from Cooper's sawmills, the roof peaked sharply in the middle of the house and at the corners, accentuating the house's four turrets anchoring its corners.

The rain wound down to a drizzle. Peter sat still in his steamy, foggy hatchback, staring up at the large corner turrets peeking behind a canopy of aged sycamore trees, almost feeling mocked by the large eye-like house windows that peered back, as if they were daring him to come back to the place from which he'd fled.

"Am I ready for this?" Peter sighed.

He turned off his ignition and climbed out. "Too late. Here we go. I'm back again."

CHAPTER 3

"HEY, BRO!"

"JJ!" Peter exclaimed.

Johnny ran to greet his brother, hugging him in a full-on tackle.

"Dude, you can't do that anymore. I'm old." Peter bent over to catch his breath.

"Whatever. You're, like, twenty-six!" Johnny said as he slapped Peter on the back. "How was the drive?"

"It was fine. I was alone so it was fine," Peter smirked. "Hey, don't you start classes soon?"

"Yeah, next week Monday," he moaned. Johnny was the youngest of the Young brothers, an All-American, blue-eyed blond if there ever was one. He was beginning his freshman year at the local state college, Grand Valley State University, and starting as a quarterback on the JV football team.

The squeal of stopping breaks caught both of their attention as their parents pulled up to the curb at the base of the house. "Come on, let's get me moved in!" Peter said.

Cooper Manor became an anthill of action as the Young clan

moved boxes and clothes and books in perfect sync from the U-Haul to Peter's room on the second floor. Peter was to share the floor with JJ. He had mixed feelings about living with his younger brother, who differed in age by eight years. They got along as far as older and younger brothers get along. JJ looked up to Peter, but they were two different people on two different paths. This added layer complicated an already delicate living situation.

"I'm surprised that piece of crap made it all this way," his father jabbed as he huffed over to the trailer.

Peter ignored the taunt and simply replied, "Me too. This box goes upstairs." Peter shoved a box of books at his father, sending him stumbling backward. Peter grinned as he walked away.

By mid-afternoon, the Youngs had managed to transfer Peter's entire life from the trailer to his second-floor room. They hauled a bedroom set, more clothes than a twentysomething male should own, several book cases, several more boxes of books, his iMac and MacBook, CDs, and the other odds and ends that Peter had accumulated in his young adult life. While not a pack rat, Peter did have a knack for saving things he had attached any significant memory to, for whatever reason.

He still had shoeboxes of family pictures he'd taken as a young boy with his pre-digital camera. There was the ball he caught at the old Tiger Stadium after it bounced off his dad's head at a family outing. And then a stack of newspapers of the same *Washington Post* issue filled one box, the one where Peter had landed on the front cover after the 2008 presidential election shouting "Hope and Change"—the election where he made his mama cry. He held on to the stack for that reason alone.

By late afternoon, Peter was spent. A break was definitely in order. After attempting to bring some order to the chaos that had engulfed his room, Peter bounded down the stairs to raid the refrigerator. He walked into the kitchen in search of some relief and found his mother at the kitchen table nestled in the knotty pine-lined breakfast nook. He wandered over, a smile curling upward with delight at what he saw.

"No-bake cookies!" Peter said with wide-eyed hunger. "And sweet tea. I didn't realize how much I'd miss that leaving DC. Glad I have my Southern belle to keep that flowing." Peter kissed his mom on her head and on a stool at the kitchen island.

Unlike his relationship with his dad the past few years, he and his mom had something of an understanding through his journey of self-discovery. Though she was certainly set in her fifty-two-year-old ways, she at least tolerated Peter's journey to understand his faith.

Maggie, a short, trim woman with blond, non-nonsense curls and the attitude to match, was the daughter of a Southern Baptist preacher from the deep South—as in Georgia deep. His was a preaching that could shake the rafters and scare the hell out of not a few wayward parishioners. She always toed the family line when it came to issues of faith and rejected anything that might differ from the male-dominant hierarchy. As the youngest of five children with all older brothers, she was bred that way. When she married, she brought that submissive posture into the marriage, sacrificing her own perspective at the altar of male headship.

But after Peter began to go his own way over a year ago, she seemed to take an interest in that journey, albeit at arm's length. Though at times his journey frustrated her, his questions—even some of his answers—caused her to wonder whether her long-held answers to important questions of faith were adequate. Which caused not a few arguments in Cooper Manor.

"So when is James coming by?" Peter asked, finishing his third no-bake cookie. "Didn't you say he was joining us for dinner?"

Maggie got up, took Peter's empty plate, and mumbled, "Yeah, tomorrow," after hearing Danny coming down the stairs.

"Did I hear JT is coming to dinner tomorrow?" Danny asked as he walked into the kitchen. "On whose invitation?"

"Mine, Dad," Peter answered with an edge of indignation. "Is that a problem?"

Sensing a challenge, and weary from the drive, Danny retreated and walked outside for the last remaining boxes.

Peter's middle brother, James Thomas Young, also lived in the area but not at home, and for good reasons. He probably should be living at home given the way his life had turned out. Earlier in the year they tried it out, but neither he nor his parents lasted more than a few months.

James, or JT as he was called, is what people from Peter's childhood circles called a wayward child. At seventeen, James got a girl pregnant, which was the final straw after a series of missteps involving various tobacco and alcoholic products. Though James owned his so-called "mistake," his life fell apart after costing his Christian high school basketball team their state championship.

At just over six-feet tall, James was the team captain and star forward who had scored more points than any other player in the history of Coopersville Christian High, mostly thanks to his killer three-point power shots. But a captain of anything in a Christian high school, much less a *student* in a Christian high school, can't get a girl pregnant and still play ball, no matter how killer or crucial of a player he might be. So when news broke of James's extracurricular actives, he was suspended from the team. What made this event in the life of seventeen-year-old James especially precarious was that it came just as the Coopersville Crusaders were headed to the state finals. While they won their playoff game without JT's history-making power shot, the Farmington Hills Falcons routed them in the championship game by three points.

Oddly, his classmates were more forgiving than their hyper-reactive parents. For months, James endured the wrath of several irate parents who said things that'd make the Virgin Mary blush. Worst of all was the loss of crucial scholarships that would have allowed him to go to college. James was never a bright kid, not like Petey or Johnny. His chances at higher education were paved with three-point power shots and under-the-basket power blocks. Since that fateful experience six years ago, a life that could have been became radically diluted into a bitter solution of drugs, underemployment, bouts with depression, and a never-again relationship with the Christian faith.

It's one of the main reasons Peter was happy to be back home, for his brother. His brother had wasted away over the past few years, and Peter shouldered part of the blame. He had wished he could have done more to help steer his brother in a more positive direction. Often Peter thought that if he had been home instead of off at college or in Washington he could have stemmed the tide of life choices that had engulfed his brother. It was a major source of guilt that still haunted him. Peter hoped coming home would allow him to make up for lost time and have some sort of positive influence in James's life.

AS THE DAY MARCHED ON, Peter's room was beginning to look like a place he could live for the next three years. After arranging the last of his books, all meticulously alphabetized by author, he began smelling whatever it was Maggie was preparing for dinner.

Mmm, lasagna! Peter's stomach echoed his sentiments. Before long, Maggie was calling for Peter to join the family for dinner.

Behave, Petey, Peter thought as he bounced down the stairs.

His parents and Johnny were already seated at the table when Peter took his place. Danny prayed for the meal, thanking God for their safe trip. Then prayed for Peter: "Lord, we thank you for bringing Peter back home again, and we pray that you would bless his studies and his new life. In Jesus's name we pray. Amen."

"Amen," the family replied.

Peter attacked his dinner, having not eaten anything but sunflower seeds and no-bakes all day. He wished he had a glass of wine to go along with his pasta, though his parents were dry as a Prohibition-era bar. They made pleasant conversation about the drive and the move as they all devoured their dinner.

"So are you excited to see your old friends at your church on Sunday?" Danny asked, stuffing a fork-full of salad in his mouth.

Peter shrugged. "I guess. But they're really not my friends anymore. And Coopersville Baptist hasn't been my church for, like, eight years."

"Well, people are sure looking forward to seeing you on Sunday," Maggie offered. "And you can enjoy our newly reno-vated sanctuary, too. It's quite the upgrade from that drafty old one you grew up in, Petey. Pastor George has even started letting us sing with a guitar along with the piano and organ."

How nice of him, Peter thought. "Sounds nice, Mom, but I don't think you should plan on me on Sundays."

"What do you mean?" Danny asked, turning to Peter with a scowl.

"I mean, it'll be nice to go with you guys *this* Sunday, but I'm not planning on putting on my choir robe and just joining back in with CBC again. I've changed too much, I can't go back." Peter returned to his plate to concentrate on cutting another piece of lasagna.

"Of course not," his dad simply said. "Because you're better than that now, right?"

"Danny, that's not what Petey meant," Maggie said, trying to play interference for her son.

"Well what do you mean, Peter? Isn't that what the past few

years have been about? Finding something better than what you grew up in?"

Peter closed his eyes and breathed. "Dad, it has nothing to do with better. I'm sorry if you felt that's what I meant. I'm thankful for what I had growing up, but I can't go back. I just think differently now, that's all. Shoot, you did the same thing when you were my age! You had no problem leaving grandpa's and grandma's Reformed church. So what's the big deal?"

"I left that church because it was going liberal. And it seems like you are, too. That's what's the big deal!" Danny said, raising his voice.

Peter laughed out loud, "Liberal? Why because I don't believe in a six-day-literal creation? Or because I think those crazy end-times books are a bunch of BS? Or is it because I don't think the only people who should be able to teach in church are those who can pee standing up?"

"All the above!" Danny roared.

Peter just shook his head. He sighed, then said, "Look, it's not like I don't believe Jesus actually arose from the dead. It's not like I even believe in evolution. For my money, I don't see why God would need six billion years to create all this, let alone six days."

He took a breath, then continued, "I'm fine with what you and Mom believe. I'm not judging you. But I've lived and worked outside this Christian bubble long enough to know there is a whole world out there that thinks we are a freak show."

"Of course they do! They're lost," Danny interrupted.

"OK, fine. But that doesn't mean they aren't seeking. Seeking after something, anything, that makes sense of this screwed-up world. And what the current Church is offering—they ain't buying! I've had countless conversations with people who have seen what the Church has to offer and have said, 'Ummm...thanks but no thanks,' and have walked out the back door."

Johnny, who had been quiet this whole time, piped in. "Is that what you've said, Petey? Thanks, but no thanks?"

Forgetting their teenage son was party to their back-and-forth argument, Peter's parents both looked at Johnny and back at Peter again, worried about what his next words might be.

Surprised at his brother's question, Peter looked at JJ. "No, Johnny. I love Jesus. I love the Church. And I love this world. That's why I moved back home to go to seminary. But things have got to change. My friends want a faith that makes sense of this world, that connects to it. Shoot, I want a faith that does that!"

Peter continued. "I'm sorry—and I don't mean to offend you, Mom and Dad, but the faith we were given just doesn't work anymore. The answers we were given don't connect to the questions of my friends. And that's why I'm on a journey to try to reimagine the Christian faith. I need to for my friends. I need to for me."

Everybody sat in silence, picking at their plates. Maggy broke the silence. "I may not get this...this journey you're on, Petey. But I'm glad you still love Jesus and the Church, and that's good enough for me, darlin'."

She patted Peter's cheek and looked at her husband, glaring at him as if she were willing a positive response from him.

Trying to contain his frustration, Danny added gruffly, "Yeah, well, I don't get it either. Never have. But maybe we could talk more about this some more sometime."

Peter was content with that, just happy to have made it through dinner, and with a minor breakthrough with his parents.

"I'd like that, too. And who knows, maybe I'll like good ol' Coopersville Baptist again! I've heard they got some good coffee, so at least they've got that going for them." He winked and offered a wry grin then went to finish his dinner, thinking how much he was already regretting coming home again.

· · ·

AFTER DINNER, Peter spent the rest of the evening putting the final touches on his new life. His bedroom was a little bigger than his former loft apartment he had left behind. His favorite chair, a reupholstered wingback chair from Goodwill he got back in DC, was tucked away in the bay window sunk into the northwest turret. On another wall sat his 40" LCD TV, a Craigslist give-away couch sat in front. Behind the couch facing the other wall was his childhood roll-top desk that came with the house. Some said it was Benjamin Cooper's own, the one he used to make his deals and trade away Coopersville's forests. The remaining walls, every inch of them, were covered with bookcases and book shelves.

Peter prided himself on his book collection. It reflected the Renaissance man image he had carefully cultivated since college. There was a section devoted to the great American novelists, like Steinbeck and Faulkner. Modern philosophy dominated his shelves, ranging from the seminal communist Karl Marx to nihilist Friedrich Nietzsche, from French Romantic Jean-Jacques Rousseau to British philosopher Francis Bacon. He was eager to add to his shelves multiple volumes of biblical commentaries and flesh out his theology section more during seminary, which began next week.

Before retiring for the night, Peter made some peppermint tea and settled into his chair in the bay window. He opened his laptop and waited for it to boot. He looked outside and saw his car parked on the street below and shook his head.

I'm actually here, back home again.

A night-time runner ran past, taking his mind back to his old home and the nights he'd spend running throughout his neighborhood in Adam's Morgan or on the National Mall at sunset. A longing for what had been began to worm its way into desire. And yet he knew that chapter was closed for good—and *for* his good.

A login screen begged for Peter's attention. He typed in his password then opened his web browser in search of familiarity: the Prosurgent website. He typed in www.prosurgent.org and smiled. *Family.*

He browsed the latest blog posts. The second post caught his eye. It was written by one of his old Prosurgent friends from DC, Darren Thomas. He was something of a mentor to Peter, walking with him through his transition from fundamentalism into a more progressive Christian faith. He was there when Peter began questioning and doubting, there when answers were as fleeting as his own shadow, there when his ministry started asking questions— there when his life took a permanent turn.

"Oh Darren," Peter said, "I miss you, Brother!"

Darren's post called for reimagining the cross as less about "divine child abuse" and more as a "divine love gift." He argued the cross was not about violence but about loving example, and Jesus' command to take up our cross was meant as an instruction to take up his future example of love in the world.

"Spot on as always my man!"

He continued to scroll down through the blog before heading for what he really came for: the directory of Prosurgent "Oasis Groups," as they called them. These groups were cohorts of similarly like-minded people asking questions about their faith, and seeking to disrupt it through deliberate acts of theological deconstruction and reconstruction. Peter credited the Prosurgent DC chapter as saving his faith. He hoped there'd be a similar group in Grand Rapids to help it evolve even further.

And there was. *Prosurgent Grand Rapids, meeting at St. Marks. Led by Rob Beukema.*

"Definitely will check them out. Especially once seminary starts!"

He sent the information in an e-mail to himself for follow-up and closed his laptop.

After a very long car ride and an even longer day unpacking, Peter plopped down face-first in his childhood bed that his mom had freshly prepared for him earlier that day. He was bone tired, enough that he didn't bother to change his clothes. As Peter began to think about his new life, he rolled over and stared at the childhood paint chipping off his ceiling.

"God, I hope I didn't just make the biggest mistake of my life," Peter prayed as he sank into his pillow.

Sleep began to overtake him. He sat up and grabbed his liturgical prayer book he had earlier placed on his night stand next to his bed. He turned to his evening prayers.

After reciting the Apostles' Creed and the Lord's Prayer, he prayed through the evening compline prayer:

> *Most holy God, the source of all good desires, all*
> *right judgments, and all just works: Give to*
> *us, your servants, that peace which the world*
> *cannot give, so that our minds may be fixed on*
> *the doing of your will, and that we, being*
> *delivered from the fear of all enemies, may live*
> *in peace and quietness; through the mercies of*
> *Christ Jesus our Savior. Amen.*

Peace and quietness. Yes. Amen.

CHAPTER 4

THE DISTANT SOUND of chirping birds and rays of morning sun peeking through pulled curtains finally brought Peter out of a deep slumber. Normally he was an early riser, but after yesterday's drive and drama, Peter gave himself permission to leave the alarm unset.

Peeling back the covers, he arched his back to stretch the ache out of his muscles. He walked over to the bay window and parted the curtains. He stood looking, fully clothed from the day before, staring at his small, rusting hatchback, a tinge of doubt creeping up his back. He shivered and took a shower to wash away the regret that needled his mind in order to start the first day of his new life.

By the time he showered and dressed for the day, his mom had left to work her job as a teller at the local bank. Dad was who knew where—hopefully chasing down a good job lead—and Johnny was manning the only TV in the house as a sniper in some Xbox game.

"So what are your plans for the day?" Peter asked his brother before sinking his teeth into an apple.

Without breaking his concentration, Johnny replied "Michigan's Adventure," then blasted a Nazi armored unit to smithereens.

"Ahh. Well, have fun. I'm heading out."

Johnny grunted an "OK" as he killed some poor digital soldier.

Peter had a busy day ahead of himself. He needed to finalize class registration at the seminary; apply at a few coffeehouses, and land a part-time job in the process; and, of course, explore his new city. He made some coffee, buttered a toasted multigrain bagel, and headed out the door for a day he hoped would not disappoint.

As he walked to his car, Peter hoped the weather was an omen of good things to come. An all-day rain transformed overnight into a warm late-August Michigan afternoon. The sky was clear, the sun was a refreshing blanket of warmth that fed the full-bloomed neighborhood. He pulled out of the driveway and headed out of town toward what promised to be a good day.

After an easy twenty-minute drive rocking out to MGMT with windows rolled wide open, Peter arrived at Grand River Theological Seminary. The parking lot was mostly empty save a few cars near the faculty and staff entrance on the east side of the building. The building itself was unimpressive: functional cinderblock architecture from the seventies. As he parked he wondered if the program would be as old and out of date.

Relax, Peter. Drop the judgment until after you start.

Peter had chosen GRTS more because of divine intervention than anything else. After he left his ministry position in DC, he felt like seminary was the next logical step. He only applied to two places: Fuller Seminary, out in California, and Grand River Theological Seminary back home. He was accepted to both. He had every intention of moving to the other coast, but for some reason he couldn't shake this feeling that God was taking him back home. Peter had never been one to make decisions based on some subjective "God told me so" feeling—he was much too rational for that. Yet the more he prayed about his future and thought about moving to SoCal, the more he was beckoned to study in Grand Rapids. There was a moment when he felt as if a voice was telling him his pride would be the only thing driving his decision to choose Fuller over Grand River. He couldn't stomach the idea of coming home to a place he vowed he'd never return, of going back to a place from where he had changed so sharply. That he was now sitting in the parking lot of GRTS was surreal.

Peter walked into the main seminary building and made his way to the admissions office. It was as functional on the inside as it was on the outside—gray cinderblock walls, punctuated by plush couches and table-and-chair setups for group studies that tried to imbue the stale atmosphere with a dose of Starbucks ambiance. Six classrooms on either side lined the single hallway that stretched from the main gathering space to the faculty offices in the back, each housing long narrow tables and chairs enough for thirty students.

GRTS was a small, quaint seminary typical of the Midwest, yet commanded a decent roster of respected biblical scholars and theologians. There was an Anglican historical theologian; an Old Testament scholar famed for his archaeological work; a younger theologian who had already written several books and was part of the conservative Reformed movement, so Peter was sure they wouldn't get along; and a New Testament professor who had written a well-received commentary on the Gospel of Matthew. Though the seminary's roots were Baptist, it had shed that cloak for a nondenominational one a decade ago. Yet it was hard for Peter not to view the seminary through his lingering stereotype chiseled and hardened through the fires of his Baptist upbringing. Peter knew it was unfair of him. He was worried his progressive,

Prosurgent views of the Christian faith birthed in DC would not be welcomed at this mostly conservative school.

"Hi, I'm Peter Young, and I need to finish registering," he said to the admissions person staffed at the front desk.

"Great! Welcome to GRTS. My name is Nathaniel, and I can help you with that." Nathaniel dutifully shuffled through a desk drawer to retrieve a catalogue, course schedule, and course registration sheet. "So what's your program, Peter?"

"The Master of Divinity program. In church planting, I think."

"Great! Here are the available classes, but the first semester for M.Div. students is generally set in stone because of how intense the program is. You'll need Greek 1, Systematic Theology 1, Program Introduction, and then either Biblical Hermeneutics or Spiritual Formation. Do you have a preference?"

"Well, what's that spiritual formation class?"

"The class is meant to help familiarize you with historic spiritual disciplines, like fasting, silence and solitude, and Lectio Divina sacred readings. It will help you spiritually form other people, but it is also meant to help you as a student take better care of your own soul."

They teach Lectio? Peter thought. *Maybe I've underestimated this place!*

He chose the class on spiritual formation and finalized his registration. His new life felt far more real after having a list of classes to look forward to, and a list of books to buy and begin reading. Yet his chest felt tight, and his stomach churned; he was unsure how this school would accept him where he was in his spiritual journey, where he was in his theology. He thought he'd go for the question that had been haunting him since mailing in his deposit and setting course for home to ease his growing anxiety.

"Let me ask you a question," Peter interjected.

"Sure thing."

"So, I grew up here and moved away for a while and changed quite a bit from the faith I grew up with. You could say I'm Prosurgent, though I really don't like labels."

"OK."

"I guess what I want to ask is, how open is this place, really? Like if I write from my own perspective in tests and papers, from my Prosurgent perspective...will that be respected?"

A knowing grin slid across Nathaniel's face. "Basically you're asking if we're some right-wing fundie school."

"Well, yes!" They both chuckled.

"I understand. I felt the same way before I started my classes. But we have a pretty diverse student body, and I think our faculty reflects that diversity, too. Now, they'll make you earn your own position and push back to make you argue your case with Scripture. But they're pretty good about respecting you, wherever you are."

Feeling a measure of relief, Peter thanked Nathaniel for his help with registering and for his reassurance. As he left the admissions office, Peter's chest felt lighter, and his stomach had stopped churning. As he lumbered down the hallway back to his car, he flipped through his catalogue, searching for the list of courses to his program. Suddenly, he plowed into someone walking the other way.

"Oof!"

"Oh my gosh, sorry! Are you OK?" Peter's face reddened.

"Yeah I'm fine," the man said looking down, holding his tie.

Peter followed his gaze and saw a large smear of yogurt running down the front of his victim's shirt and tie. The rest of the yogurt cup had splattered on the ground.

Peter covered his mouth with one hand and moaned. "Oh no! I am so sorry."

"It's fine. It was only a Father's Day present from my kids. I'm sure it'll wash out."

"Really?" Peter said horrified.

"No not really. That thing was some bargain buy at Kohl's. Anyway, I'm Calvin VanDyke," he said, extending his hand.

"Oh, hi, Dr. VanDyke. I'm Peter Young. I'm starting this fall."

"Nice. What program?" VanDyke asked as he continued wiping yogurt off his tie with a napkin he found in his pocket.

"The M.Div. program. I'm specializing in church planting, but I also have a big interest in theology. I'm excited for your class this fall."

"Really, what's your theological interest?"

Peter looked down, wondering if he should fully show his hand, knowing that Calvin VanDyke was an outspoken critic of Prosurgence Christianity. He had written a book condemning the movement as liberalism and regularly assailed their leaders on his blog.

Whatever, Peter thought.

"Well, I'm Prosurgent," Peter responded with confidence. "So I'm interested in Prosurgence Christianity."

"The Prosurgent Church, huh," VanDyke said as he continued wiping. "What does that mean, that you're Prosurgent?"

Peter must have had a confused look on his face, because Dr. VanDyke continued. "I know what Prosurgence Christianity is, but what does that mean for you? It's kind of a loaded term."

He quickly recovered, and said, "Oh, well, it means I'm interested in reimagining the Christian faith in light of our twenty-first-century world. I want a Christian faith that connects to life right now."

VanDyke smiled and gave a chuckle.

"What?" Peter said, his face twisting with confusion as much as with annoyance.

"Nothing. It just sounded like a rehearsed sales pitch out of some pyramid scheme business workshop."

Peter simply stood, not knowing how to respond.

VanDyke crumpled up his napkin and shoved it in his pocket. "Well, I hope that's working out for you—the whole reimagining the Christian faith thing. Nice to run into you, literally, but I've gotta run to Kohl's and replace my tie. My kids will be devastated if they find out it's been ruined," he winked, then added before walking away: "Look forward to having you in class, Prosurgent Pete."

"PROSURGENT PETE?" he said out loud as he walked back to his car.

He didn't like being labeled straight out of the gate of his seminary journey, especially by some conservative professor who was a vocal opponent of the movement.

And what the heck did he mean by, 'You sound like some rehearsed sales pitch?'

Rethinking Christianity was the only option Peter saw in light of the changing twenty-first-century world. He wanted a faith that made sense of his world, and he saw only one way to finding that wish fulfilled: deliberately reimagine it. While Peter was glad he got meeting VanDyke out of the way early, now his chest tightened again knowing he had been labeled and probably written off. He hoped his first impression didn't doom his academic journey, both the Prosurgent reveal and yogurt spill.

Peter drove down to the Eastown neighborhood of Grand Rapids to scope out some potential coffeehouse jobs. He had researched a few on Wealthy Street, the city's hipster stomping grounds. The street was paved in cobblestone bricks leftover from an era long forgotten. The revitalization and economic boom of the past fifteen years that transformed the city into an emerging

Midwest metropolitan powerhouse had crept toward its every corner, particularly the Eastown neighborhood. Growing up, the place had been a wasteland you dared not traverse, especially at night. Now it was home to some of the hottest spots for living and playing.

The first shop he applied to was Sparrows Coffee & Newsstand, a dive that opened a year ago. As he closed his car door he remembered visiting the place last Christmas and thinking how impressed he was at the quality of their espresso, which was why it was first on his list.

Walking in, Peter was greeted with the low murmurs of conversation, the *rata-tat-tat* of the next American novelist working out his latest story, and the hiss of the Italian-made espresso maker. He loved coffeehouses, and this one seemed glorious. The floor was a honey nut-stained hardwood floor that had seen better days, yet wore its shabby-chic look well. To the left sat an alcove of old reconditioned chairs nestled in a bay window, reminding him of Saxbys back in DC where he met with students. And to the right flowed four levels of an amazing array of magazines from a diverse cross section of high and low culture. This was the newsstand of Sparrows Coffee, the centerpiece of the shop.

Peter walked up to the empty counter and asked if they were hiring.

"Actually, we are," chirped the barista. "And I also just happen to own this joint. Alexis Watson. But people call me Lexi. Do you want a coffee or something?" She offered her hand. Peter shook her firm grip and ordered.

"A coffee would be great, Lexi. Let's go with the Fair Trade Jamaican, just black. By the way, I'm Peter Daniel Young," he offered, though he didn't know why he just announced himself in full.

Lexi smiled as she began pouring his coffee. She was a slim

twentysomething, dressed in TOMS shoes, skinny jeans, and a T-shirt with a psychedelic Bob Marley emblazoned on the front. Her hair was long and braided, like thick ropes of hemp that curled up around her head into a hive that meant business. A single small ring clung to the right side of her nose, drawing Peter's gaze.

After retrieving his coffee and taking a seat in the front windowed alcove, Lexi followed behind. "So what's your story, Peter Daniel Young?"

Peter took a sip and *mmm'ed* with approval. "That's good. Well, I just moved to Grand Rapids from DC, literally yesterday—"

"Really?" Lexi interrupted. "You moved *to* Grand Rapids? I don't know many people who move here. Usually something drags them here kicking and screaming!"

Peter laughed. "Oh, believe you me I did come kicking and screaming! But it's good. I moved here for graduate work."

"Oh, where are you studying? Grand Valley?"

Peter set his cup down and shifted in his seat. He didn't know how to describe what he was studying. How do you explain to someone you're studying to be a pastor?

"Well," Peter started, "I'm studying theology."

"Really?" Lexi said, sitting up at attention. "Now that sounds interesting. Like you're studying different religions and stuff? I'm a Buddhist, by the way."

Just put it out there Petey, he thought. "No, I'm studying to be a pastor, actually."

Lexi's face sank slightly.

Trying to recover, he added, "But not like the ones on TV or the radio or anything! Don't worry, I'm not going to try and convert you." Peter offered a chuckle and raked a hand through his hair.

"Interesting. So does that mean you can't work Sundays?"

"The morning might be tough, but I'm not opposed to working Sundays. Do you think that could work?"

"It might." Lexi leaned back, studying Peter a few seconds while chewing on her pen. "Why not," she finally said. "You seem like a decent fella, Peter Daniel Young. I can sense these things. You got a nice aura about you. So when can you start?"

Peter's eyes widened. He wasn't prepared to get a job on the spot.

"It's only part time, maybe fifteen hours, so I hope that's OK."

"No, that sounds great. But here's the deal: classes start tomorrow, and I think I'm going to need few weeks to get into the swing of things. I hate to even ask this—beggars can't be choosers, right? But could I start in a few weeks? Say, first week of October?"

"Wow, you're demanding aren't you, pastor man?" Lexi said, her mouth turning upward playfully. Lexi stood suddenly and offered her hand again. "Alright, Peter, you've got yourself a deal. I'll see you first week of October."

Peter stood and shook her hand. "Sweet! It's a date, then."

Startled by his own slip, he tried to recover. "I mean, I'll see you in a few weeks."

Blushing slightly, Lexi smiled and walked back behind the counter to serve the next customer in line.

"Leave me your number and I'll call you in a few weeks with your schedule, pastor man."

CHAPTER 5

PETER ARRIVED home from his day in Grand Rapids in time for dinner. Sitting in the driveway was an aging, rusting golden Plymouth Breeze, his brother James's car. He smiled as he slid his hand across the hood and jogged up to the house to greet his awaiting brother inside.

Though Peter and James were never close growing up, they became especially close over the past few years since James's personal life imploded. While Peter should have been one to condemn his brother's moral failings given his own black-and-white moral sentiments at the time, he was surprisingly forgiving. His parents, though, were not, which made Peter safe space for James to vent. Peter wished he would have been able to do more for his brother, but he did what he could as a twenty-one-year-old college kid. When the drug use started a few years later and bouts of unemployment and near homelessness came, Peter felt power-less to help, especially six hundred miles away. He did what he could by sending what he could, but was still haunted by guilt, believing that he could have done more to stem the tide of rot that had befallen his brother. As Peter made his way inside, he hoped he could redeem the time he lost while studying and working a quarter of a country away while his brother was wasting away. And knowing James and his parents weren't exactly on speaking terms, Peter braced himself for whatever might come that evening.

James was waiting in the living room, wearing a faded black hoodie and several days of scruff, his long wiry frame dominating the sofa. He looked much older than his twenty-three years; life had trampled him hard.

"There you are," Peter said smiling. "I wondered if you'd show up!"

"I'm only here because you're here," James replied, standing to embrace his brother. "How was the drive? Did you survive the crazies?"

"If by crazies you mean Mom and Dad, then yes, but only because I was driving separately." Peter grinned. He paused, holding JT's shoulders. "I'm glad you're here, Bro. Just try to behave yourself."

"It's not me you need to worry about. It's our crackpot pops who's got his head so far up his—"

"James. Come on, man." Peter sat down in a plush arm chair. James followed his lead by flopping on their parents' couch.

"I'm just saying. I know how to behave myself. It's Dad who seems to love picking fights about anything about my life that doesn't meet with his approval. Shoot, how many times already has he ragged on you about your car?"

"I get it. But let's try and keep the peace tonight. And I'm preaching to both of us here, because I'm about to pop myself!"

JT nodded in agreement, raking his hands through his shaggy unkempt hair. "Anyway...so seminary. Didn't see that one coming. Especially, you know, because of what happened back East."

Peter offered a weak smile and said nothing, the memory still smarting six months later.

"Hey I didn't mean nothin' by that," his brother said.

"Naw, it's fine. I'm over it."

"Well, you ready for the little white collar and life of celibacy?"

Peter laughed. "No white collar in this school and definitely no life of celibacy, either. Thank God! Yeah, I'm getting there. Classes start next week, so ask me again in a month if I'm ready to jump back into Churchland."

"Speaking of which," James said, "I started reading this new book—"

"You? Reading?" Peter interjected. "Like, a genuine book? The kind with words or pictures?"

"Dude, shut-up." JT nailed his brother's right knee.

"Ouch, hey! Kidding, kidding," Peter said recoiling.

"Just because I don't got no degree from some fancy university or a room full of fancy books from a bunch of dead white guys don't mean nothin'. And it don't mean I don't read."

"Hey, I'm just messing with you, JT," Peter said roughing up his brother's hair, and feeling not a little bad about picking on him.

While not as educated and well read, JT was a thinker. They often exchanged e-mails debating politics and religion, going back and forth through several strands before James wore Peter out. Usually James was the initiator, popping off a question about God's goodness after a natural disaster or accusations of cruelty by requiring belief in one God. More frequently, his e-mails were angry tirades against Republicans, the same ones Peter had worked for while on Capitol Hill. He wasn't a diehard GOPer, but Peter's inner debater drove him to respond line-by-line to James's Democrat talking points. Though Peter often wished he had been more available and present during James's high school experiences and beyond, he had been thankful for what relationship they did have through e-mail. Those exchanges helped connect them, if only superficially through argument and debate.

Because of his troubles that senior year, James never went to college. Not going to college was often a sore spot in James's self-esteem. Peter tried not to draw attention to this degree of separation, but sometimes it slipped. Peter tried to recover from his joke. "So what are you reading?"

"It's this new book by one of your, what do you call them, Prosurge friends? Prosurging?"

"Prosurgent," Peter corrected. "Really? Who, which book?"

"Some guy named Bryan. *A Reimagined Christianity*. You heard of it?"

"For sure. It's his new book on Christian beliefs. And you're reading it? I read his first book, *A Reimagined Christian*. Haven't gotten to his new one yet. You're showing me up, Bro!"

Peter had read most of the major Prosurgent thinkers from the new Christian movement over the past few years. He hadn't been able to digest this newest work, though, from the grandfather of Prosurgence Christianity. Having been hugely impacted by Bryan's work, Peter was something of a fan boy. A year into his campus ministry job, he had joined the conversation many other young adults had joined in small pockets of protest throughout the American Church. This was both a blessing and a curse. The Prosurgent Church was an oasis amidst the chaos that ensued from his crisis of faith. It was also the reason he lost his ministry job.

"How'd you hear about it?"

"Saw it on a table at Barnes & Noble. Thought it looked interesting, so I picked it up."

Before Peter could ask JT what he thought about it, Maggie bellowed from the kitchen, "Come on, boys. Dinner's ready."

"Well this should be exciting," JT said standing.

"Behave," Peter replied, shaking his finger playfully.

"You, too," JT shook back.

The Young men were a spoiled bunch, and they knew it. Their mom was well trained in the art of finger-licking Southern-style cooking. Tonight she pulled out all the stops, preparing the evening dinner with a special amount of flare. She cooked a pot roast in a red wine sauce, garnished with a sprig of rosemary, an irony that wasn't lost on Peter as Mom and Dad Young were teetotalers through and through. The pot roast meal was served with diced red skin potatoes roasted in olive oil and sage, grilled asparagus topped with crushed black pepper, and a loaf of freshly baked paisano bread. This was the meal Peter remembered from years long passed, and the one that made Peter feel most at home.

As the dishes were being passed around the table, Peter soaked in the rare scene before his eyes: Mom, Dad, and the three brothers seated together enjoying a family meal. It'd been a long time since that had happened. When it did, it was usually twice a year—at Christmas and Thanksgiving. With Peter living in Washington and James mostly not on good speaking terms with his parents, family dinners were a rarity. He was thankful for this moment, savoring this moment—until it happened.

"So d'ya find a church yet, JT? Or are you and Jesus still not speaking?" Dad asked as he scooped a large helping of potatoes.

"Danny," Maggie signed, clanking her fork and knife on her plate.

"What, I'm just asking."

"I'll tell you what, Dad," James started, "I'll find a church when you find a job. You and me both know that means I'm gonna be out for some time."

"You respect your father, JT," Maggie said smacking JT's shoulder.

His father offered a controlled smile, while resting his knife and fork on his plate. "Well maybe I'll go make pizzas like you down at that there Pizza Hut. Because it seems like you've got yourself a real career builder there, Son!"

"At least it's something."

"Or. better yet," Danny chuckled, "how about me and you go down to Franklin and Division and work the corner together. You know, push those little bags of grass and sugar you made a fortune off of."

"You know I don't do that no more!" JT spat angrily.

"Wait, that's right, you're a recovering drug dealer like you're a recovering Christian. Moving on to bigger and better things like flipping pizzas and yoga."

"You have no idea who I am or what I do," James said bitterly looking down at his plate. "And I'll tell you what, I experience the Divine in yoga far more than I ever did in your sorry excuse for a church!"

That drew the conversation to a halt as Mom, Dad, and even Johnny sat with mouths agape.

"Guys, cut it out," Peter interjected. "Seriously, what the heck?"

"Watch your mouth, Petey," Mom said.

The grandfather clock ticked by the minutes as the Young family sat in exhausted silence. The flame of Peter's rekindled memory quickly flickered out as he realized nothing had changed. Somehow Peter thought it would be different now that he was back. Not that he would be the savior of his family. Only that his return might be the occasion for setting aside differences, at least for one dinner. He was wrong; nothing had changed.

JT broke the silence. "You know, I haven't given up on God. I've given up on religion. Your religion," he said looking up into his father's hardened face. "And actually, I haven't even given up on Christianity. I'm like lots of other people who are trying to reimagine it. Like Petey here."

Peter looked up, face betraying his surprise that JT would

invoke him in a comment about his own spiritual journey. In that moment, for the first time, he wondered how responsible he was for where James was heading in this latest episode in his life.

"The other day, I started reading this new book by one of Petey's Prosurgent friends," JT continued.

"Prosurgent?" Danny said, turning to Peter scowling. "Nice, Peter. Now I know why yet another of my sons is wayward."

"Wayward?" he mumbled, contorting his face in confusion. "Are you kidding me? That's what you think I am? Wayward? I'm starting seminary for gosh sakes! I'm simply trying to understand how the Christian faith connects to our modern world."

"Exactly!" JT exclaimed. "You and Mom just don't get it. This guy Bryan says in his book that he no longer believes in the Christianity that's ruled the past several years, because it don't make sense no more—like the one we grew up with. He wants to believe differently, and so do I." Then he added, "And if in your eyes that don't make me a Christian or God's child or whatever—then great. Fantastic actually! Because I don't wanna be your kind of Christian."

And with that, JT threw his napkin on his plate, got up, and walked out, the backdoor reverberating throughout Cooper Manor in his wake.

CHAPTER 6

PETER CHASED AFTER HIS BROTHER.

JT had just slammed the creaking, stiff door to his rusting Breeze as he reached him.

"JT, open up. Come on back inside," Peter pleaded, pounding on the window as James tried to start his tired car.

His brother rolled down the window. "Sorry, but I'm done for the night. I've had my fill of their judgment for another few months. But if you wanna hop in and get a drink, it's your call."

Peter turned back toward the house considering JT's offer. He nodded then shuffled around to the passenger side. "I'll text them on the way. Where are we heading?"

James finally got the car started as Peter climbed inside. "The only bar that matters in GR, which is really a brewhouse. Ever heard of Founders?"

"Umm, can't say that I have. They have good beer?"

"Do they got good beer? You kidding? Their Kentucky Breakfast Stout's been rated like number two in the world. In the winter you can practically poor their Canadian Breakfast Stout on your pancakes because they age it in maple barrels. So, yeah, they got good beer!"

They drove on toward Grand Rapids, talking beer. Peter shared his experiences with East Coast microbreweries. JT filled him in on all the amazing local breweries that had sprung up and succeeded in West Michigan. The light conversation helped ease the tension from dinner. He had seen that edge on James a few times before when he visited, the reactive response to his parents' questions about his life. Sure, he got how much they drilled into him, and he had plenty of difficulty with his own parental interrogations. But that evening conversation seemed different. Something else was going on.

He hoped Bryan's new book might help JT reconsider his faith outside of what he'd always known, what he'd left behind. Peter had been meaning to read it himself, and now that his brother was into a book that could provide a meaningful guide to his own spiritual journey, he would make it a point to read through it so that he could engage JT. This would be a whole new level of engagement, which Peter hoped would take their relationship to a whole new level of deepness and understanding.

They arrived at Founders Brewing Company, managing to find a parking spot on the street out front. Peter stared wide-eyed at the big front porch jutting out from the newly built brewpub. It was buzzing with a crowd of mostly twentysomethings unwinding from the work day and classes. It was the perfect evening to enjoy a drink with his brother, and that front porch was where he wanted it.

This is my kind of place, Peter thought as they got out of the car, the tangy scent of hops floated down around the car as well as the rumble of lively conversations and a local band strumming away inside.

A big, bushy bearded man checked their IDs at the door. Peter found an empty picnic table on the porch while his brother bought their drinks. As Peter sat waiting for his brother, he marveled at how much his town had changed. Not ten years ago you wouldn't have found a brewhouse like Founders anywhere in the city, much less packed like it was that early-September evening. Through the raised garage doors that doubled as walls he saw several small groups of people in lively good-natured arguments. A couple decked out in tattoos was playing cards over a few pints, while a few more empty glasses sat off to the side. Out on the porch thick clouds of smoke hung under the eaves from pipe, cigar, and cigarette smokers. He wished he had brought his own pipe along.

James returned with two pints, an IPA for Peter and a Scotch ale for himself.

"Hey, what's up with your mug?" Peter questioned. "It's different than mine."

JT took a swig, and said, "It's my Mug Club mug. You pay fifty bucks a year to get one and some nice discounts when you fill it up. I come here often enough so it's worth it."

"You come here with a group or something? Or just yourself?" Peter asked.

"I usually just come here alone and hang out up at the bar. You meet a lot of interesting folks up there. Lots of stories come in and out of Founders each night."

Peter studied JT's mug and noticed an inscription on the side: *To the Unknown god.* He pointed to it and said, "What's that mean? To the Unknown god?"

JT turned his glass to look at the side, "Oh, that. You get to name your mug each year. You don't know what that is?"

"Of course I do. It's from Acts 17, the inscription on one of the idols in the marketplace of Athens Paul noticed on one of his trips. I mean, what does it mean, to you?"

JT shrugged. "I don't know, man. Just where I'm at, I guess. God seems unknown, foreign. So every time I take a drink I'm drinking to the god who is unknown, whoever he is. Or she, I suppose. Cheers!"

He raised his glass, Peter followed suit, clinking his brother's mug and taking a long swig. JT drained his glass and motioning to the server for another.

"I'm gonna go for a smoke. Don't let no one take my mug!"

"I'll guard it with my life."

Peter considered his brother's comment as he sauntered off to light up, the one about where he was at with God. When the server returned with JT's mug he stared at its inscription. He thought back to the dinner table conversation and JT's comments about his parents' faith, how he didn't want to be *their* kind of Christian, how he was on a quest to reimagine the Christian faith.

That's my language, Peter thought, following the grooves of the table with his fingernail, wondering if his own quest had somehow provoked his brother's.

Over the past few years, he made no small announcement about his own journey to rethink his Christian faith. At the time, his brother had been living at home, struggling to get by. They didn't talk a whole lot about it together, but James had probably heard his fair share of arguments between his parents about his theological and spiritual direction.

James returned from his smoke. He plopped down and took a long swig of ale. Peter decided he'd take a risk and ask his brother about dinner.

"So, talk to me about dinner."

JT took another swig. "What do you mean? What do you want to know?"

"I mean, you sounded pretty defensive about where you're at with Jesus or church or whatever. And what did you mean about not wanting to be *their* kind of Christian?"

"It's like what you've been saying for the past year. We need to rethink this whole faith thing, man. Especially this whole Christian and church thing. Because what we grew up with is just BS."

"You mean like what it was like at Coopersville Baptist?" Peter paused, then he asked, "Or Coopersville High School?"

JT stared out beyond the porch to the public bus station across the road. "Both." He drained his drink, then continued, "Look, I know I've jacked up my life. I know I'm not living...like a Christian should. Or whatever. I'm not a saint, alright! I know there's a god or something, and that there's some way he expects me to live or whatever. But if he's so loving, why are his people a bunch of jerks?" He slammed the table with his empty mug.

"I hear you, Bro. And I'm sorry about those years of judgment and condemnation. From those parents." Peter added, "From *our* parents."

"Yeah, well. What's in the past is in the past."

Peter took a swig. "So how are you doing. Really? How's your...usage. With your stuff?"

"By stuff you mean my drugs?" James smiled and chuckled. "Man, you East Coast urbanite turned Midwest seminarian can't picture your little brother shooting up, can you? It's better. Not good, but better. And no, you can't have some."

Peter laughed. "Right. Thanks, I think. I'm serious though, I'm worried about you. The talk at dinner. Your rust bucket car. And now you're apparently into yoga? I mean, what's that about?"

"You got your thing, I got my thing. And yoga's my thing. It helps center me. It helps me connect to the divine or whatever is out there. You should try it sometime. I go to the local Buddhist temple once in a while. I gotta tell ya, Petey, it's way less complicated than Christianity."

That one threw Peter. He could handle his brother reimagining the Christian faith, but reneging on his faith and turning to another was something else.

"So you're a Buddhist now?" Peter prodded.

"Maybe. I don't know." James flagged down another server for another refill. "You want another one?"

Peter eyed his half-empty glass. "No, I'm good. Thanks though."

"All right, your loss."

The server left and Peter continued his interrogation. "You don't know if you're Buddhist?"

"I don't know what I am. Or where I stand with God. Or even if there is a God. But I tell you what I do know is that Bryan fella knows what's up."

"Oh yeah? How so?"

"The way he talks about Christianity. Especially the Christianity of the past. The kind we grew up on. He puts it all in perspective, you know? Explaining why it was OK then, but it ain't no good no more. I definitely could be his kind of Christian!"

Sensing an opening, Peter risked making a suggestion. "Well, why don't we talk about it together?"

"Talk about what together?"

"Bryan's book. I think you're sitting under a whole lot of religious guilt crap you don't need to sit under anymore. Shoot, I'm sitting under a whole lot of religious guilt crap I don't need to sit under anymore!" Peter chuckled as the server returned with James's drink.

"Thanks." JT took a long swig. His face had a puzzled expression. "What do you mean by talking about Bryan's book? Like a Bible study?"

Peter considered that language. "Let's call it a book study. Or maybe a quest, more than a study. A quest for a reimagined kind of Christianity, a Christianity worth believing. Because there's more for you, James. More for your life. And to be frank, for your relationship with God. And I don't think your life is gonna improve all that much until you get the God thing on track."

"Preacher man's getting his preach on! Watch out, every-body," James said loudly, slurring his words. A few others looked over. Peter reddened.

"Dude, keep your voice down! That's not what I meant to do."

"Relax! I'm just messin'," he replied, slurring his words even more. "OK, a study sounds good. But on one condition."

"What's that?"

"We do our quest here, over pints."

Peter grinned. "Deal." He drained his beer and paid for both of their tabs.

As they exited Founders, James was barely able to walk straight, nearly toppling into a group on their way out.

"You OK, Bro? Need me to drive?" Peter asked.

"Yeah, maybe that's a good idea."

Peter took the keys and helped James into the car.

They drove in the silence of the late night. Peter pondered the past few days as his brother snored next to him, mouth agape. The first few days back home didn't go as he had planned. He managed to alienate his father even more than he already was. A near brawl broke out over dinner between his brother and parents. And his brother was exploring Buddhism, which seemed partly connected to his own journey toward reimagining the Christian faith. He hadn't even begun his seminary classes yet, and already he wished he was back in DC. Home was much more than he bargained for.

Peter pulled JT's Breeze into the driveway. He worried the creaking would wake his parents. The back door light was on, as well as a light in the kitchen. He saw movement in the house as he helped his brother out of the car. Just then he remembered that he forgot to text his parents where he was going. Not that he was some teenager who needed to check in with his parents. Regret needled him, nonetheless.

"Where were you guys? We were worried," Maggie whispered as they stumbled into the kitchen. James slumped down at the kitchen table.

"Sorry, I meant to text," Peter said apologetically. "We went out for a drink to catch up."

"Looks like more than one drink." Maggie huffed, crossing her arms. "Anyway, your father went to bed, and I'm heading there myself. The guest bedroom is made for James if he needs it."

"Thanks, Mom," Peter offered. "And sorry about earlier. The drive, the table. All of it. I really don't want to fight. I am thankful to be here."

"I know." She patted his shoulder on her way out, and said, "Goodnight, Petey."

James was asleep, head resting on the table. Peter helped him to the guest bedroom where a full bed with clean sheets awaited him, much more than he was normally used to.

Peter sauntered up the stairs to his new home for the next three years. He crawled into bed, hoping the rest of the week— the next three years—would be better than the past three days.

CHAPTER 7

"PETER, move it, we're going to be late!" bellowed Maggie at the bottom of the stairs.

"Almost ready," Peter bellowed back.

After taking the week to unpack, arrange his room, and venture around Grand Rapids to reconnect to a place he had long forgotten, it was Sunday morning. Which meant a trip back in time to a place he had firmly renounced. To Peter, it was a place fossilized in an era where alcohol, dancing, movies, and cards were the biggest threats to humanity—all of the devil himself. It was a time where the biggest threat to the American Church was evolution. And guitars. And the best antidote was donning your suit coat and tie, singing a few hymns, and listening to a revival preacher bring it.

"Why I ever agreed to go back to Coopersville Baptist is beyond me," he mumbled as he tucked in his shirt.

Much to his parents' chagrin, Peter refused the shirt-and-tie uniform of CBC, preferring his dark denim and vintage collared shirt on par with the vintage Christian faith he was about to partake. He grabbed his thoroughly non-KJV NIV Bible and ran downstairs to his parents' awaiting, idling car.

The drive over was quiet as the Young family continued waking up for the 8:30 a.m. service. CBC was an IFBC church, an Independent Fundamentalist Baptist Church. Or, as Peter liked to say, an *I Love Fighting and Blasting Christians* church. As a conservative assembly, they were known for their stringent fundamentalist beliefs, beliefs that kindled not a few fights with other conservative Christians who didn't toe their narrow party line.

This was the church that had shaped Peter's childhood faith, that had given rise to the very faith that provoked his quest to reimagine the overall Christian faith. His father was raised in CBC, and when he and his mom married, they made it their permanent family church home. In many ways the church made a permanent stamp on the family itself, having influenced the names of the three Young family boys: Peter, James, and John were Jesus's three closest disciples. Its impression still lingered in more ways than both Danny and Maggie could have imagined, as witnessed by the spiritual paths Peter and James forged.

"Oh, I hate walking in late," Maggie moaned. "Speed up a little, Danny, you're driving like Grandpa!"

"Dear, I'm going five over. Relax, we'll slip in our row in the back, and no one will notice."

She reached around to look at Peter who was half asleep in the back. "So many have said how excited they are to see you, Petey! Your old Bible quiz coaches, Barb and Bill Sanford, were especially eager to catch up. Remember all of those quiz meets we'd cart you around to?"

"Yeah, Mom," Peter replied with a bit of nostalgia himself. "Didn't I memorize something like six books of the Bible?"

"That sounds about right. Let's see, there was the Gospel of John, 2 Corinthians, the book of Hebrews. What else?"

"One year I remember memorizing several books. I think it was Ephesians and then 1, 2, and 3 John."

"That's right! We still have your old quiz books, you know. I ran across them while cleaning up your room the other week. Brought back such great memories."

For three years when he was a teenager Peter was part of the CBC Bible Quiz Team, an extracurricular activity where he and his teammates competed using the Bible. It was sort of like *Jeopardy!*, complete with buzzers and questions, only a book of the Bible was used as the basis for the competition. While Peter was thankful for the experience, since it had helped ground him in God's Word, and he reveled in knowing he had memorized hundreds of verses and could still quote entire passages, a few years ago he wondered if it transformed God's Word into a mere competitive device used to win competitions. Which would make sense, because the experience mirrored his church experience: Bible study and memorization was transformed into an information-gathering and cramming exercise. The Bible was reduced to something to be prodded, poked, and dissected like a baby pig in high school biology.

The Young family arrived three minutes late to the quaint, small-town church on the edge of Coopersville. The parking lot was empty of churchgoers who were already inside singing along to an old hymn. The family hustled inside the thick front doors, creaks and clangs announcing their arrival—and tardiness. A few heads turned as they took their seats in the empty unofficial Young family pew near the back.

The first song ended, and the music director, a mid-forties lifetime member with a shiny bald head, Craig Johnson, instructed people to turn around and greet their neighbor. The piano and organ continued droning on as people made their way around the sanctuary, a line forming at the back to greet Peter.

"Great to see you, Peter!" said one woman who used to

babysit the Young boys. "Welcome home," said another older gentleman who served on the deacon board with Danny.

The current pastor, Pastor George, elbowed his way down toward the back to give his greeting. "Well, the prodigal son has returned, I see."

Prodigal? Peter thought, glancing at his mother who didn't break away from looking, smiling, and nodding at Pastor George.

"I hear you're going to be a preacher? Is that right?" the rotund man asked as he tilted his head back with skepticism.

"Yes, sir," Peter replied, turning back to Pastor George. "I start classes at Grand River Theological Seminary this coming week."

"GRTS, huh? I've heard that place has gone liberal. Boy, I remember when it was a real defender of the faith back in the day."

Are you kidding me? This windbag thinks GRTS isn't conservative enough—big surprise.

"It's far too liberal for a CBC boy. Especially, for someone who's been a bit too cozy with liberalism the past few years," Pastor George said wrapping his arm around Peter, words dripping with the condescension of a kindergarten teacher.

Peter glanced at the Pastor's chubby hand now resting on his right shoulder, but kept smiling. He wondered what on earth his parents had said to this stranger, who now took it upon himself to confront him during what should have been a shallow time of pleasantries.

"Well, I think I'll be OK," Peter managed to say, maintaining his composure, fake smile firmly affixed.

The piano and organ began playing the introduction to the next hymn, willing the church to reassemble and continue the service.

"Some glad mornin' when this life is o'r, I'll fly away," belted the music director.

"What on earth was that about?" Peter huffed in Maggie's ear as the church followed Mr. Johnson's lead.

"Your father might have mentioned his conversations with you to Pastor George. He was really worried about your direction, Peter. We both were."

Peter rolled his eyes as the hymn transitioned to the chorus.

"*I'll fly away, oh glory, I'll fly away...*" the congregation continued singing.

Peter stared wide eyed at the front. He fumbled with his hymnbook to find the place, but refused to sing along.

Noticing his deliberate lack of participation, Maggie leaned over and whispered, "Why aren't you singing?"

"Because it's not true!" Peter whispered back.

"What are you talking about?" Maggie whispered back in a huff.

"The song. It's just wrong. It's about escaping this bad world to some mystical land in outer space. The song is all wrong." Noticing a few parishioners were glancing their way and giving them looks, Peter whispered, "I'll tell you later. But I'm not singing this."

Peter dutifully held the hymnal, waiting for the song to end while staring straight ahead. When it finally did, Pastor George waddled up to the podium to begin his sermon.

"The grass withereth, and the flower fadeth," he started in a low, monotonous voice, "but the Word of our God shall stand forever. Amen?"

"*Amen,*" the congregation mumbled approvingly.

What on earth does that even mean? Peter thought, furrowing his brow.

He could feel a hot wave of judgment begin to creep up the back of his neck. He was mentally preparing himself for what was to come.

Pastor George's message was one he had heard a hundredfold growing up, one that mirrored the hymn they'd just finished.

This world is not my home, I'm just a'passin' through. This world is corrupt and evil, but never fear, kiddos: we're the chosen one's looking forward to the day when Jesus comes to beam us outta here!

There was no concern about this life now, other than avoiding a whole list of things that were "of this world." Peter had forgotten that this world of fundamentalism was a foreign one, plucked from a foreign era.

Without realizing it, Pastor George was stoking the flame of Peter's resolve to reimagine the Christian faith for his day, right there in the Young family pew.

Fifty-two minutes later, the service wound to a close. But not before ending with the church's quarterly communion day.

"I almost forgot about this *lovely* experience," Peter mumbled under his breath. His mother elbowed him into silence.

This "experience" of the Lord's Supper, as it was called, consisted of individual prepackaged communion cups with an aluminum foil-seal topped with a tiny unleavened cracker.

When the tray came down his row Peter relented. It reminded him of a TV dinner. Like this staple of American consumerism, this prepackaged Jesus meal lacked substance, meaning, and community.

Popping the top, he took his little cracker and thanked Jesus for breaking his body for him and for the world. Peeling back the foil seal, he threw back the tiny plastic cup of grape juice and thanked Jesus for pouring out his blood for him and for the world. He prayed for the American Church and asked Jesus to forgive Christianity for reducing the majesty and grandeur of his sacrifice to the equivalent of a Stouffer's frozen entrée. Then he walked out of the church, the heavy, creaky wooden doors announcing his departure.

After the service ended, Maggie found Peter sitting under a large oak tree near a creek that ran along the southern edge of the church's grounds.

"Petey, I don't understand you sometimes." She planted her hands on her hips and flared her nostrils. "I get you think we're just a bunch of country nobodies who don't have as sophisticated of a faith as you do. I get it, and it's fine."

Peter stared at the ground in silence as Maggie's anger crescendoed. "But what's not fine is your level of disrespect and *judgment*."

"Disrespect? Judgment?" Peter looked up, now fully engaged. "How about you and Dad telling that joker—I'm sorry, Pastor George that I'm some backslidden liberal? Prodigal son? Please!"

Peter got up and began to walk away, a bad habit he picked up from his father. He stopped, sighed, and turned back to his mother who was still standing next to the tree, hands cemented on her hips.

"I'm sorry that I can't sing along with songs that are blatantly unbiblical. And I'm sorry that I think shrink-wrapping the Eucharist into some...some prepackaged pseudo spirituality thingamabob is borderline heresy!"

Maggie huffed and folded her arms. "See, this is exactly what we were concerned with when we talked with Pastor George."

"And what is *this* exactly?" Peter spat out.

"You abandoning the faith, Petey. Everything we taught you, everything we believe—just tossed right out the window."

"I have not abandoned the Christian faith, Mother."

"No, that's right, you're just *reimagining* it," Maggie spat back, throwing her hands up in the air with frustration.

"That's right. And this has nothing to do with what you taught me or what you believe. It isn't personal!" Peter noticed people staring from the base of the church at the top of the hill.

"Of course it's personal, Petey," she said, putting her hands back on her hips. "When you refuse to sing *our* songs and stare in obvious judgment at *our* pastor teaching from God's Word and leave in protest in *our* church because you don't like the way we practice *our* communion—you're damn right it's personal."

Rarely did Maggie cuss. When she did, Peter knew to step back and take a breath.

The way she said that last line—about it being personal—sounded as if her offense had been building for months and had finally blown. Like she had been holding her finger in a dam's leak until she could hold it in no longer.

Peter shook his head in disbelief. "Mom, where is this coming from? I knew Dad was ticked at my spiritual direction, but I thought we had an understanding."

"That was before your father explained to me what those Prosurgey...Prosurging—"

"Prosurgent," Peter corrected, before realizing he should have kept his mouth shut.

Maggie closed her eyes and paused a beat. "*Prosurgent* teachers actually meant. Nothing more than repackaged liberalism." She continued without letting Peter get a word in edgewise. "But that's not the point, Petey. At the end of the day I don't give a rat's ass what you believe. What I do care about is your high-horse attitude and your condemnation of everything what we hold sacred. That hurts, Son. Hurts something fierce."

Maggie fell silent, wiping her eyes before crossing her arms again and staring at the burnt grass with lips held tightly together.

As much as Peter's pride wanted to retort or stomp away, his heart pulled him off the ledge. He felt awful.

"Mom, I'm sorry for offending you," Peter offered, putting his hand on her shoulder, staring back at the milling crowd at the top. "I really am. My own journey has always been about me—what I need to believe. It's never been about you and Dad, and I wish you'd realize that. If I believe differently or practice differently it's not because I'm rejecting you and your Christianity. It's because this is where I feel I'm being led."

Peter leaned against the tree, staring off into the neighboring field with ripened corn stalks, unsure of what more to say.

"Johnny and your father are waiting in the car. We should go," Maggie finally said, turning toward the parking lot, her Sunday dress swishing in step with her indignation.

CHAPTER 8

SILENCE ENVELOPED the Young family as they made their way home. When they arrived at Cooper Manor, Peter dashed straight to his room and flopped on his bed. The church service exhausted him as much as his fight with his mother. Lying still, face-first in his pillow, he thought about what she said, about his disrespect and judgment. He felt so misunderstood, so alone in his faith journey. He turned over and stared at his ceiling, mentally picking at a flap of peeling paint.

"If this is what it's like at home, what am I going to face at school?" Peter wondered aloud, a font of regret welling up within.

He rolled over and saw on his nightstand a stack of books from Prosurgent authors he had yet to place in their section of his library. On top was a book from one of his favorite authors, Dale Pagels. Peter had heard an amazing podcast from the tall, gangly pastor a few years ago on the kingdom of God that helped him begin to understand the need to have a holistic gospel that included teachings about both Jesus and his way of living. After hearing it, Peter emailed Dale and wrote his ear off wondering how to implement a kingdom-centered gospel in his campus ministry. Dale was nice enough to email back and correspond through the issues Peter was wrestling through. They'd kept in touch ever since.

Peter had picked up his *A Christian Faith Worth Believing* book a few months ago, but never got around to reading it. So he reached over for it to escape the loneliness he felt on the other side of the Sunday morning drama. He turned to the first page like an infant might turn to a blanket for peace, for safety, for security. He read:

I'm in a quandary. I have a nagging inner conflict that has gotten worse in the twenty years I've been a Christian. It's the kind of problem I approach with other people with no small amount of anxiety. Yes, I'm a Christian. But I no longer believe in the Christian faith— at least the one I've believed for two decades.

"Been there, done that," he mumbled. "Am there, doing that!"

He resonated with the anxiety that came from voicing feelings of apprehension regarding current models and methods of Christianity. It was a few months into his journey into Prosurgence Christianity until Peter shared his own shift with his superiors at his campus ministry. Even longer with his parents. The reaction from both camps confirmed his anxiety and apprehension, pushing Peter to turtle back into a shell of silence. And now Peter felt those feelings rushing back to the surface with a vengeance. He continued reading:

At least, I don't believe in the versions of the Christian faith that have dominated the Church's attentions for the last fifteen hundred years, the versions that were perfectly suitable for *their* time and place but have little resonance with *this* time and place. The ones that answer the questions that no one is asking and fail to consider the ones—the important ones—that we can no longer ignore. The questions that don't jibe with who God is, who we are, and where we are going. I want to be clear: My quandary isn't over believing; I do believe. I am conflicted because I want to believe otherly.

"Exactly!" He was feeling more at east now, the anxiety and apprehension draining the longer he sat with this kindred spirit embedded in these words.

It wasn't that Peter didn't believe or struggled to believe. That's what people around him didn't get.

What he struggled with was the *version* of belief he had been handed through childhood and college, even from his campus ministry in Washington. Especially from his campus ministry in Washington! Like Dale, Peter recognized that things weren't working anymore in the version of Christianity that had been reigning in America. And he wanted to believe differently—to believe *otherly* as Dale put it. Like him, Peter wanted a Christian faith worth believing in.

A rumble of thunder shook Cooper Manor as rain began to lick his windows. Peter jumped off the bed and filled a hotpot he bought to make some tea for times such as these. He got comfortable in his vintage Goodwill chair nestled in his turret bay window, and continued reading while his water began to simmer.

Peter returned to his mentor and flipped through the first few chapters, landing on a particular passage of resonance:

> Whether we realize it, the major pillars of the Christian faith—the doctrines of God, of humanity, of sin, of Jesus, of salvation—that many of us were handed are firmly embedded in the cultural context of another time and place, so much so that they are mostly meaningless in our time and place.

"Yes," Peter whispered in agreement. Dale insisted that our Christian faith was partly the result of culture. Which meant the version we now embrace is as much a product of our modern Western world as is our music and styles of dress.

He flipped a few pages forward, Peter's confidence in his spiritual trajectory strengthened and nourished by Dale's affirming words. He smiled when he came across what had become something of his own motto for his own spirituality:

> I believe that it is the enduring tradition of the Christian faith to constantly renew, rethink, and reimagine what it means to follow God—what it means to believe in God.

"I like that," Peter said, exhaling the tension that had been building since returning back home. "Renew, rethink, and reimagine," Peter repeated.

He continued reading, feeling renewed after engaging with this book, much like reconnecting with a friend with whom he had grown out of touch. Dale's book was feeding Peter's lonely soul, giving him the permission he needed to continue down his own path of reimagining the Christian faith. It felt good to reconnect across the expanse of time and pen and ink and paper to this spiritual brother who "got" what he himself was experiencing and feeling deep down.

"I was confused by the idea that there was a separation between me and God, a massive chasm with me on one side and God on the other," Peter read as he continued drawing from the Prosurgent Church well. *"In all my life I had never felt separated from God."*

Peter turned the page, continuing to read about Dale's perspective on sin and the traditional view of God that he was removed and distant from humanity because of his holiness and our wickedness. This was a throwback to Peter's childhood, for sure.

Peter remembered being told as a kid how God was standing on one side of a chasm, while he was on the other side. His sin separated him from God, but Jesus on the cross bridged that separation. That simple illustration is what led him to pray to accept Jesus into his life when he was five.

Yet Peter had evolved in his view of human nature and sin. From his perspective, the world could definitely do without the countless sermons modeled after the famed Puritan preacher Jonathan Edwards who made God out to be an angry despot just waiting for one tiny reason to fling people into the licking flames of Hell.

Dale wrote how that illustration—a person on one side and God on the other—assumed that sin separated us from God and God from us, which Dale said simply wasn't the case.

Is sin really more powerful than God?" Dale asked. "I don't believe so, no way! I don't believe that God is hampered or hindered or handicapped by sin. My sin may have kept me from fully living into the life of God, but it wasn't keeping me away from Him or Him from me.

"Exactly!" Peter shouted, satisfaction in his Prosurgent beliefs returning.

His hotpot began screeching for his attention. He closed the book and set it down, then grabbed his favorite mug and headed for the boiling water. He flipped through a selection of various tea bags to find the right one for the occasion. Irish Breakfast. He dipped it in the steaming water, waving it back and forth to let it steep, while deep in thought.

On his way back to his chair he picked up the book that seemed to be affecting his brother's spiritual journey, *A Reimagined Christianity* by Bryan McLaughlin. Peter flipped to the first page, hoping to find comfort from another fellow reimaginer.

Bryan began the book by retelling the story of the Prosurgence Christianity movement, the band of merry men and women who set out to reimagine the Christian faith. He described that process like this:

The process was slow, moving forward a few steps only to stumble backward even more, it seemed. For several years, I felt as though I had been wading in a deepening pool of doctrinal and denominational fragments. My faith was intact—because I'd been learning there's a kind of faith that's deeper than mere beliefs—but my system of beliefs was tattered. Little by little, however, a new coherence surged forth from the ashes, like a reborn, reincarnated phoenix. I felt compelled to share what I was discovering and learning with others.

Peter re-read a line from the middle: "I'd been learning there's a kind of faith that's deeper than *mere beliefs*." Bryan wasn't seeking a new system of beliefs, but a new way of believing. Music to Peter's ears.

He continued reading when another sentence jumped out: "The way we're doing the Christian faith isn't working anymore." Peter folded the book on his lap, stared out the window through the prism created by the rain, and marinated over that middle sentence.

Exactly. Something isn't working in the way we're doing Christianity anymore.

This was the whole point of Peter's own quest to refashion his own faith.

Peter continued staring out the window, remembering back to when he first met Bryan. He had just entered a period of faith deconstruction and reconstruction the likes of which he had never experienced before, mostly thanks to Bryan's first book, *A Reimagined Christian*. The main character, Pastor Dan, was his doppelgänger, a replica of himself who was asking the same questions he was asking, and getting in trouble in all the same ways. The other character in the book series, Nelson Edward O'Donnell, served as his mentor, providing the way forward through the confusion and chaos of his crisis of faith. While Peter lived nearly forty minutes away, he felt drawn to this promised land of Prosurgence Christianity and its good-natured prophet to experience firsthand his teaching and insight into a new way of being a Christian, a new kind of believing Christianly.

Peter fondly remembered Bryan greeting him as he pensively approached him at an event his ministry had hosted that featured him and Alfred Morris on Christianity and science. There he was, shaking his hand, with his infectious grin, small Buddha belly, and trademark close-cropped beard that flowed up around his balding head. They exchanged a few words—Bryan asked

Peter what he did in the city and he mentioned he was doing campus ministry work at Georgetown University. Bryan thought that was fantastic.

A clap of thunder broke his trance. Peter returned back to his book and continued reading, coming to a section that piqued his interest:

This band of brothers and sisters journeying toward a reimagined Christian faith are beginning to reassess and repent of the versions of Christianity we've created and formed. We are acknowledging that the Christian faiths we've constructed need to be re-examined—or reimagined—and deconstructed in order to reconstruct something new for our day. We want to see our faith traditions for what they are.

"Bingo!"

What Bryan wanted was what Peter wanted: to reconstruct, to reimagine the Christian faith for his day. For the college students he left behind in Washington who grew up in the Church and left; for his friends who were trying to make sense of faith and life in a world that was so chaotic and confusing.

And now for his brother.

Peter could think of no better person for his brother's journey than his former pastor.

And yet Peter realized the stakes were higher than his own journey now, because Pastor Bryan's ideas were affecting his brother's journey. While he was mostly OK with that, Peter did wonder where those ideas might take him.

He closed Bryan's book and climbed into bed. As he closed his eyes his mind drifted from Bryan to James to VanDyke.

Peter's eyes snapped open as he remembered what would commence tomorrow: his first day of seminary. And now the anticipation and excitement, the apprehension and worry, began to coalesce to heighten the anxiety brewing in Peter.

He was excited for this new season to begin; after all it's why he moved back to his hometown in the first place. Yet there was an uneasiness that surrounded the beginning of what would be a three-year journey toward becoming a pastor and fulfilling his passion for connecting the ancient gospel of Jesus to modern twenty-first-century culture. A journey that would force him to own, hone, and clarify the beliefs that had come to define his faith the past three years. And knowing there was at least one professor who had anti-Prosurgent sentiments running through his veins—not to mention the unknown students who had similar convictions—Peter's stomach churned with a certain amount of dread.

But it also served as a challenge. A challenge to prove them wrong about fundamentalism or Calvinism or whatever entrenched, calcified conservative beliefs reigned at Grand River Theological Seminary. It was also a challenge to prove right the direction of Prosurgent, that the theology and practices of Prosurgence Christianity were a bona fide elixir to ameliorate the woes of modern Christianity.

Peter began to massage his right temple, closing his eyes to squeeze away an ache that began to needle his head. He sighed with the weight of a thousand worries. He pulled the covers tight and turned over, settling in for an afternoon nap in preparation for what would prove to be a tumultuous seminary expedition, as much as a spiritual one.

Both starting tomorrow.

CHAPTER 9

PETER AWOKE to a still-throbbing headache that had lingered from the previous afternoon. Or perhaps it resurfaced from the whiplash of a summer he'd just experienced, moving from the East Coast back to the Midwest, moving in with his parents and darkening the door of his childhood church, starting a new job and now starting classes. The summer zoomed past in a Mach-5 blur for sure!

At its start, he left his community and everything he built the past few years for a place he had sworn off since college. His parents still didn't get his faith journey, and he fought with them far more than he had cared to. JT's spiritual problems were becoming his problems, but he was also excited for the conversations that had developed around his journey. And then there was his new job. It had been a good summer, but an exhausting one, and now he was gearing up for a new chapter in his life by studying to be a pastor, a profession he had once written off and sneered at.

The school year began with a kickoff barbecue at the seminary. His drive over to begin this chapter was a contemplative one. He thought about this new path and everything that went into it: the people, the places, the circumstances, the experiences. The memory from a year ago and the ensuing fallout from leaving his campus ministry began pulsing in his frontal lobe, an experience that set him on this course in the first place.

There were times that Peter wished he was back in DC. He missed his students, missed the college campus atmosphere at Georgetown University, missed the intense conversations that pushed and pulled against his own He didn't miss the misunderstandings with his coworkers, the mischaracterizations of his own journey through reimagining the Christian faith, and he certainly didn't miss the hushed-toned conversations and penetrating stares at his every move. Though the memory of his parting still smarted, he was glad it happened. And he was ready to move on to this new chapter, though he couldn't shake the suspicion he was trading one sour tooth for another.

Peter knew he was probably stereotyping GRTS based on his own experiences with Midwest Christianity. But he was still uncertain if this school was best for him. The last thing he needed was a repeat of the past year. His encounter with Dr. VanDyke didn't help alleviate his simmering fear that it was a haven of fundamentalism.

That's probably going too far, he thought as he exited I-96 at the seminary.

Perhaps not a haven, but he did wonder how open and accepting it was for someone like him.

Peter arrived at the seminary in time for the evening's opening remarks. The front of the seminary was filled with old and new seminarians and their families.

I wonder how many of these women are pastoral students, and not just supportive wives?

Full inclusion of women in ministry was important to Peter. And he suspected that GRTS wasn't inclusive. He walked up near the back of the group just as another professor, an early forties man in a bow tie and blue short-sleeve dress shirt, began the evening.

"Welcome to Grand River Theological Seminary," the professor began. "I know you all are hungry, but we're going to begin inside at the chapel with some brief remarks by our President, Dr. Williamson. And I do promise that they will be brief!" Everybody chuckled on cue and began to file into the building.

The chapel was as modest as the rest of the building, though newer. Though there was a grand piano, rows of padded chairs, and the requisite large pulpit, the room looked more like a vaulted-ceiling classroom that was trying to pose as a chapel.

While others dutifully filled the front few rows, Peter sat at the back. Waiting for the introduction to begin, he felt his hands grow clammy. He prayed no one would sit next to him or turn around to make small talk. Peter was generally an outgoing person, but in new social situations he became awkward and shy if he didn't know anybody. This was one such occasion.

After Dr. Williams greeted everybody and opened with some pleasant remarks about their new graduate endeavors, he instructed people to introduce themselves, starting at the front. Peter was fascinated by all of the various stories floating around the room. Those stories varied by age and stage in life, they varied by academic focus and ministry goals. One story in particular caught his attention, from a stocky young guy with flaming-red hair and freckles.

"Hi, my name is Jake McAllister," he began, raking a hand through thick red hair and looking around the room. "I just graduated from Freedom University in Pennsylvania this past spring and started working at Grand Valley as a campus minister in July. And now I'm starting the MA in Adult Education part time. Anyway, excited to be here."

He offered a friendly wave and sat down.

Another Freedom grad? Who is this guy? Peter never expected to run into someone from his *alma mater* out in the real world. At least he seemed cool.

The next student was almost as interesting of a story.

"Hi, y'all!" said a tall twentysomething coed with long blond hair and curls that bounced when she talked. "I'm Isabelle Saunders, but y'all can call me Izzy. I'm from Nashville and moved up last week to begin the Master of Divinity program. Really excited to prepare to be a pastor someday. Thanks!" She said all of this in a perfectly predictable Southern twang that unpredictably blew apart Peter's assumptions regarding women students at GRTS.

She's perky, Peter smirked. *And studying to be a pastor. Interesting.*

After a few more introductions, it was Peter's turn. He stood, hands in his pockets to hide his sweaty palms.

"Uhh, hi. I'm Peter Daniel Young," he said nodding, pulling out one hand long enough for a quick wave. He cleared his throat as the room stared back. "Grew up in Coopersville up the highway past Grand Rapids. Went to Freedom University as well. Spent some time working in Washington, DC. And moved back four weeks ago to start the M.Div. program." Then he paused, not knowing if he should go there. He decided he would.

"And the reason I'm doing the M.Div. program is because I'm passionate about reimagining the Christian faith for our modern world." Peter saw some encouraging nods, and some other puzzled faces. He continued, "Someone here already called me Prosurgent Pete. That probably fits because I identify with Prosurgence Christianity, though I'm really not into labels and have never self-identified with any Christian group."

Ok, maybe that was too far, Peter thought in a panic, feeling self-aware and awkward at his vulnerability and rambling.

"And, well, I'm excited to learn with you," he quickly added before sitting down.

After two more introductions, the professor stood again to pray for the meal and send everyone on their way to the dinner line.

The buffet was catered by Sandman's Barbecue, the best barbecue north of the Mason-Dixon. Lines quickly filled up on either side of the pulled pork, mashed potatoes, baked beans, and corn bread. As Peter waited in line to take his fill, he heard a familiar voice from behind.

"It's Peter, right?"

Peter turned around to see Jake, offering a kind smile behind him.

"Oh, hey! Yeah, Peter. Peter Daniel Young. You were the guy that went to Freedom University."

"Yeah, just graduated. You, too, right?"

"Graduated four years ago. Small world. I hardly ever meet people from that place." He plopped a scoop of pulled pork on a bun and smothered it with barbecue sauce. Scooping some baked beans, he asked, "So what did you study?"

"Studied history," Jake said, making his own pork sandwich and piling some leafy greens on the side.

"So you were a track-two person, then. I was on the government studies track."

"Ahh, one of those people. So did you work in the government then? I caught you worked in DC."

"Yeah for a year. Then I got jaded. And actually I worked for a campus ministry afterward. You just started at Grand Valley, right?"

"That's right." Jake finished putting touches on his own plate, then suggested, "Do you want to sit down somewhere?"

"Sure, that'd be great."

A cluster of chairs off to the side became host to their Freedom reunion. The two sat down, and Jake shared some of his story: he grew up in the tiny Central Pennsylvania town of Shickshinny, where his dad and older brothers work the area coal mines; stumbled into Freedom University through his grandma, who paid his way to give him a proper Christian education. Peter shared some of his story growing up in Coopersville, experience at Freedom University, and a bit about his time in Washington.

"So why'd you leave?" Jake asked.

"That's a complicated story. You like beer?"

"Umm. No, I don't drink."

"Too bad. Because that's the only way you'll get that story out of me," Peter said with a wink.

"Well, look who's here," Dr. Calvin VanDyke bellowed, walking over with a full plate of food. "Prosurgent Pete!"

Peter caught himself rolling his eyes. *Yeah, that's going to get real old, real quick.*

"Hi, Dr. VanDyke," he said, recovering and gesturing to his new friend. "This is Jake McAllister. He's starting an MA program this fall. Are you going to be in his theology class this fall with him?" Peter asked Jake.

"Yeah, I am." Turning to VanDyke, Jake said, "I read your book on heaven. It totally rocked my world!"

"Thanks, I think. Glad I could rock you." VanDyke replied dryly as he chewed a mouthful of coleslaw.

The three talked about nothing in particular for the next half hour while VanDyke finished his plate. Peter had had enough small talk and decided to return home. Classes started the next day, and he wanted to make sure he got enough sleep for his new adventure.

"Jake, nice to meet you. I'll look forward to the coming year. We should hang out sometime. Over coffee of course. You do drink that, don't you?" Peter said.

"Yes, I drink coffee. And without a sippy cup." Shaking Peter's hand, Jake continued, "Seriously though, glad we met. And, yeah, it should be a fun year!"

On the drive home Peter thought about all of the possibilities for the coming year, and how thankful he was to be back home starting classes to learn how to be a pastor. Peter was especially happy a fellow Freedom graduate was with him at the start of this new journey. He figured Jake would understand some of why he was on it in the first place, considering he went to the same college. He hoped he turned out to be a true friend.

Because he sure needed one.

CHAPTER 10

THE NEXT MORNING, Peter treated himself to breakfast on his way to his first day of class. It was just him, the *New York Times*, and Marie Catrib's, an eclectic dive on Diamond and Lake on the outskirts of downtown Grand Rapids. He ordered his favorite breakfast: vegan stuffed French toast and coffee. Peter wasn't vegan, he just like the idea of eating vegan, especially with the *Times*. They seemed to go well together.

Finishing his satisfying breakfast, Peter said a short, silent prayer of blessing over his seminary journey as much as for his spiritual sanity. After gathering his things he left to face the first day of the next three years of his life.

Peter eased into a parking space just as his Greek class was starting. He slid into a seat in the last row as the professor was taking the roll. He wasn't the only nearly latecomer, however.

As Peter got settled, the perky coed from Nashville saddled up next to him. "Hi there! Is this seat taken?"

Peter looked up at Izzy, then down at the seat, then back at her. "Nope, all yours!"

"Thanks. My name's Isabella Saunders, but you can call me Izzy."

"So I heard." Peter mumbled as she started up her laptop.

"And what's your name?" She asked in her perfectly perky Southern drawl.

"Peter Daniel Young," he said, extending his hand.

She smiled and took it, and Peter took a beat too long pulling away. She grinned. He blushed.

"All right, class. Welcome to first-year Greek," intoned Dr. Greg Morris from the front, tapping the wooden lectern situated on a table, one of two New Testament professors at GRTS.

As Dr. Morris began his first lecture of the semester, Izzy leaned over to Peter. "I remember you," she said in a hushed, twangy tone. "You're Prosurgent Pete, right?"

Embarrassed, Peter nodded and half smiled. "Yeah, that's me."

"I read *A Reimagined Christian* a while back," Izzy replied. "It rocked my world."

Peter turned to face Izzy, elated she had read one his most formative books. "You did? What did you think? How did it make you feel? How did you change?" Peter peppered her with questions.

As Peter waited for Izzy's answer, an audible "ehh hem" came from the front of the room. The class turned around in perfect unison to follow Dr. Morris's gaze to the two instigators of the interruption: Peter and Izzy.

"Are you two brother and sister? Is there a family emergency?" Morris asked, with an air of irritated sarcasm.

"Brother and sister?" Peter questioned turning to look at Izzy. "Uhh, no."

"Ahh, then you're lovers, embroiled in some passionate exchange, or perhaps a dispute of some great import."

"No, sir," Izzy quickly chimed with embarrassment. "Thank you, sir, we're not."

"Well then, would you mind doing me a favor and stop talking while I'm talking?" Morris instructed with a slight Southern edge himself, Kentucky style, not Tennessean.

"Sure thing, partner," Peter replied, trying to diffuse the situation.

"Excuse me?" Morris asked with irritated surprise.

"Nothing," Peter added quickly. "Yes, sir. Sorry, sir."

Morris continued with his lecture. Peter and Izzy looked at each other and grinned like two middle school students caught passing notes under the desk.

The rest of class was uneventful as Morris began a lesson on the Greek alphabet. All the while, Peter was thinking about the mystery sitting next to him who had piqued his heart's attention.

Who is she? he wondered. He decided he would have to find that out. Just not in Greek I.

When class ended, Peter's mind was numb from Greek over-load. He had tried to grab lunch with Izzy before their theology class, but she hurried off before he could intercept her. He wandered, bleary eyed, upstairs instead to the student study hall. At one end was a gathering of couches. He chose one facing the window with a view of small lake between the seminary and the undergraduate university. He stretched out to rest his brain and rest up before his next class, closing his eyes and drifting off into sleep.

After what seemed like minutes, his phone blared his custom techno ringer, slicing through the silence that normally reined in the study hall. He jolted upright as a group of students across the room looked over in derision.

"Hello?" Peter said, throat thick with sleep.

"Are you regretting your decision yet?" James asked on the other end.

"Hey, JT. What are you talking about?"

"You know, strapping that white collar around your neck and leaving behind a life of women." Peter could hear James suppressing snickers on the other line.

"Real funny. Ha, ha. I told you no white collar at this place. And definitely no denial of marriage or the marriage bed, thank God!"

"Yeah well, sounds like a death sentence to me."

"If the next three years are anything like the first few hours, then I may just die by Greek vocab. So what's up?"

"Just wanted to see how your first day was going and see when you wanted to have our first book club."

"So far, so good. Took a nap on lunch break." Peter noticed his book bag had fallen off his lap during sleep, contents spilling over the ground. He started gathering his books, pencils, and papers as he continued talking. "Yeah, book club. Sounds great. But I think I'll have to wait for a few more weeks. I've been slammed with classes, and I think I need to get a handle on my homework for the next several weeks. How about first Wednesday in October?"

"October? What am I, chopped liver?"

"Dude, lay off. I wish it could be sooner, I do. Life is crazy right now."

"I get it. And my place in that life is, what, a distant fifth, sixth place?"

Peter inhaled deeply and raked a hand through his hair. James had displayed a similar petulance when he was in DC, trying to dominate his attention and demand time that Peter didn't always have.

"It's not like that."

"Then what is it like? I'm on the edge, man. I need to talk. I used—"

"Crap, I'm late for class!" Peter interrupted, not hearing JT's response, noticing the time on the clock across the room. "Sorry, JT, I gotta jet. I can't be late for this professor."

"Fine, go on. I guess I'll see you in a few weeks then," JT replied, sounding dejected.

"Yeah, I'll see you in a few weeks. Sorry man, I wish it could be sooner."

Peter turned off his phone and grabbed his bag without zipping it up, causing the contents to spill back out.

Peter cursed under his breath, making sure none of his new classmates heard him the first day of what would surely be a long three years.

"NICE OF YOU TO grace us with your presence, Peter Young," VanDyke remarked. The class stared at Peter in response as he tried to slink into the room.

Peter closed the door and looked around the room. The only seat left was in the first row. Not ideal, but he'd have to live with it. As he sat down he noticed he was sitting in front of Izzy. He decided he'd definitely be able to live with it.

"Sorry, Dr. VanDyke. Won't happen again," Peter said.

"Hey, man! Nice to see you again," Jake McAllister whispered as he turned on his HP laptop.

"Oh, hey. Sorry, didn't notice you. HP, huh?" Peter whispered and winked as he brought out his MacBook Pro.

Jake eyed Peter's laptop, then he looked at his own. As if feeling foolish, he gently closed the lid and slid it back into his bag as the professor began taking role. When VanDyke finished, he faced the class and began with a question.

"What is the point of theology? What's the point of that annoying word *doctrine*?"

The class simply stared back in silence.

VanDyke stared back. "Come on, why are we here? What's the point?"

"To continue painting," Peter piped up from the front row.

VanDyke turned toward Peter. He stood silently, stroking his beard with one hand while the other rested on his belly.

"And what does that mean?" he responded. "To continue painting. What do you mean by that?"

Peter took a breath. "Well, we join in with the rest of the Church and continue where they left off in defining this thing called Christianity. This thing called faith in Jesus."

"All right." VanDyke paced in the front of the room. "Anyone want to respond to that?"

"I will. It sounds like a bunch of Prosurgent mumbo-jumbo!" said someone from the back. Several people snickered in response. Peter turned around and thought he remembered the guy's name. Adam something or other.

"Well, I might agree with you, but there's a way to say that in my class that isn't a personal attack." Several more chuckled in agreement.

"I would propose this, class, and I'm going to disagree with you, Peter, which probably won't be the last time," VanDyke smiled and winked.

Peter didn't mind, though. He relished the chance to publicly disagree.

"I would like to suggest another 'P' word in place of *painting*. Jude 3 speaks of something else. The word *preserve*."

Several people nodded in agreement. Peter sat, arms folded in skepticism. He looked at Jake, who was also nodding with the rest of the class. He glanced behind him at Izzy, who was harder to read.

"'*Contend for the faith that was once for all entrusted to God's holy people,*' writes the Apostle Jude." He continued walking the length of the front of the room. "Contend. Struggle for. *Preserve* with care the one faith given to the Church once and for all. That, class, is the point of theology. The point of doctrine."

Now VanDyke was grasping the lectern with both hands, staring back for a response. Getting none, he continued.

"I want to read something from the early Church father, Irenaeus. He and others like him speak to this very thing, this idea of preserving the one faith from generation to generation. Listen to how he describes the rule of faith, the one faith given to the Church."

He opened an old, well-worn book with several strips of paper peeking up from within, marking important sections. Finding the one he wanted, he continued.

"In *Against Heresies* he writes, '*Although the church is dispersed throughout the world, even to the ends of the earth, it has received this common faith from the Apostles and their disciples.*' That common faith is listed on your handout."

The class turned to the handout as VanDyke continued reading: "'*The church believes these doctrines as if it had only one soul and one heart, and it proclaims them and hands them on in perfect harmony, as if it spoke with only one voice.*'"

He put down his book and turned to the class. "Anybody want to respond to what Irenaeus is saying here? What do you make of his belief that the Church has a single soul and heart of belief that it is pledged to proclaim?"

A few students shifted in their chairs, Peter being one of them. He squirmed at the idea there was simply one version of the Christian faith. To him, Church history seemed pretty fractured. The Church right now seemed pretty fractured. He didn't respond, though, and neither did anybody else.

"You all are a quiet bunch, aren't you?" VanDyke said. "Let me read one more line: '*The languages of the world may be dissimilar, but the message of the tradition is one and the same...Just as the sun is the same wherever it shines, so is the preaching of the truth the same everywhere in the world, enlightening everyone who wants to come to a knowledge of the truth.'*

This time Peter spoke up. "I don't buy it."

The class pivoted toward Peter. "Why not?" VanDyke asked.

"This idea that there is one message that is preached across the world and across time. Wasn't there a little thing called the Reformation, for instance?"

Peter could see a few nodding in agreement, giving him courage to go on. "And in America, how many denominations are there? The idea that there is one version of the Christian faith that's been proclaimed and believed over the past few thousand years seems ridiculous."

VanDyke let Peter's comment hang in the air. Adam from the back responded.

"Sorry about before, the personal attack and all. But yes, I'd say there is...one version, as you say. There is one way to view sin and one way to view atonement. Jesus' sacrifice for our sins and all."

"One view of atonement? Really?" Peter blurted in surprise. He muffled a small laugh before driving hard into Adam's suggestion. "I'm pretty sure there are at least five views of the meaning of Christ's death on the cross that have been believed by the Church. So which view, Adam? I mean aren't there shades of belief?"

Before Adam could respond, VanDyke cut in. "OK, there will be time to debate some of these things later. But the point I want to make is the one Irenaeus makes. The reason we study theology is to understand how the Church has believed. Yes, Adam, the Church believes something about sin. She has always believed something about sin, and those opposite views are called heresy. And yes, Peter, there have been shades of meaning surrounding those beliefs, like the cross. The Church believes something happened at the cross, but there are these shades of meaning when it comes to atonement."

He paused and took a breath, then continued, "I want to suggest that your job as seminarians, as Christians, is to understand how the Church has always believed in order to help your people believe along with the Church. Your job is to understand the pieces of the Christian faith in order to teach those pieces to the next generation. What the Church needs now is not to reimagine the faith but to *rediscover* it. Because let's face it: the history of Christianity is writ large with the consequences of that reimagining—stretching all the way to the early Church. Ideas have consequences, and Christ has given the Church the responsibility of stewarding those ideas that have always been central to the Christian faith. That rediscovery I speak of and stewardship begins with you. And it also begins with this class and the reading I've assigned for next week."

There was a collective groan as VanDyke passed out more handouts and assigned reading for the next lecture before dismissing the class.

"Wow, this is going to be quite the class," Jake offered as they exited.

"Agreed," Izzy added, joining them from behind.

"Yeah," Peter mumbled. "Quite the class."

He said goodbye to his new friends, hoping to make it in time for his family dinner. As he left the city, he couldn't shake a word that had been needling him from the lecture.

Rediscover.

Peter wondered what VanDyke meant by that word. Reimagine he got. That had been the impetus of the Prosurgent movement from the beginning, to reimagine the Christian faith. It had been his own driving force for the past year. But rediscover was a different idea altogether.

Yet he also wondered if that's what he needed. Up until he

started his ministry job, he wasn't at all interested in reading Christian books, much less ministry ones and certainly not theology books. When he did, Peter was more interested in the latest voices on blogs that were helping him navigate his crisis of faith. The majority of Peter's theological training in life so far consisted of his childhood Sunday School and youth group. Added to that was the evangelism training he received at his campus ministry work in DC. Now he thought both experiences were off-the-charts, misguided attempts to shackle the Christian faith to a rusty, stale past. So he added the voices of popular Prosurgent authors who sought to unhinge the faith from that rusty, archaic history.

As Peter merged off I-96 toward home, he wondered how those authors preserved the one faith that Irenaeus spoke of. Though he wasn't convinced there was such a thing—a common faith—he wondered where Prosurgence Christianity fit with that one soul and heart VanDyke spoke about. Given what he read on Sunday, doubts pricked Peter's mind.

"Where do I turn?" Peter voiced aloud as he turned into his driveway.

He didn't have an answer. Perhaps history had some answers. One way or another he'd find out, because VanDyke had assigned a load of reading to force the issue.

CHAPTER 11

PETER KNEW it was going to be one of those days.

He arrived to his eight o'clock Greek class barely on time. What's worse is that he wasn't able to finish his Greek translation homework. And Professor Morris called on him to translate a section from the Gospel of John that the class had been working through—the very spot where Peter had left off translating without finishing. Two weeks removed from the start of the semester, and he was barely keeping afloat.

Sitting to his right, Izzy noticed the blank spot in his homework staring back at Peter as he tried to translate. While Peter stumbled through pronouncing the verse in the original Greek before translating it, Izzy subtly slipped him her homework.

After Peter was finished translating using Izzy's notes, he whispered to her a quick, "Thanks."

She wrote 'NP' on the left corner of her notes—*no problem*.

When class was dismissed, Izzy and Peter walked out together. Peter had tried to invite Izzy out for lunch a few times before their theology class at 3:00 p.m. He thought today was as good a day as any, considering how much she saved his butt.

But as he was getting ready to make the ask, he heard his name from across the main hall.

"Well if it isn't Prosurgent Pete."

It was VanDyke. And he was making his way over to the couple.

"Hey, Dr. VanDyke," Peter moaned in disappointment.

"What, you're not happy to see me? It's probably the name thing," VanDyke said to Izzy. "All right, I'll stop. Anyway, I wanted to see if you were free for lunch."

Peter was thrown off by his invitation, and as equally bummed since it just railroaded his chance at getting to know Izzy better. He turned to Izzy, then turned back again to VanDyke, smiling. "Yeah, sure. That'd be just perfect."

"Excellent! There's a Chinese place around the corner from the movie theater, called Ming Ten. Do you know where it is? Have you been there?"

"No I haven't, but I know where it is. See you at, say, 12:30?" Peter replied.

"Twelve thirty it is," VanDyke said hustling away to his next class.

"Well, I should get going myself," Izzy said turning away.

Before he missed his chance, he said, "We should get lunch or dinner or something some time. I'd love to hear your story. I mean, since we're going to spend so much time together in these classes and all."

"I'd like that. E-mail me," she said as she walked away.

But I don't have your e-mail address, Peter thought as she left. *Ah well, another excuse to chat in class.*

AFTER KILLING some time at a local discount bookstore, Peter jumped into his hatchback and headed over to Ming Ten. VanDyke didn't seem like the person who would appreciate tardiness, Peter surmised, so he pushed the speed limit, arriving with two minutes to spare. He caught his professor on the way in.

"Professor," Peter called. "How was your class?"

"It was good. I'm teaching a seminar on Karl Barth."

"Ahh," Peter said, not knowing who he was talking about.

"You don't know who I'm talking about, do you?"

"Not a clue," Peter said, to which they both chuckled.

"A Swiss theologian, and probably one of the greatest Protestant thinkers since John Calvin. You do know who he is, don't you?"

Peter scoffed. "Yes, thank you very much. Isn't he your patron saint or something?"

VanDyke chuckled. "Something like that. Let's grab a table."

Ming Ten was a well-appointed Asian fusion restaurant specializing in lunch buffet specials. They found an open table, and then headed to the lunch trough. After tonging some fresh seaweed and pouring a bowl of miso soup, Peter eyed the offerings of the sushi bar. The attendant promised the sushi was made fresh that day. Though skeptical, Peter decided he could risk a few Philadelphia and California rolls.

VanDyke was already seated with a plateful of Moo Goo Gai Pan, a few rangoons, and a bowl of egg drop soup.

"That's it?" VanDyke remarked, eyeing Peter's plate.

"This is my first course. Plenty of room for more." He unwrapped his chopsticks and added, "By the way, thanks for lunch."

"You're welcome. I always enjoy getting to know our new students. So what's your story, Peter?"

"Well, I grew up in Coopersville. Mom's a bank teller, and Dad works for GM. Well, worked for GM. He was laid off when the stamping plant closed in Wyoming."

"I'm sorry to hear that." Dipping a rangoon in sweet and sour sauce, VanDyke asked, "Has he found work?"

Peter shook his head as he took another spoonful of soup. "He's been unemployed for almost a year. My mom has been supporting the family, the two of them and my brother Johnny."

Peter paused to sip some green tea and eat another California roll. "So anyway, I went to Freedom University and majored in government. After I graduated and moved back home I fled West Michigan to Washington, DC, and ended up working on Capitol Hill for a congressman."

"Really? As a page or intern or something?" VanDyke said interrupting.

"No, I was part of the congressman's legislative staff," trying to emphasize his position was quite a bit higher than bottom feeder high school page or college intern. VanDyke didn't seem to grasp the significance.

"Anyway, so I worked on Capitol Hill for a year and got burned out from the pace and life. And to be honest, I got pretty jaded. One of the main reasons I left..." Peter trailed off, reminiscing on this part of his story. He took another bite of sushi before continuing. "So through a series of God-moments, I found myself working at a campus ministry at Georgetown University."

"Wow, that's a career leap! Politics to religion. I bet you're a great conversationalist at parties!"

Peter chuckled. "Well, I'm not that fun at parties for a whole set of other reasons. You could probably relate."

"Hey, what do you mean by that?" VanDyke said, feigning offense. "Smart aleck."

Calvin took another chopstick full of chicken and snow peas and motioned for Peter to continue.

"So things took a bit of a turn a few months into my ministry."

He paused considering his words—considering how he would talk about his journey into Prosurgence Christianity.

"I'm listening."

Peter smiled. "I think I need another plate of sushi. Let me get that, and then we'll talk."

"You can't leave me in suspense like this! I'll join you in refilling."

Peter pilled high some more sushi, venturing out into the eel and crab categories. When he returned, VanDyke was pouring them fresh cups of green tea.

"Thanks for the tea," Peter said, settling in for his second round. "So my ministry time was spent mostly meeting with college students for Bible study and spiritual mentoring. I also met with guys for prayer and counseling. But most of my time was spent navigating their deep questions about life and spirituality."

Peter stopped again, considering his words. "The only problem is, I didn't have answers to the questions they were asking. I mean, I had answers because of my background in the Church and my classes from Freedom. But they seemed to ring hollow. Or I didn't have answers to the questions they were asking."

"Like what?"

"Well, like about life right now. Like, why is there so much suffering in the world if there is this good God? Or how to live a good life right now, not necessarily some life after death. And the thing is, when we were trained to share the Christian message, it was all about their life after death. Heaven was the whole point. But what we were offering wasn't what my college student friends were seeking."

VanDyke was listening with focused attention now, having set down his chopsticks, encouraging Peter to continue.

"They were also pretty turned off to the attitudes of a lot of Christians they knew or grew up with. Their perceptions of those in the Church were that they were just a bunch of judgmental, hypocritical homophobes who really were not interested in bettering the lives of people right here, right now. To these students, Christians seemed more interested in getting them to sign up to a long list of rules or to join their particular organization. So there were lots of emotional barriers between their interest in the Christian faith. And they were totally dissatisfied with most of the answers Christians gave to their questions."

Peter took a sip of tea while VanDyke went back to picking at his plate.

"All this to say, I felt totally ill-equipped when I jumped into this ministry work. But it also did something to me, too. It sent me down this path of sort of re-examining my own faith. I was brought into this period of faith deconstruction and reconstruction, something I had not experienced before. And in re-examining my Christian faith, I was led into this whole world of other people who were also re-examining their Christian faith. You know them as Prosurgent."

"Yes, I do," VanDyke replied.

"I know you do because I read your book on the Prosurgent Church. And I must say that I did enjoy it, even though I don't think you got some things right about them."

VanDyke furrowed his brow. "Like what?"

"Hey, this conversation is about me," Peter replied grinning. "That'll have to be for Chinese lunch number two!"

"Oh, I see how it is. Poor seminary student taking advantage of his professor friend for a free lunch."

"I gotta save my cash for my library fund. Anyway, so the past few years have been this intense journey of re-examining what I believe about...well, a whole lot of things. And so I've read most Prosurgent authors. There are some things I find suspect. But then I read their responders—"

"Like me," VanDyke interrupted.

"Like you. Like other hyper-conservative guys. Well, yes like you!" Peter said chuckling.

"Hey, I'm not hyper anything."

"That's not the point. The point is that I look back on what I believed growing up. I look at what my friends were asking and the answers I thought I had—the answers I was told to give by my ministry and the gospel I was told to teach. I look at these Prosurgent people, and think they're on to something. And then I read people who are on the other side of the spectrum responding...and I just don't know what to think sometimes!"

Peter stopped to catch his breath and take a few sips of tea.

"It's like I don't even know what the gospel is anymore. What is the gospel?" Peter said in exasperation.

"Well, the gospel is God's movement to rescue the world from sin and death through Christ's life, death, and resurrection," VanDyke replied, his voice edged with concern.

"I know what the gospel is," Peter replied chuckling. "It was a rhetorical question."

"I was never very good at those," VanDyke said with half a smile. "I hear what you're saying, Peter. I've been on that hyper-conservative, hyper-fundamentalist side myself, though you might say I'm still there! And yes, I look at what's happening in the Prosurgent Church and think they are totally off base, but for good reason."

"Because they're not a conservative fundamentalist?" Peter blurted out.

"No, not because they're not a conservative fundamentalist, but because they're not orthodox."

"By whose standard?" Peter could sense his hairs begin to prickle on end at the back of his neck and ears begin to burn with the heat of the conversation.

VanDyke stopped eating and took a few sips of tea. "When I ran into you, or should I say when you ran into *me*."

"Yeah, sorry about that."

"No matter, but when we talked at GRTS you said something about desiring to reimagine the Christian faith. And then at orientation you said something similar, that you were hoping to reimagine the Christian faith for our new twenty-first-century culture. Is that right? Is that where you're at?"

Peter considered this. "Yes, that's what I'm saying. That's where I'm at. I'm searching for a progressive Christian faith, a progressive Christianity."

"Progressive..." VanDyke said slowly, leaning back and smiling.

"Yes? Is something amusing?"

"No, it's just that I find that word so fascinating. Progressive. As if that's what the Christian faith even needs. To change and advance forward and...*progress*."

"Instead of what?" Peter said sitting back himself and folding his arms, ready for a fight. "*Regressive* Christianity?"

"That sounds about right, actually!"

Peter rolled his eyes and huffed, leaning forward to return to his lunch.

"Now hear me out, because this is what I'd challenge you with. And this is free since I'm off the clock." VanDyke shifted to the edge of his seat, readying for a lecture. "I don't think what you need is to reimagine the Christian faith. What you need is to *rediscover* the historical Christian faith. So regressive Christianity could be a good way of putting it, a sort of returning back to what the Church has always believed. After all, that's what regress means, the act of going back, a returning to what was before."

Peter leaned back again, pondering this nuance to his own spiritual quest. "What do you mean by rediscover—or *regress* as you put it? And *historic* Christian faith?"

"I mean returning back to what has always been central to faith in Jesus Christ since the early Church—the fundamentals of the faith. And yes, the dreaded, fearful, scary Reformation! But only because the Reformers themselves were interested in redis-covering the historic Christian faith from the early Church after being forgotten for centuries thanks to corrupt practices and beliefs. Maybe *vintage* is a better word. The *vintage* Christian faith. Seems more your style."

Peter smiled at this, intrigued by the idea of a vintage faith. Definitely sounded better than a *regressive* one. He was appreci-ating this conversation but felt an incredible amount of resistance welling up inside.

"Gotta admit, all this talk about fundamentalism is making me a little nervous."

"Not fundamentalism. The *fundamentals*," VanDyke corrected. "You don't need to be a fundamentalist to still hold onto the fundamentals."

"Really? How?"

"Take eschatology, the doctrine about end times. The whole left behind silliness is fundamentalism run amok. There is little basis in the historic Christian faith for that view of the end of the world as we know it. But the Church has always believed in an end, with either a positive or negative outcome. Is the end Tim La Haye's version with hero Kirk Cameron? Hardly! In fact, his acting might be cause for his own special place in hell."

The two shared a laugh before VanDyke continued. "I'm kidding, of course. The point is, you can still hold to the funda-mentals without being a fundamentalist. And that's where redis-covery comes in. Reimagination will take you to the Prosurgent Church. Like I said in class: ideas have consequences."

He furrowed his brow with curious interest at that phrase. "What do you mean by that, that ideas have consequences?"

"Whether fundamentalism or progressivism, there are conse-quences for what we believe and what we teach. Take the whole *Left Behind* end-times craze, which has tended to promote an escapism that takes Christians off the hook for what we do on

Earth now. Why care for creation when it's just going to burn? And liberalism's dismissal of judgment is dangerous at the other end of the spectrum, for it isn't honest about the clear reality of hell that the Bible teaches—which is no good for anyone."

Peter thought his point was interesting. But there it was. The 'L' word. *Liberalism.* It was sort of like another no-no word, the 'H' word: *heresy.* Peter was not fond of people throwing either of them around.

"So where does rediscovery take me?" Peter asked, folding his arms and ignoring the L word comment for a moment. "If reimagination takes me to...liberalism, as you say, then where does rediscovery take me?"

"The historic Christian faith. It sounds like you've read a lot of Prosurgent thinkers, but how many *Church* thinkers have you read? What have you read from the early Church fathers? Anything from Aquinas? How about Calvin or Luther? Or how about in the twentieth century, someone like Karl Barth?"

Peter thought he was making a rhetorical point, but when VanDyke paused and sat staring at him, he knew he was interested in his answer.

"Well...none of them," Peter said sheepishly.

The bill came, and VanDyke pulled out his credit card to pay.

"Come on, let me get that," Peter protested.

"No, no. I want to. I'm sure there will be plenty more to get," VanDyke said grinning.

He stood to go pay at the register, and Peter followed. While he paid, Peter grabbed a few butter mints for the road.

As they walked out to the parking lot, Calvin responded to Peter's answer. "Look, Peter, you seem like you've got a good head on your shoulders. I respect your own journey, where you've been with Prosurgent and all. I guess what I'd caution against is your assumption that what people like Bryan McLaughlin, Dale

Pagels, and Trevor Bohls are saying is anything new. It's not, they're not. And I would suggest you read well outside of their little club to discover what the Church has always believed."

Peter was taken aback by VanDyke's aggressiveness. A part of him appreciated it, though. "Thanks for lunch, Dr. VanDyke. And thanks for your advice. I guess I struggle with what you're saying because I just don't want to go backward."

"What do you mean, backward?" VanDyke said as they reached his car.

"Are you kidding me?"

Startled, VanDyke turned around as Peter was pointing at his car. It was an even older Honda hatchback than Peter's, but in miniature. It looked like a Mini Cooper but angular, like some futuristic wannabe. Clad in dull black paint, former rust spots were visibly patched with Bondo fiberglass putty, giving it a spotted, leopard-like complexion.

"Are you mocking my car, Peter Young?" VanDyke said, feigning offense. "That thing's been good to me. It got me through undergrad, seminary, my doctoral program. I'll have you know it's got over two hundred thousand miles, and it's still running strong!"

Peter backed up, palms raised. "Whoa, just kidding! Didn't realize you had so much history with her. Anyway, so you asked me what I meant by going backward. I mean going back to fundamentalism. That's been one of my fears coming back here."

"You've feared turning into a fundamentalist?" VanDyke said.

"I guess. But probably more the conflict between my past and where I am now."

VanDyke unlocked his car door, and said, "Well, like it or not, you're going to read some of the people I suggested because of Systematic Theology 1. But I can send off a reading list if it would help. Something to point you in the right direction."

"That would be great! If nothing else it would be an excuse to expand my library."

"Well good." VanDyke opened his door and slid into the driver's seat. Peter was amused at the sight.

"Don't laugh. This is a gift from God, you know!" VanDyke said. "Nice lunch, Peter. Take care, and see you in thirty minutes."

Peter looked down at his watch and saw it was almost 2:30 p.m. He felt like he needed a nap after that conversation before another round at SysOne.

"Rediscover," Peter mumbled as he drove back to the seminary. He didn't know if he liked that language. It sounded like a ploy to drag him back from a place he vowed he'd never return.

But it also made sense. Especially the historic or vintage Christian faith part. Prosurgent trumpeted the ancient aspects of Christianity, yet it often seemed more interested in the ancient practices, rather than ancient beliefs. Maybe there was something to peeling away the layers of crud built up over time around the central pieces of the Christian faith—of the fundamentals to the Christian faith, whatever those were.

He was reluctant to follow VanDyke's advice, though. It seemed like a step backward in his pursuit of a Christian faith that made sense in the world—made sense *of* the world, this modern one. While he wanted to reimagine, perhaps he needed to rediscover. Especially considering what he was now reading along with his brother.

Perhaps that was reason enough to take the professor's advice, especially since his and JT's first book club met the next week.

CHAPTER 12

WHEN PETER ARRIVED AT FOUNDERS, the October evening air was crisp, but unusually pleasant. Though the sun had settled, it left behind a blanket of warmth that defied the emerging autumn, as if summer was trying to reassert itself before being banished for another eight months.

The drive over was a cantankerous one, a bitter conversation between Prosurgent Pete on one shoulder and Calvinist VanDyke on the other. They personified the Yin and Yang of his theological conscious as he continued traversing the topsy-turvy road that was his spiritual journey—a journey that was about to gain a traveling companion. His brother. He couldn't shake the lunch conversation from the previous week, which both grated against his inner sensibilities yet intrigued him about the possibilities of engaging and rediscovering the vintage Christian faith.

"Rediscover what has always been central to the historic Christian faith, Peter," bellowed his professor on his left shoulder, whom he imagined wearing red-tights, wielding a pitch fork.

"No, no, no! You've got to *reimagine* the Christian faith, from top to bottom!" cried Prosurgent Pete on the other, clad in a billowing white sheet.

Shows you where Peter Daniel Young's biases laid.

Yet he wondered if the kind of retrieval effort VanDyke encouraged could be exactly what he'd needed for years. What his brother James had needed, too. Peter figured he'd find out soon enough as James was already sitting out on the front porch when Peter strolled up to the front door attendant.

"Petey!" James shouted jumping out of his bench with a half-drained beer in tow and cigarette hanging from his mouth. "I'm up here!"

The burly man with a bushy beard glanced at Peter as he checked his drivers license. "Enjoy, partner," he said, winking as he handed back his ID.

Peter waded through the tightly packed crowd, making his way onto the front porch. "Thanks for the welcome!" Peter greeted JT with a hug and sat down on a picnic table that looked to have been occupied for some time. There were empty peanut shells everywhere. Peter wondered how many times JT's mug had been already refilled. It was Wednesday, Mug Club Night, which meant he probably already had a few. Peter flagged down a server and ordered one of the tasty IPAs he'd fallen in love with last time they were here.

"So how are things?" Peter asked.

James shrugged, downing the rest of his beer. "Ok, I guess."

There was a long pause as James downed his beer, then searched furtively behind him for a server.

"So you're using again."

"Dude!" James whipped around. "What the—"

"Hey I'm just asking! Because I care man. Don't get defensive."

"Well gosh, Bro, the first thing you say to me is if I'm using again."

"No, that was the second thing I asked you. First, I asked how you were doing and you downed your beer and then searched for another."

"Smart-ass," James mumbled as he returned to searching for someone who would relive him from his brother's interrogation and bring the relief of malts and hops. After someone finally took his order, the two sat in silence for a few minutes."

"Yes, OK. Yes, I have been." James wasn't angry or huffy. Just matter of fact about it.

"OK," Peter simply said. He waited for his brother to offer more. Getting nothing he asked, "Do you want to talk about it?"

"Not really," James sighed as he looked around, running a hand through his greasy dirty blond hair. "I'm an addict, Pete. It's what we do."

"But you said you were getting better. That you'd stopped even."

"Yeah, well. There ain't no stoppin'."

Peter didn't know where to go from here, didn't really know if he wanted to. Perhaps it was the result of years of turning a blind eye to JT's struggles—out-of-sight, out-of-mind, as they say—that made him insecure. Now that he was back and sitting across from him at Founders, as his older brother he felt an obligation to help —had a desire to help, but felt utterly helpless.

"Is it pot?" Peter finally asked.

JT smirked and shook his head.

"Something harder, like *Oxy*?"

"How do you know about *Oxy*?" JT spat back.

"Hey, I know things! Is it heroin?"

James's smile fell, guilt replacing his cockiness. This was far deeper than Peter wanted to go, but obligation edged him onward. "So you're a heroin addict."

"Yes, Petey, I'm a heroin addict. Here, you wanna take pictures of my scars?" JT extended his forearms, a garden full of puncture wounds that caused Peter to take a long swig to whet his stolen breath.

"What? Mr. Know-It-All didn't know about the trail of scares heroin leaves behind?"

"No. I mean, I did," Peter said softly. "I just didn't expect to see them on my brother." He set his drink down and stared out across the parking lot.

JT followed his stare. "It's alright if you don't wanna talk about it. Hell, I sure don't! But don't worry, I'm reforming my ways."

Peter turned his head back to see a smiling JT. "Really, I am!"

"I thought you said there ain't no stopping?" Peter raised a skeptical brow.

"I mean, not like wham-bam-boom overnight. But I got me into a program and everything."

Peter felt relief, partly because he wouldn't have to step in himself. "That's great to hear. Really great!"

"Yeah, I'm done, Pete. Done." He turned around searching for his server again.

"Well you better be, Bro, because the next time I hear about you dipping or shooting or smoking or whatever the heck you do, I'm gonna kick your butt from here to Canada!"

James laughed as the server arrived with his drink. "Yeah right, you who's got like a five-inch vertical!"

"Hey, I got game enough. So you better watch out."

"Yeah," James said between sips, "Whatever."

Peter was relieved the playful brother banter helped recalibrate a conversation that didn't start as he had planned. He returned to his drinks to catch his breath and move on.

"So how are Mom and Dad? Did you go back to Fundie Freakville Sunday?" James sneered.

"Hey stop," Peter chided as his beer arrived. "No I didn't go back, which they weren't too happy about. I don't know what I'm gonna do. But I need to find something else. Hey, we should look for something together."

James huffed. "You won't find me in no church, Petey. You know that."

"I'm just saying. If you ever thought of going back..." Peter replied trailing off.

"So the book." Peter slapped the cover of his copy, trying to change the subject. He noticed JT's copy off to the side was dog-eared and well-read.

"I don't think I'm as far as you are. Looks like you've been devouring that thing."

"Yeah, I'm half-way through."

"Dang, I just started! So you're liking it?"

"Heck yeah! I'm totally down with this quest for a new kind of Christianity. I feel like this guy is giving me permission to believe the things I've been thinking for a while now."

"Really? Like what?" Peter asked.

"For starters, how he thinks about the Bible. The way Christians have used the Bible to bash others is just abusive. He says that. I've felt that. And the way lots of Christians read the Bible is totally anti-science and has allowed slavery and prejudice against gay people and the abuse of the environment. It's no wonder so many have jumped ship! I mean this way is what we grew up with, you know that Petey."

James was getting passionate, in a way Peter hadn't seen before. And the way he was describing the Bible was familiar to Peter. It's the way lots of his Prosurgent friends had talked about how the Bible has been used.

"I totally agree we need to be careful when we read the Bible. Reading it literally can lead to a whole lot of trouble. Like slavery and male dominance and an abuse of the environment. But that doesn't mean the Bible isn't true or doesn't have some things to say to us now," Peter offered, channeling some of his childhood views of the Bible he still couldn't shake.

"No, of course not," he agreed, lighting a cigarette. "Bryan's problem isn't with the Bible, but with people who read the Bible to support their agendas. That's why he says we need to think of it as a community library."

Peter furrowed a brow. "A community library?"

"Yeah, like it's filled with a number of voices having this conversation about who God is. And that conversation changes over time—from the beginning."

"So Bryan believes the Bible is human conversation about God? Not that God is saying something to us?"

"I don't know about that." JT took a drag on his cigarette as he flipped open his book. "Listen to page 81: *The biblical library is a carefully selected group of ancient documents of paramount importance for people who want to understand and belong to the community of people who seek God and, in particular, the God of Abraham, Moses, David, the prophets, and Jesus.'"

"That sounds a bit pluralistic."

JT shook his head. "I think he's just saying that people have put together this book to talk about the God the Bible reveals, like a community library has a bunch of different writers in the American History section to talk about America's history. The facts are the same, but over time those writers may change how we understand the subject. The American History section keeps all the important ideas of writers over time. He's saying the same for the Bible, which makes a whole lot more sense than what we grew up with."

Peter was flipping through chapter 8, trying to get a handle on Bryan's understanding of the authority of Scripture, not knowing what to make of what he was hearing, and reading.

"Well then where does the authority lie?" he asked.

"What do you mean?" JT asked, his voice a mixture of confusion and skepticism.

"If Scripture is just this library filled with a bunch of voices talking about God, which voice is right? Who gets to say what's right about God and what he wants from us?"

JT sat back and took a sip from his beer. "They all do. We do. God is *in* the conversation, man! God is seen in the conversation that we shape."

Peter folded his arms. "But then can't we make the Bible say anything we want it to? If God isn't saying something in the Bible, only in the...*conversation* as you put it, then doesn't that mean we're the ones that get to say what it's saying?" He cocked his head, and said, "Did that make sense?"

"Yeah it did, but don't we do that anyway? Look on page 96: '*The Bible they—*' and by they he means fundies like Mom and Dad," James added grinning. "Anyway, he says, '*The Bible they want to put us 'under' tends to be the Bible as they have interpreted it, which unsurprisingly means we are actually under their authority as they stand over us with Bible in hand.*' Boom! There it is. Case closed!"

A few patrons seated at surrounding tables and standing nearby looked over as James loudly proclaimed his win.

Peter didn't quite know what to think or how to respond. "I agreed we all bring our own interpretations to the table, but that doesn't mean the Bible itself isn't saying something. The Bible says a whole lot of things about how to live and what to believe. No, *God* is saying a whole lot of things about how to live and what to believe."

"But who gets to decide then? What interpretation is right? You're starting to sound like Mom and Dad here, Petey. I'm getting worried!" James jabbed his brother in the shoulder.

"Gosh, I hope not!" Peter sputtered. "I'll have to think more about that one. Good conversation, though."

"For sure, bro. And thanks."

"For what?"

"For this. For being here for me in my struggles. With faith. With doubt." He looked down into his nearly-empty glass, finished it in one gulp, and added, "With life."

Peter smiled. "No problem, little brother. But if you take another hit, man, I'm gonna kick your—"

"I know, I know. You gonna kick my butt from here to Canada! Let's get out of here."

THE NIGHT WAS a pleasant 62 degrees, with a clear sky and canopy of stars. It was the perfect setting for a windows-down drive while deep in thought.

Peter was delighted with the evening. The conversation was stimulating and interesting, something he couldn't say before about his brother. They had always had fun in the past, but deep conversations were never a priority, though he didn't know why.

Maybe I've underestimated him these years, Peter thought. *Treated him less than.*

Either way, he was thrilled with the discussion, though cautious about some of its content.

He was caught off guard by what he was reading and hearing from Bryan. Maybe it was because for so long Bryan had only hinted at what he was now saying in clear black-and-white terms. For years his books helped people wrestle with issues of faith, because he wasn't afraid to give voice to the questions they themselves were asking. Now it seemed Bryan had taken a sharp turn toward providing answers, alternative answers to what Peter had grown up thinking was real and true about the Christian faith.

Sure, Peter had asked similar questions and even given some similar answers to what he and his brother talked about that evening. Like Bryan, he no longer believed the Bible was in conflict with science, for instance, and many of our interpretations of Genesis were simply based on our own interpretations. But for Peter that didn't mean God didn't create the world or that evolution took over, which he had a hunch Bryan believed.

Peter arrived home near midnight, though sleep was far off. Still buzzing from his conversation with JT, he decided to make some tea and continue where he left off in the conversation on the Bible's authority in Bryan's book.

The warm mint and chamomile concoction was a pleasant combination in his chilly air-conditioned room. Peter picked up Bryan's book and turned to the section on the Bible.

As he read, Peter noticed at several points that Bryan labeled the story at the beginning of Genesis as a coming-of-age story. Bryan called the unfolding drama in Genesis *'a story about the downside of progress.'* He said as humans progressed from hunter-gatherers to nomadic herders to agriculturalists to city dwellers and finally empire dwellers, human civilization descended into shame and fear and corruption and genocide.

Well, that seems right. And we've been descending ever since!

He continued reading until the end of the chapter, when his attention was grabbed.

God's unfolding story is not shaped by the traditional version of the Christian faith, the one that imagines a realm of perfection, a fall from perfection, condemnation, salvation from hell, and then a return to heavenly perfection or eternal life. It's a different story altogether. We need to reimagine God's story as the downside of human progress—a story of our foolishness and God's faithfulness, our engagement in rebellion and God's desire for reconciliation, our intent to do acts of evil and God's intent to overcome our evil with good.

Peter set the book down and stared through his window to the large sycamore tree lazily waving its arms outside, considering what it was Bryan was getting at.

The idea that God was faithful and sought reconciliation and our good despite human foolishness and a turn toward rebellion seemed right. But then again, wasn't Bryan rejecting everything about the Christian faith Peter had known was real, much of what he still held was real?

For Bryan, there never was a time when things in the world were just right, when there was perfect peace and wholeness. More importantly, Bryan didn't believe there was a fall from this perfect state as Christians had always believed. He rejected the idea that people were born sinners in need of salvation from hell—in fact it didn't seem as though he believed in hell at all.

"What am I to believe?" he sighed.

I'm so confused. Who is right? Bryan or my childhood faith? Prosurgence Christianity or the traditional faith?

He closed his eyes and then realized something—a thought grabbed Peter in a way he hadn't thought before: these were the ideas that JT was latching onto. Peter saw how James was channeling Bryan in their conversation. Which meant the stakes were much higher than his own little inner journey away from the suffocating confines of his childhood faith.

Reimagining the Christian faith took on a whole new dimension now that his brother was doing the same.

Peter finished his tea and tossed the book next to his chair in the turret window. He knelt beside his bed, closed his eyes, and prayed a simple prayer:

"Lord, how can I know what is real about faith in you? Please show me a way."

Peter put on a t-shirt and gym shorts and climbed into bed, hoping he was ready for the journey he felt was coming his way.

DURING THE HOURS between eyes closed and eyes opened, Peter dreamt he was running down a road, an endless road that extended well into the horizon without any indication of stopping.

"How do I know which way to turn?" Peter huffed. "How do I know which path to take? Which step is real?"

Out from the midst of the wispy, black fog a voice was faintly audible, yet clear and commanding: *"I've revealed; therefore, you can know."*

"What's that?" Peter called out.

"I've revealed; therefore, you can know."

Peter looked down at his feet and noticed his path was revealed only two step-lengths ahead of where he was running. The rest was a black fog, yet before him was a crystal-clear path, electrifying its way through the fog far ahead.

I've revealed; therefore, you can know.

"I've revealed; therefore, you can know," Peter repeated again. And then again, each syllable of this beautiful sentence coinciding with every yard he pounded out as he ran.

I've revealed; therefore, you can know, Peter was mouthing as he awoke from his slumber.

He shook his sleepy head and mumbled, "God revealed; therefore, I can know."

God revealed; therefore, I can know!" He was fully awake now, his brain firing on all cylinders by the revelation.

"Yes, that's it! God has said something. Some things, many things in his Holy Scripture. It's not just human conversations about God. God himself is saying something about himself. And we're invited to listen. To take notes."

Peter awoke from his dream with a euphoric start, comforted by his God-given revelation. That euphoria quickly evaporated, however, when another realization invaded his conscious.

"But how do I know what his revelation means? So God has revealed, but how do I interpret that revelation correctly?"

Which interpretation is the right one in a sea of misinterpretations?

He wasn't quite sure. He hoped yesterday was the start of that day of discovery. Or perhaps rediscovery.

CHAPTER 13

THE FOLLOWING week after a long day of classes, Peter came home to a vacant Cooper Manor. Johnny was at a night class, and his parents were at a Bible study group. So it was up to Peter to fend for himself with dinner. He went simple that evening: PB&J, some carrot sticks, and a glass of milk.

After watching a rerun of *COPS* while eating his dinner, he went to work on a Greek translation project of a few verses from John 1 and finished a paper for his Biblical Hermeneutics course.

By nine o'clock his mind was numb, eyes glazing over from mental and physical exhaustion. He heard a commotion on the lower lever, the back door unlocking and opening. Several stomps up the stairwell confirmed Johnny was home from class. Peter retired his homework for the night and reached for Bryan's *A Reimagined Christianity*.

Since diving into the book after his conversation with his brother several days ago, Peter had been conflicted—feeling both pleased and vexed at the same time. Next week Peter was to get back together with James for round two of their book club. So as the night wound down, he thought he would read more from the new kind of Christianity manifesto written by the man who had been something of a spiritual mentor to him, diving deeper into his reimagined Christianity rabbit hole.

The topic was on Jesus—who he was, why he was important, and what he did. Peter continued his routine of tea at night with his McLaughlin reading. They seemed to go well together.

After brewing a nice Indian chai tea—not the boxed, milky stuff, mind you; this was the real, loose-leaf deal—he climbed into bed and turned to the chapter on Jesus.

In the first few pages, Bryan made the point that often Christians make Jesus in our own image—we uphold a Republican or Democrat Jesus; a prosperity-gospel, get-rich-quick Jesus; a male-chauvinist Jesus, an anti-science Jesus. Most of the chapter was uncontroversial. There was a lot Peter resonated with. He especially liked this line:

John wrote the book of Revelation to encourage Christians everywhere to pledge allegiance to the one who governs by his example of service and suffering.

Yes. Jesus rules by his example of service and suffering.

As he was finishing this chapter, Peter remembered something Bryan wrote about Jesus in the chapter before, so he flipped over a few pages to the chapter on who God was. Here, Bryan argued that Jesus brings us to a new level in our understanding of God.

Christianity's teachings on Christ being human and being God mean that we cannot begin with a predetermined, rigid idea of God taken from the rest of the Bible and then apply it to Jesus, anymore than you could pluck a great American novel from your local library's shelves and apply it to all Americans. Jesus is not meant to merely fit into our predetermined categories; he explodes through them, tears them apart; he alters them forever and brings us to a new, mature understanding of God, of the Divine.

So far so good, until Peter read the next line.

"The experience of the Divine in the man Jesus requires a brand-new definition and understanding of who God is."

The experience of the Divine in the man Jesus...

He paused and considered Bryan's wording of who Jesus is.

Is it that we experience God in Jesus? Or is it that Jesus is actually God himself?

He kept reading:

Jesus's character gives the world a unique and invaluable guide for tracing how images and concepts of God matured and developed across human history and cultures.

What is he saying here? There was more:

For the Christian faith, the most important aspect of the Bible and its teachings is the picture of Jesus it gives the world—who gives us the most developed, profound, and mature view of God's character.

"Are you kidding me?" Peter blurted out, spilling his tea on his book and pants. "Ouch, dang!"

He grabbed a shirt from a pile of dirty clothes to wipe himself off. He returned to the book, confused about what he was reading. It seemed like Bryan was merely saying Jesus gives us the highest, deepest, most mature view of the *character* of God—rather than Jesus revealing God, rather than *being* God himself.

He furrowed his brow as he kept reading, wondering where Bryan was going in his description of the person of Jesus.

God's character is like Jesus's character. When you look at Jesus, you are getting the best portrait humanly available of God's character.

He flipped to the next chapter in a panic, searching for a hint of Bryan's meaning.

Jesus is the flesh-and-bones revelation of God's character; the Divine is revealed through the man.

Peter slapped the book closed on his lap, tossed it to a pile of clothes next to his bed, and rested his head back on the chair back, staring off at the ceiling with a deep sense of unease.

For Bryan, Jesus is a man who acted like God?

Of course, he didn't come out and say it like that. But that was the logical conclusion of the language Bryan used to describe Jesus. He never said "Jesus is God." Only that he revealed "the character of God."

This changed things for Peter.

He climbed into bed, his stomach twisting with the implications, every fiber of his being set on edge. Messing with how the world was created—six literal days or six billion years—was one thing. Messing with the Church—who's in, who's out—was something else. Peter even thought various perspectives on Scripture were fine—whether as a constitution or a community library.

But messing with Jesus was something entirely different; messing with who Jesus is was off limits.

As Peter lay on his bed, eyes closed, staring off into oblivion, a number of emotions welled within.

Confusion, for why Bryan viewed Jesus in this way.

Anger, for the way Bryan portrayed Jesus.

Sadness, for how that portrayal might influence others.

Most of all, he felt betrayed. Swindled. Hoodwinked. Sold this magical new land of a renewed faith, a new kind of faith that was supposed to be truer to the traditional faith.

Bryan had been something of a mentor for Peter, though at paper-and-ink length. And yet here he was, reducing Jesus Christ to a sort of Gandhi on steroids—a really nice man who lived like the Divine and taught about love, but who wasn't actually God.

Peter reached toward the end of his bed and retrieved the book back from the top of his clothes pile. He leaned back and held it, considering whether to reopen it or not. Peter sighed and returned to his spot. He was intrigued by what Bryan was saying and wanted to continue reading to see where Bryan would continue to turn in his quest for a new kind of Christian faith.

The next chapter continued the previous section on Jesus, but centered on his works, particularly Bryan's understanding of the essence of the Christian message. As he read it became clear that for Bryan the gospel message was about the Kingdom of God, and he believed that for Jesus the gospel was about the Kingdom of God. A paragraph pinged his radar as he read about what Jesus came to do—or really what he came not to do:

Jesus didn't come to replace all other religions, or even start one himself. Instead, he came announcing a new realm, a new way of living he called the Kingdom of God, which was a way of peace and good news available to people of every religion.

Why the religion bit?

Peter bought this idea to a degree, that Jesus didn't come to start a religion. But what was going on here? He found his answer as he kept reading:

A new way of living and new Kingdom is much vaster than simply a new religious faith. In fact, this way and realm has room for many different religious traditions.

"Jesus' Kingdom makes room for other religious beliefs?" Peter wondered. "Other gods?"

He continued reading with growing interest and concern. *Is he going where I think he's going?*

The good news of Jesus' Kingdom is about God's way of living happening on earth as it is happening in heaven— for everybody everywhere. It is about God's faithful solidarity with everybody everywhere in their suffering, chaos, and pain.

There it was: universalism.

He flipped to the next chapter to continue reading Bryan's thoughts on Jesus and the Kingdom, which he continued by walking through the book of Romans. Moving through the chapter rapidly, Peter stopped at Bryan's explanation of Romans 5, our collective fall thanks to Adam. For Bryan, this part of Romans 5 related all of our divergent religious perspectives back to Adam, a common humanity.

After connecting us to our common ancestor's story, the story of Adam, Paul paints Jesus as the new Adam, a second Adam, the last Adam.

So our common humanity in Adam leads to a common humanity in Jesus?

Peter's intuition was confirmed a few lines down:

Paul's point is clear. Adam brought death and condemnation to everybody, but Jesus brings life and justification to everybody, everywhere. We're all part of Adam's original story, and now we're all part of Jesus's new story, too. A universal, inclusive story.

Peter had had his own Christian universalism impulses in his own spiritual quest. He had grown up with the idea that there was this narrow group of people who were in, while everyone else was screwed. The Christians he knew from the Christian communities he had been around seemed quite certain who was in and who was out. And they seemed perfectly fine with a God who would punish the out group forever and ever in Hell. That version of the Christian faith had worn Peter out for years, especially when he began to befriend college students who were considered part of the out group: Muslims, gay people, even Catholics were considered false Christians by most of his communities.

But while Peter had struggled with the idea that some people would be banished from God forever, he still held to this need to confess Jesus as Lord and Savior, however that looked. He couldn't shake the fact that Scripture seemed to say there were people who would be out by their own choice, and that there would be a certain level of punishment for those on the outs—justice, even, for how they had treated God and neighbor. Bryan, though, seemed to just dismiss this in one fell swoop, insisting that everybody was in, especially regardless of religious beliefs.

Peter remembered seeing another chapter in the table of contents on how other Christians should relate to people of other faiths. He turned there and started skimming, coming to a section commenting on 2 Corinthians in the Bible.

Paul says that God no longer holds humanity's sins against them. He doesn't mean just people of the Christian faith, here, but people everywhere. For generations, Christians have assumed they are on the inside, while everybody else is on the outside of God's little religious club. Thankfully, God's ways and thoughts are higher than our arrogant, exclusive, supremacist, and tribalistic ones. And God invites us into those higher thoughts, too.

Does he mean exclusive claims about the Christian faith don't matter?

He set the book down on his lap and considered this. Because it sure seemed the Bible itself made exclusive claims about Jesus. Yet it seemed like Bryan didn't care.

Peter picked the book back up and flipped a few paged forward. He continued reading:

If the Church could break free from the traditional version of the Christian faith that sorted souls into Heaven and Hell, we could offer Jesus as a gift to the world as he was meant. We would no longer think it our religious duty to insult other faiths and call their leaders demonic. We would no longer dream of a time when every other religious faith but ours would be destroyed, and only ours remained. We would no longer consider everybody else as "other" and us as God's exclusive children. We would learn to discover God in other faiths as much as our own, discovering a much bigger "us" where everybody, everywhere can be included.

There it was. A patent belief in religious pluralism and universalism.

There was a growing sense that Bryan was confirming in his book what others had been warning for years. Peter flipped the page and continued reading a section on Bryan's take on evangelism:

In a reimagined Christian faith, evangelism would stop being about proclaiming the superiority of the Christianity above all other faiths. It would stop requiring hellish, fire-and-brimstone scare tactics or slick marketing campaigns, as if Jesus and his Kingdom message were a product belonging exclusively to Christianity.

So Jesus' good news of salvation isn't a set of beliefs exclusive to the Christian faith?

Peter closed the book and took a breath. That seemed to confirm it right there. Bryan was a religious pluralist.

He closed his eyes and took a breath.

The person he had sat with as a spiritual guide for a year was claiming everybody, regardless of religious beliefs and affiliation, was simply in. That God was found in other belief systems outside of the Christian faith. Outside of Jesus Christ, even!

Peter was confused by what he was reading; Bryan's ideas conflicted sharply in his heart with the fundamental beliefs he had tried to transcend for years. Tried to *reimagine.*

For the longest time it seemed like he could reimagine the Christian faith beyond its fundamentals. It worked because he was merely asking questions alongside people like Bryan or other Prosurgent thinkers. But now, wasn't the conversation turning toward providing answers, alternative answers, to what the Church had always believed?

He was beginning to understand why VanDyke encouraged him to rediscover, rather than reimagine the Christian faith.

This flood of emotions surprised Peter. And scared him. This was the group of people who had provided an oasis in the midst of the chaos of his spiritual journey, during the time he almost walked away from the Christian faith. Bryan himself was a welcome relief in the middle of his stifling, suffocating fundamentalist Christian ministry, shepherding him as a pastoral friend through the choppy waters of his crisis.

A number of questions rose to the surface in rapid succession:

Was he now reverting back to the same fundamentalism he fled? Why was he finding himself more comfortable critiquing and pushing back against his Prosurgent friends?

Perhaps it had something to do with his brother.

He wondered what his brother was thinking as he read this book. He wondered if he was picking up on the definitions and meaning sitting underneath the bigger ideas Bryan advocated. But then he wondered even if he did, would he somehow be affected by those ideas? Would it matter to JT's own spiritual journey if he realized Bryan was arguing Jesus was simply a man who lived like God, rather than God himself?

He didn't have answers to those questions, but somehow he thought he'd find them over the coming months as they journeyed through the book together, two brothers on the same spiritual quest for a Christian faith that was still relevant for our modern world.

CHAPTER 14

THE FIRST SEVERAL weeks of the semester proved more intense than Peter anticipated. Already he'd had five Greek quizzes. In a week he'd have to wrestle with his first Greek exam. VanDyke had assigned a paper on the inspiration and inerrancy of Scripture. That was due a week after his Greek exam. The only sweet relief was his Spiritual Formation class, which visited an outdoor labyrinth at a nearby church, an unusual field trip for what used to be a Baptist school. He was barely managing to keep up with the new demands on his life, but Peter didn't mind. He was in his element most when he was surrounded by books, diving deep into new ideas, engaging in the latest arguments with other people, and fleshing out his own beliefs through writing.

Still, he was beginning to feel the strain of life pressing in against him. On top of his course work, Peter was slated to start his new job by working the closing shift on Friday evening. He arrived a few minutes before 6:00 p.m. and was pleasantly surprised to see Lexi bent over, cleaning tables.

He stared one beat too long and was caught by his new boss when she pivoted to put a chair back in place, eliciting a smile.

"Well, hello there, Peter Daniel Young. Can I help you?"

Blushing, he stumbled, "Uhh, yeah. Was just wondering where I clocked in?"

"In the back is your time card. Just write when you started, skipping the few minutes you were staring at me while I washed the tables," she said as she walked past him to go inside.

That was bold, Peter thought. *But I like it!*

"So is it just us tonight?"

"Just us and the two love birds," she said, nodding at a couple huddled in the corner. "Double date, I guess!"

"Sounds good to me."

Peter eyed the back counter stacked with coffee mugs and bags of roasted beans. Turning to the Italian-made espresso maker, Peter said, "So this thing looks scary."

"You've never worked one of these before?" Lexi asked quizzically. "You told me you had experience working with coffee house."

"I believe I said I had experience working with *coffee*," he corrected. "As in *making* coffee. The Mr. Coffee sort of way. I may have intentionally left out the part about not ever working in a coffee retail."

"Oh, now the truth comes out, pastor man! No problema. I can teach you. Saddle up, partner!"

Lexi walked him through the various components of the La Pavoni espresso maker. It was a newer machine with electronic technology that made the modern-day espresso-making enterprise much more manageable, especially for someone like Peter. She showed him how the electronic buttons controlled the espresso part of the machine, making a shot for each of them to down.

"The trickiest part is the non-electronic part, the steamer valve." Lexi grabbed the valve and turned it, shooting steam out the nozzle and startling Peter.

"Whoa! It's like something out Willie Wonka and the Chocolate Factory."

She giggled, and said, "So you place the nozzle in the milk pitcher and turn the knob like this." The steamer began to work its magic, frothing the milk while she dropped in a thermometer. "Make sure you froth the milk between 150 and 155 degrees. And don't ever froth soy milk above 125. You'll burn the soy, and that tastes just nasty. And make sure it's positioned just right, putting the tip near the top as you move along."

"This looks complicated," Peter groaned.

"Well, it is a little bit. Sort of like fly fishing, you know? It takes technique. Here, you try." She shut off the valve and dumped out the steamed milk, then handed the reins over to Peter.

After filling the pitcher with fresh milk, he put it under the nozzle and grabbed the valve, trying to coordinate his moves.

"So do you actually fly fish, or were you just being metaphorical?"

"What? A girl can't fly fish?"

"No, of course. I've just never met a chick who could fly fish."

"Peter Daniel Young, I guarantee you haven't met a chick like me on so many levels."

Peter grinned. "I like the sound of that."

He continued steaming the milk, taking care to make sure the frothing wand remained submerged beneath the churning waves of milk.

"There you go," Lexi said, encouraging him over his shoulder. "Now slowly bring the pitcher down, but be careful not to—"

Before she could finish, Peter pulled the frother down prematurely, letting the tip of the nozzle touch the top the milk, spraying milk over the back of the machine and the front of his shirt.

"Ahh," he gasped without managing to drop the pitcher.

"Oh gosh, are you, OK?"

"I'm fine.' He took a rag and wiped his front.

Lexi let a few giggles slip before offering, "Maybe we'll keep you on the coffee pot for a while, Mr. Coffee!"

Unlike the start to Peter's first evening on the job, the rest of the evening was uneventful. He perfected the art of coffee making while Lexi took point on pulling shots and crafting espresso drinks. By the end of the night, and several practice rounds later, Peter was even finally getting the hang of using the espresso maker by himself. He only managed to burn one pitcher of soy and spray two more pitchers of milk in his newbie frothing attempts. After the last customer left a few minutes past closing time, they got to work on the dishes piled around the sink.

Lexi grabbed an empty large pitcher that once held a liter of chai mix and, out of nowhere, asked the question Peter so desperately wanted to avoid.

"So seminary. You want to be a pastor or something?"

Caught off guard by Lexi's probing question, Peter dropped the milk frother he was wiping down with an echoing clang.

"Umm, sort of," Peter managed, picking up the frother and handing it to Lexi to rewash. "I mean, yeah, I want to be a pastor." He quickly added, "But not like you think!"

"And what do I think, Petey? Can I call you Petey?"

"For sure," he replied with too much eagerness. He cleared his throat and continued. "I don't know your religious background, Lexi. But I grew up in West Michigan. And if your experience was like mine, the Christianity you grew up with was judgmental, filled with rules, and totally disconnected from real life."

"Yeah, the church is pretty much jacked up," Lexi said, jolting Peter with her choice of words while scrubbing down a coffee pot. "That's why I've gone Eastern, man. The Buddha beats the pants off any slimy preacher man, hands down!" She caught herself, and let go of the rinsed pot, sending it plunging back into the soapy water. "I hope I didn't offend you!"

Peter laughed, raising his hand in reassurance. "None taken. Don't worry, I get it. I mean, in some ways it is," Peter acknowledged. "But I hope for more for the Church. A church that I might, yes, pastor some day."

"And what do you hope for?" she said, putting her rag down and folding her arms with interest.

Peter set down his drying towel. "I've been on a journey of reimagining the Christian faith for the past year or so. And what I hope is that the Church would actually connect to our world, for a Christian faith that makes sense in the twenty-first century."

"I like the sound of that." Lexi said, relaxing her arms with interest. "So what does it look like on the other side of a reimagined Christian faith, Peter Daniel?"

"That's gonna have to wait for date number two, I think."

"No! I have to know." She said hit Peter with her towel, and he playfully yelped. "OK, we should finish up anyway. We're almost done."

After finishing the dishes and counting the money for the night's deposit, the two walked out onto a leaf-covered Wealthy Street. It was midnight, and the stars were in full fall bloom. Because of the late hour, Peter walked Lexi to her car, even though it was only three cars back from his own.

"Thanks again for this job, Lexi. And for showing me the ropes tonight."

"No problem," Lexi replied smiling and peering through loose bangs. She moved them behind her ear with a single brush of her hand, and said, "You're all right, Peter Daniel Young. I mean, Petey."

You're all right, too. He turned smiling back to his car. "Goodnight," he called back before heading home for the night.

. . .

PETER WAS RIDING HIGH as he drove up 131 toward home. The job was a joy, the company even more joyous. There was something magical and mysterious about Lexi that drew Peter in.

Be careful, Peter. She's a Buddhist for gosh sakes!

While he didn't believe in missionary dating, Peter thought this could make for a blissfully appropriate exception.

As he exited the highway, he thought hard about how to make this work, plotting and scheming his next move.

What's the play, Peter wondered. Dinner? That might be too big too soon. Coffee? *Lame. She owns a freakin' coffee shop!* How about a nice drink? Did she drink? She seemed like a drinker? *That's presumptuous!*

This inner dialogue continued as he made his way around a curve toward home, distracting him from the change of circumstance occurring a few streets down the road.

It was as if he'd stepped into a puddle housing a live wire—the jolt was instant, yet also seemed to happen in slow motion.

In what seemed like mere seconds, a car a few streets down the road decided to ease through a stop sign while following his equally reckless friend. To avoid slamming into the backend of the stop sign runner, Peter slammed on his brakes and turned his wheel to the left, hoping to swerve around the car he was about to kiss with both headlights. Instead of veering into the left lane his tires failed to track the swerve, sending Peter and his Honda hatchback spinning toward the oncoming traffic emerging through a fresh green light up ahead.

"Holy heck!" Peter yelled as his car spun like a county fair Tilt-A-Whirl toward the opposite direction his automotively trained mind knew to be right and true.

His mind swam with confusion as he tried to correct and readjust his car in the onslaught of high beams heading toward his face. Cars protested this turn of events with angry horns. Luckily, miraculously, Peter managed to avoid every one of the approaching cars, somehow landing up on an embankment on the other side of the road.

Peter breathed heavily, the weight of the event sinking in, keeping pace with the angry, frightened cars.

He got out of his car to assess the damage. There were large gouges in the earth where his car slid sideways to climb on to the embankment. Nothing looked damaged from his early assessment, until he reached the other side.

It wasn't bad, but the force of the slide managed to wrench his rubber tire off the rim of his rear passenger wheel. The front tire bent slightly inward, though he couldn't tell if it was because of the force of the impact or his steering wheel was turned leftward.

"Ah crap," Peter said.

He exhaled and looked up, the blanket of stars having grown exponentially since leaving the city for the country. He weighed his options, eventually coming to the conclusion it was simply too dark to try and change the tire. Even with the full moon, the ground was too soft to jack it up, anyway. It would have to wait until tomorrow.

But no worries. He was stilling riding high off his lovestruck adrenaline, which would carry him home, and beyond.

THE NEXT MORNING, the memory of his near-accident experience and lame car hit Peter hard. He rolled out of bed and threw on his clothes from the night before to fetch his car.

When he stumbled down the stairs, he was greeted by his parents, who were at once shocked and relieved to see him.

Maggie threw herself on her son with a panicked hug. "Oh, Petey! We thought something happened to you!"

"What? Why?" Peter said in confusion.

"We didn't see your car and thought the worst," replied his father. "Speaking of which, where is it?"

Peter retold the story of his drive home, how he narrowly missed plowing into the rear end of the stop sign-running car, and how he narrowly missed being plowed into by the stream of cars coming from the other direction, resulting in his car's injuries.

"Let's go," Danny suggested.

"It's all right, I can take care of it," Peter replied, not wanting to involve his dad.

"Don't be ridiculous. It'll go better if we both go."

Without objecting, Peter grabbed a bagel and filled an insulated cup full of coffee.

"So how was your first day on the job?" his dad offered as they backed out of the driveway.

He shrugged. "It was fine."

"Good. That's good."

Danny continued driving, the silence growing. As their relationship had drifted apart over the past few years, the two found it difficult to carry on a conversation for any length of time. It was too strained, too many layers of disagreement and mutual stubbornness. But Peter tried.

"So how about you? How has your job search been? Any luck?"

"Been tough, Son. Real tough." He kept his eyes fixed on the road. "Not a whole lot out there for a guy with nothin' but a high school education. And I'm not the only one. Same sad story for everybody else who lost their jobs."

"Sorry to hear, Dad," Peter offered. He didn't know what else to say. "I'm sure something will turn up. As Mom always says, when God closes a door he opens a window!"

He silently cursed himself, knowing how weak the tired cliché sounded. He'd never uttered such a thing himself, didn't know why he did now, except he didn't know how to carry the conversation along any further.

Silence returned as they turned onto the road where his car was still sitting like a beached whale on the embankment alongside the road.

"Wow. How did you manage that?" Danny said, eyeing the skid marks still fresh on the morning pavement as he walked around to the passenger side.

Peter popped the trunk to get at his spare while his dad assessed the damage. They worked together to raise the car and change the tire. Luckily, both the rim or tire didn't appear damaged, and nothing else seemed bent either, which was a miracle considering the force of the impact of Peter's swerve.

On the drive home, Peter noticed a slight tremor, which meant his alignment was probably off.

Great. There goes my first paycheck!

After arriving home, Peter headed up to his room to jump on his computer for his morning blog-reading routine. Peter loved hopping around to a number of Prosurgent blogs to read what other people were saying about their own spiritual journeys. He felt less alone knowing there were those on the other side of the digital cloud who were wrestling as much as he was.

One of his favorite blogs was called *Jesus Creed*, by college professor Scot McKnight. He loved Scot's willingness to push the envelope while still remaining theologically rooted and biblically uncompromising. Peter felt a kindred-spirit connection with Scot and visited his blog as often as possible.

That morning, Scot had posted on the evangelical obsession with politics and vying for a seat at the political table, a topic near and dear to Peter's own heart. What Scot said wasn't anything new to him so he scanned the comments to see how people responded to Scot's pushback. One comment caught Peter's eye, a comment from a Pastor Dave Jones. It read:

Scot, what an insightful post. I have long lamented how much money and time the evangelical church spends fighting for a place at the table of power. It reminds me of a jilted lover who can't let go and obsesses over the attention of the object of their obsession. We should be obsessing over the only Lover who has given himself to us, Jesus Christ the groom. Israel was called out by the prophets for doing the same, and they had a pretty strong label for that nation: whore. Are we not the same? —DJ

"Nice!" Peter exclaimed in approval.

He had often noticed Dave Jones's comments on Scot's blog, a popular destination for the Prosurgent movement. Scot was a well-published, well-known New Testament professor at North Park University who had a special interest in the broader Prosurgent Church conversation because of his unique position at the intersection of the emerging generation and the church. Dave Jones was a frequent commenter on the site. Peter resonated with this guy.

On a whim, Peter decided to check out who he was. He clicked on Pastor Dave's profile and was connected to Dave's own personal blog. In the upper right corner was an *About Me* section, which startled and delighted Peter all at once.

"He's pastoring in Coopersville?" Fellowship Community Church, it read. "Now where is that?"

He googled the church name to find out its location. Ironically, it was just up the road from Coopersville Baptist Church, on the edge of the Main Street corridor.

"This is too good to be true," Peter whispered.

After last month's experience with his childhood church, Peter knew he could not go back, but struggled with an alternative. He knew his parents would be disappointed, and quite possibly angry, if he didn't continue attending with them. But he didn't care. He had endured stretches of churchlessness before, but didn't want to fall into that pattern so soon into this new season. It seemed like a gift from the good Lord above that he stumbled across this church possibility—and of all places a blog!

He went back to the post and replied to Dave Jones's comment: *"Thanks for your words, Dave. I linked over to your own blog and saw you are pastoring in Coopersville, MI. Lo and behold, I just moved back to my home there a week ago. And tomorrow I'm going to visit your church! See you soon :)"*

Peter closed the browser and went downstairs for the family dinner.

This Sunday, Fellowship Community Church would have one more person in their pew. He hoped they were ready.

CHAPTER 15

"SO YOU'RE JUST NOT COMING?" Maggie said with an edge of irritation, sprinkled with a dash of hurt.

Peter decided not to tell his parents until that morning that he had found another place to worship. Hence the protest.

"I just found something that I think could be a better fit," he replied, with little interest in getting into it with his mom. "It's nothing personal, I just need something else. I'll see you after church."

Peter kissed his mom on the cheek and headed out the door, cutting off the conversation.

The church was a short walk from Cooper Manor. He couldn't remember what the church looked like or place the church so he followed the directions on his phone and waited for the surprise. When he drew closer to where his phone's blue pulsing dot took him, a wave of skepticism began to crest. It looked nothing like he expected. In fact, it looked worse than he expected.

Fellowship Community Church was a small, old, white-steepled building that sat on the side of Church Street. It looked to be from the founding of the town, and the massive aging, sagging oak trees that flanked the church didn't do much for its appearance—it appeared small, overshadowed under the weight of the surrounding boughs. Off what was the main sanctuary was attached a newer edition crammed into its postage stamp-sized lot, nearly kissing the surrounding houses. While the pastor seemed progressive, by the looks of it on the outside the church seemed the furthest thing.

Several retired couples and a few families hustled into the building as he slowed to a stop across the road. For a moment he just stood there, considering if he should abandon his plans. He breathed deeply and stepped out to cross the street.

"Here we go."

When Peter entered through the large double doors, he was greeted by an enthusiastic couple who handed Peter a bulletin and welcomed him into the service. The inside of the church reminded him of a Panera Bread: cozy, inviting, and modern, a far cry from the outside for sure. He could smell coffee brewing—though it smelled like the weak and tasteless caffeine broth that tended to mark most churches. Though sparse, the church felt alive—there were lively conversations in couches off to the side, lively music coming from the gathering hall, and lively art hanging around the foyer where Peter was standing. Because the church was small, Peter began to feel increasingly self-conscious as the new guy. He quickly made his way into the sanctuary, homing in on a seat one row from the back. As he settled in, a middle-aged woman came to the front to welcome everyone and start the service.

"It is good to be in the house of the Lord today, isn't it?" she said with enthusiasm and a large, toothy smile. She was met with hearty *"Amens"* of approval.

"Can we slip in here, young man?" an older gentleman said to Peter in a thick Dutch accent as the small band started playing.

"Sure," Peter replied stepping out to let the man and his wife enter. They wobbled into the row, each bearing a cane and a hunched back.

The band was modest, a step up from the piano and organ ensemble from his previous experience with his parents, but a far cry from what he experienced in DC. A middle-aged man played an electric guitar. An older balding guy kept time on the drums. A similarly aged woman commanded the piano. And a thirtyish guy led on a mic, accompanying greeter lady who doubled as the worship leader. It was neither showy nor skimpy, but certainly reflected the quaintness of the small-town church.

They opened with a popular modern worship song. The singing felt genuine and warm. After another Top-40 Christian radio worship hit, they ended with the hymn "All Creatures of Our God and King." It was led in a way that maintained an air of tradition without being overly traditional. Peter was moved, which loosened him up and helped him to enjoy the service.

After the obligatory morning meet-and-greet, a particularly uncomfortable time for Peter as an introvert averse to small talk and strangers, an elementary school-aged boy went up to the front holding a Bible and a mic. He announced he was reading Psalm 23, then began.

"The Lord is my shepherd. I lack nothing. He makes me lie down in green pastures, he leads me beside quiet waters he refreshes my soul."

Peter was captivated by this young child reading from the Scriptures; he felt his soul refreshing.

The boy continued, "Even though I walk through the darkest valley, I will fear no evil, for you are with me; your rod and your staff, they comfort me."

This is what Peter needed this morning, the words of a child, the intimacy of a small-town church.

"Surely your goodness and love will follow me all the days of my life, and I will dwell in the house of the Lord forever." The boy ended and returned to his seat.

"Amen," Peter said quietly.

Pastor Dave thanked the boy and welcomed everyone. He began his sermon by asking a question.

"What do you fear this morning?" He paused, scanning the room, settling on Peter before continuing.

"I love this Psalm, because it gets at the heart of what many of us carry with us this morning: Fear. F-E-A-R. What a tiny word."

He paused for several beats before continuing.

"What a *big* word. There isn't a person here who hasn't struggled with fear. Who hasn't been affected or brought down by fear. We fear little things like spiders. I transform into a frightened school girl at the sight of even the tiniest of spiders."

The church laughed on cue.

"We fear big things, like how we're going to pay our mortgage or where our life is heading. Sometimes we fear really big things like the outcome of a medical test or God's silence."

That last one struck Peter in a way he hadn't considered before. Perhaps he did fear God's silence, fearing that God wasn't going to show him a way from where he came from to wherever he was going.

"So what do you fear this morning?" Pastor Dave paused again, creating space for people to consider his question. "There is a note card under your chair and a pen. I want you to take a few minutes to write down what you fear. Nobody's going to know. Just take some time for silence and solitude. Contemplate your own heart."

Peter liked those words: silence, solitude, contemplation. Inside, he was thanking God for helping him find this church.

He reached down and picked up his card along with everybody else. Peter considered the question, and then wrote down three words:

Family, Future, Faith.

Then he added a fourth that broke the three-F alliteration: Past.

Having used up the few minutes reserved for contemplation, Pastor Dave interrupted by reading the story from Mark 4 of when Jesus calmed the storm. It was a familiar story that Peter had heard countless times growing up. In it, the disciples and Jesus travel to the other side of the Sea of Galilee and are confronted by a furious squall. While the disciples were freaking out, Jesus was asleep—"on a cushion," Pastor Dave pointed out. After the disciples accused Jesus of not caring if they drowned, Jesus stood up and calmed the wind and the waves with one voice. The disciples stood awestruck by Jesus's power, exclaiming, "Who is this? Even the wind and the waves obey him!"

After explaining the story and pointing out some important parts like any good pastor, Pastor Dave said something Peter hadn't considered before.

"You know, I've often heard people say that Jesus brought the disciples into the chaos and actually created it to teach them a lesson. And he was just teasing them by faking that he was asleep to make a point. The problem with that interpretation is that there is no indication here that Jesus created this thing—that he brought them into a trial and faked sleeping just to make a point. So what's going on here? Why is he sleeping? And on a cushion?" He paused, letting the question hang.

"Perhaps Jesus knew all along what was happening while he was sleeping on a cushion—and he continued sleeping because he was resting in the *presence* and *power* of his Father. I think that's exactly what is happening here. Jesus is asleep because he is confident in God as the one who controls the wind and seas. He is confident that God is all powerful and all present with him in this amazingly fearful event. So if Jesus wasn't freaking out, why are you, dear brother, dear sister?"

Peter hadn't heard this story put like this before. He had believed that Jesus created the storm to test the disciples, but perhaps not. Perhaps he had been taken by surprise as much as the disciples.

"Jesus is calm," Pastor Dave continued. "He is at peace. He completely trusts his Father. Man, if I could just learn to respond like Jesus when life shifts, life would be so much easier, so much less stressful!"

The congregation nodded. A few groaned audible *"Amens."*

"Jesus demonstrates to us how it looks to trust God—to trust in his *presence* and *power* when life doesn't turn out right. He shows us how to *faith* instead of *fear*."

Pastor Jones ended his sermon with prayer, praying for each of those note cards. That Jesus would remove those fears and solve those fears. That those present would trust him in the middle of those fears.

At the conclusion of his prayer, along with everybody else, Peter voiced his approval with a hearty "Amen!"

The service ended, and Peter was inundated with people. As a twentysomething visitor it was hard to blend in, considering the size and average age of attendees. People introduced themselves and bore gifts of that coffee Peter smelled earlier and some cookies. And then Pastor Dave came over to introduce himself.

"Are you Peter Young?" Pastor Dave asked with a toothy grin.

"Sure am. I promised I'd be here."

"Great to meet you!" He turned to the crowd gathered around and announced, "We met online!" People laughed in response.

"So what's your story, Peter?" Dave asked. "What brings you to Coopersville? You said you moved back?"

"Right. I moved back over a month ago from Washington, DC to go to seminary at Grand River Theological."

"Really? What are you studying at GRTS?"

"I'm in the Master of Divinity program. I needed a church so I thought I'd visit. And I must say, I enjoyed myself this morning, Pastor Dave."

"Oh, just call me Dave. I'm glad you're here, Peter. Hey, are you headed off to anything in particular?"

"No, not really. I've got some pre-class reading to do, but other than that I was just going to take a nap. Why?"

"Well, my wife is away visiting our daughters and grandchildren, and I ain't got anybody to eat lunch with. Would you like to grab a bite over at the Main Street Cafe?"

Peter was taken aback. He smiled and replied, "For sure! I'd love to grab a bite to eat."

"Great! I've got to close things up here, so how about in thirty to forty minutes?"

"Sounds great. I'll see you then."

A few more people greeted Peter before he headed out the double doors and into the crisply emerging Michigan autumn noonday hour. He was regretting his decision to leave his coat at home as the temperature dipped into the fifties with plenty of bite to spare. As brisk as the day was turning out to be, he decided to take advantage of the few remaining days before the fall closed and winter officially took over by taking a stroll through town. He hoped his cable-knit sweater would work its magic!

As he wandered up Main Street, Peter thought about the service and his newfound home. *Home*, Peter thought. *Did I just find a new church home?*

It had been several months since he had been part of a church community. At the beginning of the year, he had stopped attending church. It had become too much of a rote religious exercise. And Peter needed space to figure out his relationship with church, what it meant to him and what it meant for him to be part of one. But this was different.

Somehow those concerns from the past several months fell

away. Somehow he felt comfortable in this church. And it surprised him. There wasn't much to the place. It probably should be too quaint for his tastes. Perhaps that's why he liked it. It was so unassuming that it couldn't take itself too seriously. Between its aged building, the amount of people, the age of those people, the ragtag worship team with missed beats and off-key backup, and really bad coffee—he shouldn't want to go back.

A few years in a megachurch back in DC with a double-decker parking garage, thousands of twentysomethings and young families, a laser show and a fog machine for worship, and Starbucks all had conditioned him to believe that *this* is what was important to doing church in the twenty-first century. Along with most of his evangelical generation he had been conditioned not to appreciate the spectacle he had just encountered. In his heart he knew he was being his overly critical self in cycling through the quaint features of Fellowship. But all of it is what mysteriously beckoned him to return.

He wanted to go back, he couldn't wait to go back. To go back to that old musty building. To the vacant space filled with older people. To the little-engine-that-could worship. And, yes, even to the really bad Folgers coffee.

And he wanted to get involved, which, considering Peter's experience in DC, was quite the leap. Yet somehow that leap didn't matter. Or maybe it didn't feel like a leap at all.

Perhaps Peter was learning what it meant to have faith again.

To *faith* instead of *fear*—his future, especially his past.

CHAPTER 16

AFTER TWICE CIRCLING the main town corridor Peter headed back from his contemplative walk. Peter strolled up to Main Street Cafe, finding Pastor Dave waiting outside on a bench that paralleled the street. He wore a very furry hat, the kind with large flaps you'd see in Cold War-era movies. He greeted Peter with the same jolly grin and warm personality from an hour ago.

"Well hello there, my seminary friend."

"Hi, Pastor Dave. What is that on your head!"

"A Russian *ushanka* hat I picked up last year in Ukraine. I do ministry work there from time to time. And please, just call me Dave. Davy Jones." Dave opened the door for Peter, and they took a table that had just opened near the back.

It was a quaint, modest-sized establishment typical of small towns. A faded canary yellow covered the exterior. Flower boxes with peeling white paint hung on each of the windowsills, filled with under-watered, wilting marigolds. Inside, the nine booths arranged around the perimeter and ten tables in the middle were packed with after-church patrons. Apparently, the whole town of

Coopersville decided to join Dave and Peter for lunch. The after-church Sunday lunch crowd had turned out in full force that afternoon, which made the service crawl.

"Thanks for visiting us this morning, Pete," Dave started as they took their seats. "Hope you felt welcomed. And hope we didn't scare you off!"

"Oh no, not at all! It's exactly the type of place I've been looking for. Music was inviting. People were super-friendly. And the preaching wasn't half bad either," Peter winked.

"Oh, come now!" Pastor Dave demurred, chuckling. "Well, we're a small church with a big heart. Some great folks there."

"Seems that way. I plan to be back again for sure!"

While they waited for their waitress Dave continued. "So you came across my blog from Scot McKnight's website, right? That sure is random."

"I know! I've been following Scot for a few years and came across the post you commented on, about the evangelical obsession with politics—"

"I remember that one," Dave interrupted. "Got into some hot water with that comment!"

"I bet. I liked what you said, being that I spent some time on Capitol Hill and saw exactly what you were talking about. So I clicked your profile and jumped over to your own blog, and then saw you were pastoring in Coopersville of all places. I figured that if I resonated with your words on *Jesus Creed,* I might just resonate with your words in a church service. So voilà!"

"How cool!"

Finally the waitress, a young, slight lady whose nameplate read "Cindy" came to take their order. She pushed a lock of sweat-soaked hair behind her ear, took a pen and her notepad from her apron, and asked for their order in rush.

"You look like you've been running a 10K," Pastor Dave offered.

"Yeah, it's a busy one today, darlin'," Cindy replied, relaxing the furrow from her brow slightly.

"Well, I'll make it easy on you. Club sandwich on rye with a coffee for me. Peter, what'll you have?"

Peter looked up from the menu after a long pause. "I think I'll go with a Cobb salad and some iced tea. Wait, is your iced tea freshly brewed? Or is it out of a machine."

"Machine, darlin'," Cindy replied tapping her pen on her pad with one hand, while the other rested at attention on her hip.

"Umm, OK. Let's do it."

Cindy hustled away to the kitchen, while Pastor Dave excused himself to use the restroom.

While away, Peter glanced around the cafe, taking in the sights and sounds. Sundays were still big affairs in Coopersville, and the townsfolk dressed for the occasion. There were lots of big, colorful hats festooned with feathers and flowers. Lots of older gentlemen in suits and ties best left to the eras from where they came. Boys shifted uncomfortably in their starched shirts and pants. Peter caught one bit of conversation criticizing the pastor, whoever he was, for going too long. Another criticized the worship leader for using a guitar.

Peter shook his head. *Oh, Coopersville.*

The cafe itself was painted a bland, sterile off white and had enough kitsch to rival Cracker Barrel. Memorabilia from ages gone by littered the room: there was an old town map and collections of old photos from the era of Mr. Cooper himself; a plate rail circled the cafe around the top with plates and cups and saucers; and off to the side a hutch filled with eighteen glass eyes belonging to nine porcelain dolls guarded the cash register.

Pastor Dave returned just as the dolls sent a shiver down Peter's spine, and the two of them settled into their chairs for their lunchtime conversation.

"So Peter. What's your story? I remember you said you grew

up here, moved away to DC, moved back, and now you're at Grand River Theological. But I'd imagine there is lots of color to fill in those blanks."

The coffee and iced tea arrived as Peter began to share.

"So I grew up here in Coopersville. Mom's a bank teller, and Dad worked for GM at the plant in Wyoming. He lost his job a year ago and is still unemployed."

"Sorry to hear that," Dave said with pastoral concern.

"It's fine. I mean he's coping. Anyway, so I was born and raised right here. Attended Coopersville Baptist Church all my life. Which was good and bad. Looking back, I appreciate the solid Bible teaching I got and the rootedness in the Christian faith. But the bad was that it was thoroughly fundamentalist." Peter took a sip of iced tea and added with a grin, "Which pretty much makes me a recovering fundamentalist!"

Dave gave a snorting chuckle, almost choking on his coffee. "Join the club!" he added, laughing again.

"You too?"

"I'll get to that later," Dave said. "Continue, please."

"I went to college at Freedom University in—"

"You didn't!" Dave added before Peter could finish.

"You know of Freedom?"

"Oh, I do. I know the president personally. It's a fine school, but let's just say it tends to produce a certain breed of Christian. Hope that didn't offend!"

Peter smiled. "No. Not at all. I was that breed! So I majored in government and then ended up working for a congressman on Capitol Hill for a year. That sort of started my journey to where I'm at now. It was a good experience but also disillusioning to see the inside relationship between the Church and the State."

"Really?" Dave said with a passionate interest.

"Yeah. Pretty disillusioning, actually. So I needed out and found my out through an opening at a campus ministry at a big school in DC, Georgetown University. Like the Hill, that was good and bad. Good because it was a great, enjoyable job that God provided just when I needed it. Bad because it blew my comfy, cozy Christian world apart."

The lunch entrées came. Cindy the waitress plopped them down and hustled off to the next table in need of some refills.

Dave was listening with rapt attention now. Peter's own story hit a personal nerve, connecting to Dave's own story. Peter continued after taking a bite of his salad.

"My ministry at Georgetown was basically one or two break-fasts in the morning, three, sometimes, four lunches in the after-noon, and then a coffee or happy hour meeting."

"Goodness! How'd you stay so thin?" Dave exclaimed chewing on his sandwich.

"Fitness club." Peter took another bite of salad. "Most of my job was meeting with guys for prayer and discipleship. It really was fantastic. But the questions my friends began asking...I had no answers. None! Which sent me down a path of questioning my own faith." Peter paused. "Which my ministry didn't like so much."

Dave set down his sandwich. "What happened?" Joking, he added, "Did they sit you down and tell you how backslidden you'd gotten?"

"In a manner of speaking." Peter took a bite of his salad, paused to chew and then added matter-of-factly, "They fired me."

"Fired you? Because you were asking questions? Because you challenged their neat and tidy answers?"

"Something like that. Looking back, I think they just didn't know what to do with me. And I probably didn't handle myself all that well with all the questions I was asking—let alone answering."

"Did they not like the questions you were asking? Did they

not like it that you were challenging their own answers? What was the deal, Peter?" Dave seemed to be getting ticked at Peter's ministry right there in Main Street Cafe.

"Well, it all started with Prosurgent—"

"Say no more!" Dave interrupted, raising both hands in protest.

Peter chuckled. "I picked up Bryan McLaughlin's *A Reimagined Christian* and just ate it up. He was asking all the questions I was asking, which was so…liberating. Yeah, that's the right word. And that gave me the freedom to ask more questions and also push back against the way some in my organization did things. Beginning with the essence of the Christian message, the gospel."

"Yeah, you don't mess with the way people do the gospel without getting fired!" Dave huffed, shaking his head.

"I just couldn't handle how my organization shared the message of Jesus. But what really concerned me was where they started with the gospel. They started at the end of the story—with Heaven. *'Heaven is a gift, neither earned nor deserved,'* they started. But Dave," Peter said, leaning in with an almost whisper, "my friends didn't care about Heaven! They weren't beginning with life *after* death. They were starting with life *before* death! So where my organization began the Christian message had zero connection to their lives."

Peter was becoming livelier as he relived the memory. It was the first time he had talked openly about being fired from ministry. It felt good. He sensed he had a friend in Pastor Dave, which moved this impromptu therapy session along deeper than he intended.

Pastor Dave entered the silence to add some of his own words. "Sounds like a painful time, Peter. I'm not you, so I don't want to minimize your own story when I say this, but I completely understand. I experienced a similar situation in the church I was pastoring before coming to Fellowship."

"You were fired, too? Over Prosurgent?"

"Not fired. Run out with pitch forks and torches is more like it. I started at Fellowship a year ago, right around the time you had your own problems, it sounds like. And the year before that is when things started in my previous church. Like you, I had had enough with the pitiful answers and neat, tidy box of evangelicalism. And I had begun to lead out of that as the pastor of my church. I wasn't shaping things and doing things from the Prosurgent playbook or anything, but people began to become antsy when I started stirring the pot."

Now Peter was listening with rapt attention. Dave paused, staring into his coffee before he took a sip.

"You know, people say they want their pastor to challenge them?" He continued, "That's crap." Dave drained his coffee and sat staring at its empty bottom.

They both fell silent. Dave continued, saying to no one in particular, caught in the currents of his own memory, "They don't want you to challenge them. They want you to maintain the peace. Tend the garden. Confirm what they already believe. Don't rock the boat, Pastor. Don't tweak our long-cherished beliefs. And never challenge the Popes of evangelicalism." He said that last part with an edge of bitterness.

In an instant, Pastor Dave came out of his trance-like trip into his own painful past. "Sorry about that. So Prosurgent got you fired."

"You could say that," Peter said, feeling sorry for his new friend's own painful past.

"And then you came back home to go to GRTS? No offense, but that seems kind of a step backward!"

"Yeah, I thought that myself. For a number of reasons I chose to come back again, but I gotta say I've been happy there so far." Peter was amazed at his own words, because two months ago he was second-guessing his decision.

"So Dr. Calvin VanDyke's not giving you too hard of a time?"

"Oh no, he is! But to be honest, I'm sort of thankful for how he's challenging me. He's challenged me to rethink my need to reimagine the Christian faith and instead rediscover it. Rediscover the *historic* Christian faith."

Dave smiled and looked down at his coffee again. He wrinkled his forehead, the smiling fading. "Well, I hope that works out for you. My experience with that language is that someone is part of the orthodoxy police on a heresy hunt." Again, a tinge of bitterness laced his words.

Peter didn't know how to respond. "We'll see, but Dr. VanDyke seems OK."

Another round of silence spread across the table. It was interrupted by waitress Cindy returning with the check. Pastor Dave promptly picked it up.

"Hey, I was going to get that," Peter protested.

"No way, partner. My buy. And I'd like to talk with you about something while we wait for the check."

Peter was intrigued. "Sure. What's up?"

"First, thanks for sharing your story. I resonate with so much of it, in case you couldn't tell. And I sense that we could make a great partnership."

Peter's eyes widened slightly. *Where was this going.*

"I know you're going to need a place to do your residency for your seminary program. And we need someone like you to help us out at Fellowship. In case you didn't notice, we're a bit gray," he said smiling before continuing. "Please feel free to say no or think about it more. I know we've only known each other a few hours and all...I guess what I'm saying is, I'd love for you to consider joining me at Fellowship. I'd love to partner together in ministry."

Pastor Dave's unexpected ask struck Peter off-kilter. Ever since he was fired at the beginning of the year, he had sworn off ministry work for a while. His plan was to focus on his class work, maybe join a church and just blend in. It was a year ago that things started to unravel, and the pain was still ever present.

"Wow. I'm really humbled you'd ask this of me, Dave. Can I think about it?" He added quickly, "Not because I'm weirded out or hesitant to work with you. I'm not at all! It's just that...I don't know if I'm ready to jump into ministry work again. The pain's still too sharp. Do you follow?"

"Absolutely. Yes, please think about it. And if not, no problem at all. I just wanted to try and rope you in early," Dave said smiling. "I know all too well how much the pain from ministry can linger below the surface, even though we might not even detect it. I think it still has in my own life, and it's been over two years! So think about it. Feel free to just keep coming and enjoying our gathering, if you'd like. And then get back with me. Sound good?"

"Sounds good. And thanks. For the lunch, for listening, for the conversation. Seriously, thank you."

Peter walked home and considered the lunch conversation, how it went and where it went. His soul somehow felt lighter after sharing more of his story with his new friend. Almost like he had shed a flaky, infected layer of skin. It felt good. He was touched by Pastor Dave's invitation to do ministry. It also scared him.

Am I ready to do this again?

As he considered his answer, he looked down at his watch, his eyes landing on the date, eyes widening in surprise. It was exactly one year ago from the day it all went down. One year from that day he was first brought into his boss's office and talked to about his theological and spiritual direction. He felt like it was too much of a coincidence to be asked to join the ministry of one pastor in Coopersville, Michigan, one year—to the day—after his ministry started ending.

Could this be God's movement in my life? Peter wondered. The timing seemed like something God would do to move his story forward. He'd done it before. Was he doing it now?

Shivering up the cobblestoned driveway to his home, Peter sensed the answer. He didn't understand why, but sensed it was time for him to give himself over to a group of people in ministry again. Pastor Dave seemed like the perfect person to begin exploring what it meant to minister to a group of people in the twenty-first-century church. And since it seemed like he had experienced a similar falling out while exploring the boundaries of the Christian faith, Peter knew he would be safe under him.

"Alright God," he mumbled. "I'm in. But I hope you know what you're doing!"

CHAPTER 17

THE DAYS GREW INCREASINGLY short as winter began to slowly goose-step its way through West Michigan, bleeding the palette of browns, oranges, and yellows from the area in its wake.

Peter loved autumn; it was his favorite season of the year. If he had it his way, it would fill the calendar year round in a petrified October-November state. Fall screamed romance. Not in a lovey-dovey kind of way, but in a fanciful, idealized kind of way—with its carved pumpkins, cable-knit sweatshirts, spiced cider, caramel apples, and molting multi-hued trees. Unfortunately this year, his fall was spoiled by classes, and now it was going into hibernation.

Somehow he was surviving Greek, mostly with the tutoring help of Izzy. While the first exam didn't turn out so well, thanks to her help he was now passing, but only barely.

Peter sighed as he slumped down next to her in the student study area above the main set of classrooms for his weekly tutoring session. He plopped his book bag on their table with as much force as he did his body in the chair.

"You could say that. Failed yet *another* Greek quiz. I can't get this stuff! I put more time into this class than all of my others combined. And yet another bomb. I just can't seem to get it!"

"Pour lil' thing." Izzy reached for Peter's hand. "That's why you've got me!"

"For sure. Now if only you could somehow download everything in that noggin of yours into my head, I'd be golden."

Izzy proceeded to explain the art of conjugating Greek verbs, including all of the possible tenses. Then she moved to nouns. By the time she got around to participial phrases Peter was lost.

He couldn't help noticing how she brushed up against his hand ever so slightly as she pointed out something in his textbook. So far their relationship remained as friends, which was fine. It wasn't that he found her unattractive or uninteresting; that wasn't the problem. She seemed more like the little sister he never had than a potential girlfriend. Which for the moment suited him well since his interest in Lexi had grown.

"Does that make sense?" Izzy asked, snapping Peter back to attention.

"Huh?"

"Peter, are you listenin' to a thing I'm sayin'?"

"No, I mean yes! I mean, I'm trying to. I'm hopeless, I tell you!"

"You're not hopeless. But maybe we should take a break from all of this conjugating." She stood, bracing herself on his shoulder.

Though he was barely passing Greek he was excelling in Systematic Theology. Dr. VanDyke continued to give him trouble, but a respect began to develop between the two of them, especially after Peter wrote an especially good essay on the inspiration and inerrancy of Scripture that landed him an A. VanDyke didn't agree with his conclusions, but he still wrote a touching note that Peter copied on a sticky note and placed next to his computer:

Peter, you are a good writer who writes clearly and compellingly. The Church needs you, so continue your journey of rediscovery. —Calvin

---

He was surprised to receive such a note, particularly because the way VanDyke interacted with him in class betrayed such kind regards. Regardless, it was the type of affirmation Peter needed to survive a few more weeks of the semester, and also continue down his path of rediscovery.

Having finished their Greek lesson, Peter bounded down the stairwell to return to his car to head home. His smartphone buzzed, announcing a new e-mail from Pastor Dave:

Hello my seminarian friend!

Hope your day is going well. I arrived safe and sound from Ukraine and heard you did a bang up job last Sunday preaching! Thanks for filling in for me, and for diving into the life of Fellowship. I wanted to let you know tomorrow at 10 a.m. the West Michigan chapter of Prosurgent is meeting for our monthly *Lectio Divina* service at St. Marks Episcopal downtown in GR. Afterwards we hang around for discussion. You should join us. I think you'd like it. Interested? —DJ

A few weeks ago Peter decided to take Pastor Dave up on his offer to join him in ministry at Fellowship Community Church. The Church Council had welcomed Pastor Dave's suggestion to bring Peter on as a pastoral intern, even going so far as to provide a small stipend for eight hours of work a week. When he agreed to take Dave up on his offer, he figured it'd be several months before he was doing any actual ministry work. Boy was he wrong!

The church council assigned him the task of leading the adult Sunday School class, consisting of several retirees and a few younger couples. They also wrangled him into helping with the worship band as another vocalist from time to time. And he had just filled in for Pastor Dave while he was away on a ministry trip to Ukraine. Though initially apprehensive about jumping full throttle into ministry, Peter was surprised how comfortable he felt sliding back into church work, considering how badly things ended at the start of the new year. It helped that Pastor Dave was conversant with the kind of questions and ideas that his former ministry was so resistant to, taking him under his wing to impart his forty-plus years of ministry wisdom.

Peter smiled after reading the e-mail, glad he finally had the chance to connect with some local Prosurgent followers. Over the past month, the void left not having Prosurgent DC had grown into a lonely black hole. He hoped some new friends from Prosurgent West Michigan would come alongside him in this leg of his spiritual journey.

He pecked out a short message on his phone's virtual keyboard: *'Sounds good! I'll be there.'*

The next day, Peter arrived at St. Marks before 10:00 a.m.. The neo-Gothic building is one of the oldest structures in Grand Rapids, over 160 years old. Flanked by two large columns, the facade of the stately looking church looked like something out of nineteenth-century England. It was a fitting location for the ancient spiritual practice. The *Lectio* service was held in a small chapel off the main gathering hall, a modest looking room that smelled of old wood and incense.

When Peter arrived, the space was already occupied by a few other people. Dave was seated and chatting with a man, while a woman knelt at the front by the small altar.

"Come on in, Peter," welcomed Pastor Dave. "We were just talking about you. This is Rob Beukema, the head of Prosurgent West Michigan."

Rob extended his hand; Peter shook it. "Glad to have you join us today," the man said. "Dave said you've been helping him over at Fellowship? And that you moved back to West Michigan to attend Grand River Theological?"

"Yeah, that's right," Peter replied. "It's been good to be back. I was super involved with a Prosurgent group in DC, so I'm excited to join you all this morning."

"We're glad to have you here, too, Peter. Go ahead and take a seat. We're about to get started."

Peter took his seat, and another guy walked in and sat behind him. They gave each other a nod of welcome. Besides Pastor Dave, the crowd consisted of Rob, the woman, and the guy who just sat down.

"Hi everyone," started an older woman with jet-black hair, accented by wispy strands of grey. She had a kind, worn face adorned by an inviting smile. Her neck was draped with a set of rosary beads, the kind you'd find worn by a Catholic nun. "Thanks for setting aside this hour to gather together as fellow travelers on the path that Jesus has marked out for us."

She invited everyone to kneel at the small altar situated at the front. They dutifully took their place around the railing, kneeling on thick red-velvet pads. While Peter had spent some time in an Episcopal church in DC, he was hesitant in his approach, unsure of the rhythm of this ancient spiritual practice.

In the silence between kneeling and beginning, Peter tried to remember back to some readings he did on ancient spiritual disciplines in order to prepare himself for this Benedictine practice. From what he could recall, *Lectio Divina*, Latin for *divine reading*, was a form of Scripture reading that combined meditation, prayer, and contemplation in order to cast greater meaning on God's Living Word.

The woman, kneeling with Bible open, began the service. "This morning as we approach the Living Word contained in the Holy Scriptures, we come seeking to enter it through reading, meditation, prayer, and contemplation. Listen as I read from Matthew's Gospel, chapter 9."

She paused, taking a deep breath, holding it, and letting it seep slowly out of her nose. Taking her time with each sentence, with each word, the woman read the passage.

> *Then John's disciples came and asked him, "How is it that we and the Pharisees fast often, but your disciples do not fast?"*
> *Jesus answered, "How can the guests of the bridegroom mourn while he is with them? The time will come when the bridegroom will be taken from them; then they will fast.*
> *"No one sews a patch of unshrunk cloth on an old garment, for the patch will pull away from the garment, making the tear worse. Neither do people pour new wine into old wineskins. If they do, the skins will burst; the wine will run out and the wineskins will be ruined. No, they pour new wine into new wineskins, and both are preserved."*

Silence filled the surrounding space as the woman finished her reading.

Peter stared forward, settled on the face of one of the apostles carved on the side of the ornate altar.

The woman broke the silence. "We don't come to this passage seeking to dissect it. Rather, we seek to be dissected by it. As I read it a second time, pay close attention to the word or phrase that confronts you and any feelings or emotions attached to that word or phrase." She read the Matthew passage again.

As she read the word *unshrunk* stood out to Peter. In the silence that followed the woman's reading, he meditated on the sentence that surrounded this word.

No one sews a patch of unshrunk cloth on an old garment, for the patch will pull away from the garment, making the tear worse.

Unshrunk. Fresh and new.

Sort of like the new thing that is coming out of my current reimagining, Peter thought. You don't put the new, untested cloth over an old container. You need a new one. *Like my old funda-mentalism container and this new Prosurgence container.*

"How does that make me feel," Peter whispered. He paused, waiting for a spark. Fear. Anxiety. Apprehension. Possibilities. As the spectrum of emotions continued cascading, he also mouthed "Hope."

Hope...that it'll be OK, that God will show a way forward from one wineskin to another.

The woman broke his concentration by announcing she would read the passage again. "This time as you follow along in your inner being, voice the passage as a prayer."

As she read the passage again, Peter followed along in his own Bible, mouthing the words in sync with the woman's intonation.

Again, silence invaded the space upon the completion of the reading, allowing room to offer any further petitions to God in response to the passage.

"As we close this sacred reading of Matthew nine," the woman began again, "we come to contemplate, to enter the thin space where time and eternity almost touch in order to move beyond the words to reach union with Christ. This time, let us recite the passage in unison."

With one voice the small gathering read Jesus' words aloud. A growing sense of mission and purpose gripped Peter as came to the part on which his own heart landed.

No one sews a patch of unshrunk cloth on an old garment...

You can't dress up past expressions of the Christian faith.

...for the patch will pull away from the garment, making the tear worse.

A reimagined Christian faith won't work with old fundamentalism.

Neither do people pour new wine into old wineskins. If they do, the skins will burst...

Which is why we need a new wineskin.

No, they pour new wine into new wineskins, and both are preserved...

Which is why we need to rethink the Christian faith.

"Amen," said the woman, wrapping up the service. The others *Amened* in agreement and made the sign of the cross.

Peter echoed their *Amen* and followed them with the sign.

Peter went back to his seat. The woman came over to introduce herself.

"Welcome," she said. "I'm Hannah. This your first time?"

Peter smiled and shook her hand. "Yes it is. Dave invited me. I'm serving with him now at Fellowship. He said I needed to meet you folk, so here I am."

"Great! Glad to have you. Are you able to join us for coffee?"

"A poor seminarian never misses the chance for free coffee and conversation!"

AS THEY MADE their way to the fellowship hall Rob came alongside him. "So how is VanDyke treating you? Does he know you hang around with the Prosurgent crowd?"

Peter chuckled. "Oh yeah. I somehow let it slip I was into

Prosurgence Christianity, and he decided to call me Prosurgent Pete."

"Prosurgent Pete, huh?" Rob said. "Did you hear that, Alex? Peter's got his own nickname from VanDyke! Have you met yet?"

"No," he said turning around to shake his hand. "Peter Young."

"Alex Schneider. Nice to meet you."

Alex was tall and thick with thinning hair and a large tattoo extending from under his left sleeve, though Peter couldn't tell what it was.

"You know Dr. VanDyke? Did you take classes with him or something?"

"Naw. He's just our nemesis," Alex said, eliciting some laughter from the others. "We've just read some of what he's said about the Prosurgent Church movement and think he's full of it."

Nemesis? Peter thought. *That's odd. They don't even know the guy.*

He let it go as they entered the downstairs gathering space where no doubt countless potlucks were held over the years. A few women left the kitchen attached to the hall, having finished their task of brewing the coffee and arranging the pastries.

The group doctored their coffee with sugar and powdered creamer, grabbed pastries, and sat down in a grouping of comfortable chairs arranged around an aged fireplace at one end of the hall.

"So I finally picked up Bryan's book and started reading it," started Alex, biting into a chocolate-covered donut.

"About time!" Rob replied. "And?"

"I don't know yet. Some of it I like, some of it I don't."

"What's not to like? He's turning Calvinism completely on its head and saying the Christian faith doesn't have to be *that*. It can be something else."

Rob was getting animated now, waving his half-eaten donut

around to make his point.

"I disagree," replied Alex.

"Ha! Classic Alex. Is there anything you say besides *I disagree?*"

"Yes I do, and here I go!" Alex said interrupting. "I think the guy is too innovative sometimes. Like he tries too hard at what he's selling."

"You'll have to forgive him," Rob said with a sneer, turning to Peter. "Alex isn't a true believer."

"It's not that I'm not a believer in what Prosurgent is trying to do. I just think it's becoming too much like what I left behind. And McLaughlin is like that blowhard Reformed pastor from Minneapolis driving the Prosurgent ship."

Hannah and Pastor Dave piped in with Rob to boo Alex down. One of the women who had returned to clean the kitchen stared at their good-natured fun. Peter didn't know what to make of it all.

"We're just messing with Alex," Pastor Dave said. "He's our fellow Plymouth Brethren contrarian. You know Bryan was Plymouth Brethren, don't you Alex?"

"Sure do. It's not that I don't appreciate what he's saying. It's just that I don't buy all of it."

Rob shook his head and turned to Peter. "So have you read his *A Reimagined Christianity?*"

Peter didn't quite know how to reply to Rob given the beating Alex just received for his contrarian views. "Yeah, I started reading it a few months ago."

Peter went silent. Rob waited a few beats then asked, "And? What did you think of it?"

"I'm digging most of it so far. It is interesting how this time he's giving way more answers than merely asking questions like he did in the past."

"What do you mean?"

"Well, like with his first book, *A Reimagined Christian*, he sort of hints at thinking about sin and Jesus and the Bible differently through the questions Pastor Jack asks. And then sort of hints at answers through his spiritual friend Nelson. But this time he just lays it out there. I'm not saying it's a bad thing. It's just an interesting shift from simply trying to connect the Christian faith to our world as missionaries in our postmodern, post-Christian world, to now actually writing theology. It seems the conversation has shifted from a missional one to a theological one."

"I'd agree with that," interjected Alex.

"Again, not a bad thing. It's also different this time around because now I'm reading it with my brother, who's sort of going through a crisis of faith, actually. We have sort of a book club at Founders."

"Really?" Rob asked. "We hit up Founders at least once a week for our own pow-wow. You should come sometime. It's sort of like this, but we trade the coffee and donuts for beer and peanuts."

"And way rowdier," Alex added.

"Sounds like fun," Pete said. "I don't think I can make this week. But maybe I'll drop by next."

"We'd love to have you," Rob offered.

"Cool, I'll see you guys in a few Wednesdays then." He thanked them for their hospitality, then headed out the door to the seminary for Systematic One.

Peter was buzzing with excitement after connecting with another community of people on the same journey that he was on. And the deeply spiritual encounter he had in the chapel added even more to his excitement.

Unshrunk cloth, Peter thought as he turned into the GRTS parking lot.

Old wineskins. New wineskins.

He had heard this language before, even hearing it applied to the Prosurgent movement. But somehow this mystical encounter in the small chapel of St. Mark's gave new meaning to these words.

"That's totally it!" Peter shouted out his rolled-down window as he parked his car before noticing a group of classmates walking into the seminary building. He smiled and nodded at them in embarrassment.

Of all the metaphors to describe where I'm at, that's it.

Old wineskins and new wineskins.

As he grabbed his backpack from behind his seat, his cell phone vibrated and chirped with a number he didn't recognize.

"Hello, this is Peter."

"Pete, it's Alex. From the Prosurgent West Michigan group."

"Hey, Alex, what's up?"

"Not much," Alex replied. "Not sure if you're busy but I thought I'd give you a call to see if you were free for dinner tonight. I got your number from Dave Jones. Thought it would be worth getting to connect with this Prosurgent Pete guy I've heard so much about."

"Prosurgent Pete. Nice." He hustled into the building as class was starting. "Sure, that'd be great. What were you thinking?"

"Is Founders OK? Say around 5:30?"

"Founders works. See you then."

He had been looking forward to connecting with Alex since they met at the service that morning and the conversation at the fellowship hall. They were the same age and Peter sensed an ally, a fellow journeyman in Alex.

Peter pulled into his normal seat just as VanDyke took to the lectern, eyeing Peter suspiciously as he grinned from the new connections he'd made with Prosurgent. He said a silent prayer of thanks as he opened his laptop to listen to a lecture that would surely counter the community he hoped would once again feed his lonely soul.

CHAPTER 18

"I DIDN'T peg you as a hog guy," Peter shouted.

Alex was standing next to a gleaming Harley Davidson motorcycle, removing his helmet.

Peter walked up to greet Alex when an unknown number popped up on his caller ID.

Who is this? Peter wondered, sending the caller to voicemail.

"I've gotta get as much ride time in before the flakes start falling." He rubbed his hands together and blew to warm them. "You ever ridden before?"

"Yeah, no. Never had an interest."

"You're missing out, man." Alex slapped Peter on the back as they headed into the building.

The two found a seat in the back of a vacant Founders. The dinner crowd had yet to come out in force. Apparently they were leading the way.

"Prosurgent West Michigan seems like a great group of people," Peter offered after the server left to fill their drink order.

"They're fantastic, man. They've become something of a second family to me after moving here."

"So you're not from around here?"

"Naw. I moved to GR a few months ago."

"You moved *to* Grand Rapids? What, for some chick or something?"

"Actually, yeah," Alex said laughing.

"Really? Where from?"

"Pittsburgh. Thanks," Alex said to the server as she set down two pints brimming with Founders's thick brew.

They each took a sip. "*Mmm*, that's what I'm talkin' about," Alex said in reply. "Have you had their Breakfast Stout yet?"

"Not really into stouts. IPA is more my style."

"Aww, dude you've gotta live a little, man!"

"I'm good," Peter said smiling. "So you move to Grand Rapids for a chick. She your girlfriend?"

"Yeah. I actually lived here a few years ago. That's when we met. We were both working at a church in the area. I left to go back home. We stayed in touch and started doing the long-distance thing. And when I needed to get out of town, it seemed like the right thing to do to come back."

Alex gave just enough detail to answer Peter's questions without painting the entire picture. Peter took note, but moved on, "So are you working, or what are you doing?"

"I'm figuring that out. Sammie, my girlfriend Samantha, works at the hospital in town. So it's all good right now." Alex attended once more to his beer, draining it halfway. "So what about you? Why's a guy like you going to GRTS?"

Peter laughed. "I'm not sure to be honest! It's been fine so far. Met some cool people who seem normal enough. And VanDyke isn't a total pain. Yet. Although I had lunch with him a month ago, and he suggested I should abandon my progressive Christian faith and replace it with regressive Christianity."

"Seriously?" Alex sneered. "You're joking. Please tell me you're joking."

"I cannot tell a lie," Peter said, making his best Boy Scouts hand gesture. "Although he did call it the vintage Christian faith, which I found interesting."

"Oh my word. Well that about sums it up, doesn't it? I mean, when I heard you were attending GRTS I wondered what a guy who is into Prosurgence Christianity was doing there. Or maybe I should say, I wondered what a GRTS guy was doing at Prosurgent West Michigan gathering."

"GRTS is more open than people think. But I do feel a little out of place."

"How did you end up there? And how did you end up in Prosurgent?" Alex inquired.

Peter thought for a second about how to answer both of those questions. "For the first question, it was one of those things where I felt called back home. I know that sounds so cliché, being called and all. But I really believe God called me back here for whatever reason."

"You say return. You from here? What led you to come back?"

"Born and raised. Actually, I vowed I'd never return. Funny how that works out." Peter grinned and drained his beer. "I came back because I was kicked out of ministry, actually. I had a pretty serious crisis of faith while working for a campus ministry. That's when I got into the Prosurgent Church conversation. It was exactly what I needed at the right moment. And my ministry really didn't get what it was all about. So they let me go."

"They fired you? Wow! Sorry to hear that, man."

"No, it's fine. I'm over it. So now I'm just trying to figure out this whole Church thing and what it means to do ministry in our changing world."

"I hear that," Alex voiced as he finished his own drink.

"Yeah?" Peter said as Alex flagged down another server. The two ordered another round and some sandwiches.

"You talk about being kicked out of a ministry. Try being kicked out of a church."

"What do you mean, kicked out of church?" Peter asked.

"I mean kicked out. The elders of my church didn't like the questions I was asking. Said I was rocking the boat too much—infecting the minds of their young with my Jedi mind trick Prosurgent voodoo," Alex said this as he wiggled his fingers on either side of his head.

"Are you kidding me? What kinds of questions were you asking?" Peter asked.

"Oh, you know, questions like: Why can't God and evolution both be responsible for the universe? How do we know we have the right understanding of Scripture? Are we really totally depraved—to the point we can't love or create beauty or do remarkably good things for people? What does it even mean to be saved? Is it a prayer? The right combination of words? Something someone does or doesn't do? And why oh why do we think hell is this forever punishment of burning fire when our view of hell is influenced more by Dante than the Apostle John? So, questions like that. The simple stuff." His mouth turned upward with a wry grin as he ended his monologue.

He took a large swig of his drink, and added, "Oh, and I smoked and drank occasionally. And to be honest, I think that's what tipped them over the edge."

"Yeah, the whole smoking and drinking thing will get you every time," Peter said. "But seriously, gotta love how grown adults get scared out of their minds at questions. Mere questions! Sounds a lot like my experience in DC. Was this your childhood church?"

Their server interrupted the conversation by plopping down two thick sandwiches. Then the same number that rang an hour ago appeared on Peter's phone. He hit *Ignore*, returning to their conversation.

"Yeah from birth," Alex responded.

"So probably had altar calls and the whole bit?"

"Dude, every Sunday was altar call Sunday!"

"Did your pastor go on and on, claiming the Holy Spirit was telling him there was that *one person* who needed to come forward to repent of their wicked ways?"

"One time we sat there for seriously seventeen minutes until this thirteen-year-old boy was dragged to the front to confess he had bought an 'N SYNC CD!"

"Well obviously. Because anyone who bought an 'N SYNC CD should do penance a hundred times over!" Peter roared. "But of course that makes sense, because worldly music like 'N SYNC might put all sorts of sinful ideas in the minds of our youth—"

"Yeah, like dancing."

"Exactly!" Peter said, pointing his finger at Alex. They both exchanged laughs and took swigs of their brew.

Alex asked, "Dude, did your church ever have Apocalyptic Sunday where you studied the 'end times' and stuff?"

"Complete with diagrams and charts and timelines! In fact, our pastor did a two-freakin'-year, verse-by-verse study on Revelation."

"Oh man, that's brutal."

"You're telling me. And I credit that whole series with the reason why I wrote a high school essay saying the Catholic Church was the whore of Babylon." Peter hit his fist on the table in protest to that memory.

"You didn't!"

"Sure did. Said the Catholic Church was a tool of Satan. And the worse thing was that my English teacher was Catholic."

"No...So what happened?"

"He was going to fail me, so I brought *him* to the principal's office and claimed religious discrimination!"

Alex shook his head, and said, "Man, they breed us fundies well, don't they?"

"Sure do," Peter said laughing. "OK, this is too scary how similar our backgrounds are."

"Yeah, for real. What did you grow up? Baptist or something?"

"Ever heard if IFBC?"

"I Fight and Blast Christians?"

Peter almost choked on his beer. "That'd be the one."

"Unfortunately, yes. They're basically kissing cousins with the Plymouth Brethren," Alex moaned.

"Isn't it fascinating how most of us Prosurgents are recovering fundamentalists? There has to be some sort of study of this phenomenon somewhere. I mean, you don't find liberals jumping their mainline ship to become Prosurgent. It's the crazy conservatives who are jumping out of one boat and into another."

"It is sort of amazing. I'll tell you what, though, I'm not sure I would be a Christian still if it wasn't for Prosurgent, especially this group here in Grand Rapids."

"I hear you on that," Peter said, raising his glass in a toast; Alex joined. They clinked their glasses and promptly drained them.

"Don't get me wrong. My faith in Christ is huge in my life, and it's not dependent on some group—whether the Brethren or Prosurgent," Alex added. "And I've got my share of disagreements with Prosurgent, too. It's just that I haven't found another group that's as interested in asking questions and being OK with the ambiguity of the answers than the Prosurgent Church."

"Totally. Especially for us post-Evangelicals. Because I don't know about you, but I'm not interested in leaving the conservative camp only to become a liberal."

"For sure," Alex agreed. "Prosurgent is the closest to a third way as I've ever seen."

They both drank some of their water as the conversation seemed to come to a close.

"Man, this was great," Peter offered. "Thanks for sharing some of your story, Alex."

"You, too. This was rad. You should join us for our Wednesday Founders night. It's like this but multiplied by twenty."

"I will one of these nights, for sure."

The two paid their tabs, walked out, and parted ways. As Peter walked back to his car he was amazed at the common threads of their individual stories. He was also amazed at yet another ally God had provided him.

During his drive back home he reflected on the events of this new development. Between his new job, new church, and these new Prosurgent friendships, Peter couldn't help but feel blessed beyond all measure. It didn't seem like there was anything that could disrupt the flow of positive energy coursing through Peter's life.

PETER DROVE with the windows down and heat at full blast as he drove home. The combination of late-autumn chill and heat invigorated his senses. *The Killers* were blaring away, so was Peter. His moment of drive-time ecstasy was rudely interrupted by the repeat caller beckoning him on his cell.

"Who on earth is this," Peter complained. On the fourth ring he decided he should answer the call, imagining the wrong number was having a major meltdown.

"Hello, this is Peter," he bit into the phone.

"Petey," moaned someone on the other end of the line.

He sat up straight, heart galloping forward with recognition at the voice.

"Yes? Who is this?" He rolled up his window, turned down the heater, and turned off Brandon Flowers.

"It's me, Petey. JT."

Peter's heart sank below the floorboards. "James, what's going on? Are you OK?"

The line went silent, except for a few clanks in the background and strained breathing.

"JT. Hello? Bro, are you there?" Peter's voice strained with concern.

"I did too much this time, Petey."

Peter closed his eyes and tilted his head back, leaning it against the car window. The drugs.

"Where are you?" He got nothing but static in reply.

"Hello. JT?" he asked with voice raised. "You there?"

"I'm at home. Come quick, Bro. They're out there."

"Who's out there? Where are they? What's going on?"

"I hear 'em, man," JT moaned in a panic. "They've been after me."

Peter was getting increasingly confused and concerned by what his brother was saying. If there really were people stalking outside his brother's house he didn't want to deal with that problem. Should he call the cops? He decided to wait until he got there. Which made him realize he had another important problem: he didn't even know where James lived. He knew it was somewhere in Grand Rapids. Probably off of Franklin in the South East, or Plainfield in the North, the new epicenter of crime and drugs in the city.

"I'm coming. Just tell me where you live."

CHAPTER 19

AFTER MANAGING to coax the address out of his stoned brother, Peter followed the blue ball on his phone's map to a street off of Coit Avenue just north of downtown. It was dusk, so he was nervous as he parked in a very unfamiliar part of town marked by the obvious signs of desperation and poverty.

Several yards were well overgrown. A faded, cracked baby swing laid toppled over in one front yard. Moss was growing on several roofs way past their life expectancy. The smell of pot still hovered in the early-November air. Nearly every lawn was covered by a blanket of still-unraked leaves. Thankfully it didn't appear as though there was anyone else around the house.

Must be the paranoia, Peter thought as he sat idling, contemplating his next move. Finally, he put his hatchback in *Park* and shut off the engine, then he got out.

He carefully closed his door so as not to wake the neighbors. He padded toward the front of his brother's house and jumped back a step as he caught a glimpse of a figure sitting in the shadows next door. A neighbor eyed Peter from his front porch, sipping from a can of Bud Lite. Peter went for the knob, but curiously the door was cracked open.

Not good, Peter thought. *Maybe there was somebody—or somebodies—already inside.*

He pushed his way into the two-level split condo, and said, "Hello, JT? You in there?" The heat and smell of the inside slapped him in the face as his voice echoed back to him.

His brother's place was a mess. Empty TV dinners sat molding in a corner. Flies were buzzing the windows, looking for relief from the stifling, dark living room. The bare floors creaked as he walked farther into the house. Movement upstairs caught his attention. A moan, then a thud.

Peter took the stairs two at a time in haste. When he reached James's room, he wasn't prepared for what he saw.

A lone shadeless lamp bathed the room in an eerie twilight glow. On a dresser, the light reflected off of three syringes. There were a few little baggies of what looked like baking soda. Some lighters and a big spoon, with two razor blades. And JT, shirtless on the bed, glistening with sweat, bony and pale. Around his upper right arm was a rubber hose tied tight. His eyes flickered opened, looking at Peter standing in the doorway, with mouth opened in disbelief.

"Hey, Petey," James managed to grunt, his eyes rolling in the back of his head.

Peter snapped out of his trance and hustled over to his brother. "What happened? What do you need?"

"Stop stuttering. Jacked myself up good this time. Heart feels like it's gonna explode. Can't breathe right."

"Dude, you need a hospital."

"No!" his brother said, eyes wide and wild with fright. A set of tremors took hold of his arms.

"My God..." Peter said, hand covering his mouth in shock.

"You look like you're burning up. And you called me over here, so now we're gonna do things my way."

Peter reached down to lift his brother. He was soaking with sweat. James didn't fight him, but he didn't help either.

They drove to the emergency room of a hospital in downtown Grand Rapids. JT was admitted quickly, finding relief from Valium administered by a freshly graduated physician's assistant.

Peter sat out in the waiting room while James recovered, drifting into a deep sleep, trying to escape the nightmare and positively spent from the encounter.

In his sleep world, he entered into a dream world much like his own. Although within what seemed like minutes he was transported to a small country church, at least that's what he thought it was. It was like the one in *Little House on the Prairie*, except the walls seemed to have a hard time staying still. On second thought, he was the one moving, walking up toward the front.

Peter swam through the air up the center aisle in slow, undulating waves of dreamy movement. He was in some sort of line, making its way up to the front. In fact, the others in line along with him were his family: his mother was dressed in a billowy black dress; his father and brother in matching black suits.

He looked around him and saw a mostly empty room, except for a few faces he couldn't recognize peppered around the modest-looking country church sanctuary. Looking back toward the front he saw what appeared to be a large, long box. Its walls were about two feet high. Inch by inch, he swam his way to the front until he arrived. He didn't understand it, but he felt compelled to look inside the big box.

He grabbed the sides. They were hard and rough, wooden to the touch. His nose came alive with the smell of fresh-cut Christmas trees. It was a long pine box.

Peter tried to look inside, but his body felt heavy, weighed down by an unseen force. Then he began to shrink in size, so that even on his toes he could not see. With all of his might Peter persisted in stretching to reach the top until he managed to hoist himself up along the edge. What he saw made him regret his persistence.

Inside was his brother James, dead. His face was ashen and had a sunken quality to it, so that his cheekbones jutted upward at ghastly angles. Peter clung to the sides staring at his dead, ghoulish brother, not knowing what to do or say. Something caught his eye as he stared. It was a book, his brother was clutching it. It was hard to make out what book it was. Peter strained with all of his might to focus on the very top row of words that peaked over his brother's bony, skin-stretched hands. The words were only partially visible, but then it hit him. He could make out what looked like an M, L, and A.

McLaughlin.

As he strained at the book, a moan began to well deep within the decaying shell of his brother. As it grew louder, the leathery skin on JT's skull began to stretch and thin, his bloodshot eyes bulging beneath until the skin melted off entirely. When it did, the moan turned into a macabre screech as the stiff jaw of JT's corpse flew open, uttering the words "Ideas have consequences."

"Ideas have consequences, Petey," the decaying corpse said again as spindly fingers wrapped around Peter's wrists.

Peter let go of the edge of his brother's pine casket and tried to wrench his wrist free from the mouse-trap grip of JT's boney hand, all the while his brother screeched on, channeling his systematic theology professor in an other-worldly séance.

"Ideas have consequences, Petey. Ideas have consequences."

Peter finally managed to wrench his hand from his brother's grip, sending him tumbling into a dark oblivion.

He awoke with a start, banging his head on the waiting room wall.

"Ouch," Peter moaned, leaning forward and rubbing the tender knob forming on his skull. His eyes strained against the fluorescent hospital lights as he panted from a dreamy adrenaline rush as much as from the sudden awakening jolt. He sat back and noticed the outline of a dark figure standing in front of him.

"Hey, Sleeping Beauty. You ready?" James grunted.

Peter rubbed his head in momentary confusion, staring at the man with long scraggly hair, matching his disheveled dark clothing and even darker eyes set within puffy sockets. The memory of the dream smacked him again, and so did the vision of a dresser piled with syringes and bags of white powder.

"You all right?" Peter asked, standing stiffly, still groggy from his dreamland experience. "How long have I been out?"

"A few hours. It's morning. I'll be OK, they gave me some pills. Let's get out of this hellhole."

THE DRIVE back to JT's house in the early morning hours was a silent one. Peter didn't know what to say, and James wasn't in the mood for talking.

He parked in front of his brother's house, and they just sat together in the car, staring out the front windshield.

"Well, thanks, Petey. For everything," James finally managed. Reaching for the door to make his exit, he added, "I owe ya one."

"Wait a minute. That's it? I get a *Thanks for everything*?" Peter said, filled with an equal amount of concern and irritation.

"What do you want me to say?" James huffed, turning back into the car.

"How about telling me why the heck you nearly died of a cocaine overdose up in that stuffy craphole! Or why you were doing drugs in the first place? I thought you were over that!"

"Craphole? Look man, don't you dare judge me—"

"I am not judging you," JT shot back, turning to his brother.

"But you sure as hell scared my pants black! I drive up here not knowing what the heck is going on after receiving some cryptic call. And then I see my younger brother doped up and nearly dead."

Peter stopped and took a breath, shaking his head and running a hand through his hair.

He continued, "I'm not judging. I'm pissed. But more than that, I'm scared stiff for you! I almost lost you, bro. And I want to know what the deal is. What happened? Did you try to kill yourself?"

"No, I didn't try and kill myself," JT finally broke in.

"Well then what?"

"I just over did it!" JT shouted. "I've been having a rough time, and so I wanted to peace out for a few hours. I swear I've been clean. Look at my arms."

James showed Peter his arms, a graveyard of several older scars but only one fresh puncture, the one in his right arm.

Peter looked away. He couldn't face this reality, that his brother was an addict, or at minimum had a reoccurring drug problem. He looked out at his house, then to the other side of the road, his gut churning at the scene of desperation.

"Petey," JT grunted, "say something."

"I...don't even know what to say." He stopped. He stared into the silent November morning before continuing. "Is this what you really want? All of this. This house. This street. This trip to the ER. This puncture mark and those puncture marks! Is it?"

His brother recoiled with a look of surprise. "You think I chose this? This chose me! I wish I could have something more, but I'm that throwaway toy that's not ever gettin' played with."

JT threw open the car door, got out, and slammed it as he started up toward his house.

Peter didn't know whether or not to follow after him and

continue a conversation he knew his brother didn't want. He watched his brother stagger up the stars and decided to follow.

"JT, wait up," he yelled as he closed his door, running after him.

James reached the porch and sat down. Peter joined him.

He said, "I had a dream about you, you know. When I was waiting for you in the ER. It freaked me out, JT."

"About what?"

"Well, you died."

"Sounds about right," James said with a chuckle.

"I was at your funeral, I guess, and there you were. In some cheap pine box in some country church."

"Sounds about right, too."

"I don't want you to die, James!" Peter said, his throat growing thick with emotion. His eyes started to leak; he couldn't help it. "There's more for you. I haven't given up on you. And neither has God."

James laughed. "People gave up on me years back. And so did God."

"OK, do you want me to get my preach on?" Peter replied jabbing his brother in shoulder.

"Nobody for a mile wants that!"

"I'm serious about this. There is more than those damned lists of rules we grew up with or judgmental stares the past few years. And I aim to prove it to you."

JT looked at his brother, the hostility and tension draining a bit. He smiled skeptically. "How are you going to do that?"

Peter considered his question. "Well first, I'm going to clean your room out. Of everything."

JT didn't seem to like that one, but relented. "Can I at least keep my bed?"

"I don't want to touch that nasty thing."

The brothers stood in unison and embraced. JT sauntered off

to take a shower. Peter went up stairs and cleared out his brother's drugs and other paraphernalia, tossing it all in a plastic grocery bag he found in the kitchen. He looked through his brother's room for anything that looked like it might be drugs, or used to cook or shoot them.

As Peter was searching he came across JT's copy of McLaughlin's book. It looked like he was three-quarters of the way through. He marveled at the sight of several dog-eared pages, underlines, and even some notes scribbled in James's illegible handwriting. This is what Peter himself did with all of his books, but he never would have guessed his brother did the same. He didn't read the notes; he knew better than that. But he did smile. And he looked forward to the next trip to Founders where he could explore those notes more with his brother.

Peter finished as James came out of the bathroom, towel wrapped around his waist.

"Is that all of it?" he asked, holding up the plastic grocery bag clinking with his prized finds.

"Yeah, that's it," James replied, eliciting a skeptical gaze from Peter. "I'm not playing. I swear that's it. I want it out." He added, "I want out."

Peter didn't know whether to believe him. James had made similar promises to his parents, and the law, in order to evade punishment and jail time—only to relapse using and dealing again. While he managed to get out of the dealing business, he knew there was a massive gravel road from being an addict to a recovering addict.

"I hope you do, JT. And if you do, I'm here for you," Peter said as he hugged his brother's frail body.

They said their goodbyes, hugged again, and Peter headed back home to end a day he never expected.

A day he never wanted to relive.

CHAPTER 20

PETER ARRIVED home as the sun was just starting to wake up his neighborhood to the start of the crisp November morning. As he approached the back door he hoped Cooper Manor was still tightly tucked into bed. The smell of eggs, bacon, and burnt toast trashed those hopes.

Peter opened the door that led into the kitchen and saw that the family was already gathered around the table.

"Where the heck have you been?" his mother exclaimed from behind the stove flipping several pieces of bacon. "I've been worrying myself to death all morning when I woke up and saw your car was gone, yet again."

His dad barely looked up from the newspaper as he agreed with Maggie. "Yeah, Petey, it'd sure be nice to at least let us know when you decide to burn the midnight oil. For your mother's sanity. Where were you, anyway?"

Searching for words, Peter demurred. "Umm, I spent the night hanging out at JT's place."

"Gosh!" Danny spat as he returned to his paper. "I hope you de-lice yourself after spending a night in that rat's nest!"

"Good morning, anyway, sunshine," Maggie said, she said kissing Peter on the cheek. She poured him a mug of coffee and put it in front of him as he sat down to join the family.

Peter sat still and silent, sipping his coffee and keeping the previous night's events to himself. Internally, he was still reeling but refused to bring his parents into his brother's drama.

It was rare everyone was together in the morning during the week, but Mom worked the later shift that day and Johnny didn't have class until the evening. Sometimes Peter felt insecure about living at home with his family at the age of twenty-six. It was days like these, though, that he was thankful to have a family he could eat with. He thought about James, how he didn't have what he was experiencing right now. Some of that was on him; some of that was on his parents. Either way, he felt sorry for him and wished he was sitting around the table to add his wit and stir things up. Instead, he was slumming it in that split-level in Northwest Grand Rapids. Hopefully sober, hopefully clean.

"We missed you for dinner yesterday, Petey," said Danny as he poured milk and sugar in a fresh cup of coffee.

"Yeah, sorry about that. I ended up going out for dinner with a friend after class. I should have let you know. Class was good, though. You would have been proud of Dr. VanDyke" He shoveled a forkful of cheesy eggs into his mouth and washed it down with another swig of thick, black coffee. His mom knew how to do coffee right—he had trained her well.

"What do you mean, that we'd be proud?" Danny questioned, peering over his newspaper with raised right eyebrow.

Peter sensed a land mine and wanted to diffuse the situation quickly. "Nothing. I just meant that he was encouraging us to rediscover what the Church has always believed. To hold to the fundamentals."

"Got that right," his dad replied, crunching on a piece of overcooked bacon. "Maggie, dear, a little less crunch next time, please."

"Then a little more help next time, please," Maggie shot back as she took her seat to enjoy the family breakfast.

Peter looked over at his mom and then at his dad. He returned back to his plate, and continued, "Yeah, but he also said we don't need to become fundamentalists, either."

"What's that supposed to mean?" Danny said, throwing down his newspaper.

"It means I can believe that God created without believing that Alfred Morris has the final word on how he created. Or that there won't be an end to the story without it being defined by Tim LaHaye's *Left Behind* escapism."

Both Morris and LaHaye had become symbols for Peter of everything that was wrong with the fundamentalist version of the Christian faith he had grown up with. Morris had said once that one could not be a true believer unless they believed in a six-day-literal creation. LaHaye had made something of a fortune off of a fictionally contrived tale of the end of the world, emphasizing the destruction of the world and escape of believers from that world. He also jump-started Kirk Cameron's career again, which Peter felt was equally as horrifying.

"Why are you so eager to abandon what we've raised you to believe?" Maggie asked. He could feel the same tension he witnessed several Sundays ago at CBC bubbling beneath the surface in his mother's question.

"As I've said before, this doesn't have anything to do with the beliefs you raised me on," Peter replied, growing tired of this back and forth with his parents. "I'm talking about the general tendencies of conservative Christianity. Yes, some of what I was given from CBC, but also what I was given at Freedom University and then my ministry in DC. And I gotta tell you, outside this Christian bubble, that faith doesn't hold a lot of weight with people."

"Of course, it doesn't," Maggie replied, "because the world loves the darkness rather than the light. That's Scripture."

"I know it's Scripture, but a bigger reason is the emotional barriers people have to the Christian faith because of Christians. To religion in general, really." Peter was getting exhausted, and it was only just after nine. He realized the time and was thankful for a way out.

"Sorry, but I should be going." He got up and cleared his leftovers in the trash. "Thanks for breakfast, Mom. I won't be back until later. Have a good day!"

PETER SLAMMED the car door and jammed the key in his car's ignition. He revved the engine in frustration and backed out of Cooper Manor in a way that visibly expressed the annoyance he felt inside. He was tired of having these conversations with his parents. It was the same tired circle of personalism and attacks, and he was over it.

"They should be freakin' excited that I'm being challenged to come back again to their side of the theological fence!"

He hit the steering wheel, sliding through a four-way stop at the end of his neighborhood. He brooded all the way from Coopersville to Grand Rapids, feeling like he would never please his parents, never believe and behave in a way they would find acceptable.

As he made his way to Wealthy Street to begin his 10:00 a.m. shift, he hoped his day got better. Somehow he thought it would as he parked and saw Lexi setting out the trash.

"Need some help?" Peter asked as he walked up behind her, making her drop the black bag.

"You scared the crap out of me!" Lexi exclaimed, clutching her chest.

"Sorry! Didn't mean to scare you. Let me get that." Peter picked up the bag of trash she dropped and set it in the bin.

"No, it's fine. I startle easily. Classes going well this week?"

"Other than Greek...they're fine."

"What's wrong, Pete? Not as excited as you thought you'd be?"

Peter looked up. "No, it's not that. I just came from a frustrating conversation with my parents. That's all."

"Aww. Well, I'm sure it's nothing a good cup of coffee can't cure!" She held the door open for him as he walked inside.

Already the place was abuzz with the morning crowd, filled with moms and their kids, cramming students, and a few freelancers. Instead of the promised cup of coffee, Peter pulled himself a shot of espresso. After a month on the job he was finally getting the hang of the espresso maker, even making descent lead patterns with the milk, like the experts.

"So what happened at home that's got you so frustrated?" Lexi asked.

"It was just this breakfast conversation. About my faith, actually."

"Say no more!" she exclaimed, putting up her hands in protest. "Been there. Done that."

"Oh yeah? What for?"

She dunked a frothing pitcher under the suds and began to explain. "I grew up in a pretty strict Christian Reformed home. No work on Sundays, which meant either napping or playing in my room with my sister, which I didn't so much like. And of course church stuff three days a week. And people pointing fingers at your every failing. And a complete disconnect between my church's teachings and the way the rest of the world worked."

She started scrubbing a pot caked with leftover oatmeal to work out her frustration at the recounted memory.

"And then one day—I was probably seventeen—I was just

like, screw it. I stopped going to church, which pissed my parents off. They tried to get me to keep going, but I just refused. Haven't gone back since."

Peter could tell the memory throbbed with more layers than she was sharing. He left it alone and brought the conversation back to himself.

"The funny thing is I was sharing how one of my professors encouraged me to rediscover the Christian faith through the historic Church."

Lexi looked up from washing to listen.

"We had lunch together, and he challenged me to not reimagine the Christian faith, but to rediscover it. He said basically the same thing in class. So I thought they'd be happy for me..." Peter stopped and smiled. "But they couldn't even get there. Instead, they got all offended at something I said."

"What'd you say?"

"Just that he thought I could hold on to the fundamentals of the faith without becoming a fundamentalist."

Lexi raised one eyebrow. "Like them?"

Peter offered a wry grin. "Basically. That's not what I meant to say, but yeah."

Lexi laughed and started washing another pitcher. "What do you mean by that, anyway? That you can hold onto the...the fundamentals of the faith, as you put it, without being a fundamentalist Christian. What's that about?"

"I know, it sounds kind of scary and super backwards and traditional. I'm not entirely sure what to make of his...encouragement, I'll put it. What I got from it was that I could still believe we were created by God without being anti-science. So the fundamental of the faith is that, for example, God created us and this world, however he worked that out. And VanDyke would say I can hold onto that without going all fundie and saying it all happened in six literal days. Stuff like that."

Lexi nodded in silence as she continued to wash.

"I don't know," Peter demurred, shrugging his shoulders. "I'm not entirely convinced, given how burned I've been by fundamentalism. I've got some reading and studying to do about it, so we'll see."

"Well, Peter Daniel Young, let me know what you find. I've pretty much given up on organized religion, but maybe there's something there for me, too."

Oh, I will.

CHAPTER 21

THE PAST SEVERAL months had been a whirlwind for Peter. Coming back home again, reopening old wounds and debates with his parents, entering into his brother's journey, starting a new job, and starting seminary had been more than enough for one person to handle. Ending the new year on most of these notes was definitely unexpected. And on top of all of this change, he was beginning to wrestle again with his faith. It was a year ago all over again.

That experience back then was world rocking. Not only did the foundational assumptions of Peter's childhood faith crumble around him, leaving him with the task of picking up the pieces to reconstruct a new version. His relationships were challenged and strained, too. Back then, some of his friends didn't understand what he was experiencing. His parents certainly didn't, which led to a near breakdown in their relationship. One of the hardest experiences, though, was the collapse of his ministry and the way his coworkers turned on him.

And now it seemed as though an impending storm was brewing just over the horizon, a familiar storm that threatened to engulf Peter's life once again. Just as the pink, newborn skin of his new faith was settling into a firmer, developed membrane, the impending cyclonic forces imperiled that new flesh once again.

Peter was deep in thought at his desk as dusk quickly closed the day. He preferred to keep the lights low but for his banker's lamp that lit his Cooper-era antique desk.

He was anxious. The fear of regressing back to his fundie youth threatened much of what he had built. Yet alongside that inner turmoil rested the slightest hint that what was coming was OK. That not only was it almost inevitable, but he should embrace it.

He imagined himself standing in an open field, surrounded by tall grass swaying in protest to the gusts of wind leading a summer storm's procession. As if on cue, the rain came in buckets, trampling the grass and soaking him from head to toe. Instead of hunkering down inside to wait out that storm, he felt he should run out into the open to feel and experience its full downpour weight.

Peter decided to answer the storm's call.

He grabbed VanDyke's lecture notes and his theology textbook. Yes, he had no choice but to jump in, because his seminary career depended on it. But he decided to take VanDyke up on his challenge to rediscover the historic Christian faith—the *vintage* Christian faith, as he called it—with measured willingness. Perhaps this was the path to extending what he'd begun a year ago: connecting the ancient Christian faith to the twenty-first-century world. Perhaps his reading would finally put the pieces together to satisfy this longing.

After making himself a steamy cup of Earl Grey to keep him company, Peter decided to start with some reading from *A Reimagined Christianity*.

It'll jump-start my brain enough to engage my class material, Peter thought.

He snatched the book from under a pile of dirty clothes and turned to Bryan's chapter on the authority of Scripture.

My journey seeking a reimagined Christian faith has forced me to ask some hard questions about our most cherished book, the Bible. We have to face the fact that we can't reimagine the Christian faith without also reimagining our approach to Scripture—because we've messed things up with our cherished book.

So far, Peter was with him. His seminary classes had taught him the Bible is far more complex than we generally give it credit. We need to pay close attention to how we interact with it, how we interpret it.

Peter continued, noting that for Bryan the way we've read the Bible has gotten us into trouble with science, slavery, women's rights, and the environment. Bryan believed that we've read it more like many read the U. S. Constitution in our country—as a set-in-stone document to be read literally and interpreted word for word. According to him, this is misguided:

It shouldn't be read and interpreted and applied like some do a constitution, as if it were an absolute authority on everything in life. Instead, the Bible is a community library.

Peter remembered JT talking about this comparison a few weeks ago and considered it again. Constitution vs. community library. Growing up, he saw how literal, rigid, constitutional readings of the Bible had contributed to racism—even in his church. He recalled an experience from his quiz practice days, when his coach misread a verse in 2 Corinthians based on such a reading. His coach thought that when Paul asks "What fellowship can light have with darkness?" in his discussion on believers not being "yoked together with unbelievers," that it was biblical grounds for preventing interracial marriage.

Peter shook his head at such a reading and view of Scripture. He wondered what Bryan would suggest instead. He read:

Whatever our beloved book is, it is not a constitution and shouldn't be read like a constitution. Instead, it is like a grand community library, filled with the culture and community of people tracing their heritage back to the forebears of our collective faiths—Abraham, Isaac, and Jacob. Understand that the biblical library is a carefully curated collection of ancient documents of utmost importance for those people who want to understand and be part of the community of people who are seeking to know and be with the God of Abraham, Moses, David, the prophets, Jesus — even Muhammad.

Peter set the book down on his desk. He leaned back and considered this definition of the Bible, that it was a select grouping of really important documents for a religious community.

Is that what the Bible is?

Seemed humanistic. It was as if Bryan thought the book was merely a collection of documents compiled by people, where some documents were chosen over others, without any guidance by God himself.

Where was God in the writing and compiling process? And what was this Muhammad bit? He continued reading:

This inspired library conserves, protects, informs, and inspires a continuing, lively conversation about God. This collection of documents provokes a living and vital discussion into which we are all invited to take part, a discussion through which God himself is revealed.

"So God is revealed through human conversation? Not through the Bible itself?" Peter asked, crinkling his brow. "And the Bible is just a history of our discussions about God? Is God himself *saying* anything?"

He flipped to the next chapter, continuing to plow through Bryan's argument.

God's revelation happens through our discussions and arguments. God is revealed when communities of people who share the same basic questions come together to discuss those questions. Revelation unfolds as people come together, interact, and share their ideas.

There it was. For Bryan, revelation was about human conversation about God, rather than God revealing himself to humanity.

Peter recalled the dream he had a few weeks ago, how God had seemed to remind him that he was the one who revealed, therefore Peter could know lots of things about himself. Bryan seemed to be saying the opposite: knowledge of God doesn't come from God, but from human debates and discussions.

As Peter thought about the implications of what Bryan was saying, he remembered that his theology reading—the one he was woefully behind on—pertained to this very topic. He took out his book on ancient Christian doctrine and turned to a section on the Bible as our basis for our knowledge of God.

The section quoted an early Church father, Clement of Alexandria. Peter read the quote and felt conviction rising.

> The Bible is the criterion of our knowledge. What is subject to scrutiny is not believed until it is subject to this test...

Exactly. Whatever we talk about in the Christian faith must be put to the test by Scripture; it's how we know what we know.

He continued reading, coming to a comment from the second century African Church father Tertullian:

> The Apostle Paul was guided by the same Spirit as the author of Genesis was, and the same is true of all the Scripture.

Yes! From Genesis to Revelation, God himself is speaking—and in one voice.

Peter remembered something else, from a lecture the other day on God's revelation to us about himself. He opened his laptop to find his notes and pulled out a handout with some quotations from Barth, that twentieth-century Swiss theologian VanDyke had asked him about.

"There it is," Peter whispered.

VanDyke taught about how we know what we know about God. He used the teachings of Barth to explain that we really can know and understand aspects of God because God has chosen to actually say something to us about himself. Peter started reading from the handout VanDyke referenced in the notes.

God encounters man in such a way that man can know him. He encounters man in such a way that in this encounter he still remains God, but also raises man up to be a real, genuine knower of himself.

VanDyke had explained that, rather than being hidden and concealed, God can be known because he has placed himself before humanity to be known. We really can know God, Barth insists. God has made himself "clear and certain to us." God does not remain hidden away, playing hide-and-seek with us. We can actually know God because he has given us knowledge of himself by speaking to us.

Peter's pulse quickened as he read through his notes and assigned reading, feeling as though he were on the threshold of a breakthrough in his own understanding of God. He continued reading:

God makes himself known and offers himself to us, so that we can in fact love him...and he creates in us the possibility—the willingness and readiness—to know him.

Back in his notes, VanDyke explained that genuine knowledge of God is possible because God has spoken to us about himself in a number of ways: through creation, his mighty deeds, our moral conscience, the Bible, and through Jesus Christ.

Peter closed his laptop and set aside his handout, a satisfied grin inching across his mouth at the idea that through his grace and love God has revealed himself to the world.

But as he continued meditating on this truth, his face began to sink. Peter considered something else in the equation.

What about the human element? We all bring something to Scripture. None of us comes to the Bible with clear, clean lenses. So God revealed. OK, fine. How can we be sure what we've read from Scripture is real, and not just our own interpretation?

He rolled these questions around in his mind for a while. As he considered them, something seemed to surface.

Perhaps that's why we have the Church. Especially the historic Church. If the same Spirit guided the authors of Scripture from Genesis to Revelation then wouldn't he still be guiding us? Today? Maybe not in the same way by actually writing revelation, but wouldn't he be guiding us to interpret it? And wouldn't that interpretation be unified, like God himself?

Peter thought he was onto something there. He felt a tinge of giddiness as he pieced things together. Until he was brought back to the reality of so many diverse interpretations throughout Church history.

Or was it that diverse? Maybe there was a strand running from the early Church until now. A strand that connected God's story bit by bit into a grand, magical, revolutionary Story of Rescue.

Hope welled up deep within Peter. A hope that he was on the brink of finally finding what he'd been looking for the past few years. His palms still grew clammy when he thought where this new leg of his journey might lead him.

"God, I hope this doesn't lead me backward, toward my fundie faith!" Peter petitioned.

Yet deep down, as much as it might take him to the brink of

fundamentalism, he had this intuitive sense this wasn't going to happen.

But then the conversation with VanDyke over egg rolls and Moo Goo Gai Pan barreled through his mind. "I hope I don't regress!" Peter hissed as he sat up, thinking that's exactly what he was doing.

He considered that word, how it provided an odd counterbalance to the word progressive that VanDyke had dismissed.

Regressive Christian.

"Regressive Christianity," he said.

It did have a nice, ironic ring to it. Because while it could be taken as a negative, perhaps it was more of a positive than he had initially given it credit for. If Peter was honest with himself isn't that what it meant to rediscover and retrieve the historic Christian faith? Wasn't he being beckoned and wooed to return, to go back again?

Even to his childhood faith?

A shiver ran up his spine at the idea. By following VanDyke's advice he was returning to some of the roots of that faith, yet transcending them all at once. Because while fundamentalists insisted they were the ones preserving orthodoxy, there were aspects of their own beliefs that were other than how the Church has always believed.

"Not regressive Christianity," Peter murmured. "*Vintage* Christianity. That's it!"

An object on his desk caught his eye. His old eMate 300, a vintage laptop if there ever was one. He received the Apple product that was part of the ill-fated NewtonOS line of personal digital assistants as a high school graduation gift. His parents though it would be useful for taking notes and writing papers for college. It was. And in the past year he reclaimed the obsolete mini-laptop as a distraction-free writing machine.

The hyperconnected, always-online world of Facebook and

Twitter had proved a debilitating distraction for his creative life. His progressive MacBook technology actually became a hindrance to his creative life. It harmed it more than it helped move it forward like it promised.

In order to move forward in his writing and thinking life he had to move backward in his technology.

Perhaps the same was true in his spiritual life. Not progress, but regress by going vintage.

By rediscovering and retrieving the historic Christian faith.

Peter felt as though he were an ancient explorer who was stepping into a special new world teaming with new, undiscovered life and cultures and customs and personalities. Of course it wasn't actually new and undiscovered. For Peter it was; for the Church it wasn't. He longed to know what She knew. He longed to rediscover what She had faithfully preserved for two millennia. What She had given life and limb to contend for. To *preserve*, like VanDyke said.

The thought overwhelmed Peter. But he was ready. He was committed to rediscovering—whatever the vintage Church had locked away for safekeeping.

CHAPTER 22

FROM SEPTEMBER through December Peter struggled like a goose against a strong nor'easter headwind. His first semester was intense; it was gale-force wind strong. And it was capped by the bane of his semester existence: Greek. Throughout the semester he was five steps behind where he should be. So he was unsure how he would end the semester. He had been hovering around a C. If he didn't pass this exam his seminary career would be over. Greek is one of those gatekeeper classes, as they say, designed to sift out the wheat from the chaff.

By the time Peter had ended his exam he was convinced he was the chaff. His brain was mush as he struggled to translate several sentences, correctly identify Greek vocabulary, and conjugate those bloody parts of speech.

He found Izzy and Jake waiting in the lobby of chairs and couches. He walked over to them, plopping down next to Jake.

"Greek exam didn't go so well?" Jake asked.

He sighed and shook his head. "Not sure. I think I did OK, but I have no sense either way. I'm just plain exhausted from the thing. Either way, at least I'll pass. I think."

"I don't know. I found it rather invigoratin'," Izzy said. Both Jake and Peter looked at her like she was mad.

"I know what we need," Peter said standing up.

"What's that?"

"Sparrows."

"We need little birdies?" quipped Jake, eyebrow raised in question.

"Sparrows is the coffee shop I work at, nerd. Let's get coffee before SysOne to celebrate the end of the semester."

"Ooh, I like that idea," Izzy said jumping out of her seat.

"Let's do it," Jake agreed.

"Cool. I'll drive." Peter offered.

Jake and Izzy climbed into Peter's hatchback, huddling in his back seat because the passenger door didn't work. The three had formed a little seminary clique over the past few months. This celebratory drive was the perfect cap to their intense communal learning experience.

Fifteen minutes later, Peter eased the car into a parking spot under a naked oak tree capped by snow one block from Sparrows. He mastered his parallel parking skills on the streets of Washington, DC, which resulted in not a few parking tickets and almost as many orange boots after the parking tickets were left unpaid. The crew tumbled out of the car and rushed into Sparrows to find relief as snowflakes made their way down across the Wealthy Street landscape.

"Petey!" exclaimed Lexi when she saw Peter follow Izzy and Jake through the door.

"Petey?" said Jake with a raised eyebrow and mocking grin.

"Yeah Petey. As in P.D., my initials."

"Right..." He added in a whisper, "Sounds more like a pet name from a star-crossed lover."

"Whatever," Peter hissed back, giving Jake a stern look that demanded silence.

"And who do we have here? Fellow partners in Churchland mischief?" Lexi said with a wink.

Peter chuckled. "Churchland mischief. I like that. This is Jake and Izzy, fellow students at GRTS. We needed a caffeine boost, and of course there's only one place to get that fix along with the service and smile of a Greek goddess."

Way too obvious, Peter thought, red creeping up around his neck and to his ears.

"Greek goddess? Sounds like you've been drinking something else on your way here, Peter Daniel Young!"

Izzy rolled her eyes and sighed at the obvious flirtation between the two. Jake looked on with amusement.

"Will you have your usual?"

"You know it. Black coffee," Peter said.

Izzy ordered a chai and Jake requested a carafe of loose tea. To the protest of the other two, Peter paid for their drinks while getting his free.

"Don't worry about it. Go get a table. I've got these."

"Greek goddess?" Jake jabbed Peter when he returned a few minutes later with their drinks. "You got a little thing for your hippie coworker there, Pete?"

"Shut-up. She's not a hippie," Peter replied, refusing to play into Jake's other question. "She's a great gal. She is into yoga, though, but that doesn't make her a hippie. Though I think she's into Buddhism or something. Sort of spiritual but not religious."

"She's a Buddhist?" asked Izzy. "She doesn't look Asian."

Peter looked at Izzy with a look of confusion, shared by Jake as well. "Well, you don't need to be Asian to be into Buddhism. Not sure what it's like down South, but plenty of full-blooded Americans are into the religion. Or at least Western versions of it. And actually a lot of former Christians are into Buddhism now, like Lexi, even though they grew up in the Church."

"Really?" Izzy said dumbfounded. She looked back at the

woman. "I wouldn't have guessed she was ever a Christian. Why did she leave the Church?"

Peter felt this sudden need to protect Lexi from his seminary friends. "Well, she grew up in a version of the Church much like my own childhood. It was judgmental, legalistic, hypocritical. And I think that's why she peaced out." Peter left it at that, seeking to move the conversation along past Lexi.

"Is that why you went Prosurgent?" Jake asked.

Peter turned to him, now feeling this sudden urge to protect himself. He didn't know if it was a challenge or just an innocent ask from someone interested in his journey. Either way, he proceeded with caution.

"Well, I'm not one for labels—"

"I believe you're the one who called yourself Prosurgent Pete," Jake interrupted, sipping his tea.

"No," he shot back, "that was VanDyke! I mean, yeah I appreciate Prosurgence Christianity and appreciate the conversation, but I wouldn't say I'm Prosurgent, per se."

Jake gave a slight grin and nodded as he continued sipping his tea.

Peter huffed. "Anyway, yeah the last few years I've been on this quest to reimaginer the Christian faith, and that's probably in large part to the type of church I grew up in. The same type that Lexi grew up in. And for a while now Prosurgence Christianity has helped me recover." Peter drained his coffee and announced he needed a refill.

When he returned he shot back with his own question. "I'll assume from the tone of your question that you haven't felt the need to think about your faith for yourself?"

"Whoa, man," Jake said, sensing a challenge. "I didn't mean to offend. I respect your desire to rethink some things. Shoot, I even understand it. Remember we went to the same college!"

"Hey, fellas. Do you wanna go outside and duke it out?" Izzy said, trying to ease the tension.

Peter took a break to simmer. He had had enough experiences with people challenging his journey that he was through letting people challenge him without his own pushback. But he knew he did need to learn not to get so defensive, which he recognized he was failing at that moment.

"How about you Izzy?" Peter said, deliberately turning away from Jake. "I can't imagine you grew up in a church that was OK with a woman going off to seminary to be a pastor!"

"No, I didn't," Izzy chuckled.

"Then what changed for you?" He asked, intrigued about the underlying story that led Izzy to move 600 miles north to a former Baptist seminary to become a pastor.

"I think it unfolded in a series of moments just seeking the face of Christ."

Her reply sounded like the kind of quaint Christian cliché you might find slapped on a bumper sticker. He sensed it was genuine, though, and wanted to drill down into that.

"I don't understand. What do you mean?"

Izzy looked up from her chai. "I just mean I stopped caring what other people thought about where I believed Christ was taking me. Lord knows it ain't easy being a Southern female with the call of God on her life! I've been shut down and put down more times than I'd care to count. Yet I never read no where in my Bible where the only people God called to be his hands, feet, and mouth were the ones who could pee standing up."

Peter and Jake both cracked smiles at Izzy's feistiness.

"Listen, Hebrews 12 talks about running the race marked out for us and fixin' our eyes on Jesus, so I've tried to do that. I've just tried to run the race God's laid out for me, while fixin' my eyes on Jesus. And then unfixin' my eyes off of everyone else and their opinion of whether or not I should or should not be permitted to teach his Church."

"I like that," he said quietly. It was simple in its own Southern way, but profound nonetheless. Her answer also spoke of a freedom that Peter found allusive.

"So much for a light, friendly conversation over tea and coffee," Jake said.

Izzy and Peter both looked at Jake with a hint of irritation. Izzy answered Jake's sarcasm. "Well, OK, Mr. Sarcasm Pants. How about you answer Peter's question."

"What question?" Jake asked defensively.

"The one about owning your faith for yourself. Or do you still believe and practice your faith like you always have?"

Jake shifted uneasily in his chair and sipped some more of his tea before he answered.

"I don't think I've had too traumatic of a faith experience. I mean, I listen to you and Petey here and I can't relate. I haven't been traumatized." Sensing protest coming from the two of the them Jake quickly added, "And I'm not judging you both in saying that. Maybe traumatized isn't the best word. I just meant I had a somewhat normal church experience. If one can have a normal church experience. Does that make sense?"

"I hear you," Peter said. "I'm not offended. Your story's your story. But you're in campus ministry at Grand Valley. That experience hasn't influenced how you view Scripture or the Church or anything? That's what sent me down this journey in the first place!"

"Well, I didn't grow up in a Christian home and I didn't grow up going to church, so maybe that's helped."

"You didn't grow up in the church and you went to Freedom University? How did that happen?" Peter asked in amazement. Izzy also asked what an unchurched guy was doing in seminary and working for a campus ministry.

"I had a rich grandma," Jake replied. "Seriously, I grew up with nothing and had no way to get to college. I would have ended up like most of my friends. A drunk, a dad, or a dirt back."

"A dirt back?" Peter asked in confusion.

"A coal miner. It's a nickname my friends and I gave our dads who worked the coal mines. Most of them have joined their dads in the family business. And they're dads a few times over, too. With a few different gals. And also drunk most of the time. So I could have been there…" Jake trailed off, staring deep in thought.

Peter and Izzy left him to his memory and waited for him to continue.

"For me I didn't have any baggage from the Christian faith because I had no faith. College was a good experience that gave me a good grounding in the Bible. So I haven't felt this strong need to reimagine the Christian faith, as you say Peter. Because for me, I've just been discovering it." Then he paused and added, "Perhaps you need to rediscover it Pete."

Peter's head snapped up to attention. "What did you say?"

"Which part?"

"Never mind," Peter said.

"I guess we should get back to it," Izzy offered. It was nearing lunch and the three of them had work to do before SysOne class. Peter picked up the three empty glasses and walked them over to the dishpan situated on a shelf above the trash.

"I gotta take care of something before we leave. You guys go to the car. I'll meet you there," Peter said as he walked back over to the counter.

But instead of going to the car the two of them stood by the door, looking on as Peter made his move.

"Slow morning?" Peter asked as Lexi was washing several plates and mugs.

"Yes, but it's been a good morning. Your friends seem nice," Lexi said, nodding in the direction of Jake and Izzy.

Peter turned and saw his friends still standing at the door. A look of horror crossed his face, weakening his confidence as he geared up for his next move.

"Oh, yeah, umm...they're great. Hey listen," he continued in a whisper. "So, you got any plans anytime soon?" *Smooth, real smooth, Peter!*

"Date night with me and Rufus tonight," she said, dunking a glass in the soapy water.

Peter's shoulders sunk slightly in reaction to that news. "Oh, you and Rufus. Cool!" He said, trying to hide his disappointment.

"Yeah. He's a big hairy beast, but he's my big hairy beast. And he's a great Gilmore Girls companion."

Big hairy beast? Then it hit him.

"Oh, Rufus. Your dog!"

"Yeah, my dog," Lexi replied with a look of confusion. "Why? You have this shifty-eyed look about you, Peter Daniel Young."

He let out a nervous laugh then wiped his palms on his pants to dry away the accumulating perspiration. He looked over at Jake and Izzy who were still standing near the door with a hurry-up-and-get-to-it-so-we-can-go look of annoyance.

"Peter," Lexi said, holding a dripping frothing carafe, snapping him back to the moment. "What's up?"

He took a breath and blurted out, "You wanna get sushi?" Peter was shocked at his own forthrightness as much as Lexi. "I mean I don't wanna get in the way of your Rufus and Gilmore Girls time and all, but I just thought it'd be fun to get to know each other more—you know, outside of work."

Lexi stopped washing the dishes and smiled. "Well, as awesome as Rufus and Gilmore Girls are...your invite sounds way better!"

"Great" Peter said relieved he made it through the "ask" unscathed, finding success on the other side.

"So I get off at five. How about you pick me up at my house around six?"

Peter paused, confused. "Oh, you meant tonight?"

Lexi raised her eyebrows. "Didn't you mean tonight?"

"So...I'm an idiot," he whispered, head hung down.

Lexi snickered. "OK."

"In my rush to ask you out I totally biffed it."

"You...biffed it?"

"Yes! I can't go out tonight. I mean, I want to go out, I do. But with the semester winding down I've got papers out the wazoo. And then with the holidays..."

"Petey, slow down, spit it out."

He took a breath. "Can I take a rain check? Until, like, after the New Year?"

Lexi laughed. "I see how it is. Ask a girl out and make her wait a month, string her a long a little. I see how you work Peter Daniel Young!"

"No! That's not what meant to do," Peter said in protest.

"Relax pastor man, next year is fine. But you better go," she whispered, "I think your friends are running out of patience."

Peter spun around to see the two still standing by the door. Izzy's arms were folded and Jake was leaning against a table.

"Right. See you!"

He hustled to his friends, and they as Lexi said goodbye to the gang.

"Way to go bro! Smooth, real smooth," Jake offered as they walked back to the car.

"Yeah, marvelous," Izzy said.

On the way back, Jake and Izzy got into a heated debate about whether Macs or PC's were more superior, Izzy having owned Macs since childhood and Jake the same for his collection of HPs. As they rehearsed and rehashed the same tired arguments since the '90s, Peter tried to contain his giddiness at both his bravado and Lexi's interest.

Peter was glad the two were wrapped up in an argument because it also gave him a chance to consider their Sparrows conversation. It was an ironic conversation one, because everything about his current juncture in his spiritual journey should agree with Jake, at least in part. He felt this growing need to rediscover the faith himself. Yet why couldn't he just agree with some of Jake's critiques and let him in on his own journey of rediscovery? Why did he get defensive whenever someone challenged or even inquired about his desire to rethink Christianity?

Peter was intrigued to hear more of Jake's story, how he never grew up with the Christian faith and then when he encountered it he wanted more. And then there was Izzy, and her cryptic '*I'm fixin' my eyes on Jesus, while unfixin' my eyes off of everything else*' bit. What was that all about?

For the first time in a while he didn't feel alone. Perhaps these were the allies he had been waiting for to help him along in his own spiritual quest.

However that looked right now and wherever that quest was taking him.

CHAPTER 23

IT WAS SNOWING AGAIN. Seemed like it never stopped snowing in Michigan, which made him. More than once Peter felt his hatchback drift toward the edge of the highway as he snaked his way toward Grand Rapids to meet his brother for their pre-Christmas rendezvous. He passed an SUV that had slid off and down into some trees, hazard lights flashing in protest.

They're always SUVs, Peter thought as he shook his head, thankful it wasn't him.

Though the roads were treacherous Peter wouldn't let anything stand in the way of meeting with his brother, even a lake effect snow warning. When he pulled into the small Founders parking lot he noticed a healthy group of people wouldn't let the snow sidetrack their festivities, either.

Peter spotted his brother in the back, already cradling a drink. As he approached him he saw something else setting in front of him—an oddly shaped item wrapped in what appeared to be newspaper, the comics section.

That's right, a present!

Peter had forgotten JT mentioned getting him something for

Christmas. And he had neglected to return the favor in the hectic end-of-the semester activity.

"Dude, what's this?" Peter said embracing James.

"Your Christmas present."

"I feel like a total schmuck because I totally forgot yours!" It was a minor fib meant to avoid the fact he forgot to buy him a gift in the first place.

"Don't worry about it. I'm sure I'll see you again in another couple of months. You can give it to me then," James grinned as they sat.

"I know. I'm a bad brother, OK?"

"Whatever, just shut up and open your gift."

Peter eyed it suspiciously and started picking at the corners, choosing one flap that wasn't taped down completely. He began to tear at it, revealing a clear object of glass beneath. As he continued tearing he saw the Founders logo.

A Founders mug? Peter wondered as he completed the unveiling. Etched into the glass were the words *GRTS Mafia* and below it the number 446. James had gifted Peter his very own Founders Mug Club membership.

"It's a Mug Club mug," JT said.

"I don't know what to say." Peter turned the object around in his hand. "This is seriously the best gift I'll get this year!" He looked up at his brother who was grinning with pride. He smiled, emotion rising in his throat, and said, "Thanks, James."

"No problem. Now you're legit."

"For sure. But GRTS Mafia?"

"Yeah. Because you're like a backslidden criminal coming in here and drinking beer. Pretty sure those Baptists wouldn't be too happy knowing their precious pastor student was drinking!"

Peter laughed. "Probably not. But I know of a few professors who drink, so I figure if they wanna kick me out they gotta kick half their faculty out, too."

A server walked up to their table, and Peter promptly ordered his first Mug Club drink. JT drained his own mug and ordered another.

"So how are you? Have you been good?" Peter said, tilting his head like a parent to a toddler coming back from a trip.

"Yeah, I've been good."

He shot him a skeptical look.

"Seriously, I haven't used!"

"Alright, bro. Good thing, too. Because you know next time you do I'll kick your butt from here to Canada."

"Oh, I know! Not that you could or anything."

They both laughed as their drinks arrived. They clinked glasses, cheering Christmas and the end of another year, promptly taking celebrator swigs of their brew.

"So you got your first semester under your belt," JT said. "Feel good? Did you learn anything useful?"

"I can't believe it," Peter said, shaking his head. "And, yeah, I actually learned some things."

"Like what?"

"Aside from a hundred Greek vocab words I'll never use...I think I'm beginning to understand the importance of rediscovering the historic Christian faith."

"What is *that*?"

Peter shifted in his seat, anticipating a confrontation from his brother's tone. "I mean...like...the faith from the past. From, like, the early Church. My professor jokingly calls it regressive Christianity." He laughed, trying to deflate the punch from the loaded idea.

"*Regressive* Christianity?" JT slurred, wearing a look very much like Peter imagined he himself wore when VanDyke said the very same thing.

"Vintage Christianity, really," Peter said defensively. "Like going back to the basics of how the Church has always believed."

"Like our childhood fundamentalism?"

"Not fundamentalism. But maybe the fundamentals. Like what's always been central to the faith from the beginning."

"Like what?"

Peter took a big breath. He breathed it out through puckered lips. "Well the authority of Scripture—"

"But *whose* authority?" JT interrupted. "Because by my guess, there've been thousands of authorities on the Bible. Some of them even burned some others at the stake!"

"Well sure, but the Bible itself has authority for what we believe and how we live, doesn't it?"

"Yeah, but it's interpreted. And how many interpretations do we have? Shoot, we can't even come to an agreement on a single *translation* of the Bible, let alone a single *authority* on it."

Peter was taken aback by his brother's aggressiveness. "All I mean is that the Bible is saying something. God is saying something through the Bible to us about himself and his world. And *that* has authority."

"Whatever. What's the next fundamental?"

Peter didn't know how much longer he wanted to do this, but he liked engaging his brother, so he continued. "Well, another one would be the exclusivity of Jesus—"

"Exclu-what?"

"Exclusivity. Like salvation by grace through faith in Jesus Christ alone."

"Like Jesus is the only way to God?"

"Exactly.'"

"That's total BS," JT sneered, leaning back again as he drained his beer. He set his mug down with a degree of force that underscored his disapproval.

Peter scoffed. "What do you mean, that's BS? That's, like, basic. That God has provided rescue and recreation through Jesus."

"If you're a Westerner, maybe. But what if you're born in Iraq? Or China? Or some African country? Then, what, you're screwed?"

It was clear that the handful of drinks James already had was lubricating his tongue, and his attitude.

"Bryan has a great chapter on that one. You should read it." JT said.

"Oh yeah? What does he say?"

"First of all, he calls out our horrible record of demonizing other religions. Then he says that God doesn't show favoritism to one religion and that we don't need to go around fighting so that only our religion survives. Especially because Jesus is a gift to the entire world. Even other religions. We need to discover God in the other, because he's already there." JT moved in closer to the table, then continued, "Petey, Christians are so caught up in dividing *them* from *us*, but the thing about it is, that '*us*' is way bigger, and people of all faiths are included!"

Peter sat wide-eyed and still, not knowing what to do with James's admission of religious pluralism.

"So what was the point of Jesus?" Peter probed.

"To show us who God is. To show us a better way of being human. To model for us how we are supposed to live this crazy life."

"OK," Peter replied, searching for where to take the conversation. "And so what are we called to do? Does Jesus benefit us in anyway?"

"Yeah, it's like I said. He shows us how to live. How to live your best life now."

"And how do we do that?"

"By following him. By obeying his teachings and living the Kingdom. And here's what's great!" JT was getting animated now, fueled by another round of drinks. "Bryan thinks it's fascinating to think that thousands of Muslims and Buddhists and

Hindus—even atheists and agnostics—everyone from everywhere will enjoy the Kingdom of God in ways even Christians won't!"

"Really?"

"Sure. And why not? I have a Muslim coworker who is more loving and more Christ-like than any Christian I've ever known. I mean, why can't someone follow Jesus's life and teachings and still be a Muslim? Especially if all they've known is that religion?"

"Because it doesn't work that way!" Peter blurted out, frustrated at how the night was going and what his brother was believing.

"So my Muslim friend is screwed?"

"No, your Muslim friend isn't screwed! God loves your Muslim friend. In fact, he loved him so much that he died for him—"

"Oh, don't feed me that fundie BS—"

"Dude, stop saying that," Peter interrupted, rolling his eyes. "It's not BS, and it's not simply *fundie!*

"Oh, no, right. It's *regressive!*"

Peter regretted his vulnerability as much as where this conversation had gone.

"James," Peter began, then paused to take a breath and calm himself. "What I was going to say before you interrupted me is that God loves your Muslim friend. He loved him so much that he died for him. He wants nothing more than a relationship with him. And I believe he is not at all interested in screwing him over. He's been on mission to rescue him and put his life back together again, in Christ—as much as me or you. Look, all I'm after is what the Christian faith has always believed, that's all."

"Yeah, well, that's why I'm not a Christian anymore."

Peter was blown back by James's confession. He sat back, cocked his head slightly to the right, and stared back, not knowing what to say next. Then he asked, "Is that why you're not coming over Friday? Because you don't want to celebrate Christmas? A *Christian* holiday?"

"Maybe that's part of it," JT admitted. "I mean, what's the point? The guy was born, lived a great life—the best life, I think—and then died. A religion formed around him and grew, just like any other religion, by the way. And I mean, I like the guy, his teachings and all. But all of the religious and hocus-pocus, mumbo-jumbo stuck around him...I just don't buy it anymore."

The way JT described his affection for Jesus sounded like how one idolizes Gandhi or Mother Theresa. He appreciated him as a great model for living, but nothing more. Certainly not as God or Savior.

"Don't look so gloomy, Petey. Gosh, you look like I murdered someone or stole your child!"

In a way he had committed murder. *You've bludgeoned your faith to death*, Peter thought. But he kept his thoughts to himself.

"Dude, it's the beer," Peter managed, yawning and searching the room for their server. "I've had my fill. And it's late."

"I'm feeling it myself. I should go."

Their server brought over the checks and they each paid cash.

"Great chatting again, Petey," JT said.

"For sure. Always great. And thanks for the gift." Peter grabbed his empty mug by the handle, looking it over. "Seriously, the best gift ever!"

"I figured with our regular book club and all, a poor student needs to save a few bucks on his beer."

Peter laughed as they stood. He stretched and they walked out together into the crisp December night. The snow had stopped, and it seemed to have warmed a notch.

"Well, Merry Christmas, James. I can still say that, right? Or will you, like, break out in hives or something?" Peter smiled as he hugged his brother.

"Just as long as I can say Happy Hanukkah or Merry Winter Solstice."

"Deal! Also, thanks for sharing. I'm not sure what I think about it all—I mean I am training to be a Christian pastor," Peter smirked. "But I'm happy you're wrestling with this stuff, man. I've never heard you talk like this—like, ever. But it's cool."

"Yeah, well, I guess I just decided to own what I believe for the first time, you know?"

"I can appreciate that." If there was anyone who understood that impulse it was Peter. That same desire had launched Peter into his own spiritual journey two years ago. In many ways, it was what kept him going still, even in seminary.

"And I may not be in seminary or anything, but I can read; I can think for myself."

"Sure you can. You've definitely bested me at Bryan's book, that's for sure."

James blushed slightly and turned to leave. "Merry Christmas, Petey!" he yelled as he shuffled through the snow to his car.

"Merry Christmas, James," Peter mumbled to himself as he watched his brother slip away into the night.

PETER JUMPED on 131 to head home and was feeling a bit light headed. Thankfully, the snow had been on the wet side, covering the roads in a layer of melting slush, rather than packed dry snow. He also had the company of the local jazz station to keep him focused, and also cheer him up.

As he drove, mesmerized by a smooth number by John Coltrane, Peter meditated on the evening conversation, particularly his brother's attraction to Bryan and his theology. He was pleased that his brother had taken such an interest in spiritual things, especially theology. This was new for James. Peter couldn't remember an instance growing up where his brother took such a strong interest in church or faith, much less reading—and a faith-oriented book at that.

But where the book was taking his brother, Peter wasn't thrilled. In fact, it depressed him. It was clear James was taken with Bryan's religious pluralism—even universalism. And because James didn't have a firm biblical foundation, what he was reading was filtered through his own situation and ideas.

Then again, what harm was there?

As a child, James prayed to receive Jesus as his Savior, as Peter had. And at least he was now interested in God and Jesus, even if his understanding of both was skewed. And Bryan himself was a pastor, although he had clearly taken an odd turn by Peter's estimation. And the Prosurgent people also loved Jesus and were trying to find their own way forward.

"What is the harm, really?" Peter voiced while Coltrane blared out a saxophone solo.

Then it started to hit him: his brother had voiced belief that everybody was 'in,' as if a universal salvation ruled the world. He also voiced belief that God was in other religions, that God's family is bigger than the Christian faith.

"Can someone believe that and be a Christian?" Peter asked out loud, staring at the bright full moon lighting his way home, glistening and reflecting off the fresh blanket of snow.

His question haunted him. Again, he felt he was channeling his fundamentalist past, but to Peter believing that everybody was already rescued and "in" and that God was in every other religious faith was incompatible with biblical Christianity, with the vintage Christian faith. Bryan's reimagined Christian faith, his new kind of Christianity, seemed to be pushing the opposite of historic Christianity, that a twenty-first-century Christian identity needs to respect other religious faiths and embrace a belief in a God who already accepts humanity.

Then what's the point in declaring "Jesus is Lord" or believing

God raised him from the dead? Peter wondered, pulling into his driveway.

It was nearly midnight as he crept inside Cooper Manor and upstairs to his bedroom. He heard someone downstairs go into the bathroom as he closed his door.

As Peter changed he looked at his textbooks strewn about around his desk. The ones that caught his eye were from his Systematic Theology class. Throughout the semester, VanDyke had gone on about how the earliest of Christian thinkers gave life and limb to preserve the faith entrusted to the Church. Literally. He told moving stories culled from the annals of early Church documents of men coming to the earliest Church councils missing arms and eyeballs, hobbling for miles on mangled legs and raising stubby arms in agreement to council business. These men were the ones fighting to preserve what the Spirit of God himself through the Apostles had passed down to the Church, even to the twenty-first-century Church that Peter and James and Bryan and the Prosurgent group was part of. VanDyke's point was that we disrespect their legacy when we reimagine the faith they died to preserve. We also disrespect the Holy Spirit who has been actively preserving the faith once and for all entrusted to God's holy people, the Church. What a shameful thing it is to disrespect and flat out deny what both the Communion of Saints and the Holy Spirit have preserved for us.

Peter crawled into bed, exhausted from the evening and still buzzing with alcohol. His mind was consumed, though, with the thought of his brother being swayed and taken in by Bryan's latest theological musings.

"Ideas have consequences," Peter mumbled, remembering something that VanDyke said in class and at lunch. He'd repeated it again a month ago when he had been talking about early Church heresy. Yes, they do. But what kind of consequences would they have for his own life? For his brother?

Peter resolved to find out. While he wasn't turning his back completely on Prosurgent, he was resolving to take a more active role in being responsible for the faith of his brother. Perhaps that's part of what Jude meant in his letter when he talked about contending for the faith, struggling for the faith given to God's people. Perhaps it was less about ideas and more about people, actual people, whose faith was in danger of being snuffed out for a variety of reasons, including faulty ideas.

Yes, Peter thought. *I will contend for my brother's faith.*

Part of what he knew that meant was countering the false teaching that seemed to be embedded in Bryan's book.

This was entirely new territory. The idea of challenging and confronting Prosurgent thinking was something he wouldn't have considered a year ago. Challenging his fundamentalist roots, yes; challenging his new Prosurgent branches, no way!

Perhaps challenge was the wrong word.

Too strong, Peter thought.

Perhaps contend and guard were better.

"That's it," he mumbled as he drifted into sleep. Peter knew he needed to contend for the faith of his brother, to guard it by talking through some of what James was reading, and now believing.

Rediscovering, not reimagining, the vintage Christian faith would be his agenda for his brother as much as for himself.

CHAPTER 24

PETER RUNG in the new year with as much flurry of activity as when he returned home in August. While the eight-week break from regular class work was nice, Peter replaced Greek vocabulary and theology papers with lattes and scones by working overtime at Sparrows. Not that he minded. Not only did it pad his bank account in time for the coming semester, it allowed him to spend more time with Lexi. Something was happening between them that only Cupid could ascertain—or perhaps devise. Regardless, Peter planned to make good on his date invitation soon. After his second semester was underway, that is.

He pulled into his second semester just as Jake was getting out of his car. Izzy walked over to Peter's hatchback as he pulled it into the parking lot a few spaces down.

"Hey, fellas!" Izzy said, her feet bundled in white Uggs and body wrapped in an over-sized white fur coat.

"You look like a polar bear!" Jake said.

Izzy punched him playfully in the arm.

"Ouch!" he said, recoiling dramatically and rubbing his arm.

"Future pastors can't go around hitting people. Not good for the resume."

"Well I think you look positively splendid, Izzy," Peter said. "Like you just popped out of the wardrobe of Narnia."

He snickered, earning him his own slug. "Ouch!"

"If you were where I was the past eight weeks," Izzy said, adjusting her fur hat, "you'd come back bundled up, too."

"And where was that?" Peter asked.

"Alabama. With my memaw."

"Your...me-what?" Jake asked as he looked at Peter in confusion.

"My memaw. My *grandmother* for you Yanks."

"You people are so weird. It's like a whole other country down there!" Peter said.

"Weren't you going home to Knoxville?" Jake asked.

Izzy's face dropped. "Well...I had some family problems that didn't lend themselves to going home."

The two glanced at one another as Izzy continued. She sighed, and said, "Daddy left Mama. Kicked her out, actually. Said it was his house and that was that. Which is *so* ironic considering..." She trailed off, as if she wanted to reveal more of the story but couldn't bring herself to face what had befallen her family.

Jake put his arm around her and offered a short side hug. "Sorry, Izz. How crappy."

She dabbed a tear from her eyes with her white leather gloves and pushed back a loose strand of hair from her face. "No matter. I had a blast with my other family! It was fine."

Peter walked over and gave Izzy a hug. "So sorry, friend."

"If you want, I'll go beat your dad up for you," Jake offered.

"Yeah, me, too! Jake and I will be, like, a double-man hit squad or something."

Izzy giggled. "Thanks guys, you're the best!"

"Unfortunately, I was busting my tail pretty much the whole break between work and that blasted Greek."

"But at least you got to hang with your lover," Jake said, arm still around Izzy in comfort. "Speaking of which did you ever take her out on that date you promised?"

He shook his head. "No, not yet. Soon, though."

"Dude, you better get on that. You're not getting any younger."

Peter rolled his eyes, and the three of them walked inside. The atrium was buzzing with activity as students arrived and caught up before classes started. Their Greek professor, Dr. Morris, lumbered over to the three of them with a very large Starbucks coffee.

"You ready for our little celebration, Peter Daniel Young?" he asked, grinning widely.

"One hundred percent, chief. Just hope it's not as lame as the last test."

"Ooh, that's good," he said after taking a sip of his coffee, then clucked his approval. "Well, we'll see if you're whistling the same tune when I'm done with you."

Dr. Morris winked then walked away to another group of students, asking the same question.

"So are you really ready?" Jake asked.

"No, I'm pretty much screwed," Peter moaned before sauntering off for his Greek "celebration."

Two hours later, he wrenched his stiff body out of his chair, handing his test back to Dr. Morris. He was one of two students remaining as the end of class drew near.

"Not all that lame was it?" Dr. Morris said smiling with an air of cockiness.

Peter simply smiled back. "Nope," he said and walked out.

Truth be told it wasn't as bad as Peter feared. But it sure was a stressful way to start the semester. He flopped on a couch in the atrium, closing his eyes in exhaustion before Systematic Theology 2 started in thirty minutes.

After traipsing through dreamland a half hour later, a deep baritone voice called through his sleepy haze.

"Happy New Year Prosurgent Pete."

Without opening his eyes he knew who was disturbing his R & R. "Happy New Year to you, too, Dr. VanDyke." He kept his eyes closed, willing his professor to leave him alone with the few more minutes he had before class.

"You ready for another semester with your favorite theology professor?"

"Wouldn't miss it for the world."

"Then why are you laying on this sofa when you should be sitting in my class?"

Peter jolted upright and glanced at his watch: 10:13. He looked up at his portly professor wearing an amused grin while cradling a cup of coffee.

"Here, drink this and come to class. Next time I'll let you sleep and mark you absent."

Peter grabbed the mug before VanDyke left. He shook his head to clear the sleep away, drank some coffee as he grabbed his bag, then hustled to catch caught up to VanDyke.

"Nice one, bro," Jake whispered as Peter sat down.

"Welcome back and happy New Year," VanDyke said from his lectern at the front. "I hope you behaved yourself while you were absent. Especially you, Peter."

Peter smirked and nodded as the class laughed on cue.

He continued, "This semester we are covering a big chunk of systematic theology, beginning with the Church's understanding of human nature and sin. We want to begin in an unusual way, because rather than jumping to the orthodox view we're going to begin with the unorthodox view. With the heresy known as *Pelagianism*."

Peter recoiled at the word *heresy*. From his experience, people tended to throw out that word whenever they disagreed with an opposing view.

"Pelagianism is named after Pelagius," VanDyke continued, "a theologian of British origin and was made famous for his heated debates with another famous Christian thinker. Anyone know who that was?"

Blank, bleary-eyed students stared back in silence as he awaited a response.

"Yes, Adam?"

"Augustine," he said.

"Right. At least someone's made it back safe and sound from Neverland," VanDyke mumbled before continuing. "Now, Augustine is mostly known for his beliefs about human nature and sin. When you hear someone say that person or belief is *Pelagian*, they're usually referring to that person's belief about human nature. Pelagius believed that the original spark of divine goodness from the garden was still present in humanity. He believed that we are not fundamentally cracked and broken image bearers as Augustine and other early Church fathers believed. Instead, he insisted we are by nature good. We're still born with the original goodness of our ancestors, Adam and Eve."

As Peter took notes on the lecture he realized he hadn't heard of Pelagianism before. He had witnessed these teachings first-hand, however, reading Bryan McLaughlin's new book.

VanDyke continued. "So if we are still by-nature intact image bearers of God—meaning the original spark of divine goodness in humanity isn't broken or tainted, well then why do we sin? Pelagius gave four reasons."

He turned to the dry-eraser board and began writing.

"First, he said we sin out of *ignorance*. We don't know any better or we don't have the right information about how we are supposed to live. He also said we sin because of *bad examples*, which leads to *bad habits*. And over time, those bad habits form *patterns and systems of sin.*"

VanDyke paused, letting the class catch up with their note taking.

Returning to his lectern, he continued, "Here's what's important about Pelagius's beliefs: he believed that people were capable of choosing, on their own, either good actions or bad actions. For him, nature does not compel a person to sin. A sin nature that is bred into people from birth does not cause people to sin. For Pelagius and others who follow his teachings, ignorance, examples, habits, and systemic patterns cause us to sin. So, because the divine image of God is still intact, and merely tainted or off-track, people can choose, on their own, to do acts of goodness that lead to salvation."

He paced away from the lectern, hands in his pockets, and continued teaching.

"You've probably heard the saying *We sin because we're sinners. We're not sinners because we sin.* For Pelagius, it's reversed. For him, we don't sin because we're born sinners, born bad. Instead, we are born good and then *become sinners* when we do bad things out of ignorance, bad examples, and habits. Make sense?"

He waited for confirmation either way, receiving some head nods.

"You might think this is just some ancient, boring heresy that reared its ugly head 1600 years ago. But there are plenty of examples throughout history of people saying the same thing. That's why they're called Pelagians. Let me give you some modern examples to show you how this thinking gets filtered into the church. I'm actually going to read from a few of your pals, Peter."

Peter's head rose upright from his note taking. His face flushed, both from being called out and also from the beating he was anticipating.

VanDyke returned to his lectern and opened a book. "One of the loudest voices in the Prosurgent movement is Dale Pagels, author of *A Christian Faith Worth Believing*. His book is classic Pelagianism. Listen to what Pagels writes: *'The theology of human depravity made sense when Christians held a view of humanity being something less than what God had intended when he created them.'*"

He closed the book, and continued, "For Pagels, original sin was a cultural response to wrongly held beliefs that human nature was less than the original condition in the garden. He says this false belief has led to false doctrine on human nature, and even salvation and judgment. Instead, Pagels believes *'the reasoning behind this view of humanity has outlived its time. It's dated, expired, and so too the theology that came from that view.'* Notice that he is rejecting original sin, the teaching of Augustine and the historic Christian faith, which we'll get to later."

VanDyke flipped forward to another pre-marked spot. "Now listen to what he says on pages 129-130. He's talking about the nature of Adam and Eve in the garden and he writes, *'Their nature did not change, their DNA was not transformed...The story of our ancestors never says that the sin of Adam and Eve sent them into a state of depravity.'*

"He goes further: *'we are still able to live as God's children because people still possess God's light within them. That light might glow bright or fade dim as a person lives like God or leaves God, but the light is never snuffed out.'*"

VanDyke closed the book again, keeping his finger inside to mark his spot and turned to the class.

"Like Pelagius, Pagels is saying that we are born good, that the light of our goodness brightens or fades with how good or bad we live, and that original goodness is never extinguished. Well, what affects that original goodness, then?"

He paused waiting for an answer.

Adam answered from the back again, "Ignorance, bad examples and bad habits?"

"Exactly, Adam. Good."

Peter rolled his eyes as VanDyke continued.

"Pagels gives an example of a newborn baby to argue his case that we are born good and godly. Examples, habits, and ignorance from our life taint our in-born goodness, just like Pelagius. He says in the case of a newborn, we should not view him as full of evil, but instead should understand that this baby begins life entirely good. That good child is affected, trained, and drawn into sin because of the examples other sin-trained models provide. Children sin because they practice what is modeled for them by adults or older siblings, continue in those practices and form habits, and simply do not know better. So just like Pelagius, Pagels believes that sin manifests itself and affects people from the outside in, rather than the inside out. For him, our nature is not broken, but our examples, habits, and knowledge are."

Peter had enough. He threw down his pen with enough force that it slid off the table. VanDyke glanced over at him and scowled.

"Care to add something to the discussion?" he asked.

"Yeah, I do." Peter took a breath, trying to dampen his irritation for VanDyke using Prosurgence Christianity to make a point. "So we are so far gone that none of us can do any good? We're totally depraved that we're just disgusting, wretched, sinners? Is that how you see things?"

"Well, Augustine said—"

"I don't care what Augustine said," Peter interrupted. "I want to know what *you* say?"

The class went silent as Peter's challenge punctuated the air.

A slight smile flashed across VanDyke's face. He took a patient breath before speaking. "What I was going to say, is that Augustine responds by explaining how post-Fall, the nature of all people is corrupted, because Scripture says so. Psalm 14 says that there is no one who does good, not even one. In Romans 5 Paul makes it clear that in Adam all have sinned, that all were *made* sinners."

Peter became more agitated. He had grown up with the idea that everyone was just a bunch of worthless sinners, in the hands of an angry God as one preacher put it. He'd rejected that idea as well as the hyper-emphasis on sin that marked his childhood faith. And now VanDyke was bringing it back front and center.

"Let me continue, because the real danger isn't so much with how we view our human nature, but how we view *salvation*. Pelagius said that our human nature actually has the ability to not sin at all. Folks, this is where the real danger lies. Because what he promoted, and even what Prosurgent promotes frankly, is self-salvation."

VanDyke paused to refer to his notes, then said, "In response, Augustine offers a line from the Lord's Prayer: *Lead us not into temptation, but deliver us from evil.* We've all heard that line, right? Augustine asks, '*If they already have capacity, why do they pray? Or, what is the evil which they pray to be delivered from?*' I think that's a fair point. Augustine is saying, why should a person pray to be delivered from evil if he can save himself all on his own by not sinning? Augustine continues, '*Behold what damage the disobedience of the will has inflicted on man's nature! Let him be permitted to pray that he may be healed! The nature is wounded, hurt, damaged, destroyed. It is a true confession of its weakness...It requires the grace of God.*'"

He set down his notes, then offered an explanation. "In response to Pelagius's belief that human nature is not corrupt and is capable all on its own to not sin, Augustine replies that human nature must be delivered from evil because it must be healed. That healing comes not from our own works, but from the grace of God."

Several students nodded as they finished their notes. Peter sat staring at the front dry-eraser board, arms folded and legs outstretched.

VanDyke looked at the clock, its hands commanding the class's release.

"Alright, I think that's enough for today. Make sure you begin your assigned reading, because this semester you've got a lot of it. Coming to class prepared will be important for our discussions."

In unison, the class rose from their seats to head off to their next destination.

"Peter, you got a minute?" VanDyke said.

Peter closed his eyes and sighed. Jake slapped him on the back and whispered, "Good luck, buddy."

CHAPTER 25

PETER WALKED over to Van Dyke as he was finishing gathering up his notes.

"Look," he started, "I don't mind the back and forth, but let's cut the attitude."

Peter hung his head in embarrassment at his outburst. "I'm sorry. I didn't mean any disrespect." He continued staring at the ground while VanDyke continued to put away his notes.

"Apology accepted. Just watch it, OK." Before Peter could leave he continued. "And can I ask, is everything alright? You seemed overly agitated today." He finished stuffing his notes into his satchel and began to leave, nodding toward the door for Peter to follow.

He did, and they walked back to his office. "I just feel like everybody is against me when it comes to faith and spirituality and Christianity. I can't please anybody!" Peter's indignation bounced down the office hallway as they continued to walk. "Not my parents, not my friends, not my brother..." Peter trailed off as they reached VanDyke's office.

"And not me, either, right?" VanDyke asked, unlocking his office.

"I guess," he sighed, slumping down into a chair in front of VanDyke's desk. The spacious office was lined from top to bottom with books from both present and past thinkers, giving the modern room an old library feel and smell.

VanDyke took a seat at his desk and swirled his chair over to face Peter. "I'm not against you, Peter. I'm definitely for you—"

"On your terms!"

Another interruption. And there was the attitude again. He rolled his eyes and apologized.

Peter closed his eyes and sighed. "I'm sorry. Again. Why do I keep doing that?"

VanDyke stared at him across his desk. "Because you're living with a whole lot of tension, Peter."

"Living with tension? What do you mean?"

"You're living in the tension of reimagining on the one hand—reimagining the Christian faith, reimagining the gospel, reimagining Church. And then rediscovering on the other—rediscovering the *historic* Christian faith, the historic understanding of the gospel and the Church. I've seen it in class. I've seen it in your papers. It's a good thing. But it's also painful. Especially if you've got relationships involved, other people who are on either side of that tension. There's bound to be blow-ups."

He paused, then added, "As long as it's not in my classroom."

He winked and smiled. Peter let out a deep, weary sigh.

"Sounds about right. And, yes, people are involved."

"You mentioned your brother? What's that about?"

"I thought I mentioned him before. Maybe not. He's basically a drug addict who's latched onto Prosurgent."

"A stoned Prosurgent Christian? How cliché."

Peter suppressed a laugh. "I'm serious. It's not funny. He got super close to overdosing a few months ago—actually, maybe he did. I'm not sure what the technicalities of it all is. Anyway, he almost died."

"Goodness! Sorry, Peter. Had no idea. So what's the deal with his Prosurgent interest?"

"Well, I think I had something to do with that."

He paused, staring off toward a row of faded, crusty books.

He took a breath, then said, "He'd heard about my own spiritual transformation and journey while I was in DC, and I guess he was intrigued. He bought Bryan's new book thinking it would encourage his own battles and demons with the Christian faith. And when I moved back home, I suggested we do a book club together to discuss it. He absolutely devoured the thing. Dog-eared pages, underlines, and all. And it changed him. Now he's basically written off the Christian faith. At least the *vintage* Christian faith, as you would say. Believes that all religions are equally valid. Everyone is already 'in.' I guess now he's Prosurgent James as much as I was Prosurgent Pete!"

VanDyke picked up on an important slip of the tongue. "As much as you *were* Prosurgent Pete?"

A smile crept across Peter's face. "I guess...I don't know. I mean, yeah, I think a lot of what Bryan is saying now is wrong. I said so in my last pow-wow with James. But I also don't wanna go back to where I was. Where I believed that we were all just wretched spidery sinners hanging above the flames of Hell by a single thread, while this vengeful God mustered up all of the grace he could spare to keep us from frying forever."

He was getting animated now as he confronted the fear of returning to his fundamentalist roots.

"So you're saying you're stuck in the middle of fundamentalism and Prosurgence Christianity?"

"Exactly!"

VanDyke whistled, leaning back in his chair and putting both hands behind his head. "That's a tough spot to be in."

Peter waited for more, but got nothing. "So what do I do?"

VanDyke looked at him with a knowing look, but said nothing for several more seconds. "I don't think I can tell you what to do. I mean, for starters, you can ratchet it down a notch in my class."

"I know, sorry."

"But seriously, I don't think I can tell you what to do. Part of what this journey is all about, not only in seminary but our own spiritual development, is living with tension. Is it uncomfortable? Definitely. Is it awkward? It's supposed to be! But I'd imagine sooner or later you'll find your answers to whatever it is that you're seeking."

Peter didn't like the cryptic, Jedi Master routine. Although he also appreciated VanDyke for not merely telling him what to do or how to believe.

He sighed and sloughed lower in his chair. He put a hand on his head and said, "But what do I do about my brother?"

VanDyke considered this question. "That's another question, isn't it. Because as we've said in class, *Ideas have consequences.* And the ideas that we gravitate toward and trumpet will inevitably spill over into the lives around us, won't they? Especially people who are already struggling and searching."

Peter felt a pang of guilt and shame for the responsibility of James's spiritual trajectory. He knew VanDyke didn't meaning to cause that pang. But his words sparked them, nevertheless.

"Thanks for the chat, Dr. VanDyke. Except next time, let's do Asian food." Peter smiled as he stood and retrieved his book bag.

"Sounds good." VanDyke stood, shook Peter's hand, and escorted him out of his office. As Peter turned to leave, he had one more thing to say.

"And, Pete. It really will be OK."

"I sure hope so," Peter replied before heading out into the rest of his day.

CHAPTER 26

DING, dong.

Peter waited at Lexi's front door, listening as a large, loud beast inside bellowed in protest as the doorbell announced his arrival. He had finally made good on his date offer.

The large animal could be heard running around on hardwood floors just beyond the front door as he stood in the mid-January cold, palms sweating and hands fidgeting while he waited to be let in.

Lexi's voice punctuated several large barks trying to quiet and calm Rufus down before letting in her evening date. The heavy deadbolt was unlocked and security chain was unhooked. She opened the door wearing a pair of skinny beige corduroys accented by bright red TOMs shoes. A coral colored turtleneck peeked out underneath a knee-length peacoat.

"Hi, come on in. Sorry about the dog," she said, ushering Peter in to escape the cold.

"No, not at all. I love dogs. Rufus, right?"

"Yes, that's your name isn't it? Rufus, Rufus," Lexi said to her massive English mastiff, whose whole body waged in agreement.

Peter smiled as he watched Lexi on bended knee make faces as she talked with her companion, rubbing his face with affection.

She stood and walked farther into her craftsman-style home. She continued walking, and said, "I'll be right back. I need to feed Rufus and make sure he has enough water."

Peter was left with Rufus while he waited. He tried not to make eye contact with his new friend.

Rufus stared back at him, eyes squinted and tongue hanging with skepticism at the guy who invaded his territory. He broke the silence with a massive sneeze that shook the entry way and made Peter jump with surprise.

"God bless you, Rufus!" Lexi said as she came back. "He didn't try and do anything did he?"

"No, he was great. I love dogs," Peter repeated, even as he was deciding if he liked *this* dog.

"You be a good boy," she commanded as they left the house.

They scampered down the snowy sidewalk to Peter's awaiting ride parked on the road.

"Nice car," Lexi said as they reached his awaiting hatchback.

As they climbed inside, Peter couldn't tell if she was joking or genuinely admiring his ride.

"What can I say? It's a college car."

"And a pastor man car."

He smiled and started her up. "Exactly." He pulled out onto the ice-crusted streets, and said, "Sushi, right? Does that sound OK?"

"Sounds perfect," Lexi said smiling, sending Peter soaring.

He had been flying high all week waiting for the night when he would be taking Lexi out on an official date.

"What would you like to listen to?" Peter asked as he punched his radio on.

"I don't know. What do you got?"

"Do you like Daft Punk?"

"Shut up!" Lexi exclaimed, turning half-way in her seat toward Peter. "I *love* DP!"

"Then DP it is," Peter chuckled as he found the playlist on his phone.

Instantly Lexi started treating Peter's hatchback like a club. He tried to keep his eyes on the car in front of him, but Lexi was tempting his focus with every twist of her arms and head.

"Wow. You've got moves, girl!" Peter said.

"Come on, join in," Lexi said as she continued gyrating.

"I think I'll concentrate on getting us to dinner alive. I'll leave the entertainment to you. Besides, you don't want to see my moves."

"Why not? You don't like to dance?"

"It's not that I don't *like* to dance. It's that I just feel awkward in front of people." Peter quickly added, "Especially people who've got moves straight out of the 80s!"

"Is self-assured Peter Daniel Young afraid of making a fool out of himself in front of a chic?" Lexi taunted.

"No, it's not that," Peter said, trying to recover.

"Then come on then. Bust a move!"

Peter just shook his head and smiled, turning onto Division Avenue a few blocks from their sushi destination.

As Daft Punk moved on to a more downtempo song, he slid his hatchback into a metered spot across from Republic, an American fusion joint that had a metropolitan feel.

"Alright Lady Gaga, let's role!" Peter said, exiting the car.

He waited for Lexi and the two of them hustled across the slushy street as a city bus lurched toward them from the north. They passed a homeless man huddled in the doorway of a bar next door. Lexi broke from Peter's arm to offer a few crumpled dollar bills. He accepted her offer, smiling and nodding in thanks.

Peter held the door for her when she returned. Smiling, he said, "Man, you put me to shame."

Lexi turned to him in the entrance as she stomped the accumulated slush off of her TOMs. "I figure if that was me, I'd want someone to notice and drop a few dollars. Didn't some spiritual teacher say something about doing to others as you'd want done to you?"

"Yeah. That was Jesus."

"There you go, pastor man."

After hovering around a few tables in wait, one finally opened. They grabbed it out from under two college couples who were similarly hovering.

"So what's good here?" Peter asked, eyeing the menu.

"Everything, but you definitely can't go wrong with their sushi."

When their server finally arrived Peter ordered three rolls for them to split, in addition to a fruity drink for Lexi and a glass of Syrah for himself.

"So Lexi..." Peter said, trailing off.

"So Peter Daniel Young..."

"I realized as I was picking you up that I really don't know your story. I mean, I've gotten to know cool things about you—like how you can bust a move with the best of them." The two shared a laugh. "But the rest is blank. So help me out. Who is Alexis Watson?"

"You don't mess around do you?"

"Nope," he said, winking as their drinks arrived.

"What is that thing?" Peter inquired of the electric purple concoction placed in front of Lexi.

"It's a pomegranate martini. It's *so* de-lish. Do you want a sip?"

He shook his head and took a sip of his Syrah. "I'll pass. I think my lips would pucker the rest of the night from that thing."

"That wouldn't necessarily be a bad thing..."

Peter chuckled before taking another sip. He smiled, then said, "So, your story."

"Yes, my story," Lexi smiled back. "What do you want to know?"

"For starters, are you from here?"

"Yes and no. I was born in Grand Rapids and spent some of my childhood here. But then I spent a good chunk of time oversees in Thailand."

"Really? Was your dad in the military?"

"You could say that," she smirked. "My parents were medical missionaries when I was in high school."

"You're a missionary kid?" Peter said, eyes widening with surprise.

"MK and proud of it," Lexi replied, taking a sip of her electric drink.

"Didn't see that one coming." Peter took another sip of wine, hesitating to approach the subject. He went for it anyway. "Can I ask, is that one of the reasons you left the church?"

"Yes you may. And, yeah, it probably is. Not because my parents did anything wrong or were to blame. They were mostly great. It was the CRCers that were part of our group."

"Ahh, so this was a Christian Reformed Church outfit?"

"Yeah. I was born and raised in the CRC. My parents are surgeons in town and in eighth grade they had this...calling from God, as they put it, to go overseas and take Jesus with them. If you ask me, their so-called *calling* came more as a result of their fortieth birthdays than from God."

"So they just uprooted you and your...you have brothers and sisters, right?"

"Yeah, oldest of four. I have three younger brothers. And yes, when I graduated from middle school, we packed up everything and moved to Thailand for three years."

"That's crazy. So what was it about your time there that made you leave church?"

Three trays of sushi rolls arrived. He picked up his chopsticks to dive in, but was stopped by Lexi.

"Don't you wanna say a little prayer or something, pastor man?"

"Oh, sure," Peter said, startled. Setting down his chopsticks he closed his eyes and offered a blessing. "God we thank you for this evening that we can spend getting to know each other. Thank you for this food, which we know is just a small representation of your goodness to us. We bless you for it and ask you bless it to our bodies. Amen."

"Amen," Lexi said with a grin after watching Peter pray.

He returned to his chopsticks and grabbed a roll with a large tentacle sticking out from the middle.

"So Thailand," he said, dipping it in soy sauce. "What about that experience made you leave behind church. And leave behind Christianity?"

Lexi put her hand in front of her mouth as she chomped on a roll. She took a sip of water to answer his question.

Swallowing hard, she said, "Well for start the missionaries had zero respect for the Thai people and their culture and their history. They were the respectable, sophisticated in-the-know white people who were coming to educate the heathen savages. And then the way they talked about Christianity with them was just nutso to me."

"How so?" Peter asked in the middle of chewing some seaweed salad.

"By the way you can eat all that green string stuff. *Blech!*"

"Don't tell me you're anti-seaweed. How could you? No matter, more for me." He stuffed some more of the translucent green noodles into his mouth and grinned.

She made a face, and said, "Where was I?"

"You were disturbed or something about how the CRC missionary peeps talked about Christianity."

"Yes! So it was like they were Kirby vacuum salesmen, selling some mystical land out in outer space called Heaven."

"Let me guess," Peter interjected. "The first line of their sales speech '*Heaven is a gift that's neither earned nor deserved?*'"

"That's it! How did you know?"

"Because that's the same canned speech *I* gave to college kids in DC!" Peter exclaimed loudly, drawing stares from the two college couples they had earlier elbowed out of their table.

"So the same speech about Heaven being the point of Jesus you gave to American college students was the same speech those missionaries gave to my English-speaking Thailandese friends?" Lexi said, voice raising in shock.

"Afraid so."

"Wow. That makes me even more mad. I mean, not only did they make Jesus about securing your butt in the after life—totally ignoring the big everyday concerns they had in *this* life. But they did it in a way that wasn't at all contextual! As if everybody in the world thinks about things through a freakin' Western American lens!"

Lexi threw her napkin down on the table in a huff and crossed her arms, staring at nothing in particular.

"Yeah, well, I had the same issues with my thoroughly Western American ministry. And I got fired for it."

"You did," Lexi exclaimed, coming out of her thoughts and slapping her palms on the table, rattling everything on it. "Sorry!"

"Whoa there, sister. Maybe we should take it back a notch," Peter said as he pulled Lexi's electric purple drink a few inches back.

"Hey! I need that. Especially so I can talk about my story with church. It's my antidote for the pain." She drained her drink and flagged down the server for another.

She said, "So you got kicked out of ministry, huh. I had no idea you were such a rebel!"

"Oh, yeah. And probably for the same reasons that tweaked you. I mean, when did Jesus ever say, '*I came that you might have Heaven.*' No way! Jesus said, '*I came that you might have life, and have it in the full.*' As in *this* life. Right now, as much as the next one. And of course he said he was life itself."

"But he also said he was the way, the only way. And if no one came to God through him, then, well, you're screwed. Which of course for my CRC peeps meant that if you weren't chosen by God in the first place, which meant you were definitely screwed!"

Lexi was becoming animated now. A second pomegranate martini came, and she took a sip. She hummed with please, then continued, "And I just began to reject that idea. I made so many great friend among those people. Got to know their religion, how deeply spiritual they were, how it filled every aspect of their life. They didn't care just about the next life. In fact, they believe that the next life is an extension of this one. That what you do now matters. Unlike my CRC peeps that said you were sealed forever if you were chosen and if you prayed a prayer, regardless how you lived."

Peter sat on the edge of his seat, his pulse quickened as he hung on every one of her words, marveling at the depth of this woman in dreadlocks and piercings sitting across from him. In the distance he heard his name.

"Peter? Peter!"

He snapped back and realized it was Lexi calling out above the din of conversations, music, and his own distracted heart.

He chuckled. "Sorry! Just entranced by your little soapbox episode there."

"So what do you think?"

"About what?"

"About what I said about my spiritual Thai friends being lost forever unless they're randomly chosen by some god?"

He took a sip of wine and cleared his throat. "I'm with you, for sure. I think that's bunk. And I get your frustration. I mean, a lot of your own complaints led to my own crisis of faith that I told you about. But that's why Prosurgent has been so important for me."

"Yeah, tell me about this Prosurgent thingy you keep going on about."

"When I was working in college ministry I kept running into students who were asking questions that I didn't have the answers to. Questions that had nothing to do with getting to Heaven or whether Earth was created in six literal days or millions of years. They were asking the same questions you've been asking. Which got me asking a whole lot of the same questions."

"Like what, Peter Daniel Young?" Lexi leaned in closer while cradling her martini in one hand.

"Like the fairness of a God who chooses to save some while damning a whole helluva lot of other people to Hell. Whether Jesus has any relevance for my life now. What someone has to do to actually *get* saved. Is it a prayer? Chanting a certain set of words? Something people have to do day-after-day? And what about people who didn't have the privilege of being born in a country like America whose dominant religion for over 200 years has been Christianity?"

"OK, so lots of questions! Where does Prosurgent come in?"

"They were my lifeline, the reason I'm still a Christian. It was an organization of people, a movement really, who were asking the same questions I was, especially how on earth it looks to connect the Christian faith to our twenty-first-century modern world."

"Sounds badass."

Peter sputtered on a sip of his wine. He chuckled and

finished his sip. "Oh, it is! And they basically saved my faith. They gave me permission to ask the questions I never asked growing up." Peter paused, and sighed. He continued, "The questions my parents really weren't interested in me asking even as a young adult."

Lexi set her drink down and reached over to Peter's hand that was resting on the table. "So your parents went ballistic, too?"

Peter appreciated the empathetic gesture. "Oh yeah. I remember one phone call after a series of blog posts questioning my beliefs of my childhood."

"Wait you have a blog?" Lexi said, interrupting. "I didn't realize you were so famous!"

Peter blushed. "*Did*. I really don't pay attention to it anymore. And it certainly didn't make me famous. But it was great for helping me work through my stuff. Anyway, so for months I was working through all of these questions swirling around. And then I came out against not even core Christian beliefs. First, I said the whole end-times escapism that says we're just waiting for God to beam us out of here so that he can blow this place up—" He made an exploding gesture with his hands, and the appropriate exploding sound effect to go along with it. "I said it was just ridiculous because it was a recent teaching, from like the nineteenth century. But the real kicker was when I challenged the whole women in ministry view by suggesting that God does indeed call and gift women to be pastors."

"Now that's trouble. God knows the world would end for sure if a skirt manned the pulpit!"

"I know, right? My parents didn't like that one, especially Dad. He sent me this long article that defended my childhood view of the end of the world. Then I got this lengthy e-mail saying he and Mom couldn't believe I was turning my back on the faith. All for suggesting women have the right to pastor!" Peter raised his voice in a void of silence as the DJ changed songs, receiving several glances from the surrounding tables.

He took another sip of wine and continued. "A few weeks later, I went home for Christmas and we got into it, about me leaving the faith. Finally, I was like, I'm not leaving behind the Christian faith, I'm leaving behind my *childhood* faith. And is that gonna be a problem? Are we not going to talk anymore because I don't believe like you do?" He paused and took another sip. "Mom didn't like that very much and started crying."

"You made your momma cry, Petey?"

"I did," Peter said smiling. "I felt bad and all, but I was trying to make it clear that I wasn't changing. That I *had* changed already. And they needed to get on that choo-choo train because it had definitely left the station."

"When I announced I wasn't going to church anymore my parents went ape. Looking back, I think they were just so fearful," Lexi said, reliving her own coming-out experience. "Fearful of what their friends would say. What all their church peeps would think when they didn't see little Lexi toting Mommy and Daddy on either arm. Fearful of where I would go. Fearful of losing me, losing their *control* over me." She paused giving thought to that last insight. "I think a lot of it was they couldn't control me anymore. Not that they were all that controlling. But parents can't let go in general. And letting go of their child's faith journey has gotta be on the top of that list."

"I hear that. For so long they could control what I believed. What I read and heard that made me believe what I believed. Did you ever see that M. Night Shyamalan movie *The Village?*"

Lexi furrowed her brow and shook her head. "I don't think so."

"So it's about this old village that looks like it's set in, like, the 1800s. They raise chickens, milk their cows to make cheese. And they live in constant fear of these unnamed monsters in the woods. They have this sort of truce with them, that they don't mess with them and they don't go out into their woods. They even set up this sort of fenceless wall with large posts and lanterns to let the villagers know where they can't cross. Well, this seven-year-old boy dies—"

"Thanks for ruining it for me!" Lexi said, huffing and throwing her hands in the air.

"What? I'm sorry!"

"No, no, no I'm teasing! Keep going this sounds interesting."

Peter took a breath, then continued, "OK, so this seven-year-old boy dies and one of the characters wants to go into the woods to get medical supplies in a nearby village. Well, his mother rebukes him and reminds him they can't. No can do because of this truce with the monsters. This guy totally breaches the invisible line anyway and goes into the woods, but comes back. After that, splashes of red paint mysteriously start showing up all over the doors and walls of buildings. One evening the monsters are even spotted and scare the living daylights out of the kids."

"Creepy!"

"For sure. But here's the thing: it was all a total farce."

"What?" Lexi asked, crinkling her forehead. "What do you mean?"

"The boundary, the village itself, even the monsters—all of it was fake! In fact, the elders of the town *are* the monsters! And it's not 1800 something but the 2000s. The village was some compound started by some hippies in the 1970s as this social experiment to create a secluded utopia. And they use fear to keep their families from venturing out into the world. They wanted to keep their kids from '*wicked places where wicked people live.*'"

"No way!"

Peter nodded. "And in the final scene you realize that adults have been trying to keep their kids away from the modern world.

And they used the fear of wicked people, fear of communal disruption, fear of imaginary monsters to do so."

"Oh my gosh that was *so* our lives!"

"Wasn't it? Such a brilliant movie. And I think that's what happens with our parents when we cross the line. They start splashing red paint all over the place, accusing us of abandoning the family or our childhood faith or whatever. Like you said, all out of fear."

Lexi sat back, buzzing from her martinis and the conversation. "You're a very wise man, Peter Daniel Young."

Peter smiled. "So they say." He finished his glass and peered down at his watch. "Wow, it's getting late. I should get you back home."

"Do we have to?" Lexi whined as she began draping her scarf around her neck.

"Afraid so. I don't wanna tick Rufus off on our first outing by bringing you back late on a school night. But I gotta say, this has been one awesome night."

"Agreed! So let's make sure we do it again soon."

"I'd definitely like that."

After Peter paid their bill, he retrieved his car and drove Lexi back home. When they opened the door, it seemed to barely register with Rufus that they had arrived. Rufus simply yawned and turned over in his bed.

"So much for impressing Rufus by bringing you home early," Peter complained. He turned to Lexi, and said, "Thanks for sharing your story with me. Sorry for all of the pain and confusion the Church has caused you. Believe me I understand!"

She smiled, and said, "And thank *you* for sharing some of your story, too. You're a pretty swell guy."

"Swell, huh? Man, what'd I do to earn *that*?"

"I'm serious," Lexi said, slugging Peter in his left arm. "And

I'm also serious about doing this again sometime soon. I enjoyed it. Really."

"Me, too."

Before Peter could turn away Lexi leaned in and gave him a peck on the cheek.

"Thanks," Peter replied weakly, eyes wide with both shock and delight.

"You're welcome. Now you better get off to home. I don't wanna tick off Mama Maggie and Papa Danny by getting *you* back late on a school night."

Peter said goodbye and headed back home, pondering along the way what God felt about a seminarian falling in love with an ex-Christian Buddhist.

CHAPTER 27

PETER ARRIVED a few minutes before 7:00 p.m. to a full Founders for brother bonding time. They hadn't connected since Christmas, causing not a small amount of guilt for Peter. He hoped James was doing alright, especially with his drug problem. He tried to check in more, but busyness was proving it difficult to keep track of his brother as well as his own life.

He parallel-parked into a tight spot along a side street near the brewhouse, tapping the bumper of a nice SUV a few times in the process. When he walked in, the place was buzzing with beer-infused conversations, the scent of hops and peanuts delighting the senses. A band was setting up some equipment on the stage in front of a set of massive windows that looked into the brewing warehouse. Peter walked up to the bar and ordered his IPA and his brother's Scotch ale.

He managed to find a table near the closed garage doors that opened to the porch out front in the summer. A couple had just left as Peter was walking around aimlessly with his two beers in tow. He settled in and enjoyed the soundcheck from what sounded like a post-rock indie band. The lead singers soft, droning voice at irregular intervals reminded him of the high-pitched velvet tones of Sigur Rós frontman, Jonsi.

"Well you don't look much older than the last time I saw you, but then again I can't remember when that was." JT plopped down in a chair across from Peter.

"Dude, how long are you gonna keep razzing me about that? I'm a jerk I know!"

"Probably a few more times," his brother replied with a smirk. "Here, have some peanuts."

"Do you know who this is playing?" Peter asked, motioning to the group on stage as they were winding down their soundcheck, trying to make conversation.

"Naw, never heard of them before." JT took a few long swigs of his drink.

"Whoa partner, pace yourself! We're gonna be here a while."

"I know. It's been a day..." he popped a few peanuts as he looked around the room.

"Did something happen?"

"Yeah, Jenny left me."

Peter had a momentary look of confusion before realizing Jenny must have been JT's girlfriend. Peter felt foolish. He didn't even know JT had a girlfriend. He nodded to try and cover his ignorance and looked down into his drink. In that moment, he realized he didn't know all that much about his brother. Between college and moving to DC, it's like he just dropped his family from his life—like a family of orphans dropped off at a halfway house, never to be thought of again. His brother was no more known than the bouncer he passed on his way in.

"Sorry, bro," was all Peter could manage in reply, continuing to stare into his drink. "Can I ask what happened?"

"I caught her cheatin' on me. She found someone else, I guess." JT drained his first round and waved the server over to order a second. "Probably for the best anyway. But it does make you wonder…"

Peter lifted his head. "Makes you wonder what?"

"If the universe or God or whatever has it out for me." He chuckled and shook his head. "I feel like I've gotten screwed more times than a guy deserves. I mean we had talked marriage, you know?"

"No, I didn't know."

"Probably for the best. What's that phrase? *'God works all things out for the good'* or some BS like that that mom used to say." He huffed and leaned back, stretching his long basketball player legs out under the table. "Screw that. Wanna join me for a cigarette?"

"Sure why not."

The two brothers went outside, leaving their coats to guard their table. When they returned three other guys were hovering over it in search of a vacancy as the main hall grew more crowded once the Sigur Rós wannabe band started up. They were deciding if it was vacant or still in use.

"Peter Young?" Peter heard shouted as he walked toward the table, making out a man as Rob from the Prosurgent West Michigan group.

That's right! Wednesday is Founder's group night.

Peter had totally forgotten his other commitment to join them for their Founders night discussion group. Along with Rob was Alex and then a newer guy who introduced himself.

"Hi, I'm Clinton." Clinton had short blond thinning hair. He had a frazzled look about him, like he had just woken up out of bed with baggy, wrinkled clothes.

"Is this your table?" Rob asked, shouting over the din of the band and conversations.

"Yeah, we went out for a smoke," Peter said turning to introduce his brother. "This is my brother, James. People call him JT."

"Hey JT. I'm Rob."

"Alex," Alex said, extending his and over the table.

"Clinton," the new man said again.

"Can we join you? Is that OK?" Rob asked as he was picking up an unused chair from an adjacent table.

"Sure, sit. Sit!" Peter motioned toward the table.

The server returned with the two brothers' drinks and took an order for the other three, all Mug Club members.

"You're a Mug Club member? Nice!" Rob bellowed.

"Yeah, JT got it for me for Christmas. Best gift ever!"

"So I heard you were in DC," Clinton said. "What did you do there?"

"Originally I moved to work in congress. Did that for a year and then worked in a campus ministry for a few years before returning back to GR in September."

"Wow!" Rob said. "Sounds like quite the trip."

Peter nodded. "It was. By the way, I met Bryan McLaughlin a few times while I was out there."

"You did? I've known Bryan for years," Rob replied. "How was that?"

"Amazing! He's such a cool dude. Gave some real helpful spiritual advice when I needed it."

"Yeah, Peter's a recovering fundamentalist like me," James interjected.

"Join the club!" Clinton said laughing, raising his glass in agreement.

"I'm not a recovering fundamentalist as much as a recovering Calvinist!" shouted Rob as he popped a few peanuts.

"Recovering fundie here," said Alex, raising his hand. "Pennsylvania Plymouth Brethren." He stopped and took a drink, then said, "Enough said." The table laughed with recognition.

"But then Petey found Prosurgent and pissed off our parents big time," JT offered, words tinged with a slight drunken edge.

Peter gave a short laughing snort, feeling a little embarrassed to be at the center of attention.

"They got pissed, huh?" Rob said, draining his first beer.

"Yeah. And then he introduced me to it all, which pissed them off even more!" JT roared, slapping his brother's back.

"So have you read some of the Prosurgent people?" Alex asked JT.

"Just finished Bryan's new book."

"See, even Peter's brother has read it, Alex," Rob said, smacking Alex's right arm.

Alex scoffed. "I said I started it. Lay off!"

"What did you think of it?" Rob inquired.

Peter was interested to see where this conversation was going to go. So far it had just been the two of them conversing about the book, which was more contained than this setting. It allowed for him to interject and correct where he felt his brother needed some help with the big ideas Bryan was presenting. This was a different story. Peter had felt uncomfortable with some of what Bryan was saying, but voicing that here might be more difficult than in a setting with just his brother.

"I think for the first time religion makes sense," JT said, finishing his beer and searching for the server to order another.

Peter found it interesting that JT said *religion* rather than the Christian faith.

"What do you mean by that?" Clinton said. "And keep in mind, I haven't read it yet and don't plan to."

"For the love of—Oh go on and read it!" Rob bellowed. "You're such an oppositionalist sometimes! You'll have to excuse Clinton. He's in our camp but isn't into anything that's establishment."

"You bet I'm not, and Prosurgent's falling into the same trap the Religious Right did a decade ago."

"They are not!" he bellowed again, throwing his arms up in the air in mock disgust.

"Fellas, fellas," Alex interjected. "Let's let JT answer the question."

Rob and Clinton both apologized and told James to continue.

"Thanks," James said as he reached for his drink that had just arrived. He took a swig, then said, "It's like Bryan says. We need to find God in the other. We need to realize that our religious 'us' is bigger than just us, you know?" Rob nodded in agreement. JT continued, "That, and in the end all will be well, man. All will be well."

"Exactly!" Rob exclaimed. "All the energy that's expended deciding who's in and who's out is such a waste because God's family is bigger than our 'us.' Bigger than what we make of it." The rest nodded in agreement as they swallowed mouthfuls of beer.

"But you're not suggesting that people who don't believe in Christ are saved, are you?" Peter said as they were drinking.

"Sure am!" Rob replied.

"I disagree with that," Alex said, interrupting Rob before he could continue.

"Of course you do! That's his favorite line. He's even got it on his mug, look."

Rob turned it toward Peter and JT for a closer look. Sure enough, etched on Alex's mug was the phrase 'I Disagree.'

Alex said, "I'm just saying we should be careful to dismiss the exclusivity of Christ along with embracing the openness of Christ."

"Come again?" Clinton asked.

"So Jesus is the only way of salvation, but that doesn't mean the boundaries of who are in are restricted to a select few. Jesus invited anyone who was weary and burdened from life to come to him for rest and rescue. But that doesn't mean everybody and every religious person is in."

The group grew silent. Peter was pleased. He liked this guy Alex from their first conversation, and even more now.

"But then what about the *all things* of Colossians," replied Clinton, continuing the conversation. "Scripture says that Jesus reconciled all things to himself. All things."

"Exactly!" Rob said, eating some more peanuts.

"Yeah, and isn't that Bryan's point with his understanding of Jesus and his Father's house," JT said, surprising Peter. "Bryan says that Jesus doesn't mean it's out there in outer space down the road. Instead, God's house is Spirit-filled people living right now. And everyone is part of that!"

He was getting animated now, feeding off the affirmation of Rob and Clinton. He took a long swig, and said, "Jesus isn't owned by Christianity. He's owned by everybody!"

"Exactly!" shouted Rob. "Get this guy another beer!"

Throughout the night Peter didn't say much, preferring to listen to the group and to his brother. JT was clearly taken by Bryan's book, and now he was finding affirmation for his new beliefs through the group. Peter was alarmed at some of what was said at the table, especially from Rob. He was excited for gaining a new ally in Alex. He seemed like someone Peter would resonate with, someone who had grown up under fundamentalism, someone who had broken out but had also remained in the realm of Christian orthodoxy.

After JT had finished his fourth beer, offered by Rob as payment for his brilliance, Peter suggested they call it a night. By that time James was becoming visibly affected and Peter worried for his safety. Luckily for Peter, he didn't put up a fuss and agreed. They both said goodbye to the other guys who stayed for another round.

JT happened to park a few cars behind Peter, so they walked in the crisp February evening together.

"You good, bro? Should you ride with me?" Peter offered as they walked, concerned he was too drunk to drive.

"Naw, it's OK."

"Are you sure? It's not a problem—"

"Seriously," JT interrupted, slurring his words. "I've driven in worse than this. But hey, thanks for the night. Thanks for listening. You're a good brother. A good brother."

James gave Peter a hug, an unusual sign of affection. Peter hesitated at first, but then hugged him back.

"And thanks for getting me that book, bro. It's helped so much."

"No problem. Glad it's helping." Peter didn't quite know how to respond since he was beginning to regret the gift. "Alright, JT, drive safe."

"Good night, bro,"

PETER SLUMPED in his car and shut the door. He leaned back and stared forward at the bumper of the other car ahead of him as his brother drove past.

He didn't know what to make of the evening conversation, what to make of how it revealed the new terrain of JT's beliefs. Any hope Peter held that he would be open to believing even a progressive version of the basic beliefs of historic Christianity were firmly put to rest. James had rejected orthodox Christianity. What exactly that meant for his brother was unclear as Peter continued staring in silence.

Peter shivered in the midwinter night, his breath clouding in front of him and crystallizing in sheets on his windshield. He put on his stocking cap, rubbed his hands together, blew warm air to heat

them, then started his car. He pulled onto Wealthy Street, still both-
ered by the evening. The image of his brother surrounded by
affirming voices and backslaps made his stomach turn. It turned
even more when he realized he had brought those voices to the table.

Anxiety gripped Peter as he sat waiting for the light to give
him permission to turn on to the highway toward home. When it
did, he had a desire to talk to someone about his frustrations as he
sped down the ramp. It was far too late to talk with VanDyke.
Same for Pastor Dave.

"What about Jake?" he asked himself as he drove on the I-96
overpass.

Jake would be perfect, considering his own story of late
conversion and spiritual struggle. But was it too late to chat? He
looked at his watch as he approached the exit toward the seminary where Jake lived. Just after 11:35 p.m.

Peter cranked the wheel to exit, hoping his seminary friend
wouldn't mind an unexpected pop-in.

Ten minutes later, his shoes crunched on freshly fallen snow
as he made his way through the seminary student parking lot to
Jake's apartment. When he arrived at his friend's door, he
wondered if it was really necessary to wake him at midnight to
unload his feelings about JT.

He brought his finger up to the doorbell, hesitated, but
pushed it anyway. He heard the bell chime and then nothing for
several minutes. Peter noticed a MacBook laptop box sitting next
to an overflowing trash can outside of Jake's door, wondering if he
finally traded in his HP for a real computer.

He heard a rattle behind the door before it opened, revealing
a barely awake Jake in flannel pajama pants and a gray T-shirt.

"Petey?" Jake asked in sleepy confusion. "What happened?
Why are you here?"

"Did I wake you?"

"It's midnight. Safe to say you woke me. But come on in." He turned on a lamp in his living room. "Do you want some tea?"

"Actually that would be nice, thanks." Peter sat down on a brown corduroy recliner. "Nice place you got here."

Jake laughed. "It works." He finished putting a kettle of water on the stove, then flopped on a sofa across from Peter. "So what's up? Why the midnight visit?"

"Yeah, real sorry to drag you out of bed. I feel almost foolish now, realizing how late it is..." Peter trailed off, staring at the floor.

"No, buddy. It's all right. You wouldn't be here if there wasn't something the matter. So what *is* the matter?"

"It's James," Peter said, looking up.

"Your brother? Is he all right? Did he OD again?"

"No, it's not that. Well, I don't know if he has or not. No, I just got out of Founders with him. You remember that book club we have going on?"

"I remember you mentioning something about that. What happened?"

Peter took off his scarf and bunched it up in his hands. "I don't know how to describe it. We got together for our club and then a few guys from Prosurgent West Michigan showed up. So we hung out with them instead. But that's when it got...interesting."

"Interesting?" Jake asked, raising an eyebrow. "Aren't those Prosurgent peeps your buds?"

"I know. They are, but the way the conversation went..." Peter trailed off, stopping to sort his thoughts. "It's like I saw myself at that table from a year ago."

"And that worried you enough to wake me up at midnight on a school night?"

Peter sighed and rubbed his face. "I know this isn't making any sense. And I'm sorry for dragging you out of bed."

"No, it's no problem," Jake said on his way to get the steaming teakettle. "What'll you have?"

"Do you have Earl Grey?"

"Early Grey? This late at night? Yikes!"

"Hey, don't judge."

Jake brought Peter his tea and settled back on the sofa under a thick quilt. "So what's the deal with your brother?"

Peter blew across the top of his mug and took a long sip of tea. The satisfying taste of Bergamot helped dissipate his anxiety. "It's like he's abandoned Christianity, but hasn't abandoned Christianity, you know?"

"No, not really," Jake replied, carefully sipping his own tea. "I thought he was coming back to the faith with this new Prosurgent book."

"Not coming back to the *Christian* faith. Coming back to faith maybe, and even then more like coming to Jesus. Or some pseudo-spirituality built around him."

"Hold up," Jake interjected, setting down his mug. "You're calling Prosurgence Christianity a pseudo-spirituality built around Jesus? This from Prosurgent Pete?"

"I know! I mean I still value the whole Prosurgent conversation, how they're challenging traditional Christianity and all. But after reading some of the things Bryan is saying now and then seeing how JT has latched onto them like a hungry piranha..." Peter trailed off.

Jake waited for Peter to continue as he searched the pained expression of his friend.

"It sounds like you're having an identity crisis as much as JT," he said finally said, taking another sip of tea.

"You're right. I probably am." Peter looked down and shook his head. "So what do I do about it?"

"About your fear of abandoning Prosurgent and going back to

fundamentalism? Or your fear of your brother abandoning the Christian faith and going toward Prosurgent?"

Peter raised his head at Jake's probing questions, saying nothing.

Jake continued, "I mean isn't that what you're really asking?"

"I...I guess," Peter stammered. "I didn't really think of it that way. Like I'm fearful of JT becoming part of Prosurgence Christianity."

"I mean I could be wrong, but let's face it, Bryan and Dale have gotten a bit loony of late, haven't they? And now there's that Trevor character, spouting off in his new book that what Jesus meant by Heaven and Hell isn't at all what the Church has meant by it over the years. That in the end love will win and everyone gets a jolly good 'Get out of Hell Free Card!' And now here's your brother, finding spiritual solace in their ideas. They may have been helpful once upon a time. But now they're just crazy!"

"They're not either!" Peter sighed, feeling defense creeping up his spine once more.

"Alright," Jake said raising his hands in defense. "You're the one bustin' up my sleep parade because you're concerned about your brother. If that's not it, then what is it?"

Peter huffed and folded his arms. After a few seconds, he relaxed and let out a sigh. "OK, fine. Maybe you're right. I am scared." He looked up at Jake. "Of both."

"Now that's more like it. Things go a lot smoother when people just agree with me." Peter rolled his eyes as Jake sat up. "Do you want some more tea?"

"No, I'm fine. So what do I do, Jake?"

"Truth and love, Pete. Truth and love."

"You sound like a fortune cookie."

"Actually, it's John. As in the Apostle. You know, the one who wrote the fourth gospel and that book about the end of the world?"

"Funny. But what does that have to do with anything?"

"Everything!" Jake exclaimed, shifting back under his quilt. "John says in chapter 1 that grace and truth came through Jesus, while the law came through Moses. Grace and truth. You need both, I need both, and James needs both. Love on him by being present with him, by listening to him. But also give him the truth. Because if you're not honest about what's what, then you're not at all loving."

Peter was quiet, letting Jake's words sink deep down into he being. "Grace and truth." Peter finally said. "Is that what did it for you? What brought you to faith?"

"That, and a really faithful friend who wouldn't let go. Something tells me you're good at not letting go. And for that, JT's a pretty lucky guy."

A smile crept across Peter's face. *You bet I'm not letting go,* Peter said to himself. "Thanks, Jake. For your words. For letting me wake you up."

"Yeah, you definitely owe me, like, a year of free tea for that one."

Peter smiled and stood. "I think I can arrange that."

The two embraced and said goodbye.

The air seemed to have grown more bitter over the hour. Peter hurried to his car and eased it out of the seminary housing parking lot.

Grace and truth.

I can do that, Peter thought. *I'm not letting go, James. Not on your life.*

CHAPTER 28

PETER AWOKE to a frigid early-March sun streaming through his window.

Dang. Overslept.

It was Monday, so he didn't miss any class, but he hated sleeping past 8:00 a.m. He felt the day was almost over once the ten o'clock hour rolled around—and his alarm clock registered nearly 10:30.

He picked up his phone to check his e-mail and noticed he had a text message, though he didn't recognize the number: *'Hi, Peter. Pastor Dave here. Missed you the past few weeks. Hope all is ok. You free for lunch today? Best, PDJ.'*

How nice, Peter thought.

He had missed the past three weeks at Fellowship Community Church because of increased hours at Sparrows and falling woefully behind in his second semester schoolwork. Luckily his day was free enough to fit in a lunch.

'Sure thing! How about 1:00 p.m. at MSC?' he texted back.

Peter set the phone down to grab come coffee and a bagel from downstairs. The rest of the Cooper Manor household had already gone about their day. Peter was left alone to do his thing, which suited him fine. After he brewed a pot of strong Guatemalan coffee he had brought back from work, he returned upstairs to plot his day.

Waiting for him was a reply already from Pastor Dave: *'Right o, Pete. C u at Main Street Cafe at 1!'*

He jumped into the shower and then jumped on his Greek vocabulary work. As a first-year seminary student he was ruled by Greek vocab. Greek work never ended. Thankfully, he was beginning to get the hang of it, mostly thanks to Izzy's tutoring; he had a shot of pulling a C, maybe a C-plus for his second semester. By lunchtime he finished racing through nearly a hundred vocal words. He was looking forward to his time with Pastor Dave, especially since he wanted to pick his brain about his confusing and conflicting feelings over Prosurgence Christianity.

Though spring should have begun to emerge out of winter's slumber, patches of snow still clung to the ground and Peter could see his breath on the air as he huffed through his neighborhood. Coopersville was already living the day in full-force by the time Peter wandered out of his home, strolling the short distance to Main Street and taking advantage of the sun-drenched, late-winter afternoon. A group of kids played loud schoolyard games, only outmatched by another group arguing about something or other. One older couple was trying to unwind their Christmas lights from their bushes in preparation for the closing winter. Peter passed a young mother taking a young child bundled in a cocoon of blankets for an afternoon stroll.

As Peter wandered through his hometown he wondered how the Christian faith would connect to these people. He wondered if it still mattered to their lives, many of whom struggled each day to pay their bills and hold their families together.

Did the Christian faith still work? Did it still matter to these people?

While still searching for answers, he arrived at Main Street Cafe. Pastor Dave was waiting outside on a bench that paralleled the street, greeting Peter with the same jolly grin and flappy Russian hat.

"Well hello there, my seminary friend!"

"Hey, Davy Jones," Peter said in his best pirate interpretation.

Dave chuckled and opened the door for Peter. "Good one!"

"We've missed you the past few Sundays," Dave started as they waited for a table. "I hope everything has been all right? I hope we didn't scare you off!"

"Not at all!" Peter exclaimed, feeling bad for his absence. "I've felt bad for having to miss, with being a paid intern and all. Life has been real crazy with work, and I've fallen behind in my course work. That's all."

"Oh, good. Not about falling behind, but that you haven't been scared off by Fellowship!"

"Don't worry about that. I plan to be back this coming Sunday for sure. No more playing hooky for me."

A hostess ushered the two to a booth near the bathrooms. Main Street Cafe was bustling with as strong of a lunch crowd as the first time they ate together. Upon sitting, they were promptly greeted by an old friend.

"Hello there, gentlemen," said Cindy, the frazzled server who had waited on them that first Sunday. "How 'bout some water to start while you look over the menu?"

"That's fine for me," said Pastor Dave. "How about you, Pete?"

"Iced tea with lemon?"

"Sure thing, darlin'." She shuffled off to clear the adjoining table while Dave and Peter looked over the menus.

"So what's been going on, my seminary friend? Is VanDyke behaving himself?"

Peter laughed. "VanDyke hasn't been too much trouble. I've kept him in line. And surprisingly, I've learned a thing or two from him and his theology classes. Which has created some...problems, shall we say."

"Oh? Do tell."

Cindy returned with Peter's iced tea and Pastor Dave's water. "There isn't any lemon in here," Peter complained.

"Sorry 'bout that, darlin'. I'll get you a bowl of 'em," Cindy replied, with a hint of irritation masked by her plastered smile. "So what can I get you boys?"

"Club sandwich for me. Pete?"

"Cobb salad, dressing on the side."

"You and your salads! Are you on a diet or something?"

"Hey, I'm not getting any younger. Plus that whole freshman fifteen thing is a killer."

Pastor Dave laughed as Cindy shuffled away. "So you said Dr. VanDyke's theology class was giving you problems?"

"Well, not so much the class as the reading. And also my brother..."

"Your brother? James, is it?"

"Right, James. I'm concerned where he's going. Spiritually, I mean. Like what he's starting to believe about God and the Bible and Jesus and faith. It's like Prosurgent has given him permission to just abandon everything from his childhood faith."

"Well, you've sort of abandoned your own childhood faith, haven't you?"

Peter shrugged. "I guess. Yeah, a lot of it, for sure. With James, though, it's...different. It's like Christianity doesn't even matter anymore. I mean, he says he likes Jesus, just not the Church."

"I sort of like Jesus but not the Church, too!" Pastor Dave interrupted chuckling. "It sounds like he's on something of a similar journey that we've both been on."

"Maybe, except he's also into Buddhism. And Bryan's new book has got him on this new universalism kick..." Peter trailed off. Shaking his head he continued, "I thought Bryan would be helpful for his spiritual journey. Then I thought Trevor Bohls, that pastor from outside the city with the new book out on hell, would also help bring JT back by helping him see the Christian faith was still relevant, just like these thinkers did for me in helping me navigate my questions. Instead, they seem to be destroying his faith."

"Destroying his faith? You sound like one of those silver-haired TV fundies, Pete."

"I know! That's what also concerns me."

"Concerns me, too!" They both laughed.

Peter continued, "I do feel like I'm in some ways going backward. Studying and reading more on the historic Christian faith has changed me. It's like awakening me to maybe some of the not-so-good side to the Prosurgent Church."

"Like what?" Pastor Dave prodded as their food arrived.

"Umm, Cindy? Hate to be one of those customers," Peter said, "but I still haven't got my lemons."

"Yes, dear. I'll get right on that." She hustled away to the back. Peter thought he heard her huff and could sense her eyes rolling in irritation.

"Where were we?" Peter asked, taking a sip of his naked water.

"You were going to explain how you've become anti-Prosurgent," Pastor Dave said grinning.

"It's not that I'm anti-Prosurgent. I'm just beginning to question some things."

"Like what?"

"Like the way Bryan views Scripture, as this community library filled with human voices saying things in different ways about God. That's odd to me."

"How so?" Pastor Dave said after biting into his sandwich.

"It's like he says the Bible is merely human conversations about God, rather than the other way around—rather than God saying something to us about himself." Peter drizzled some dressing over the top of his salad and took a bit of his own.

"Or maybe he's trying to get at the fact the Bible wasn't beamed down to Earth in its entirety or the authors weren't Dictaphones typing out every word that God gave them. Maybe what he's doing is trying to recapture human authorship?"

"That could be true," Peter said, taking another bit of his salad. "But then take his view of creation and sin. He clearly thinks we evolved from nothing. And then he seems to say the Fall story is actually a coming-of-age story. Like it's not about rebelling against God, but rebelling against some sort of human potential or ideal or something. Very humanistic."

"You gotta realize, Bryan grew up as a Plymouth Brethren. A hyper-fundamentalist denomination of Christianity that's pretty anti-science and has a strong emphasis on depravity."

"Well then what about his view of Jesus?"

"What about it?"

"Nowhere in the book does he say that Jesus is God. It's all *'Jesus is the highest representation of the* character *of God.'* What's that about? Jesus shows us God's character?"

"Doesn't he? What's the problem?" Pastor Dave retorted, sounding mildly defensive.

"Of course he does..." Peter said trailing off and folding his arms. "It just sounds like Jesus is more like the son of Gandhi than the Son of God. Like some great guy who lived and loved well. A Gandhi on steroids!"

"OK," Dave replied, searching for a response. "So what does this have to do with your brother?"

"Oh, right. Like I said before, it's given him permission to just leave whatever he didn't like from Christianity. And even sort of meld it with his Buddhism. So sin for James is now about doing really bad things that make your life suck. Jesus is this really great example we follow in order to live our best life now. Nothing about repentance. Nothing about Jesus's payment for the cost of our rebellion. Nothing about Christ in us producing good works. It's humanistic spirituality!"

"Repentance? Payment for our sins? Man, you are sounding like those silver-haired TV fundies!" Pastor Dave jested.

Peter laughed and took a sip of his tea. "Don't get me wrong, there are things I still appreciate about Prosurgence Christianity. So I'm not just tossing it out. There're just some red flags going up. Especially since someone else is involved, my brother. And he doesn't have the biblical and theological knowledge I do, you know?"

"I think I hear what you're saying. But what's the alternative? Six-day-literal creationism, total depravity, election?"

"I don't know," Peter exclaimed, "That's why I'm in a funk!" He leaned back and sighed. "Because all I see is either fundamentalism and a hyper-Reformed version of the Christian faith, or Prosurgence Christianity. Although getting into the historic Christian faith in Systematic Theology is showing me maybe there's another way."

"It'll be all right, brother. I remember when I was about your age and finishing up seminary back in California. There were all of these new ideas that didn't seem to make sense because they clashed with what I knew growing up. And then later as a pastor there were more ideas that seemed foreign and scary. In fact I remember in the early '8os there were huge controversies about spiritual gifts. And then the big doozie with the whole openness of God brouhaha."

"Openness of God?" Peter asked.

"Yes. There was actually a book by the same name that made huge waves because it challenged the conservative ideas of God's foreknowledge and human free will. And then in the mid-'90s another group of Christian thinkers developed the idea of open theism even more."

"Open theism. I remember VanDyke talked about that in SysOne. You can imagine he's definitely not a fan."

"Of course not, he's a Calvinist." Pastor Dave spit out Calvinist as if it were a sour grape. "You remember from your class discussion that determinism says that God fully determines every minute detail of the future. Including hurricanes, parents backing over their children accidentally...even the salad you dropped on your shirt."

Peter looked down and saw a dressing-soaked leafy green had dropped and smeared down the front of his shirt.

Davy Jones giggled. "So that means we don't have free will, that we can't really make free decisions. Or if we are free it's fake because our acts must always be compatible with God's determining actions. That also means all of the bad stuff that happens is planned by God. So some people came along and said, *'Wait a minute. That's not the God we find in the Bible. What we see is a God who is living and personable and relational and good and loving.'* So open theists argue that determinism is bunk. The idea that God is this Watchmaker who winds up the universe and sets every detail into motion is totally at odds with the very personal God of the Bible."

"I remember all that from class. So what was your point?"

"Sorry, got off track. What I meant with all of this was every generation is called to reimagine what it means to be Christian, Pete."

Every generation is called to reimagine what it means to be Christian? Interesting...

"In my day it was reimagining the doctrine of God. In your day it's other things—like Hell and other religions, perhaps."

Something about that didn't sit right with Peter.

Pastor Dave finished the last bite of his sandwich, waiting for Peter to respond. Grinning, he said, "I see your wheels turnin'. What's up?"

Peter hesitated, not knowing how to respond. "I hear what you're saying, Dave. But is reimagination really what's needed? And besides, it seems more like Prosurgent is redefining the Christian faith as much as it is reimagining it. I mean, take Trevor's new book. He's saying that what Heaven and Hell really mean is way different than what Christianity has always said they mean. He's redefining Heaven and Hell altogether. I'm all for rediscovering what the Christian faith is. Like maybe Hell and judgment is more along the lines of annihilation than eternal, conscious torment. The Church has believed both and maybe we need to rediscover how the Church has talked about Hell and what the Bible says about it. But reimagining Hell for a new day? I'm not so sure about that..."

Peter trailed off as Pastor Dave sat and listened with a look of amusement. "You better be careful, Pete. Before long you'll be quoting Jonathan Edwards's *Sinners in the Hands of an Angry God* sermon!"

Pastor Dave laughed, trying to be funny but instead bore an edge of condescension that Peter did not appreciate.

"Hey, I'm my own thinker! I'm not some VanDyke lackey—"

"No, I didn't mean anything by that," Dave interrupted, putting his hands up in surrender. "I just think you should give yourself permission to reimagine."

"Yeah, maybe I should..." Peter glanced at his watch. "I also should be going. Greek is seriously kicking my butt," he offered as an excuse to exit a conversation that had grown uncomfortable.

"Well, we wouldn't want it to win, that's for sure! We need you, Pete. The Church needs you. Honestly."

He smiled. "Thanks, Dave."

"I'm serious. You're a precocious guy. I love your curiosity.

Never stop being curious. Never settle for the way things have always been. Or the way things have always been *believed*, either." Pastor Dave winked before getting up and grabbing the check.

"I was going to get that!" Peter protested, trying to snatch it back.

"No way," Pastor Dave said as he hugged their bill. He stood up, bolted for the register, and whipped out his credit card before Peter could catch up.

"Thanks for lunch," Peter said as they walked out into the chilly air, the sun hidden behind a thick bouquet of clouds.

"No problem, partner." Dave put on his black, furry Russian hat to guard his balding head. "Let's do it again soon! See you Sunday?"

"For sure! I'll be there."

Peter stuffed his hands in his peacoat. Unfortunately, his head and neck weren't as lucky as Pastor Dave's. He'd left his hat and scarf at home. As they parted ways, Peter replayed their conversation.

Reimagine what it means to be Christian. Peter considered Dave's words again, becoming more uncomfortable. It seemed like he was as interested as Prosurgence Christianity was in tossing every belief up for grabs.

In the end, isn't their quest a redefinition? Don't they want to redefine Christianity for our new age?

That's why James seemed to be so taken by people like Bryan and Trevor. They were giving him a reason to believe—not because of the weight of tradition behind those beliefs, but precisely because they were untraditional. Because they redefined those traditional beliefs to make more sense in our modern age.

And there was Pastor Dave, joining in with the Prosurgent Church's quest for a new kind of Christianity.

But what do I know? Peter thought as he huffed his way back home.

Dave had been through more church shifts and theological controversies than he had. Maybe there was something to Dave's permissive words. Something to his encouragement to refuse to settle. To not settle for the way he has always believed.

The way the Church has always believed.

Yet, he couldn't shake his professor's warning: *Ideas have consequences.*

Sure do, Peter thought.

His mind jumped to his brother, and how the ideas surrounding a reimagined, redefined Christianity had caused him to lose his faith—to walk away from it.

Where those ideas would ultimately take him, Peter could only guess.

CHAPTER 29

PETER PULLED into the parking lot at Woodland Mall a little before two o'clock. After driving around for several minutes, he found a spot what seemed like a football field away.

An uneasy dread began surging in his belly as he walked toward the Barnes & Noble store that anchored the mall's south entrance. Peter had come to meet his brother for Trevor Bohls's appearance there that day. Trevor had been something of a local celebrity thanks to his successful megachurch built in a former local shopping mall.

For the past few weeks, he had been promoting his new book *Love Will Win* on a national book tour and the national morning talk shows, creating a national uproar among evangelical Christians along the way. In the book, he questioned the prevailing Christian claim that Hell was for real and forever, arguing for a universal salvation. JT bought the book the day it released and devoured it in one sitting. He'd been ecstatic to learn Trevor's last stop on his tour was Grand Rapids, and dragged Peter along for company.

Peter was apprehensive, knowing what Trevor was arguing

and what James was beginning to believe. But he came along, figuring it was another way he could be part of his brother's spiritual journey.

As Peter approached the entrance, he could see James standing outside motioning him with his arms to hurry.

"Come on, Petey!" James yelled with obvious impatience. "Hurry it up, we need to get in line pronto."

"Dude, where's the fire?" Peter said as he jogged up to his awaiting brother.

"There's a massive crowd already here. And they're talking like we might not even get in!" James seemed panicked.

"All right, bro. I'm sure we'll make it."

The two walked through the double doors of the big-box retailer to a large group of people gathered near the base of the escalator.

Goodness, a crowd fit for a rock star, Peter thought as they waded through the herd of people and up toward the second floor.

"Look at all these people!" James glowed as he clutched his copy of Trevor's book. "See, Pete? There are lots of us who are sick and tired of how Jesus's story has been hijacked."

Over the past few weeks, Peter had noted a growing hostility from James, ever since *Love Will Win* came out, even parroting its language and turns of phrase. After Peter had voiced his concerns, James became more resolute in his quest for reimagining the Christian faith. And consequently less interested in what Peter had to say, especially in regards to his own journey to rediscover the historic Christian faith.

Peter rolled his eyes, but stood still and silent.

When they reached the top, the floor was humming with enthusiastic conversations and reunions as fellow journeymen gathered in the romance section to sit at the feet of their spiritual guru. James immediately gunned toward two open seats positioned on the aisle near the front. Peter followed as James plowed through a group searching for their own place to roost.

"Perfect!" James said, plopping down in his prized seat. "Hey, do you mind getting me something to drink while I hold our seats?"

Annoyed, Peter slung his coat over his seat, almost hitting the older lady seated behind him. "Fine, what do you want?"

"Just some green tea. Thanks, bro!" James said as he extended his long legs underneath the chair in front of him, making himself comfortable for the event.

"Don't mention it," Peter mumbled as he walked toward the escalator.

Riding down, he looked across at the people riding up the other side, considering the various persons who somehow found hope in what Trevor was offering them through his latest book. There were young, middle-class parents with toddlers in tow. An older gentleman clutched a copy of *Love Will Win*. What looked like a four-person group of college students in baggy black clothes filed up the escalator. As he reached the bottom he guessed many were congregants from Trevor's church. He also guessed some of those attending were people like him, concerned Christians interested in the conversation he sparked and curious about how he would talk about his book's themes.

Peter entered a long queue inching its way toward the cafe counter. In front of him were two young adults. As he waited in line to retrieve his brother's tea and his own latte, Peter couldn't help but overhear their conversation as they were obviously there for the book signing.

"I just really like his message and his ideals," said the twentysomething clad in dark-gray skinny jeans and a red plaid shirt.

"Oh, I know!" said the twentysomething's female companion ensconced in the same hipster attire. "I can so relate what he teaches to everyday life."

"For sure. And I'm not having something shoved down my throat," the guy continued. "I just feel like I can be myself."

"You've read it already, right?"

"Finished it the day it came out. Totally blew my mind!"

"I can't believe there was so much controversy," the young hipster gal protested. "I mean, get a life, people! If you don't like what someone says that's your deal. Just shut up and keep it to yourself."

"Yeah, and what the heck's so wrong with telling people that God is love? That he loves everybody, and everyone is invited to the party? It's this Hell-and-judgment language that's turned me off from church for so long."

Peter stood listening, fascinated at the conversation happening in front of him. It mirrored ones he'd been having with himself for the past few years, the ones he'd been having with his brother the past few months. He felt sorry for what they felt about and experienced in Christianity. There was also a growing part of him that felt sorry for what they had found, the alternative Christianity that redefined the faith entirely.

Where's the hope in that? Peter thought as the pair finished ordering their drinks and he ordered his.

As Peter retrieved his drinks, he heard an employee announce over the intercom for people to take their seats. He snatched their drinks and made his way into the still-swelling crowd at the base of the escalator.

Lord, I'm not looking forward to this, Peter prayed. *But I'm here for the sake of my brother. And if I can contend for his faith and help steer him back to you, the pain will be worth it!*

"Hello, everybody and welcome," a chipper Barnes & Noble employee greeted the crowd as Peter took his seat.

"Thanks," whispered James after Peter handed him his tea. He promptly took a sip and settled in for the afternoon.

"We've got a real treat for you this afternoon. Obviously you are here because you know that." Taking a piece of paper, he began to read, "Trevor Bohl is a pastor, a best-selling author, international teacher, and highly sought-after public speaker. His newest book, *Love Will Win*, has just hit *The New York Times* Bestseller List, which of course is why we're here today. At age twenty-eight he founded his church, and under his leadership it's one of the fastest-growing churches in America. For many of you he needs no introduction. So please give a warm welcome to our very own Pastor Trevor Bohl!"

"Sunday afternoon at the mall. Can I get an 'Amen' in Barnes & Noble?" Trevor said as he walked out to the front of the cheering crowd.

He was wearing his trademark black, thick-rimmed glasses and close-cropped hair with a white high collar bomber jacket and black pants, accented by a white shirt and black wool vest. He looked like he just walked off a fashion runway, rather than the platform of a church.

Several *"Amens"* rippled around the two-hundred-plus crowd. There was even a loud *"Hallelujah"* in the back, eliciting a few chuckles, and a *"Here, here!"* from James.

Peter rolled his eyes as he looked over at his smiling, transfixed brother.

"It's great to be here this afternoon. I want to begin by saying that Jesus did not come to Earth with an established doctrine. He came, and he said, *'I am the bread.'* He said *'I am the living water.'* Try making a dogma out of that. Jesus came to announce that you have always been loved. And I think it is time to reclaim the essence of this message. Which is why I set out to write this book about Heaven and Hell. Because over the years what's happened is that these living, breathing ideas have become misguided, toxic, calcified doctrines that ultimately subvert the contagious spread of Jesus's message of love, peace, forgiveness, and joy that our world desperately needs."

He paused, allowing his opening line to soak into the crowd. Several people around Peter voiced their approval.

James mumbled, "Absolutely."

Trevor continued in a methodical rhythm, moving back and forth at the front of the crowd, like a Southern Baptist preacher building momentum up toward an altar call.

"I think it's important to point out how Jesus actually talked about Heaven. For most people in our culture, the fundamental way we talk about Heaven is evacuation. Essentially, Jesus is the ticket, and if you believe, say, confess, repent, or however the different tribe does it, you then go to someplace else. Somewhere other than this place. So then all of the dominant images are of clouds and puppies and perfect hair."

The crowd laughed on cue.

"But Jesus's fundamental question was how do we bring Heaven here? His prayer was '*Father, your will be done on Earth as it is in Heaven.*' So his understanding was the union of Heaven and Earth. And this is an invitation to take part in the life of Heaven now, which is really huge."

As Peter looked around, the majority of the crowd was in obvious agreement with Trevor's mini-sermon. James was sitting on the edge of his chair, his legs bunched up in front of him as if he were going to spring to his feet to accept the preacher's call to come forth.

"You and I have this invitation for love, joy, peace," Trevor continued. "We can forgive our enemy, or we can throw a stone back. We can create all sorts of Hells right now if we wanted to. Genocide. Rape. Abuse. Financial schemes.

"At the core of the human experience for thousands of years has been this longing for justice. Something within us says that the tyrannical dictator who is killing innocent people must be held accountable. That person needs to be brought to justice. It's part of both the Christian and the Jewish traditions. The prophet

Amos says let justice roll like a river. So this is a profound human longing we should hold on to.

"The problem is when it becomes *those* bad people. As if my hands are clean. And then Hell becomes *this*, it's all for those people who are terrible and wrong. And it becomes a way to not own up to your own contribution to creating Hell right now.

"We see people choosing Hell around us all the time. We see people in the face of the invitation to love your neighbor exploit the neighbor, abuse the neighbor. So I begin with the reality of Hell here and now. I also begin with the reality of the life of Heaven here and now. Jesus kept saying the kingdom of Heaven is here and now, it's among you, it's upon you."

Trevor had the crowd right where he wanted them.

Man he's an ingenious communicator, Peter thought as Trevor began his final descent.

"God loves everybody everywhere. God loves people who don't love God. God's love is as wide as the universe, and God's love is as close as your next breath. Now stand up and accept that you're accepted. Thank you."

As if accepting his invitation, the crowd rose to their feet and gave Trevor a sustained round of boisterous applause that echoed throughout the big-box bookstore. Trevor took their accolades in stride as he sat down on top of the table he'd later use to sign his book.

"OK, now who's got questions?" he announced as people returned to their seats. "You there in the back. Young guy in camo."

A young man with a camouflage jacket in the back stood up. "Hi, Trevor, thanks for all you do. My question is what do you say to all of these blogs who are saying you're a false prophet, you're committing heresy? Because you've come under a lot of vicious attacks."

"Thanks for the question," Trevor said. "I am deeply compelled and fascinated with Jesus. And I think the orthodox, historic tradition is this vast, diverse conversation that's been going on for thousands of years. And I think that Jesus can handle the discussion, I think he can handle the debate. I'm interested in his good news right here, right now. OK, another question. You there in the pink hat."

A middle-aged woman in a bright-pink hat stood and took the mic. "Thanks, Trevor. I've been thinking a lot about what we've been seeing in Japan with the tsunami. As a pastor, why would you say God allows this suffering to happen? And are they condemned to Hell because they are Shinto believers?"

"Excellent question! Thanks for asking it. First off, when there is human suffering and we shed tears, I believe that God sheds tears, too."

On cue, several people murmured *"Amen"* in response.

"So I begin with a God who identifies with our pain and suffering. I don't have a conception of a God floating on clouds out there in outer space. Sort of going, *'Well, you got yourself into this mess.'* My understanding is of a God who deeply, deeply cares. Who sheds a tear like we do. And I also begin with the assumption that God is love. And that God's love is a vast, wide, expansive, indestructible reality. OK, who's next?"

Immediately James stood up. "All right, I guess we have a winner!" Trevor said, the crowd laughing in agreement.

James looked around, saying "Oh sorry. I guess I should have raised my hand!" bringing another round of laughter, even from Trevor.

"Go for it, buddy," he encouraged.

"For the last few years, I've been questioning my faith. I mean, really wrestling with it like never before. And my family, well, not my brother, Petey, here," James said as he motioned to Peter.

Peter reddened and sloughed lower in his chair as James continued, becoming more animated the further he went.

"It's my parents, man. They can't handle questions about the faith. What would you say to them about that?" Before he sat down, he said, "Oh, one more thing. And what would you say to them about everyone being saved? I've never felt accepted by God, like I'm going to Hell because church doesn't agree with my life. What would you say about that?"

"Man, great questions," Trevor replied as James sat down. "Thanks, partner. Those are deep! So let's see if I can make it. First, it's not a threat to ask questions. In fact, I'd say to your parents it's honoring the mystery of God's love. The Bible itself is a conversation. A question is not a walk away from God. It's a walk toward God. It's all orthodox. It's all part of the tradition."

Trevor took a breath, and continued, "And on the topic of universalism, I think the real question in all of this is 'Is God a universalist?' Is everyone invited or not? Is God love or not? The way I read Jesus is that everybody's invited to the party. So I assume that freedom to accept extends beyond when you die. And this business of deciding who goes to Hell—that's God's job. And I'd suggest that God is way better at it than we are."

Trevor paused staring out into the crowd, nodding in silence. "OK, I'm getting the cue from our helpful Barnes & Noble employee that we've gotta wrap it up. But I want to end with the final words from the book."

He found his place toward the end and started reading. "Love, that's the reason why I wrote this book. It's also what I want to leave you with. May you," Trevor started, looking up at the gathered crowd adding, "Grand Rapids, Michigan, may you experience this massive, expansive, infinite, indestructible love that has accepted you all along. Accept that this love accepts you, a love that's as vast as the universe and as tiny as the cracks in your heart that no one knows are there. And may you know deep down, that love will win. Thanks, everybody."

James rose to his feet to once more clap his approval, his eyes pinching several tears as he blinked. Several others joined him in a short ovation before the signing.

Peter left James at the book signing queue, telling him he needed to get back to his Greek homework. In reality he felt depressed and sickened by the false ideas Trevor was peddling to the unsuspecting crowd. To his unsuspecting brother.

As he drove back home he thought about the course of the afternoon, especially the end when his brother rose to applaud Trevor, and with tears streaming down his face.

"What does he find so attractive about Trevor's teachings?" he wondered out loud as he raced home. He continued pondering the question, and a word struck him.

Hope.

James found the hope he had been looking for, perhaps his whole life, in Trevor's gospel. To James, how Trevor talked about sin, Jesus, Heaven, and Hell was far more hopeful than what he'd heard before. Than how the faith of his childhood talked about these important Christian ideas.

While Peter was happy for James's newfound appreciation for the Christian faith and theology, he wondered where these ideas might take him. If he was honest, he was concerned.

I'm not jumping on the heretic train, Peter thought as he continued processing, *but Trevor's gospel doesn't seem complete.*

He couldn't quite put his finger on it, on the dissonance he felt listening to Trevor's talk. Which for Peter was plenty uncomfortable, because of how much he'd been affected by Trevor's ministry over the past decade. From his books to his short films and his sermons, Peter owed his own spiritual development in part to this mentor as much as Bryan McLaughlin. Yet here he was, questioning him and his teachings with the same unease as Bryan and the rest of Prosurgent.

Ideas have consequences.

That annoying phrase that wouldn't seem to go away needled his mind as Peter eased his car into the driveway of Cooper Manor.

What kind of consequences could Trevor really have, though? Peter wondered.

Only time would tell.

CHAPTER 30

SPRING WAS IN THE AIR, but not in the way that West Michigan expected. By the beginning of April, the ground should have been thawing, birds should have been migrating back home, and temperatures should have been turning toward the forties. Not this year. Old Man Winter had returned with a vengeance after Mother Earth had teased the Lake Shore area just two weeks ago with a heat wave of mid-sixties, sunshiny weather. Yet one week later, Mr. Winter decided Grand Rapids hadn't had enough.

They call them snow squalls, sudden, moderate snow fall with strong, gusty winds thanks to Lake Michigan. This round of lake effect snow dropped a few inches on Grand Rapids and left the streets a slick mess. The wintry event recalled a memory from Peter's childhood: his parents had to cancel his third birthday party at McDonald's because of a blizzard. While not a blizzard, such weather should have passed by now.

Yes, spring was in the air, but not because of the weather. It was in the air only because Peter and Lexi were going out for another round of sushi.

Bundled up yet again in a sweater and wool coat, Peter stood at the front door ringing the bell while Rufus bellowed on the other side. He heard Lexi hurl a string of curse words to quiet her furry companion before undoing the heavy locks that guarded her Eastown home.

"Hello," Lexi said out of breath. "Come in, come in." She ushered Peter inside and closed the large wooden door with purpose. "This weather is killing me!"

"Tell me about it. If I have to commute another day to class crawling along I-96 through one more, what do they call them? Snow squalls?"

"Snow squall," Lexi agreed while she poured Rufus a cup of food.

"One more snow squall and I'm permanently moving to Arizona. I don't care how hella hot the summers are!"

"No fair! What about me?" Lexi whined.

"Well, we've got social media," Peter offered.

Lexi socked him one in the right arm as she grabbed her scarf.

"Hey, that hurt! Seriously, it's like the universe just has to dump a pantload of snow every Monday and Tuesday night, just before classes."

"That's because the universe doesn't want you to be a pastor man, pastor man," Lexi said ushering them out the door.

"You try driving forty-five minutes on the highway in this thing," Peter said as he opened the passenger door for Lexi.

"No thanks. I much prefer my walk up Wealthy Street each morning."

Peter climbed in and started the car. With 200,058 miles, it's a wonder that she still started. He faithfully changed the oil every three thousand miles and other fluids as needed, and so his old Honda hatchback obliged him every start, without fail. So far.

He eased the car onto the congested cobblestone corridor, making his way up Wealthy Street to their usual sushi place,

Republic. For a small business owner and seminary student, the happy hour was a win-win for them both: $5 rolls and small plates, $3 local beers and cosmopolitans. What could be better?

They arrived at the side parking lot just as an attendant was unhooking the chain that kept out would-be parking squatters. Once inside they promptly ordered three rolls and spinach artichoke dip. Peter ordered a local brown ale and Lexi the cosmopolitan.

"I'm exhausted," Lexi said stretching her arm across the table, resting her head in the crook of her arm.

Peter was staring off, watching the snowflakes dance across the large window facing Division Avenue. "That's too bad," he said weakly, continuing to stare.

Noticing he had zoned out, Lexi followed his line of sight out onto the street. "By the way, I thought this would be a good time to mention I'm pregnant."

"Oh, sorry to hear that," he said matter-of-factly as he sipped his ale, entranced by the dancing snow. A beat later he was jolted from his trance and started coughing.

"Oh no, are you OK?" Lexi said, covering her mouth with her hand to suppress a laugh.

"No, I'm not," Peter replied weakly as he continued coughing.

"I'm kidding, by the way. Kidding!

He hacked again. "You really know how to kill a guy."

"Oh come on I was trying to catch you off guard, to see if I could drag you away from whatever show had grabbed hold of your attention out there."

Peter sipped some water and finally recovered. "Sorry. I guess I'm just distracted."

"By what, Petey?"

"I don't know. My journey, I guess."

"That narrows it a bit."

"My *spiritual* journey. You know how last time we talked about how important Prosurgent was for my crisis of faith?"

"Yeah, you said it was crucial. And I saw how you just caught yourself when you said *was*. It's not anymore?"

Peter paused, rotating his glass in a circle, staring into its dark, chocolaty liquid.

"Peeeteeey," Lexi said, trying to catch his eyes.

"Oh, I'm doing it again."

She smiled back. "Yep."

Peter sighed. "Well, I feel like I'm letting go of Prosurgent. Or moving beyond Prosurgent, or something."

"Interesting. Tell me about that."

"So for the longest time Prosurgent was really interested in connecting the Christian faith to our changing culture. They helped me wrestle with a whole lot of questions at a time when I needed to do some wrestling. They gave me the freedom to explore the boundaries of my faith, and really get down to what mattered to the Christian faith. They helped me peel away all of the crap that my fundamentalist past had stuck around Jesus."

"So what's the problem?" Lexi prodded.

"What if they're exchanging one village for another?"

Lexi took another sip of her cosmo just as their food arrived. Peter drained his beer and ordered another round for them both before the happy hour special ended.

"What do you mean, one village for another?"

"Like that village movie. So there's the fundie village over here," Peter said, setting his glass of water to his right. "And Prosurgent village over here," he said taking his empty beer glass and setting it to his left. "Each village stands for a set of ideas. Each village guards a set of ideas with an invisible boundary."

"OK. Then you left one village for another. What's the problem with that?" Lexi wondered.

"Nothing, per se." Peter paused, choosing his next words. "I guess, I think I'm realizing that the one is almost as extreme as the other. Like I've gone all expat on one nation for another nation with just as many problems."

"Like what?" Lexi said, sitting up straight and furrowing her brow. "From everything you've described about Prosurgent, they seem like the only sane village in all of Christendom!"

"That's what I thought. And I thought by offering something new and some fresh version of the Christian faith they were taking us back to the beginning. Back before fundamentalism got hold of Christianity, back before the Enlightenment got hold of the faith, back before the Romans with Constantine and the Greeks wrapped their hands around the Church. In other words, back to Jesus himself."

"But isn't that true? Aren't they peeling back all the layers to what's important? I remember you saying something about a centered faith."

"A centered-set faith," Peter corrected.

"Right, a centered-set faith where Jesus sits at the center of our beliefs, rather than an arbitrary boundary dictating our beliefs. Which of course shifts with every Christian village that has a different boundary."

"Right," Peter agreed getting more animated. "But what I'm saying is what if the Prosurgent village is just as controlled by a boundary set of beliefs as the fundie village? And it's actually just as toxic to the Christian faith as fundamentalism?"

Lexi nearly choked on a piece of sushi at that statement. "Toxic? OK, that's a new one."

"It is for me, too!" Peter exclaimed throwing his arms up in the air. "That's what I'm saying. I mean, I've been reading such interesting things from the historic Church for my theology class. And we've had these discussions in class about what's central to the historic Christian faith. And it seems like there's this one single strand weaving the Christian faith that binds each belief together, like a string of popcorn garland on a Christmas tree. VanDyke says there's one single story that the Church has given Herself to...and, I don't know, I think he's right."

"One story? There are like a bazillion stories!" Lexi exclaimed in protest, becoming as animated as Peter. "I mean, you've got the Catholic story and the Reformed story and the Baptist story. And then something like Russian Orthodox and Romanian Orthodox and Ukrainian Orthodox."

"That's fair," Peter said in agreement. "But there are still shades of that one story I think."

"OK, but what's the point?"

"The point is I get this sense that Prosurgent just wants to throw out that story! Or at least significantly rewrite its script."

Lexi sat back, crossing her arms with a look of confusion. "I don't understand. In all of our conversations you seemed totally gung-ho for this whole Prosurgent thing. So, what, now you're selling out? Setting sail from the Prosurgent village back home to Fundieville?"

"No, way! I hope not. I know I was sold out. I've been living and breathing all things Prosurgent for half a decade. I feel genuinely trapped, Lexi. Between the two villages. Like I'm a man without a home."

Peter sighed and shook his head before continuing. "I had absolutely sworn off here," he said as he picked up his glass of water. "I fled, vowing never to return." He dropped his glass with a loud thud, sending water up and over the side.

"And then I found solace and a home and a community here." Peter picked up his half-full beer glass in his left hand. "I became a full-on citizen of Prosurgentville. I mean, I'm known as Prosurgent Pete!" They both laughed.

"But now...I just don't know." He paused. "I feel alone. Just like I did a few years ago when I started this whole blasted journey to begin with. And it scares me, Lexi."

Lexi reached one hand across the table, grabbing Peter's free one. She used the other to help him set down his beer glass in order to take both hands in her own.

"You're not alone, Peter. I'm with you." She held his gaze, reassuring him she was standing with him in his journey.

"Thanks," he softly mustered, his throat rising with emotion. He choked it back with a drink of water.

"I know this has been so emotional for you," Lexi continued. "You lost your ministry. You sort of lost your parents. You look like you're losing your faith again. But you are so strong. You give me strength for my own spiritual journey."

"I do?" Peter wondered, meeting her gaze.

"Yeah! I haven't told you this, but I started reading through the Gospel of Mark the other week."

"Really?" Peter said, wide eyed with surprise.

She laughed. "Yup. Haven't picked up my Bible in four years." She paused. "Which is ironic, because now that I think about it I'm pretty sure I started my own journey out of Fundieville the same time you did! Crazy. Anyway the point is your journey is affecting my journey. I think of you as this loyal radical. Someone who is bucking the status quo, challenging convention, shaking his fist at the Christian Man...well not Jesus, but like Jerry Falwell or Pat Robertson or someone."

Peter laughed. "Nice."

"You're that guy, but you're also loyal. Unlike me, you're not leaving Christianity. You're actually training to be a pastor man, which I still can't get over sometimes, but still. You're doing what so many of our peers can't do. Won't do. And it's inspiring. It's why I've started reading my Bible again."

"Loyal radical, huh?" Peter said, considering her thoughtful, encouraging words.

"And that's not easy," Lexi added. "And that's fine."

Peter smiled, overjoyed that he had her as a traveling

companion for a journey he sensed would have plenty more bends on the road ahead.

He squeezed her hand. "Thanks, Lexi." He paused and smiled. "What worries me the most, though, is not my own journey, but JT's."

"Your brother's?"

He nodded. "I told you about how we've been doing that book club at Founders."

"I think that's rad, talking Jesus and theology over pints!"

"It has been. The past few months have been great seeing my brother wrestle, really wrestle, with issues of faith and spirituality. But he's leaving the faith, Lexi. I mean he left it a while ago, by going all Buddhist."

"Hey, I'm Buddhist!" Lexi interrupted in protested.

"Oh, right." Peter began to panic. "Did I offend you?"

"Sort of," she said huffing. She leaned back in her chair and crossed her arms.

"Gosh, I totally didn't mean to. Sorry, Lexi."

Her eyes narrowed. "What *did* you mean by your 'he's going all Buddhist' comment?"

Careful, Peter. Diffuse, diffuse, diffuse—pronto!

"I just mean I had hopes of helping rekindle his love for Jesus and the Church. Does that make sense?"

That seemed to mollify her as she relaxed and let down her arms. "I guess. But what if he wants to be a Buddhist *and* follow Jesus? Like me?"

Peter felt trapped. His mind spun, considering the myriad of ways he could respond. This date was not going anywhere near as he had planned.

He took a drink of water, then said, "Look, what I'm trying to say is that I'm just realizing how important ideas are. That ideas have consequences. No idea is neutral."

Confusion reigned on Lexi's face. He could tell she was

trying her best to follow along and hold back whatever emotions were ready to pounce.

"I totally respect my brother's journey. I respect your journey! But obviously I'm training to be a pastor. A *Christian* pastor. And I believe that through Jesus God is rescuing and recreating the world."

Peter waited for a shoe to fly across the table. None came.

"I'm not saying I've got it all figured out or Buddhists are idiots and headed to Hell. Or you can't somehow embrace the cultural aspects of Buddhism and still embrace Jesus as Lord and Savior...like your Thai friends."

Lexi's demeanor loosened, the scowl on her face relaxing.

"I'm just saying ideas matter; they have consequences. And I'm wondering what consequences these Prosurgent ideas JT has been feeding on for months will have in his life, that's all."

After a few seconds of painful silence, Lexi final said, "I think that makes sense." She squinted her eyes as if still considering Peter's monologue. "As long as you're not saying all Buddhists are going to Hell like my parents do!"

Peter laughed. "Not at all! I haven't figured out how other religions and spiritualities play into God's plan of rescue."

He wasn't lying, exactly. He believed Jesus and Jesus alone provided the rescue from sin and death we humans so desperately need, not Muhammad and the Buddha. He just didn't know how God might use other religions to draw people to himself through Christ. But that was for another conversation, one far, far away from this one!

"I'd wager we're not going to solve all the world's problems on date two," Lexi said winking.

Good, she's back!

"Probably right," Peter said smiling. "But darn it, we were so close! All right, let's get you home. Daddy Rufus awaits."

. . .

PETER'S BRAKES squawked as he saddled up to the curb in front of Lexi's house, the rear skidding toward the right in response to the thick padding of ice. He parked the car and turned off the ignition. They both sat still in the silence of the crisp, moonlit evening, warmed by their blossoming affection.

"Tonight was…" Peter said, stopping to find his next word. "It was amazing. Thank you."

Lexi blushed beneath the view of the full moon, hidden from Peter's own view. "I had quite the night myself, Peter Daniel Young."

Peter smiled and looked down at the floorboards, not knowing what to say next. "Well, cool," he managed.

"So, are you going to walk me to my house, maybe?" Lexi said.

"Of course," Peter said, feeling foolish and realizing how cold it was getting after shutting off the car. They both stepped out.

"Whoa…" Peter exclaimed, sliding on a patch of unseen ice as he went to close his door. Grasping for the door handle to stabilize himself, he tore it off, sending it flying over the top of the car.

"Ouch! What was that?" Lexi said as Peter flayed himself out on the road. She ran around to the other side. "Are you OK?"

"I think that was my car door handle," Peter moaned as he gathered himself up from the ground.

Lexi stood next to him covering her mouth, trying to suppress snickers, though a few managed to slip through.

"You laugh? I could have died. Got run over by some SUV as I went down thanks to my crappy Honda," he said, starting to laugh along with Lexi.

As Lexi helped Peter limp to the front door, the security light turned on, eliciting a round of barks from good ol' Rufus who was tucked away warmly inside.

"Sorry about your car door," Lexi said, frowning as she stood in front of Peter.

"I'm sorry about your head!" Peter chuckled. "Is there a bump?" he asked, leaning in closer for a better look. He felt the top of her head and suddenly looked down at her, realizing the razor-thin gap between them, their warm breath filling the void and inviting Peter to make a move.

He closed his eyes, lowered his head.

Peter's phone buzzed and cackled, ruining the moment like a sour note in the closing measure of a Mozart concerto.

They both laughed as they exhaled their pent-up emotions from the evening.

Annoyed, Peter retrieved his phone and stared at its face. "It's my mom," he said, reddening with embarrassment.

He started putting it back in his coat pocket, but Lexi protested. "No, take it. Come on, it's your mom!"

Peter smiled and laughed, whispering *"Sorry"* as he answered it and put it to his ear.

"Hey, Mom. What's up?"

He was met only by silence on the other end, punctuated by what sounded like soft sniffles.

"Hello? Mom?"

"Peter, it's James."

Time stood still. Peter's pulse stopped, and worry flooded his face. He glanced quickly at Lexi. She could see his demeanor had shifted. She tilted her head, crossed her arms, and stared back in worry.

"Mom, what do you mean? What's wrong? What happened?"

"He's dying, Petey."

She said it so matter-of-factly that Peter's subconscious disregarded her response as if it never happened.

"Mom, answer me. What happened?"

"Peter, I just told you," She said with an emotional firmness that snapped him back into focus. "He's in the hospital...dying. The police are over here. You better come."

Peter put a hand on his head and looked back at Lexi, face twisted with disbelief. She came next to him and put her hand at the middle of his back to let him know she was with him in whatever was happening.

Before Peter could utter another word, Maggie broke through the emotionally taught silence.

"And Peter," his mom added with a heavy, breathy throat, "they're saying it might not have been an accident."

CHAPTER 31

THE DRIVE TO THE HOSPITAL, while short, was chaotic. The roads were slick and slushy. Peter's mind suffocated under the weight of disbelief. An endless geyser of fear and disbelief clouded his vision. Lexi would have driven had the car been an automatic. Instead, she clutched his right hand in silence, trying to reassure him that it was going to be OK.

This can't be happening…Was it more coke? He was sure he had stopped using. Or at least lessened his use.

I should have got him checked into a group, Peter continued in silent self-flagellation, bearing the responsibility of the chaos that had engulfed his family. That had engulfed James.

This is all my fault. A repeat of last fall, only worse. And…suicide worse?

Maggie had said his being in the hospital may not have been an accident—hinting that it may have been self-inflicted.

"Suicide…"

He mouthed the word again, unable to grip this revelation. It was unacceptable, not possible.

Not James. Not his brother.

They arrived at St. Mary's a half-hour after Maggie's phone call. Peter raced inside, Lexi in tow. It was only when they were ascending to JT's intensive care unit room that Peter remembered Lexi had joined him.

"Thanks for coming," he managed, gripping her tight and burrowing his face in her shoulder. "This can't be happening..."

"I know, Petey. I know. It's gonna be OK," she whispered, trying to bring Peter some kernel of reassurance.

They stood holding each other, surrounded by the silent hum of the rising elevator.

The elevator *dinged,* announcing their arrival to the ICU, interrupting their moment of comfort. They released each other as the doors opened. Peter stepped out holding Lexi's hand, searching left and right for the right direction. He found it when he noticed his father leaning against the wall down a hallway to his right. Two nurses had just walked in after a doctor had exited.

Peter stiffened as he glided down the hallway, half aware of what his body was doing.

"Dad," Peter said softly, waking Danny from his silence.

Seeing Peter, Danny exhaled the full weight of the evening and embraced him.

Peter felt his father's wet cheeks against his own damp face. He had never seen his dad cry in all of his life.

Over his dad's shoulder Peter saw his mother hovering over the exposed feet of James at the end of the bed. She looked up and over at her two embracing men as Danny began to sob in soft spurts.

"I know, Dad, I know," Peter reassured his father, still clutching his neck.

"I was too hard on the boy. I, I, I shamed him. I pushed him away." Danny couldn't stop giving voice to the cascading flood of regret.

His mother walked out to meet him, followed by Johnny who had been hidden around the corner, seated next to his brother.

"Hi, Mom. Hi, Johnny," Peter said.

"Hi, baby," Maggie replied, eyes bloodshot, face reddened, body limp from the emotional trauma. She kissed his cheek and stole him away from her husband for a round of hugs and sobs herself.

Johnny stood to the side, hands cupped in front of him, staring white and wide-eyed through and past his embracing mother and brother. Peter released the grasp he had on Maggie in order to bring his younger brother into the fold.

"How you doing, baby brother?" Peter asked. Johnny's face felt cool and clammy against his own flush, moist face.

"This sucks," Johnny managed.

Meanwhile Lexi stood at silent, supportive attention off to the side, allowing the Young family to grieve in peace. Peter noticed her and pulled back from his family.

"Everyone, this is my friend Lexi. She's the one I've told you about." They exchanged hellos before Peter crept into his brother's room.

Entering, he saw a nurse working on the other side of the bed, checking his monitor and logging the results. She saw him and offered a small smile of sympathy. Peter hesitated for a moment from walking farther inside. When he did, he was unprepared for what awaited him.

The first thing that caught his attention were the tubes. He could barely identify his brother through the tangled web of tentacles attached to JT's nose and mouth, arms, and chest. He walked over to the side of the bed, resting a hand on his bundled chest. Even through the layers of blankets he felt boney, like someone out of a World Vision fundraiser. His face was even more gaunt than he last remembered it, skin stretched tight across his sharp features. Those features were why he was so popular as a teenager. Now they were a pale reflection of those better days. Nearly all color had drained away, leaving behind the look of death itself—a putty-pale doppelgänger of the former James Thomas Young.

The nurse left the room as the Young family filed in behind Peter. They positioned themselves around the bed, and Peter asked the obvious: "What happened?" He looked at his dad and then his mom, searching for an answer, any answer to make sense of what lay before him.

His mother couldn't form words, so his dad sighed and took over. "His landlord came over to collect his monthly rent. Apparently, he had fallen behind. So he came knocking. When JT didn't answer he unlocked the door and found him on the couch." He stopped, glancing at Maggie and gathering his breath. "He was shaking real violent like. Seizing, they call it. He was having a seizure. Apparently, that's what happens with a cocaine overdose."

Peter went pale, remembering that fateful fall experience the first time he straddled overdosing. He listened to his father describe how the landlord called for emergency help and the doctors tried to revive his brother. He'd been in a coma since the doctors stabilized him. They didn't expect him to come out of it.

His father stopped, using his handkerchief to wipe clear, salty liquid draining out of his nose. He sniffed and continued more emotional. "I knew his life was bad. But not this bad. Thought he'd drop that crap after he stopped dealing."

"I knew," Peter said stone faced, staring at JT.

Peter repeated himself, looking from his mom to his dad. "I knew he was using. He called me after an episode he had a few months back. Brought him to this very hospital. Wasn't as bad as this, and I thought he was done. He *promised* me he was done." He paused, looking back at his motionless brother. "I guess I was wrong."

Maggie slid next to Peter, putting her arms around his waist. "Honey, this wasn't your fault."

He stood, unable to speak. Unable to coax himself away from self-blame. "Yeah," he managed, glancing at his mom. "I know."

Peter turned back to his brother, wiping his moistening eyes on his shirt sleeve. "You said it may not have been an accident when you called."

"What?" Maggie said, breaking her trance.

"Yeah, like it may have been—like he may have tried to..." He trailed off, unable to finish the unthinkable.

She wiped her eyes and tried to form the word Peter himself couldn't. She looked to Danny, who spoke up. "The police or doctors or whoever, said this could be a suicide attempt. That James could have been trying to kill himself. Apparently, they found some sort of note."

"A note?" Peter asked in confusion. "Like a suicide note?"

"Something like that. It was more like a diary," Maggie muttered. "And the final entry was yesterday sometime before... Before he—" She stopped, unable to continue.

Peter held his mother as she began to sob. A moment later Peter asked, "Did you see any of it? Did they read it to you?"

"No, no, we didn't read it," Maggie answered dabbing her eyes with tissue. "Honestly, we haven't thought much about it since we were called down here. The police mentioned it, but we've been so wrapped up here..."

Peter turned back to his brother, considering this added layer to an already complicated situation.

He wrote some sort of suicide entry, Peter thought.

A loud buzzer began sounding from the monitor next to James, jolting Peter from his disbelief.

"What the heck!" he said, jumping back, hitting his head on the wall. "What's going on?" Peter demanded of the nurses and doctor rushing to his brother's side. "What's going on?" he said with more force and volume.

"Hold on, son," his father cautioned Peter. "Let them work."

The medical staff ignored his question, not by intention but by necessity. They were hard at work trying to revive James, whose body was crashing.

"No, James! Don't go. Don't leave us!" Maggie pleaded from the foot of the bed.

Peter stood helpless along the back wall next to his younger brother as he saw the O2 levels plummet on the monitor. JT's heart rate dropped dramatically, then jumped up and back down again in erratic fits. Lexi had moved to Peter's other side, grabbing his hand to announce her solidarity with him in the chaos.

The doctors worked quickly to try and revive James. His body was giving in to the shock from the overdose. One nurse administered epinephrine at the doctor's order. It did nothing to slow the rate of oxygen loss and stabilize his heart.

Then the heart rate monitor flatlined.

His family turned in one accord to the continuous monotone emanating from the device next to JT's bed.

"James!" Peter shouted in agony. His mother and father joined him.

"James, no!" Maggie cried.

"Bring him back!" Danny shouted at the doctor.

"Nurse, get them out of here," a doctor instructed the nurse closest to the Young family.

"Come on, we need to let them work. Let's go into the hallway." She gently herded the emotionally wrought family out of the room.

Maggie started sobbing in Danny's arms. Peter held Johnny. Lexi held them both.

Time hung. It taunted them with worry and fear. It finally

snapped back into motion twelve minutes later when the doctor emerged from JT's room.

The Youngs unfolded from their embrace, peppering the doctor with questions.

Holding up both hands to quiet the family, the doctor updated the family.

"We've stabilized him—"

The Youngs and Lexi interrupted the doctor's report with a collective good-news sigh of relief.

The doctor continued, however, with the full clinical details. "We've stabilized him, but the news is not good." He waited for them to give him their full attention before proceeding. "Unfortunately, the amount of cocaine James took on top of the years of using has left his body in a weakened state. And the coma that resulted from this overdose is permanent. He won't come out of it. And if we remove the breathing tube he will not breathe on his own. He's in a permanent vegetative state."

Shock and disbelief engulfed the Youngs as they stood holding each other.

Maggie spoke first. "So you're saying there's nothing more you can do? Can't you administer some sort of anti-overdose medication?"

The doctor shook his head. "I'm sorry, he's going to remain in this state. There's nothing more we can do." The doctor paused, raking a hand through his salt-and-pepper hair, positioning his arms back in front. "And here's the thing, we don't have on record any consent to maintain or end life in this type of scenario."

He turned to Maggie and Danny, addressing them directly. "Because you are his parents we need you to decide what you'd like to do with James. If keeping him in this state is best. Or if you'd like us to stop all life-maintaining measures to let him go."

The family wasn't prepared for this. Prepared for him dying, yes, somewhat. Prepared to make the decision to let James die, not at all.

Maggie and Danny stared at each other in horror. No parent should have to bury their child, their twentysomething child no less. And no parent should have to make the decision to pull the plug that leads to burying that child.

Danny spoke first. "Is he in pain? Will he be in pain?"

"We've got him on a constant morphine drip, so no. If you choose to remove life-sustaining measures, we will make him very comfortable as he ends life."

Peter turned to his parents and said with determination, "James would not want this. He would not want to be kept alive. Especially if he indicated as much with this note they found. For whatever reason, he wanted out."

The rest of the Youngs nodded in agreement.

"I know this is difficult, but would you like to remove the life-sustaining measures, then?" the doctor asked. "We need consent."

Peter answered for the family. "Do it."

The doctor looked at Maggie and Danny.

They nodded in agreement.

CHAPTER 32

PETER FELT OUT OF BODY, a poltergeist levitating above
the medical drama.

He had long ago learned to detach himself from circumstances and people as a way to protect his heart from pain. There
was no detaching himself from this one, however. Though he
mentally pushed himself out of body in order to float above the
moment to shield himself from the ever-present dread pervading
the room, his heart brought him back to Earth. There was no
detaching from this one. While Peter might be able to peel back
his emotions for the moment, the sense of responsibility was too
strong—bone-deep strong.

The Young family and Lexi stood to the side, motionless as
the hour glass was set draining away the sands remaining in their
son's and brother's life. The nurses removed the breathing tube
feeding air to James. Another nurse injected his IV with a clear
liquid. Peter presumed it was the happy drugs the doctor
promised would make him comfortable. It was the last hit James
Young would ever take again.

When the nurses had finished their work, the doctor reassured them that James was comfortable, that he was pain free in his march toward the end.

"How long will it take?" Maggie asked.

"It depends," the doctor replied, "though my sense is it won't take long."

"How will we know?" Danny asked.

"See those numbers on the monitor?" The doctor pointed to the screen to the right of James's bed. The room turned toward the monitor as the doctor explained the blue number was the oxygen reading and the red one the blood pressure reading. Once those numbers started falling the end was at hand.

The family thanked the doctor for his help before he and the nurse left them alone with James.

"I'll come back in about twenty minutes to check in," the nurse whispered as she closed the door.

No one walked into the day thinking they were going to be standing around the hospital bedside of JT, saying their final goodbyes.

How does one go about that? Peter wondered, having never dealt with death before.

The room was still, but for the clock ticking above the door. It smelled of rubbing alcohol and static electricity, the kind of smell after a summer rain—adding a sterility to the stillness that made it all the more unbearable.

"I love you, son," Danny said, finally breaking the stillness. "I know I didn't tell you that much." His voice cracked with emotion. He shook his head before continuing. "I'm so sorry about what happened your senior year of high school, Jimmy."

Peter hadn't heard that name since before middle school.

"I should have stood with you instead of...of shaking my finger at you," Danny continued, spittle flying out of his mouth as he started weeping.

Maggie clutched her husband around the waist, trying to keep him steady.

"I need a chair," Danny said. Lexi brought one over to the bedside. He dropped into it with leaden force, sighing as he wiped his eyes with both hands. He sat still, staring at JT while Maggie rubbed his shoulders.

"I'm proud of you, son," he managed. "You hear me, JT, I love you. I wish I'd done better by you." He finished, grasping JT's hand, massaging it with his other.

"Do you want to say anything, dear?" Maggie said turning to Johnny who was stoic, still, silent in the corner. He hesitated and then walked over to the bed. Peter motioned him to the other side opposite Danny, placing him at the front of the bed.

"I, uh," Johnny started, grasping for words. "I love you, James. I'm sorry for all the things I ever said to you that were mean and hurtful." His throat was thick with emotion. His eyes began to well; the dam was beginning to burst. "I'll see you in Heaven, I guess..." Johnny finished, turning away, hands coving his face.

Peter looked up at his mom, nodding for her to go. He looked over at the monitor, noting the blue number was now in the eighties and the red number was hovering around one hundred. Peter knew what that meant: the sand was running out.

Maggie traded places with Danny, she grabbed JT's hand and took over massaging it with her other hand. "Baby, it's Mom. It's gonna be all right. Jesus is waiting for you, my sweet son! You can go to him, you trusted him way back when. I was there. You were six, and I was right there when you prayed."

Peter shifted from side to side as he stood listening to his mother. It was as if she were reassuring herself more than reminding James. Peter's gut clenched in agony listening to her.

Maggie placed her head on the bed besides James's pillow, sobbing with short bursts of pained emotion. "I love you, baby.

I'm so proud of you!" She sat back in the chair, wiping her eyes. Danny wrapped his arms around her, kissing her head.

The numbers kept falling on the monitor above James's bed. Peter knew the time was near, though when he went to speak, his mind went blank. No words. His ears were cottony with silence. His vision was coned, as if the world were dimming.

"I love you, bro. James I've always loved you, man," he managed. He stopped, searching for words. He started again, "And I'm so sorry that I wasn't more available for you. I'm so sorry that I wasn't there for you when you needed me most."

Peter stopped again. His lip began quivering. His throat grew thick, neck muscles straining under the weight of his effort to hold back the floodwaters waiting to burst through—until he could no longer keep it inside.

"I failed you, James," Peter whispered, tears leaking through and tumbling down his face. "I failed you! I didn't contend for you when you most needed me to fight for you. For your...for your faith!" Now spittle was coming from Peter's mouth as months of emotion cascaded out from the depths of his beaten, battered body. "And now look at you, bro. Look at you!"

Maggie and Danny looked at each other, confused by his references to JT's faith as Peter continued bearing the weight of James's mistakes and choices.

Peter stopped to catch his breath. Lexi joined him at his side, seeking to bring some measure of comfort in his hour of darkness. She touched his back reassuringly, but he didn't notice. Peter took his shirtsleeves and wiped both eyes. "I have so many good memories of us together. Especially our talks the last few months. You're loved, JT."

He stopped again, staring at the closed eyes of his dying brother. "Go with God, James. Go with God."

Silence ruled the room for several minutes, punctuated by sniffles, coughs, and short sobs.

There was a knock at the door. The attending nurse had returned. She came around the corner, searching for that monitor above the bed. Without the family noticing, the red and blue numbers had transformed into blinking blank lines.

"How's he doing?" Maggie asked.

"Let me check," she said working her way past Peter. "Excuse me."

Peter stepped out of the way and looked on as she brought her stethoscope to bear on James's chest. She pressed it in a few places, searching for whatever sign she was searching for.

When she was finished, she removed the two ear pieces. And looking around the room she said with delicate care, "He's passed."

"THE LORD IS MY SHEPHERD," Peter intoned, reading Psalm 23 from his phone. "I lack nothing. He makes me lie down in green pastures, He leads me beside quiet waters, He refreshes my soul. He guides me along the right paths for his name's sake. Even though I walk through the darkest valley, I will fear no evil, for You are with me; Your rod and your staff, they comfort me. You prepare a table before me in the presence of my enemies. You anoint my head with oil; my cup overflows. Surely your goodness and love will follow me all the days of my life, and I will dwell in the house of the Lord forever."

"Amen," Peter said, closing his phone.

"Amen," everyone muttered in unison at the foot of JT's bed.

The family chose not to invite a hospital chaplain or the Coopersville Baptist Church pastor into their time of grief. Peter acted in their stead. It had been an hour since James's passing. Peter prayed for his broken, shocked family. And he prayed for James. His mother and father offered their own prayers.

"Jesus, we thank you that James asked you into his heart as a little boy," Maggie said between sniffles. "We thank you that he was sealed in your family, and we thank you for receiving him in Heaven. We thank you that we can know he is in Heaven with you because he asked you into his heart as a little boy." Then in a whisper she added, face buried in her hands, "Please bring him into your Heaven." She broke down in sobs that made her shoulders bob up and down.

Danny wrapped his left arm around his wife, adding to her prayer. "Yes, God, we thank you that James was your child. We know he didn't live right his whole life, but we trust that his prayer as a boy was genuine and brought him salvation. We trust he is with you." He paused, adding, "And we thank you for receiving him." Danny bowed, joining Maggie in her sobs.

Peter stirred in his chair, feeling uncomfortable at the petitions for James's entrance into Heaven. It was as if his parents were willing their son into the presence of God because of the prayer he prayed as a small child. While it made him uncomfortable, he actually thought about joining them. Peter wasn't one to question somebody's salvation, and he certainly didn't want to do so in this moment so close to his brother's death. But the last several conversations with James about the afterlife and faith had given Peter great concern.

What happens to a person who prayed a prayer, lived a life in devotion to himself, cavalierly dismissed judgment, and wrote off Jesus as the one path to God?

A frigid shock reverberated through Peter's spine as he contemplated this question. His mind began to reel with the implications of its answer for his now-deceased brother.

Peter stood in response to that jolt, in response to the questions and implied answers worming their way through his heart. He walked to the window, staring out at the city emerging from its slumber. The rising sun cast long shadows draped by fiery hues of burnt oranges, bloody reds, and peachy yellows.

This is the way life works, isn't it? Someone dies, and the world continues on.

As Peter contemplated the complexities and meaninglessness of life and death, he noticed something on the ground peeking out from underneath his mother's coat. He reached down and grabbed a notebook, one of those cheap books of lined paper bound with a spiral of hair-thin metal.

Peter's hands began to tremble, knowing what he was holding. He opened it to the first page and read the first line: '*These are some random thoughts about my messed-up life. I may also throw some ideas about God, too. If anyone reads this, I will mess you up. SO STOP NOW!!*'

Peter whipped around, spitting out, "You've had James's diary this whole time?"

The room turned toward Peter as one. "I had forgotten all about it!" his bleary-eyed mother responded. "The police left it with us. Said they'd determined there was nothing useful in it for their investigation. Except the last page. It's why they thought it was probably a suicide instead of just an overdose."

"Why didn't you tell me you had it here?" Peter bit back with obvious irritation as he flipped through the book, the night's toll making itself known.

"Petey, we forgot. Don't get this way!" Danny shot back.

"Sorry," Peter offered as he continued flipping, settling on an entry dated a week ago. He read:

The Buddha says '*Believe nothing no matter where you read it, or who said it, no matter if I have said it, unless it agrees with your own reason and common sense.*' I totally think he is right on. Which is why I cannot believe in Christianity anymore. It doesn't add up. All my life all I've ever known is Christianity. But now it just doesn't agree with my reason and common sense. It don't make no sense that God will let people fry forever for being bad for a short time. It don't make no sense that out of all of the world religions only one is the right one. It don't make no sense that people need to speak the right words to some prayer to 'be saved' as I was told, even if I live a life of hatred and selfishness. This Trevor guy basically says the same thing, which I dig. And he's starting to help me realize that my childhood religion doesn't add up. Judgment and Hell and condemnation aren't the center of God. Love is the center. And he has always loved me. I just need to accept that love. I don't need to be a Christian to have that love and sign up to a list of religious rules. As he says, '*Our invitation is to trust that we are loved and that a new world has been spoken about us, a new story is being told about us.*' I don't know if I can accept that new world and story, because mine is pretty screwed up and hopeless. But maybe I can trust and accept this love and move on...

The entry ended cryptically, indicating he had disavowed the Christian faith while also inching closer toward disavowing life itself. *Love Will Win* didn't lead him to overdose. But maybe it helped it along a little by giving him the confidence that he was accepted by God, a confidence that had eluded James for years.

Peter felt the urge to hate Bryan and Trevor for permitting James to shift so radically. So permanently. But hadn't he undergone the same radical shift? They could hardly be blamed for James's desire to end a life that had spiraled down well before reading them. And yet...had their misgivings about the Christian faith greased the skids leading to James's drastic end?

Perhaps Peter should hate himself for introducing his brother to the ideas that gave rise to his shift. That gave rise to the ensuing consequences.

He fought back a swell of anger toward the Prosurgent ideas that for so long he had embraced. VanDyke had warned Peter that ideas have consequences. He just hadn't considered what might happen if Prosurgence Christianity fell into the hands of someone less knowledgeable and discerning—even less stable—like his brother.

As Peter stood staring at the breaking dawn, the questions returned with a vengeance, coming in rapid-fire succession: How did he die? In what state did he die? Was he in Christ when he died? Did he fall away? Outside of fellowship with God? Outside Christ? Does that mean he's not with God? Not in Heaven?

Is my brother in Hell?

The questions were vice grips pressing in against his soul, suffocating what life he had left on the other side of the night's trauma.

"I need to go," Peter said abruptly, waking Lexi who had dozed off. She looked up and around the room, landing on Maggie and Danny, who glanced at each other.

"We need to make arrangements, Peter," Maggie said.

"I know, but I can't stay here anymore. I got class," Peter offered in excuse.

"I'm sure they'll understand, Petey," Danny responded.

"I just need to get away," Peter bit back, grabbing his coat off from Johnny's chair. "And I gotta get Lexi back home. I'll see you guys later." Lexi looked back toward Peter's parents as she followed Peter out of the room.

"Is everything all right?" she asked, trying to catch up as Peter fled down the hall.

He punched the call button on the elevator and stared at the numbers ascending to their floor, breathing heavily.

"Petey, did you hear me?"

"What?" he said turning to Lexi, pale and dazed.

"I asked if you were OK. What's going on?"

"I just couldn't stay there anymore. I couldn't breathe in there anymore. Not with my parents' prayers. Not with James lying there." He stopped, adding, "Not with these questions."

"Questions?" Lexi asked as they stepped into the elevator.

"Nothing," he said, hitting the down button with purpose.

Lexi let it go, choosing to stand beside her friend in silent solidarity as they descended back to life.

CHAPTER 33

THE DRIVE back to Lexi's house was painful, slow, silent. And cold. Overnight, the hatchback decided she didn't need her heater anymore, adding an extra pound of misery to an already wretched morning.

They turned onto Wealthy Street, crawling up the long corridor back to Lexi's house. Peter finally broke through the icy silence. "The last conversation my brother and I had before he died was about his peace with the afterlife, you know."

Lexi turned to look at Peter, who was staring straight ahead with moist, glassy, unblinking eyes. She didn't respond, letting him continue at his own pace.

"He said he'd finally come to peace with his life. That he was already accepted, that he accepted that acceptance, and that God was at peace with his path. And he was ready." Peter was trance-like as he recalled the final conversation from a few short days ago.

"But the thing is," Peter continued, blinking away the gathering head of tears, "James told me he rejected the faith we'd grown up on. Everything. Heaven and Hell. That we're sinners separated from God. Even down to Jesus as the only way to God."

Lexi sat pensively, folding her hands on her lap and starting at the gathered bits of Peter's life on the car floor. She sat listening, waiting for him to continue, waiting for the cue that Peter needed her. He didn't, however. Silence engulfed the two as they continued driving through the frigid Grand Rapids dawn.

When they arrived in front of Lexi's home Peter sat, waiting for Lexi to leave.

"How about you come in for a quick breakfast?" Without giving him the chance to object, she got out and waited for him at the end of the sidewalk leading to her front door.

Peter sighed and shut off the engine. He exited, bracing himself on his car as he walked over the freshly frozen cobblestone road.

The two walked in silence into Lexi's house. They were greeted with the pungent aroma of dog pee.

"Oh, Rufus," Lexi moaned as her half-asleep dog lumbered over to them for his morning greeting. "Sorry, buddy. It's my fault, not yours. Let's go outside. Come on!"

Rufus lumbered along as Lexi opened the slider, leading her faithful companion to relieve whatever was left.

"I'll clean up his mess," Peter offered.

"Thanks," Lexi shouted on her way out the door.

Peter grabbed a wad of paper towel and began sopping up the large puddle in the kitchen. "At least it was on linoleum," he mumbled, scrunching up his face in protest. After Rufus finished with round two outside, he bounded straight for Peter, toppling him over like a sack of upright potatoes.

"Rufus, no! Stop, buddy," Peter pleaded as the dog attacked him with his oversized tongue. He seemed to be going for his eyes, perhaps trying to wipe away the sorrow as much as lick the salty residue left over from the night.

"Come on, Rufus, let's get some breakfast," Lexi laughed as she pulled her dog off from her helpless friend.

"Instant oatmeal alright for you?" Lexi said, rustling through her pantry closet. "It's about all I have at the moment unfortunately."

"That'd be fine. And thanks. For everything. For coming with me to the hospital. For just being present with us in our grief."

Lexi turned around to find Peter standing behind her smiling. He kissed her on the cheek. Then hugged her, holding her, refusing to let her go.

Lexi allowed herself to be held, holding Peter and all of his pent-up emotional weight. As they stood, Rufus chomping in the background, she whispered, "What do you mean it's your fault, Petey?" She was met with silence.

A few seconds later, Peter came out from their embrace. With head down, he sighed and said, "Our conversations. The books. All of my talk of Prosurgent and reimagining the Christian faith."

He sighed again and turned toward a stool at the island in Lexi's kitchen. He sat, and continued, "I mean I know I didn't cause his death. James had lots of demons. I get that. But his final words just haunt me, Lexi. Haunt me with questions and what ifs and lost opportunities. I failed him—"

"Wait a minute, Peter Daniel," Lexi interrupted, holding her hand up to emphasize her caution. "Failed him? How?"

"I should have fought for his faith more. Guarded his faith!" His raised voice cracked with emotion.

Lexi walked over to him and held his face with both hands. "Peter, you are not responsible for James's faith. Or whatever direction he took his faith. James was on his own journey. It sounds like he made peace with that journey. And whatever that means for his death, you don't own that."

A piece of the weight of responsibility Peter had been bearing since reading his brother's diary back in the hospital seemed to float away. Lexi released his face, placing both hands on his shoulders. He closed his eyes and sighed, still searching for a way to make sense of what had happened to his brother.

"It's not going to make sense, Petey," Lexi offered. "Trust me, I know."

Peter raised his head to attention, searching for the rest of the story. Lexi's eyes moistened herself as she rekindled a memory long buried.

"I know," she started slowly, "because my dad ended his life a few years ago."

The questions fell out of Peter in wide-eyed disbelief: *What? When? Why didn't you tell me?*

"It was three years ago this past Christmas," she offered, taking a seat on the stool across from Peter. "We were in Chicago, celebrating New Year's. My mother and my brothers and I were at the pool a few hours before the ball dropped. My dad said he was feeling tired and was going to go back up to the room. He kissed my mom who was lying by the pool. Gave me a kiss on the forehead. Hugged my younger brothers."

Lexi paused, replaying the reel containing her potent, precious childhood memory. A single tear rolled down her cheek as she continued.

"I didn't think anything of it, but looking back it was so final. Like he was saying his final goodbyes to us. Anyway, he left, and we continued playing and swimming. A little bit later there was a commotion outside the pool area. Lots of people were gathering and muttering up the hall in the lobby. We were like 'What's going on?' I overheard someone say something about somebody jumping. Sure enough, somebody had jumped from their balcony and landed on the pavement out front."

Peter sat listening, his brow furrowed with horror. "Oh, my gosh." He leaned back, placing his hands on his head.

"It wasn't until we went to our room an hour later that we found out what happened. I remember how crazy cold it was. We had a suite, and the door to the balcony was wide open." Lexi blinked away tears from both eyes, staring off into the distance. She looked at Peter and said, "We had no idea. Not a clue this was coming. We never found out why, either. No note. No nothing. Something snapped. Something caused him to think that jumping off a balcony of a Chicago hotel while on vacation with his family on New Year's Eve was the only way out."

Lexi paused for several seconds, reliving feelings not relived for years. Wiping her eyes on her sleeve, she continued, "Peter, it's not your fault. Whatever led to that overdose was inside James. I know you want answers. You want to figure out why and what you could have done differently to help and fix whatever was going on inside his head. Whatever was going on inside his heart. It's useless, Peter. Believe me, I know. My brothers know. My mom still doesn't know, but she's getting there."

Peter breathed in this advice and Lexi's own story, letting it melt away his feelings of responsibility and brotherly incompetence. He couldn't shake this nagging feeling, though, that the ideas he and his brother had been batting around since his return had shaped him somehow. Had seeped into his story in a way that wrote this tragic ending.

"Thanks," he said softly, choosing to keep these thoughts to himself. He stood and took a step toward Lexi, still seated. "Thanks for sharing your story. I'm so sorry, Lexi. I couldn't imagine losing my dad, and in that way...Anyway, thanks for your words. I know you're right. It just might take awhile to get there."

"Oh, it will," Lexi said, trying to reassure him. "But you'll get there. Your whole family will." She grabbed Peter's hand, giving an added measure of reassurance. Smiling, she said, "Now how about some nice, homemade microwaved oatmeal?"

"Sounds perfect."

CHAPTER 34

AFTER A LARGE BOWL of maple brown sugar oatmeal and a mug of fresh ground coffee, Peter thanked Lexi once again for coming along with him to the hospital and for her reassurance.

"I'm so lucky to have you in my life, Lexi," Peter said, holding Lexi in her doorway, refusing to step away.

When he finally did, Lexi replied, "I'm here for you, Peter Daniel Young. In whatever way you need me. I'm here for you."

He leaned in and, rather than pecking Lexi on the cheek as she expected, pressed his lips against her own. The dam of emotions built up in Peter's heart burst forth in a torrent of passion in the dawn's early light.

"Thanks, darlin'," Peter said after withdrawing from his love, leaving Lexi speechless for once. Without letting her reply, he walked back to his car.

"How can you just kiss me and walk away?" she shouted, her arms raised in protest.

Hands in his pockets, Peter turned around and smiled, shouting up the walkway, "Because I'm Peter Daniel Young!"

Lexi laughed. "Oh, please! Hey, be careful out of there."

"I will," Peter said after reaching in through the passenger side to open his driver's side door. His feet slide on the road as he made his way around to the other side of the car.

"Don't worry, I'm OK!" he shouted back.

Lexi laughed and waved him off as he drove away.

Peter was riding high, still breathing heavily from his impulsive moment of passion. He had been longing to show his affection for Lexi. Her care and vulnerability gave him the courage and permission he needed to make good on his desire. And it didn't hurt the morning sun was beginning to melt away Nature's final one-two wintry punch!

As he drove down Wealthy Street, past St. Mary's Hospital, the high began to fade as reality rose back to the surface. Along with reality arose the questions that percolated in Lexi's kitchen.

Why didn't I see this coming? Could I have done something to give James hope? Did our conversations somehow lead to this? Was it something I said? Did our conversations about God and salvation and the afterlife give James permission? Was it something he read? Something I encouraged him to read?

Damn those books; damn those ideas!

Peter continued cursing himself and cursing the ideas he had for so long embraced with abandon. While those ideas had given him new life, while they had breathed new life into his faith, he was blaming them for the death of his brother.

As he made his way onto 131 to head back home he found himself becoming angrier at Prosurgent, at the ideas and people who gave rise to the ideas he believed caused something to shift, something to break, inside his brother.

I need to talk to someone, Peter thought. *But who?*

He didn't think Alex or anyone from Prosurgent West Michigan was a good candidate. Too close to those ideas Peter was beginning to despise. Neither was Pastor Dave, given his own views.

What about Dr. VanDyke?

Peter knew VanDyke's morning was free as he usually spent working in his office. Approaching the exit that led to school, Peter took it, hoping his professor friend was free.

Maybe he can sort all of this out…

Fifteen minutes later, Peter pulled into the GRTS parking lot and spotted Calvin's identical hatchback. He pulled alongside it, parked, and ran inside hoping he could still catch him.

He arrived at VanDyke's office, only to see him meeting with another student. He caught Peter peering through the door window and motioned for him to come inside.

"Good morning, Peter," VanDyke said.

"Sorry to bother you, I didn't mean to barge in on a meeting," Peter replied, embarrassed and out of breath.

"No, it's fine. We were just finishing up anyway."

VanDyke turned back to engage the student Peter had interrupted, telling him to make the necessary changes to his paper in order to resubmit it. The student agreed and got up to leave. Only then did Peter see that it was Adam.

"Hey, Adam," Peter offered as he walked out in irritation.

"Have a seat. What's going on? Is everything all right?"

Peter sat, realizing he hadn't showered or changed into new clothes since the previous morning, on top of not sleeping in over thirty hours. It was starting to show.

"I've been at the hospital."

"The hospital? Are you alright?"

"I'm fine. It wasn't me. It was my brother." He paused, staring at a stack of papers on the corner of VanDyke's desk. VanDyke sat back waiting for Peter to continue.

"He died of a drug overdose early this morning."

It took a moment for Peter's words to register. "Oh no…" VanDyke leaned across his desk with a pained mixture of shock, horror, and sympathy. "You said he died of a drug overdose?"

"Yeah. It's a long story," Peter said shaking his head. "James has had a rough few years, and he thought drugs would help him cope." He paused, continuing to stare at the pile of papers. "He was brought into the ER unconscious yesterday afternoon. His landlord found him that way. By the time I got to the hospital he had slipped into a coma from all of the cocaine. And we decided to pull the plug early this morning."

"I am so sorry. I can't imagine what your family has been going through. What you have been going through..."

"Not gonna lie, it's been a rough night." Peter paused before adding the bit of definition that was particularly shocking. "What makes it worse is that the police found a diary at the scene. And they think the last entry was some sort of goodbye note."

"A goodbye note?"

"As in a suicide note. Well, they're not entirely sure. Sort of reads that way."

That pained look washed over the professor's face again. This time he wheeled his chair around closer to Peter, as if this revelation of suicide somehow deepened the importance of their conversation.

"How are you doing?"

Peter sighed, searching for a response. "I mean, obviously I'm devastated my brother's dead. Actually, I don't think it's really hit me. Still numb, you know?" VanDyke nodded with empathy. "But the thing that's just...eating me inside is this feeling that I somehow had a hand in all of this."

Peter's self-confession took VanDyke by surprise. "What on earth do you mean you had a hand in all of this? In his suicide?"

"Yeah. Sort of. Not directly, of course. But I told you how we've been having all of these conversations about his spiritual journey and what's real about the Christian faith."

"I remember you mentioning something about that a few months ago."

Peter continued, "We did this book club thing with Bryan McLaughlin's new book, thinking it'd be a great way to engage my brother on his journey. Found out that was a big mistake!" Peter shook his head, chastising himself in silence. "Then a few weeks ago he picked up Trevor's new book, and it totally changed him."

"What do you mean it changed him?"

"I mean, this peace came over him like I hadn't seen before. Like he'd made peace with all of his questions and problems with Christianity. Something gave way inside."

"So where do you come into all of this?" VanDyke asked, probing Peter like any good professor.

"I feel like I caused that breaking! Like my own questions and problems with Christianity were some sort of model for James. I mean, I introduced him to this idea of reimagining the Christian faith. I encouraged his questioning. I even encouraged some of the answers he found."

Peter's throat grew thick with emotion as his brother's death became more real with each passing moment—as he relived his relationship with his brother as teacher and student the past few months.

"Peter," VanDyke offered, breaking through Peter's inner turmoil. "Brother, this isn't your fault—"

"I know..." he interrupted.

"No, listen," VanDyke interrupted back. "I don't know James's story; I don't know what's been going on in his head and in his heart. But you can't blame his death on your conversations. You can't blame his death on whatever Prosurgent ideas he was latching on to."

"But I read some of his diary! Before he died he wrote he had made peace with his questions thanks to those Prosurgent ideas. He decided to finally accept that he was accepted by God, that he had realized God had simply accepted him regardless of what he believed. Regardless of what his childhood faith required him to believe."

VanDyke leaned back in his chair and stroked his chin, as if pondering this revelation.

"Peter, only James and God know what James believed or didn't believe. What he accepted and what he rejected. It sounds like James would have eventually stumbled across all of those ideas you talked about on his own. He was searching for answers, searching for something different than the faith he grew up on. It was his search, his journey, his deal. Not yours. And certainly not your fault, brother." He paused, letting his words find a place to sit in Peter's aching heart. He continued, "Again, we don't know what James believed or didn't believe. Maybe what we take away from this is how important ideas are."

Peter looked up and tilted his head. "What do you mean?"

"I mean, it seems like whatever questions James had he found some answers he liked. He found some ideas that he liked and latched onto them. Those ideas weren't your fault. It seems you'd been trying to help him navigate his questions with good pastoral care."

Peter began to warm up to what VanDyke was saying with growing recognition.

"You've been on a remarkable journey of your own the past year," VanDyke continued. "And what is the one thing I've been saying in our own conversations?"

He waited for Peter to answer. Peter knew what he was looking for. "Ideas have consequences," he mumbled.

"Right, ideas have consequences. Now I don't think we should say whatever ideas James latched on to led to his suicide. I don't think that's healthy or helpful."

"No, but we do know they brought him hope. And that hope is what gave him permission to peace out. As false as it was..." Peter said drifting off.

"Maybe that's true." VanDyke paused, choosing his words. "Either way we're all responsible for our own journey with God. You're responsible for yours. James was responsible for his. Although, I will also add that we teachers are also responsible for the journey of those whom God has entrusted to us. That's why the Apostle James says that people shouldn't presume to be teachers, because they'll be judged more strictly. They'll be held more accountable because of all the people they shepherd. Whether in the pews through sermons, or on the couch through books. Honestly, this is why I've taken so much interest in you, Peter."

The end of his mouth curled in a smile. "What do you mean?"

"I mean, I see lots of potential in you. And I guess I just don't want to see you—"

"Use my powers for evil?" Peter said, finishing VanDyke's thought with a menacing growl.

VanDyke laughed. "Exactly!"

Though the pain of the past day was still fresh and deep, Peter felt somewhat lighter after talking with his professor friend.

"Ideas have consequences," Peter recited.

"Ideas have consequences. Again, not blaming these ideas on your brother's death, but it just goes to show how weighty that maxim is. The real lives of real people and their real eternal outcomes are at stake. Which makes getting the ideas right about the Christian faith—about faith in general—extremely important. Extremely important! Not only for ourselves, but also for the people God puts in our paths."

Peter sat in silence, his chest tightening again given the weight of VanDyke's words.

"I hope I didn't just reopen your wound," he said chuckling.

Peter smiled, trying to reassure him. "No, you're fine! I'm just tired and wrecked from the past day. These are good words, so thanks. Lots to consider here."

Peter got up from his chair, signaling his intent to leave. VanDyke got up as well.

"Pete, I hope you release yourself from any responsibility."

"Thanks. I think I will, eventually."

"Come here," VanDyke said, embracing Peter in sympathy. "Let me know if you need anything from me, alright?"

"For sure, Dr. VanDyke. And thanks for letting me barge in on you this morning. I'm sure you had better things to do."

"Not at all! You're always welcome. Blessings, brother."

Peter left his seminary for home feeling slightly better, as if a piece of the boulder of regret sitting in his gut was chipped down to size a bit. He had begun to accept that what happened to his brother wasn't his fault. James was on his own journey, a journey that was heavily influenced by Prosurgent authors. The very same authors that had influenced his own journey. And the very same authors Peter had introduced to James.

Not my fault, Peter reminded himself.

Their ideas were their ideas, not his own. He reminded himself of this, reminded himself that he hadn't taught the things that seemed to bring James hope and peace. In fact, he pushed back against those very ideas in conversations with his brother.

As he drove, a new resolve began to quicken in his belly. A resolved to take ideas more seriously than he had been. Sure, VanDyke had nurtured such a passion within him over the school year. But this personal tragedy had opened his eyes wide to the potent potential toxin ideas carried. And their consequences.

"Ideas have consequences," Peter said, gripping the steering wheel. "So what does this mean for me?"

He decided he needed to get away to process these things. To process the death of his brother. To process how, if at all, Prosurgent ideas had influenced that death.

Peter knew just the thing to help him process.

CHAPTER 35

"MOM, I'LL BE FINE," Peter said as he continued packing for an impromptu backpacking trip to Manistee National Forest. He stuffed his sleeping bag at the bottom of his backpack. "I've done this plenty of times before."

"But why now? We've got preparations to make," Maggie complained.

Peter huffed at his packing troubles as much as his mother's nagging.

"Because I need to get away. I need to process what's just happened...what's happened to JT." Peter shook his head and returned to his packing. "Besides, I'll only be gone overnight. I'll be back in time to help make arrangements for his funeral later this week."

It was clear his mother didn't like Peter's response. She stood still, hands at her hips before switching gears.

"But what if something happens to you out in the middle of nowhere. I can't stand to lose two of my babies in a week!"

Peter rolled his eyes before turning around smiling to put his mother at ease.

"Mom, I'm not going to die. If I can survive a week on the Appalachian Trail, surely I can survive one measly night along the Manistee River."

"What about the snow? You could catch your death of cold out there!"

"I've got my thermal sleeping bag and a sweatshirt," Peter said, continuing to pack. "And believe me, I've camped in worse weather than this. Besides, the weather man says it's going to warm up into the 50s."

Maggie wasn't going to win so she left Peter to finish his packing for his overnight trip into the wilds.

Peter heard about the park in *Outdoors Magazine*, and was surprised by its high marks. In DC, hiking and backpacking had become an obsession. He spent hours walking the Billy Goat Trail along the Potomac and days backpacking in the Shenandoah Mountain. He even hiked part of the Appalachian Trail. Hiking gave Peter calming, centering therapy in a way nothing else did. He hoped the mighty Manistee would prove to be the soothing balm he needed for such a time as this.

He managed to escape Cooper Manor by midmorning after leaving the coordinates to the parking lot where he would eventually abandon his hatchback in favor of trailblazing along the mighty Manistee River. With nothing but his pack full of the necessities, he set off for the two-hour drive up M-37.

Underground electronic music from Europe kept him company. They provided the soundtrack for his adventure into the depths of his soul. He didn't let himself contemplate the gravity of his brother's death. Not yet. That would come later.

He wiped his eyes threatening a deluge, forcing his emotions back where they belonged, at least until he reached Red Bridge River Access.

Thankfully, Sigur Rós came to his rescue. *Hoppípolla* sent him soaring above the emotional fray.

Peter breathed slowly, in and out, feeling lighter as he turned left onto M-55, a fifteen-minute drive from the trailhead. He rolled down the windows to breathe in the forest that awaited his return, anticipation growing in his belly for the reckoning that was awaiting him regarding his brother's spiritual journey into, through, and beyond his own.

After parking at the access point, Peter hoisted his fifty-pound pack on his back and began setting off toward the trailhead that kissed the North Coates Highway. By the time he set off, it was late morning. There was a lingering bite in the air, but the day was beginning to melt away winter's final swan song.

As he made his way through the Manistee River trailhead, the stress and frustration that had piled high over the past several months began to recede the farther he left his car and outside world behind. Peter breathed deep as he made his way over a boardwalk through a swamp. Waist high wet grass brushed against him like a carwash, helping wash away the dirt and grime and sorrow that had accumulated from life's trauma.

He had forgotten how important backpacking had been for re-centering his life. Something about casting one's frail existence before the mercy of nature for a few days, removed from the trappings and stresses of modern-day living, infused the essence of life back into his bones.

On the other side of the swamp, he somehow felt lighter, like his the core of his being had been freed from deadened weight, allowing him to begin focusing on why he came to God's country in the first place.

James's impending funeral began to needle at his brain as he ascended a cliff hugging the mighty Manistee. He held it at bay, however, with every pump up the incline. He wasn't ready yet to confront what had transpired a few short days ago. Instead he considered his spiritual journey, what had transpired over the past eighteen months into, through, and beyond Prosurgence Christianity.

He traced the contours of his memories backward until they arrived back at Clint Wilson, the college student friend who started it all. It was his abandonment of Christianity and the questions about faith and life that left Peter flatfooted, that led him to rethinking what it meant to be a Christian in the first place. Then he remembered his first Prosurgent DC meeting and the mentorship of Darren Thomas who shepherded him beyond his fundamentalist past. There was the *Everyday Evangelism* training that finally sent Peter over the edge. Then of course Freddy Morris and his debate with Bryan McLaughlin at Georgetown University, organized by his ministry that confirmed the Church was wildly out of touch with people's questions, especially his young adult friends.

Never would he have guessed he'd say "goodbye, Prosurgent," having abandoned fundamentalism in favor of the progressive Christian movement. Yet having sat with the deeper teachings of Prosurgent authors and having begun to rediscover the historic Christian faith—vintage Christianity, as VanDyke put it—he knew there was no going back.

Especially after the death of his brother.

It had been over an hour since he'd left his car. He had drained both of his Nalgene bottles on either side of his pack from physical exertion and the increasing noonday heat. Setting his pack down along a creek that ran over the trailhead, he withdrew his hydration pump and began filling his bottles.

He heard a noise up the trailhead through the thick forest of northern Michigan pines.

There they were. A doe and her fawn. He finished pumping the one bottle and left his water gear behind to get a closer look.

Peter measured his steps one by one, hunched over slightly to balance his weight forward in an effort to make as little noise as possible. Standing thirty feet away from these two beasts lifted his spirits even more. He sat on his haunches as the two foraged for food at the forest's floor, nibbling at the emergent foliage beneath the towering trees.

In an instant, the mother deer lifter her head and sniffed the air, just as the wind began to shift toward Peter's back.

It's all right, girl. I'm not going to hurt you.

The doe's instincts took over, however, and she scampered off with her baby out of harm's way back into the woods.

Peter returned back to his water, thankful for the gift of experiencing God's creation up close, a small gift that made him smile inside and out.

Before returning to his hike, Peter examined the map of the Upper River trailhead he'd printed off the Internet. Judging by the landmarks on the map and signs he'd seen along his hike, it looked like he was near mile marker eight, which meant he was making good progress. He stuffed the map back into the Ziploc bag for protection and hoisted his pack back on his shoulders. Clicking the pack's hip belt in place and adjusting the straps, he headed back out on the trail in search for the perfect campsite for the evening.

Another hour into his hike, Peter came upon a clearing deep into the woods off-trail that seemed to buttress the river. Abandoning the trail, he headed toward what looked like the perfect camping spot.

And it was.

The forest floor had been trampled and cleared by scores of tenters over the years. They'd even established a makeshift fire pit, still filled with ash and a few unburnt logs from the previous campers who must have left the day before. A few trees provided overhead protection, but the main selling point was the view.

The site did indeed sit along the snaking Manistee, facing west. Not ten feet from the site a cliff dropped at least sixty feet down sharply to the banks of the river below. The view snatched Peter's tired breath as he dropped his pack and drank in the view. A family of hawks hovered above a sharp bend in the river, a baby floating effortlessly around its mother and father.

This is the life, Peter thought as he stretched the sore out of his back and shoulders.

Off to the side, a narrow trail snaked down somewhere near the river, providing a much-needed source of water for his camp. He retrieved his hydration pump and bottles again to prepare to settle into his home for the next day.

AFTER SETTING up his tent and arranging his camping gear inside, Peter took a small sack he'd packed away filled with his journal and some blue pens to help him do what he had come here to do in the first place yet had been avoiding since leaving Cooper Manor: process his brother's death.

How do you even do such a thing? he wondered, plopping down on the dusty ground overlooking the river, his legs dangling over the edge.

He sighed and reached into his sack, dumping the contents on a grassy patch next to his perch. Along with his blue pens and journal dropped a sealed paper bag. It felt like it held a book, similar to the Moleskine journal he had brought along. He flipped it over and noticed a note stuck to the bag. He snatched it off and opened it. It was a simple white card with his mother's handwriting:

Petey,

James would have wanted you to have this.

—Mom

Peter set down the card and opened the bag, finding his brother's journal inside. He held the modest book before him, its weight growing like a phone book—from his weariness, from its significance. He hadn't returned back to it since the hospital.

As he sat on the edge of his campsite he contemplated whether to dip into the depths that awaited the cover's turn. He held it close to him, like an archaeologist might hold a precious relic from ages past. JT's journey was that meaningful, that holy.

The cover was stained with what Peter hoped was coffee, though its still-lingering odor was too pungent to simply be dried Folgers. Its pages were also laced with the trace scent of earthy spice, citrus, and flowers. "Marijuana," Peter snickered, shaking his head as he continued flipping.

Each page was filled from top to bottom with his brother's messy script. He remembered several lines from the hospital when he first encountered this testament to James's inner thoughts on faith, life, and everything in between. There was the entry about his first experience at the local Grand Rapids Buddhist temple. There were entries devoted to his myriad of questions: How could a good God allow people to burn in hell forever? Why did Jesus have to be the only way? What is needed to "be saved" as they say? What's on the other side of death? He wrote about his frustration with these questions, his frustrations with how his childhood Christian faith answered them—his pleasure at how his newfound Buddhist faith answered them.

Peter continued flipping until he reached more recent entries, the ones dated since his arrival back home: *"This Bryan dude has got it right! He gets what's wrong with Christianity. I like the way he wants to change it. I'm so glad Pete introduced me to it, and I can't wait for our book club to start."*

A pang of regret twisted in Peter's gut as he was confronted yet again by the role he had in his brother's spiritual journey. He knew it started innocently enough. After all, he wanted to help his brother navigate his spiritual questions and do what he himself wanted to do—what he thought was best to do—and that was reimagine the Christian faith for his twenty-first-century world. In this case, for his brother's life.

He thought about those words, reimagine the Christian faith. And he laughed and shook his head. How arrogant! To think the Christian faith needed reimagining.

To think I have the right to reimagine it!

His thoughts took him further, though, plumbing the depths of regret even more.

For the first time he realized something he hadn't seen before about Prosurgence Christianity: It was a faith tailor-made for the well-educated, well-cocooned soccer moms and business men and angsty young adults with middle-class sensibilities who haven't a care in the world, who haven't tasted the injustices of a world in open rebellion against God.

Someone like Peter Daniel Young.

But hand Prosurgence Christianity to someone like James Thomas Young—someone who struggled to keep a job, was addicted to drugs and alcohol, and questioned the reason to continue living—and, well, it was a whole other story.

This version of Christianity wasn't created for him; it was created for Peter.

And that's what Peter hadn't realized before. He didn't see how the progressive religion of Prosurgent would feed the broken aspects of James's life with the false hope of a false antidote.

It didn't require anything from James, since tolerance rules this religion. And so the kind of change James needed wouldn't come in the first place because there was nothing beckoning him into transformation.

It didn't offer power because the true source of power for this religion was the self, rather than the Spirit. Even if James wanted to change he couldn't, because human-centered salvation is no salvation at all. It takes the power of God to break the chains of sin and death, in all of its forms.

It wasn't at all hopeful because it wasn't at all honest. The Prosurgent religion isn't honest about the human condition, that we're busted beyond all self-repair and in desperate need of rescue. It isn't honest about who Jesus is as the only fix for our hopeless condition. It isn't honest about what Jesus did to bring and bear our remedy, the death he died to pay our price in our place. And it isn't honest about the end, the reality that every person on the planet will be judged—either in Christ or outside of Christ.

On the other hand, it was a religious experience and religious system of beliefs tailor-made for someone like James who wasn't biblically or theologically literate enough to discern how different Prosurgent was from what the Church has always believed—from the vintage Christian faith. It played off of James's need to be accepted without requiring anything from him in return. It leveraged his frustration with conservative fundamentalism by offering liberation from any sort of demand to faithful living. And it plied him with the false security that God's love trumped his justice, that in the end he'd be "in" by nature of his existence, without any final reckoning for his life lived from birth to death.

And Peter had offered up this false religion on a silver platter.

His throat stumbled over itself as the weight of his responsibility grew all the more heavy.

Did I do this?

Peter clenched his eyes, tears threatening to burst forth. Regret twisted in his gut, the weight of his part in introducing this new religious expression to his brother bearing down on him.

He wiped his eyes, heaved heavy breaths, and pushed past the feelings of responsibility by flipping more pages, reaching the end of the journal, James's final entry.

Peter closed his eyes and closed the book, contemplating

whether he wanted to invite whatever awaited him in James's final words. He started to open it before slamming it shut again.

After another minute, he decided he needed to know where James was at in his head, in his heart, before ending it all. He cracked the back cover and peeled it back to get to the awaiting entry. It was dated the day before his death.

> I'm finally at a place of peace. Trevor says that '*Love is what God is, Love is why Jesus came, and love is why he continues to come, year after year to person after person.*' I think I can finally say that I know that love. And I accept that I am in that love because that's what God is. God is love. As Trevor says it's been mine all along, but I haven't had a religion that has helped me see that. I see it now. I can't go on though...

Peter inhaled sharply, eyes widening as he read his brother's pre-overdose confession. He continued reading.

> I've screwed up my life to the point of no return. I hope people realize that. But it's all good.

Then the final words in the final entry before he died:

> I accept that I'm accepted. Not because I believe in Jesus as the only way or believe Christianity as the only religion. But because God believes in me. Sure I've made my mistakes, but I've made peace with my journey and

life and eternal future, wherever that might be. Whatever that might be like.

I've made peace with my journey and life and eternal future. Wherever that might be? Whatever that might be like?

Peter set down JT's journal on his lap and looked out over the raging river below.

"Those damn Prosurgent ideas!"

He clenched his fist and twisted his face in repulsion for the beliefs he'd once fought for. The beliefs that got him fired.

The beliefs that killed his brother.

But is that right?

Was it fair to say Prosurgence Christianity caused James to end his life? Probably not. No, it wasn't. But as Peter processed these final words and the conversations the past year at Founders, he began to see more clearly how those ideas had influenced James's decision. Maybe not so much the decision to end things with drugs—that was JT's choice. But certainly his decision to forsake the fundamental beliefs of the Christian faith, even Jesus.

"It's all just game, isn't?" Peter sneered. "A damn game of one-upmanship and silly, juvenile speculation with no regard for the consequences of such ideas!"

He stared down the cliff, his revulsion beginning to match the churning waters beneath.

"Well, it's not a game! The real lives of real people and their real eternal outcomes are at stake!" He was shouting now, his rage ricocheting throughout the river valley bellow.

And that's what the Prosurgent Church didn't get.

All of the speculation about the origins of the universe, the existence of Adam and Eve, our human nature, our depravity, Jesus' divinity, what happened at the cross, whether Jesus physically arose from the dead, the afterlife—all of it mattered. The way one answered the big questions of life has a direct impact on the lives of real people.

It's not an intellectual game; it's a spiritual death match.

And JT lost it several rounds in.

Peter closed the journal and leaned back, the afternoon sun slicing through the brisk air and heating his face as it began setting lower on the other side.

He said a prayer seeking God's forgiveness for the part he played in introducing Prosurgence Christianity to James. As he prayed, verses came to mind speaking about the weighty responsibility to steward the ideas of the faith well—to steward the sacred souls of those entrusted to leaders of God's people well.

"The book of James says, '*Not many of you should become teachers, my fellow believers, because you know that we who teach will be judged more strictly.*'"

Father, forgive me for my failure to teach well. By your grace and mercy spare your judgment. Please still consider me worthy to be a teacher over your people.

There was Paul's instructions to his coworker, Titus. When speaking of elders and teachers in the church, he instructs that they "must hold firmly to the trustworthy message as it has been taught, so that he can encourage others by sound doctrine and refute those who oppose it." Later he says they "must teach what is appropriate to sound doctrine."

Lord, Jesus Christ Son of God, have mercy on me for not encouraging James by sound doctrine, and teaching what the Church has always believed.

And further instructions to Titus to "set young men an example by doing what is good," and in teaching them to "show integrity, seriousness and soundness of speech that cannot be condemned..."

I condemn myself! For introducing James to dishonest, trivial, superficial, unsound teaching. And now look at things...

He could bear the reckoning no longer. What's done was done. James was gone. And it seemed like the ideas that seemed so innocent enough opened a path toward his end.

Peter closed his eyes and closed JT's journal. He brought it up to his face and breathed in deep the scent of his brother's words. He clutched it to his chest and started rocking front to back as the pent-up emotions that he had refused to let loose began cascading out from the depths of his being.

At first it was a muffled pant, like a newborn baby waking from sleep in search of his first morning feed. Then it grew into a torrent of deep, guttural heaving, the roar of tears matching the raging river below. Peter set the journal down and clutched his face with both hands, trying to stem the tide of emotion, but to no avail. The soft spot in Peter's emotional core busted wide open, taking his body with him in a sobbing fit.

It would be a long day as he let himself fully enter into the pain of losing his brother. It would be an even longer night as he continued making peace with the role he played in introducing him to the ideas that brought the confusion that led him to forsake his faith.

That had even perhaps led him to end his life.

CHAPTER 36

PETER ARRIVED back home to a Cooper Manor ablaze with activity. Maggie, Danny, Peter, and Johnny spent hours combing through a pile of photo albums that chronicled the life of their family to prepare for the funeral of their now-dead son and brother.

There were the photos of James's birth, and the proud parents displaying him for the camera. In one photo three-year-old Peter looked on in Maggie's hospital room as she held his new brother. Other photos captured James's first bath, his first pose as a newly standing baby, his first time on the potty with Superman Underoos around his ankles. There were many more "first" photos that captured the young, developing life of JT. Later photos captured the rising sports career that later ended in disappointment. T-ball, baseball, soccer, basketball—you name it, he did it. And it was captured in full Pantone color, neatly arranged as memory books long forgotten.

"What's this chest, Mom?" Peter asked, heaving the heavy wooden box over before his seated parents.

"Oh, that's JT's memory chest." Maggie paused. "It *was* JT's memory chest. You've got one, too. So does Johnny. Go on, open it."

Peter turned the knob that held the chest closed. Inside sat all of the things that had given definition to James's life.

His varsity jacket was neatly folded on top, with several trophies hidden underneath. A sheet of paper with a gold-foiled seal marked James's baptism in a park along the Grand River. At the bottom was a tattered black-leather book, the outer rim stained red—James's confirmation Bible. *Holy Bible* had been rubbed off from the front so that it looked like any other book. Peter closed his eyes and gently rubbed the face of his brother's old Bible, considering his brother's spiritual journey.

"It'd be good to put some of this stuff out at the visitation," Danny said, standing beside Peter as he poked and prodded the relics from distant family memories. "Maybe on a table next to his pictures or something."

"I like that, Dad," Peter offered as he set his brother's Bible aside for his own keeping.

Tomorrow was to be the visitation along with the funeral to follow that afternoon, both held at Coopersville Baptist Church. Peter was sure James would have protested those arrangements with all of his might. He himself felt compelled to protest on his brother's behalf, but thought it unwise. He and his brothers grew up in that church, so it was fitting that James was memorialized there. It wasn't worth fighting his parents over something that was clearly important to them. And besides, he didn't know where else to have the funeral considering how detached James had been from church.

What Peter did protest, though, was his parents' suggestion that Pastor George perform the memorial service.

"No way!" Peter said, his face beginning to redden with frustration. "James would have enough of a fit knowing that his funeral was being held at CBC. There's no way he'd go for Pastor George."

"What's wrong with Pastor George?" Danny roared. "I know you can't stand our pastor or our church, Petey, but don't make this about your issues."

Peter's mouth dropped an inch without any conscious movement. He was too stunned to give any sort of auditory response. So he just stood there, a geyser of emotion making its way up to the surface. A mixture of pain, offense, anger, hurt, resentment sat churning in Peter's throat. He swallowed hard before responding. Before he could croak out a response his mother cut him off.

"Danny, stop!" Maggie exclaimed with an unexpected firmness. They both turned as Maggie continued with a slight tremor, spitting the next set of words out. "Just stop it. Today is not the day! Peter didn't mean anything by it."

She paused, collected herself, and continued in exasperation as she repacked James's chest. "Honestly, I don't think Pastor George is a good idea, either. James wouldn't want it."

"Then who, Maggie?" Danny asked, sitting down. "JT didn't have no church."

She stopped her packing and turned to Peter. "I think you should, baby."

It took a moment for her words to register. When they did, he stepped back, overcome with the weight of the ask. "Me? I don't think that's a good idea."

"Why not? You both were so close the last few months. I don't know who else *should* do it."

Peter sat down, unable to accept the weight of the role his mother was asking him to bear. It was one thing to stand alongside his brother through his spiritual journey. It was quite another to dot the *i*'s and cross the *t*'s on its closing sentence.

His father interrupted Peter's silent contemplation. "I agree, Petey. It does make sense. And sorry about my words earlier."

Peter looked up at his father. He continued, "I think you'll do great, son. Will you help us bury James?"

Now Johnny was now looking at his brother, smiling with reassurance and nodding with the same ask.

"OK," Peter exhaled. "It'd be my honor."

PETER FLOPPED face-first on his bed, anxious from his parents' request. He hadn't a clue how to perform funerals—the order of the service, which passages worked, which ones didn't. And now he was being commissioned to bury his dead brother?

"What on earth do I say?" Peter said, breathing deeply into the pillow. And then it hit him.

Thomas.

"Thomas," Peter said as he turned over to stare at his ceiling. Thomas was his brother's middle name. It was also one of Jesus's disciples, the one who doubted.

Peter sat up and reached for the Bible that sat at the corner of his nightstand. Turning to the Gospel of John, he found the passage that spoke of Thomas's own doubt, John 20:24-29.

"Unless I see the nail marks in his hands and put my finger where the nails were, and put my hand into his side, I will not believe." Then he said to Thomas, "Put your finger here; see my hands. Reach out your hand and put it into my side. Stop doubting and believe."

Adrenaline nurtured a low-grade panic deep inside Peter. "But he did doubt. He didn't believe."

This realization hit Peter hard, knocking him back onto his

bed. The reel from the past few months' events replayed inside his head as he closed his eyes, meditating on these words of Jesus.

Stop doubting. Believe.

Despite how troubling those commands were, despite how troubling they were to James's own story, he knew this was the sermon he needed to preach. The sermon he himself needed as he wrestled with doubt.

Who knows who will be there, Peter thought. *Who knows who else needs these words.*

Ideas have consequences. VanDyke's words again sang a loud tune inside Peter's head, combined with these words of Jesus.

The sermon began to write itself as he lay thinking about his brother—his brother's choices, his brother's journey—choking back the regret and feelings of missed opportunity.

Peter knew what he needed to do. So he got to work, writing the most important sermon of his life.

CHAPTER 37

THE DAY TO memorialize and bury James Thomas Young came as swiftly and harshly as that fateful day when JT was brought to the hospital. While the day was not unexpected, it still stole into their lives like a late-summer tornado, ruining and ravaging their lives. By the time the day arrived, the family had almost forgotten why they were gathering in the first place. The past two days helped numb the shock and pain from the death of their son and brother.

Saturday turned out to be a beautiful Michigan spring day. The sun bathed the Youngs in comforting, reassuring rays as they drove to Coopersville Baptist Church. The trees were in full bloom, dancing in the soft breeze, waving to the grieving family as they drove to the church. The birds themselves seemed to have sensed the day's heaviness, manufacturing a dirge appropriate for the somber day of mourning.

Danny, Maggie, Peter, and Johnny rode in silence, bearing their grief individually. Maggie wore a loose-fitting black dress and a large black hat festooned with red roses. She dabbed her eyes every so often and arranged her hat to hide her grief, even from her family. The men each wore black suits with white shirts and gray ties. Peter shifted every so often in his seat, feeling uncomfortable in the straitjacket he'd sworn off since leaving Capitol Hill. Johnny sat stock-still, hands folded on his lap with the same distant expression he'd worn in the hospital. Danny stared straight ahead driving with his face set in stone—pale, stoic, unemotional.

The family pulled into the parking lot of the country Baptist church. Every heart quickened as they saw the gleaming hearse parked at the front of the church beneath the main stairway, waiting to take away their troubled son and brother to his final place of rest. Danny parked behind the black Cadillac as reality finally came rushing to the fore.

The family made their way through the main entrance, being greeted by Pastor George.

"Hi, Young family. I'm so sorry for your loss." Pastor George gave Maggie a short hug and shook the hands of Danny, Peter, and Johnny. "Can I get anything for you?"

Maggie looked at Danny. "No, Pastor, thank you. I think we're all set. Is there a place we can sit?" She stopped, then added, "And can we see James before people start arriving?"

"Yes, of course. Right this way."

He led the family to a small sitting area just off the main sanctuary where the viewing and then memorial service would be held. James's casket was already in place at the front of the sanctuary, flanked by a few modest bouquets of memorial flowers. Pastor George led the way up toward the front. The family slowed with every step as they inched forward, repelled by an almost magnetic force the closer they got to James's awaiting body.

As Peter made his way to the front, the dream from several months ago that haunted his hospital emergency room visit came rushing back from memory. He felt now just as he did then: a floating poltergeist, unable to face what lay within the modest pine box that held the shell of his deceased brother. When he arrived, he forced himself to look inside, unprepared for the sight that awaited him.

James was cocooned in garments his parents purchased from Macy's, matching the rest of the Young men: black suit, white shirt, gray tie. The clothes betrayed the actual life he lived, but nicely covered it up as well. His thinning, long hair looked clean and well groomed. Again, a far cry from what it actually looked like most of the time. His face was a pale reflection of his former self—gaunt, stretched, and caked in heavy makeup.

Maggie trembled in Danny's arms, while Johnny stood behind and off to the side, silent as ever. Peter was the closest to the wooden box. He placed his hand on James's chest. A dose of adrenaline shot through his body, quickening his pulse and bringing tears to his eyes.

James, I'm so sorry. I'm so, so sorry I didn't do more...

He blinked, allowing the rising wave of emotion to overtake him. He began to convulse. Then uncontrollable sobs overtook him. Peter felt out of body: he heard his cries; felt his body shake; heard the comforts from his parents; felt his family's embrace, yet he was wholly unaware. He experienced it all in a way that was detached from the experience itself. The week's chaos had finally caught up to him, and he was allowing himself to break down in response.

Minutes passed, and then more until the tsunami finally subsided. His mother continued for another moment. He even heard his brother finally let go, too.

"OK," Peter finally said, unwinding from his family's embrace, wiping his eyes with the sleeves of his suit, trying to recompose himself. "Where's that sitting area?"

For the next twenty minutes the Young family sat and paced, waiting for eleven o'clock when the visitation would begin. When it did, they made their way back out into the sanctuary, standing to the side of James's casket. Soft music played in the background as the doors to the sanctuary were opened, indicating the start to a very long day.

The Youngs greeted family and friends who were as shocked and saddened by the horrendous turn of events. Grandparents, uncles, aunts, and cousins arrived to pay their respects to the family. James's friends and coworkers from the pizza joint came as well. Even his girlfriend who dumped him a few weeks prior came to say goodbye. She was a basket case in desperate need of a box of tissues.

After an hour of greeting mostly nameless faces, Peter caught a few familiar ones standing halfway in line. Izzy and Jake. He smiled, warmed by their solidarity during this dark time. He caught their eyes and nodded in appreciation. When they arrived at the front he gave them a large, long hug of gratitude.

"Thanks for coming," Peter whispered, his eyes misting.

"We're so sorry, Peter," Izzy said in her sweet Southern drawl.

"Yeah, so sorry," Jake agreed, patting his hurting friend's shoulder. "I can't imagine losing my brother. How are you?"

"I'm making it. I can't believe it, really. Sort of in a daze from it all. But we're managing."

"Let us know if we can do anything for you," Izzy offered, giving one of her tissues to Peter.

"Thanks," he said, taking her gift and using it to blow his nose. "And thanks for coming. I really appreciate it."

He gave them each another hug before they made their way to seats near the back of the sanctuary.

After sending his friends along, another familiar face rushed into the sanctuary. Lexi positioned herself in the back of the line, but Peter waved her forward after catching her attention.

"Excuse me, sorry," Lexi apologized as she hustled forward to Peter.

"I'm so sorry I'm so late," she apologized as she embraced Peter. "Things got crazy busy at Sparrows, and I couldn't get away."

"It's no problem," Peter reassured her, rubbing her arm. "I'm just thankful you could make it. Really, I'm glad you're here."

"Hello, dear," Maggie leaned over.

"Hi, Mrs. Young," Lexi said, giving Peter's mother a quick hug of sympathy. "So sorry for your loss."

"Thanks, darling. I never got the chance to thank you for taking such good care of my boy here."

Blushing, Lexi replied, "Tt was nothing, Mrs. Young. Glad I could help."

"Well, I thank you just the same."

"You remember my friends Izzy and Jake," Peter said to Lexi.

"Yeah, I met them a few months ago at the shop, didn't I?"

"Exactly. Well, they're here sitting toward the back." Peter pointed in his friends' direction. "I'm sure they wouldn't mind you sitting with them."

"Oh, that'd be great. I should let you go." Lexi gave another reassuring hug to Peter whispering, "You'll get through this. It'll be OK."

Peter grinned. "Thanks."

As Lexi left for her seat, another familiar face trailed her, Pastor Dave, that toothy smile bringing a measure of comfort and relief.

"Davy Jones," Peter sighed, emotion threatening to arise in gratitude. "Thanks for coming."

"You bet, my man," Dave said as he bear-squeezed his seminary friend. "How you holding up? How's your family holding up?"

"As good as can be expected." Peter motioned toward his parents to make an introduction. "Mom, Dad, this is Pastor Dave. The guy I work with at Fellowship Community Church."

"Hello, Pastor," Maggie said.

"Hi, Pastor Dave," Dannie said, shaking hands. "Thanks for coming. And thanks for looking after our boy over at Fellowship. Hope he's behaving himself," Dannie smiled weakly.

"He's a good troop. And can preach a mighty fine sermon!"

"That's our boy," Maggie offered.

"Well, I'll leave you all to the rest of your friends. Again, so sorry for your loss."

"Thanks, Dave. Seriously, thanks for coming. Means a lot."

"You bet. And give 'em Jesus, partner," he said, offering a reassuring squeeze as he left to find a seat.

The line continued for another twenty minutes as two o'clock approached, the start of James's memorial service. As the hour drew nearer Peter became more agitated, anticipating the sermon he was about to deliver. Toward the end, another familiar face came to pay his respects and share his sympathies with the family.

"Hi Peter," VanDyke said. He gave Peter's mom a hug, shook the hands of Danny and Johnny, and then gave Peter a sympathetic embrace.

"Thanks for coming, Dr. VanDyke. Really appreciate it."

"Of course. I know this has been a rough few days. So asking how you're doing is pointless."

"It's been rough. But we're making it."

"Good. Hey, I saw you were giving the sermon."

"Yeah, we agreed it would be best."

"That's great, Peter. That's great. I was just a little older than you when I did my first funeral. And someone gave me some great advice I've carried with me ever since."

"What's that?"

"Never give false hope. But don't take it away, either."

Peter was struck by the depth and simplicity of VanDyke's advice.

He smiled, another wave of emotion threatening to burst. "Thanks for that."

"You'll be great, Pete." VanDyke left to take his seat in the back along with Izzy, Jake, and Lexi.

THE TIME HAD COME to memorialize James Thomas Young. Though the Youngs weren't ready, they took their seats. The room settled into stillness as Peter rose and made his way to the pulpit to begin the service that would lay his brother to rest.

When he reached the platform, he looked out at those who had come to remember the life of JT. He paused, his sweaty palms gripping the sides of the pulpit with nervous energy. After taking a deep breath, he began.

"Hello and welcome. On behalf of my parents, Daniel and Margret, my brother, Johnny, and myself, I want to thank you so much for coming to this memorial service for our son and brother, James Thomas Young.

"This afternoon we are here to remember and to celebrate the amazing man we came to know. We come to celebrate all of what he did and all of who he was. We also come to mourn. We come to mourn the loss of our son, brother, and friend."

Peter paused, scanning the room full of people who cared so deeply for his brother.

He continued, "Let's be honest, none of us want to be here. Oh, we tell ourselves he's in a better place—I've been trying to tell myself that the past few days. And that's true because of his faith in Jesus. But I want to say that it's OK to come in here grieving and weeping and confused—even a little angry. Because we know deep down that death isn't the way it's supposed to be. That *this*, isn't the way it's supposed to be, because James died too soon.

"But while we may have come in here weeping, we will not leave that way. We don't mourn like those who do not have hope, because death doesn't have the final word in James's story. One day, when our Lord and Savior Jesus Christ returns to finally put this world back together again, he will raise JT back to new life. And for that we have hope."

Peter sat down, and Pastor George stood to lead the assembled group in singing a rendition of *The Old Rugged Cross.* Maggie and Danny insisted that their pastor play some role, and Peter relented.

"On a hill far away," they sang, *"stood an old rugged cross, the emblem of suffering and shame; how I love that old cross where the dearest and best, for a world of lost sinners was slain."*

The song transported Peter back to hot, sticky summers past when he and James as kids would get into trouble most Sunday mornings while singing hymns like this one. Peter was often the instigator, throwing something at James or pinching him when his parents weren't looking. It often ended with James getting into trouble, accused of causing the ruckus. His parents had seemed to have this innate skepticism about JT, even before all of his troubles started.

The final verse brought Peter back from his memory: *"To that old rugged cross I will ever be true, its shame and reproach gladly bear; then he'll call me some day to my home far away, where his glory forever I'll share."*

Peter noticed his parents sang the final refrain with particular gusto, tears streaming down their faces, ending with the chorus: *"So I'll cherish the old rugged cross, till my trophies at last I lay down; I will cling to the old rugged cross, and exchange it someday for a crown."*

After the singing ended, Pastor George stood again. "As Peter said," he began, motioning toward Peter who was seated behind him, "none of us want to be here. James died too soon. But we do indeed have hope, like he said. We don't mourn like those who do not have hope. I want to read a small section from the Apostle

Paul in 1 Thessalonians. Paul was comforting people who had lost loved ones, just like you."

Pastor George found his place in his Bible and began reading:

> *Brothers and sisters, we do not want you to be uninformed about those who sleep in death, so that you do not grieve like the rest of mankind, who have no hope. For we believe that Jesus died and rose again, and so we believe that God will bring with Jesus those who have fallen asleep in him. According to the Lord's word, we tell you that we who are still alive, who are left until the coming of the Lord, will certainly not precede those who have fallen asleep. For the Lord himself will come down from heaven, with a loud command, with the voice of the archangel and with the trumpet call of God, and the dead in Christ will rise first. After that, we who are still alive and are left will be caught up together with them in the clouds to meet the Lord in the air. And so we will be with the Lord forever. Therefore encourage one another with these words.*

Pastor George said, "Amen," and took his seat next to Peter.

On cue, Daniel Young rose from his front row pew and made his way to the pulpit in order eulogize and pay tribute to his son. Peter smiled reassuringly as he approached. Danny smiled back through a pale, tear-stained face.

"Thank you for being here this day to remember and honor my son," Danny read. "I never thought I'd be doing this. It's not right for a father to have to bury his son. But here I am."

He continued by chronicling James's life, beginning with his birth in a downtown Grand Rapids hospital.

"Secretly, I had wanted a girl," he said, "but I was happy to have another boy. And what a boy he was."

Danny went on to talk about how James would get into everything growing up. "Every unlocked door, cupboard, window, bucket, mud puddle, dead squirrel–you name it James was in it," he said to a round of chuckles.

He continued talking about how proud he'd been when James made his first sports team, T-ball, and then more after that. "Pee-wee football, soccer in late elementary, basketball in junior high and high school. If it had a ball, James was there." Danny paused, adding as his voice cracked with emotion, "And he was good, real good."

To everybody seated in that room the pride was obvious. To Peter, so was the pain. The pain from James's youthful indiscretions, the pain from James's public humiliation, the pain from James's life spiraling out of control. The pain from his death, his probable suicide.

Danny's lower lip began to tremble as he continued. "He also had his share of pain and pitfalls." There was so much embedded in those two words, *pain* and *pitfalls*. Danny decided not to delve into those layers and instead end with his own self-confession. "And I regret not supporting him more in those pitfalls and in that pain."

He stopped to wipe his eyes before continuing. "James, son, you were such an amazing young man. You had your struggles, but you struggled on. I'm sorry for how little support I gave you. I'm sorry for the fights and arguments. I'm sorry for not telling you how proud you made me as a father. Most of all, I'm sorry for not telling you how much you were loved. I loved you more than you knew. And I just wish you knew that before..."

He stopped again, regretful emotion barricading his breath in his throat. "Before you left us." Danny tried to suppress the rhythm of sobs that began overtaking him. Having finished memorializing his son, he took his seat, finding consolation from his tearful wife.

Peter looked at his family before approaching the pulpit for the home stretch.

Here we go...

He rose to preach the most important sermons he would ever give.

CHAPTER 38

PETER ARRANGED his message notes and opened his Bible to the passage he had chosen, pausing to scan the room to prepare for this important moment.

He could see Lexi smiling, cheering him on from the back. Izzy, Jake, and VanDyke exuded the same look of confidence. Near the back he spotted James's former high school girlfriend and mother of his child, who had slipped in when the service started. In the front row sat his parents and brother, waiting for a word from the Lord that would ease their suffering.

And Peter was the one who would bring that word.

He took a deep breath and settled into place, then began, "A professor of mine from seminary, Dr. Greg Morris, has said that being a Christian means embracing the fact that life sucks until Jesus returns."

Peter paused, chuckles making their way around the room.

He smiled and nodded. "So true. This sucks. None of us want to be here. Yes, we tell ourselves that he's in a better place. But I still want to say that this sucks, because death sucks. It sucks that my parents are burying their twenty-three-year-old son. It sucks that my brother Johnny and I are saying goodbye to our brother. It sucks that some of you are saying goodbye to a friend."

He paused to scan the room, noticing several nodding heads. He continued, wondering how his honesty would be received. "And it sucks the way James died. I mean let's be honest about that. James died of a drug overdose. And it seems like that overdose was by his own hand."

Several eyes stared back wide-eyed at hearing this revelation.

"Most of you don't know this, but James kept a journal. I know, I can't believe it either," Peter said eliciting a round of laughs. "He wrote about everything he was struggling about in life, especially his spiritual life. Listen to one of the entries he wrote a few weeks before his death. Take a listen:

> All my life all I've ever known is Christianity. But
> I haven't always been a Christian. I'm not sure
> I am one now. I don't understand how a good
> God could allow people to burn in hell
> forever. I don't understand why Jesus has to be
> the only way. I don't understand what is
> needed to be saved as they say. But I have
> come to believe that God accepts me. I haven't
> always felt that way. But now I do. I accept
> that I'm accepted. I've made peace with my
> journey and life and eternal future—

Peter stopped, considering whether to read James's final words. Taking a breath he took the plunge, "wherever that might be. Whatever that might be like."

The room reverberated with the final words of the dead man they came to memorialize. A few people shifted uncomfortably. A few others gave confused looks to their neighbor. Others looked shocked at what James had written, and perhaps Peter's inclusion of those words in the service.

For Peter, reading them was important. He didn't want to shy away from the obvious. That the life his brother had traversed was one of struggle. Struggles with life itself, struggles with issues of faith. It mattered that people realized this, as much as it mattered to Peter's own self-memory. Perhaps it was selfishness on his part that drove him to include the weighty revelation. But he needed it for his own self-realization of the consequences of ideas for the journey of all.

Peter turned the page of his manuscript, continuing as James's words lingered. "My brother's middle name was Thomas. He was given this middle name after my grandfather, Thomas Young. But I think this name fits my brother well because it was also the name of a well-known Apostle of Jesus. Many know this Apostle as doubting Thomas for his famous skepticism of Jesus's resurrection."

Picking up his Bible, he turned to the Gospel of John chapter 20, the heart of his sermon.

"When Jesus was resurrected from the dead," Peter began, "he appeared to several of his disciples, but Thomas wasn't one of them. So when he heard that they had seen Jesus he was like, 'No way! Unless I see the nail marks, unless I put my finger in those holes and my hand in his side, I will not believe.'"

He paused, put down his Bible and then asked, "How many of us have been there? With God, with faith...with Jesus? My brother was there." Peter paused again and smiled. "In fact, we ran up a pretty hefty Founders tab talking about those doubts and his questions."

Several people laughed. His parents shot each other a look of embarrassment.

"James doubted just like Thomas doubted. Just like some of us have doubted. And the same words Jesus had for his disciples are the same words he had for James and many of us here today. *Stop doubting and believe!*"

Peter turned back to the Gospel of John and read:

> *A week later his disciples were in the house again,*
> *and Thomas was with them. Though the doors*
> *were locked, Jesus came and stood among*
> *them and said, "Peace be with you!" Then he*
> *said to Thomas, "Put your finger here; see my*
> *hands. Reach out your hand and put it into*
> *my side. Stop doubting and believe."*

Peter paused, and then exclaimed, "*Stop doubting and believe!* Honestly, that's what I wish I could say to James right now. Bro, stop your doubting and just believe already!"

He paused again, looking at his friends seated in the back row for reassurance. Izzy smiled at him, cheering him on. Jake nodded him along, too.

"Honestly, it's what I want to tell myself today. You see, a few years ago I had what I would call a crisis of faith. I doubted, and then I gave up everything that I had believed as a child. And so I began to reimagine Christianity in order to make sense of our modern world, in order to make that faith relevant to our modern world. When I returned back to the Grand Rapids area to go to school to become a pastor, I took that same attitude with me. And I brought James along for the ride.

"But what I've been realizing the past few months is that what I don't need is to reimagine the Christian faith. What James needed was not to reimagine the Christian faith, either. No! What we needed was to stop doubting and just believe. Stop *reimagining* and start *rediscovering* what has always been central to belief in Jesus as Lord and God."

Peter caught Maggie and Danny nodding in agreement.

Surprise and delight had taken hold of them as they watched their son voice what they had been insisting on since he'd returned.

"And right here, Thomas does just that. He exclaims, '*My Lord and my God!*' You see, he cast aside his doubt because of his experience with Jesus. And so he believed once more. But Jesus says something very interesting in response. Listen to verse 29, '*Then Jesus told him, "Because you have seen me, you have believed; blessed are those who have not seen and yet have believed."*'"

"Great Thomas! Jesus says. You've experienced me and seen me with your own eyes. Of course *now* you believe. But blessed are those people who have not seen me and yet have left their doubts behind and believe. Believe that I died for the sins of the world. Believe that I was raised back from the dead and actually defeated death in the process. Believe that you might have life by believing in my name!"

Peter received several *"Amens"* of hearty approval. He paused, remembering what VanDyke had told him. *Never give false hope. But don't take it away either.* His advice gave him courage to press forward to say what he wanted to say next.

"James may have struggled with doubts," Peter continued, "but he believed. Sure, he pushed back against his childhood faith, but as a child he put his faith in Jesus. Sure he hadn't gone to church in a while, but that didn't mean he gave up on God."

He struggled with how to put into words what he hoped to be true: that though James had strayed, he remained in God's family. He decided to cut it off and go into his closing.

"Sure, it sucks that James Thomas Young died so suddenly and so early. But here's the thing: it's not the end of his story. Death doesn't have the final word—God does. James's story isn't over because James embraced God's story. While James didn't attend church and he struggled with life, he did come to the point where he gave his life over to God. You all know that it wasn't James's way to make a big fuss about things, and so I won't either, but I'd like to invite you all to bow your heads with me. And if something I said resonated with you and you'd like to follow James's lead in finding your story in God's Story you can do what James did."

Peter stared out at the room full of bowed heads and closed eyes and then continued. "Right now you can *confess* you are a rebel in need of rescue. *Ask* God to forgive the things you've done against him and your neighbor. *Receive* Jesus as your King, and *trust* in Jesus's death and resurrection for your own new life. If you'd like to do that now, in the quietness of this moment silently pray this prayer:

> *God I confess that I am a rebel*
> *I've not loved you with my whole heart*
> *I've not loved my neighbor as myself*
> *I am truly sorry and I humbly turn from my way*
> *   of living*
> *For the sake of Jesus Christ*
> *have mercy on me and forgive me.*
> *Jesus, I believe that you went to the cross for me*
> *   and I thank you for that sacrifice.*
> *Jesus, I believe that you paid the price for my*
> *   rebellion and I trust in that payment for my*
> *   rescue.*
> *Jesus, I believe that God raised you from the dead*
> *   and I want to experience that new life myself.*
> *Now, God, take my life, I give it to you*
> *and let it be all for you and for your glory.*
> *Amen.*

The room sighed a collective "*Amen.*"

"Yes, this day we mourn the loss of our son and brother and friend. But we do not grieve like the rest of the world, because we have hope. We believe that Jesus Christ has died, he has risen from the dead, and he will come again. And we also believe that God will bring with Jesus those who have died in him. Right now, James is with his Savior, but one day when Jesus returns, James will be brought back to life along with all of us who have joined James in giving our lives to Christ. So, this day, be encouraged by these hopeful words, because we and James will be with the Lord forever. Amen."

Peter made his way down off the platform and sat next to his father, who took his hand and squeezed it. He looked up at his dad, who was beaming with pride, tears streaming down his face. His mother smiled and mouthed "Thank you," giving Peter the same encouraging squeeze.

The director of the funeral home who had prepared James's body and casket made his way to the front and announced the conclusion of the memorial service. He invited the pallbearers to the front in order to bring James's casket out to the awaiting hearse.

Peter and Johnny got up, along with four other cousins. Maggie and Danny also stood in order to follow their son out of the church, and then out to JT's final resting place on the edge of town.

A SMALL GROUP gathered at Coopersville Cemetery just north of town. The Young family and extended family were invited to pay their final respects to James. Before he was lowered into the ground, Peter read from Revelation 21, the passage of Scripture that promised *'a new Heaven and a new Earth.'* When he read the verse about God *'wiping every tear from their eyes'* and there not being anymore *'death or mourning or crying or pain,'* Peter added "or drug overdoses or suicide," giving voice to the gathered groups' collective pain and frustration.

When Peter finished, he sat on one of the velvet covered chairs along with his parents and brother. The cemetery attendant began lowering James into the ground. As the ground consumed his brother's body inch by inch, Peter's mind wandered once more to the preceding months, to the conversations he had with his brother about faith, life, and everything in between.

Unlike before, however, regret didn't chase his mind's wandering. Instead, he was thankful. Thankful to have had the opportunity to walk with his brother through one of the most important moments in his journey. Thankful to have spoken the words he did and have at least some impact on the very words he read that afternoon from his brother's diary.

But alongside that thanksgiving came confusion. Confusion about why his brother had made peace with his life, made peace with death and his "eternal future," as James put it. Confusion about what his brother believed. Confusion about where his brother was on the other side of death.

What kind of God would send James away to be punished for millions and millions of years? Peter wondered, the agony becoming more than he could bear alongside his brother's descending shell.

He pushed this thought away, resisting the urge to make final judgment, realizing that he could never know. Not that it didn't matter, but that at this point it was between James and God.

The modest wooden casket arrived at its destination with a muffled thud. The finality of the moment began to settle into Peter's consciousness in a way he hadn't fully considered. He looked around at the surrounding green plots that held hundreds of other brothers and sons, sisters and daughters, parents and spouses. He looked back at the empty space above the hole in the ground where his brother's casket had just been sitting.

Unlike at any time since this ordeal began four days ago, it hit him brutally hard that his brother was actually dead. That he was gone and would never again roll up the drive way in his rusty, creaky Plymouth Breeze. And that meant no more Founders, no more book club, no more discussions and conversations about deep things. When he married, JT wouldn't be standing next to him. His future kids wouldn't know their Uncle James or benefit from his wisdom and kind-hearted care.

The weight of this realization became heavier with each passing minute. He joined his parents and brother by throwing a flower into the black hole that had just become his brother's final place of rest.

CHAPTER 39

THE SCHOOL YEAR ended with a flurry of activity that nearly buried Peter.

The first was a Greek translation project on the first three chapters of the Gospel of John. It wouldn't have been so bad, except Dr. Morris was keen on having his students outline every aspect of the adjectives, prepositions, nouns, articles, and verbs in every verse. It was death by conjugation for nearly two weeks.

A group presentation on the major literary genres of Scripture was almost as equally painful because it required Peter to work with a group, which as an introvert was as painful as the Greek translation worksheets. Surprisingly, not every final assignment felt like work.

A paper on personal spiritual formation helped Peter plot a routine that would help him pray, read the Bible, and engage spiritual disciplines in a way he'd always wanted but never got around to doing.

His final paper of the semester was for VanDyke's class. This juicy assignment forced Peter to articulate his view of God's revelation of himself to humanity and the nature of the Bible. He relished the assignment because it gave him a chance to spar with his favorite professor.

While the end-of-the-school-year pace had worn Peter down over the past four weeks, it served as a welcomed distraction from the loss of his brother and fallout from his death. Peter had locked away unaddressed feelings that he'd much rather avoid than confront. Most of them had to do with his brother's journey. Others had to do with his own. The past several months walking alongside his brother in conjunction with his seminary journey had created discordant tension, the likes of which Peter hadn't dealt with since the first time his faith ruptured back in DC. He sensed a similar breach was forming thanks to James.

And thanks to Dr. Calvin VanDyke. He was greeted by this man and nicknamed Prosurgent Pete even before his first semester began. Now he was ending the year with an exam for his class, typing the final lines of his final exam.

Peter insisted that it was all VanDyke's fault for the fissures that had formed in the bedrock of his Prosurgent faith. And now he was working on his final exam for the very class that gave rise to those fissures.

It was a fitting end to this first leg of his seminary journey, pecking away at his laptop answering questions on the nature of revelation, nature of Scripture, and God's attributes. Because not only had he come back home to his Coopersville home again, he had pivoted back toward his spiritual home again, too, thanks to the guidance and teachings of VanDyke.

"That should do it," Peter mumbled, typing a period at the end of the final sentence of the final question of his eight-page theology exam. He saved the document to his thumb drive in order to print it out in the computer lab next door. As the printer spit out the pages to his exam, Peter considered everything those paragraphs represented.

Growth, knowledge, wisdom, change, shift.

He thought of another as he grabbed the final page: *backwards.*

Am I moving backwards?

He allowed the word to tumble around in his head as he walked back to his SysOne classroom.

He remembered voicing such a fear to VanDyke over their first lunch, fearful that he would move backwards by reconsidering the fundamentals of the Christian faith. Standing next to VanDyke's own rusty Honda hatchback, Peter recalled voicing his fear of turning back toward the version of the Christian faith that had ruled most of his life. It was one of his fears of returning back home in the first place. For him, diverting from the his current Prosurgent path meant returning to fundamentalism. He couldn't see any other way around it, and he'd die before he'd allow that to happen.

Die before becoming a *regressive* Christian.

VanDyke looked up from the book he was reading as Peter walked back into the classroom.

"So is this for the heresy pile or historic orthodoxy one?" VanDyke smiled as Peter stapled his exam.

"Probably a little of both," he shot back, handing in his exam.

VanDyke whistled as he thumbed through the stack. "Eight pages? And single spaced? Do you want to send me to my early grave?"

"Hey, it's your fault. You wrote the exam. So now you get to live with the consequences."

"I guess you're right," VanDyke said smiling. Drawing more serious he continued, "So how have you been the past few weeks, Pete?"

Peter shrugged. "Alright, I guess. As well as anyone can be after losing someone. Especially to a drug overdose."

"Sure. Well, I've been praying for you and your family. And I hope now that the semester has closed you can have some down time to take a break and process."

"I appreciate that. I think the summer will be good for processing for sure. And thanks for the school year. Haven't always seen eye to eye, but you were respectful and challenging, which I appreciated."

"I try to be. Even with heretics," VanDyke said with a wink.

Peter laughed. "And also thanks for talking with me as I work through this whole Prosurgent thing and historic Christian faith thing." He paused and smiled before adding, "And for helping me consider becoming a *regressive* Christian. Not that I am one or anything," Peter quickly added. "But thanks just the same."

"My pleasure, Prosurgent Pete!" VanDyke smiled. "Seriously, I've enjoyed our discussions and it's been great to see you grow."

"You mean, it's been great to see me become more like you, right?" Peter said, his mouth curling up in a wry grin.

"No, though that couldn't hurt. I mean, you've grown because you're really wrestling through the ideas. You're not just swallowing the latest Christian fad. I think you've seen that ideas have consequences, like we talked about in my office a month ago."

Ideas have consequences. Peter was reminded of his brother.

He took a breath, and said softly, "They sure do. Thanks again for everything Dr. Van Dyke. See you in September."

Peter left behind the school year as he left his final class of the semester. Waiting for him in the lobby were his two faithful friends.

"OK, I don't know about you but that test was wicked crazy," Jake said next to Izzy as Peter walked over, plopping on the couch on the other side of Izzy.

"Oh it wasn't so bad," Izzy said.

"Wasn't bad?" Jake exclaimed, turning to his Southern friend. "Those questions were way too sneaky."

"Sneaky? He gave us the questions beforehand!"

"Whatever," he said, folding his arms in a huff. "That Dr. Van Dyke is a trickster for sure."

Peter and Izzy just smiled at each other, letting it go.

"I'll tell you one thing, I won't mind not seeing that trickster for a few months, that's for sure!" Izzy said, opening her laptop to check her e-mail.

"I don't know, he's sorta grown on me," Peter said, drawing stares from his two companions.

"Sounds like you two have a little thing going on, Prosurgent Pete," Jake jabbed.

"We have lunch sometimes," Peter said reddening. Changing the subject he asked, "So what's the plan for the summer?"

"I'm spending it with my memaw in Louisiana," Izzy said. "I'm taking a few classes over the Internet and gotta get a jump on that Hebrew we start this fall."

"Of course you do," Jake said, rolling his eyes. "Can't you take the summer off like the rest of us normal people?"

"Just because you're merely in an *M.A.* program doesn't meant the rest of us get to slack off," Izzy retorted, shocked by her condescension. "Oh, my! That sounded way more condescendin' than I meant for it to, Jake."

"Don't worry, us mere M.A. students don't offend too easily," Jake replied under his breath. "And why aren't you going home to Knoxville? Still trouble in paradise?"

Izzy looked crestfallen. Peter and Jake looked at each other as Izzy's eyes and head went down. "Actually, yes. There is." Looking up she said matter-of-factly, "My parents announced last month they're splittin'. I mean, Daddy had already kicked her out on the street with nothing to her name. But a month ago he made it official."

"I wish my parents would split," Peter mumbled, not thinking anyone heard. They did, confirmed by Izzy's look of horror. "I'm kidding! But definitely not a cool joke. Sorry. And I'm sorry your parents are divorcing. I remember around Christmas you said things were rough between them. What happened? Unless you don't want to talk about it..."

Izzy shook her head. "No, it's fine. It's so cliché, really. So typical of Southern men. Well, men in general." Taking a deep breath she revealed, "My mom caught him cheatin'."

"How horrible!" Jake said, shaking his head in disgust.

"And to make it worse, it was a lady from her church Bible study. Again, so cliché. So that's why I can't go home. And I really don't want to talk about it anymore." Izzy folded her arms and immersed herself in her e-mail.

"Real sorry to hear that Izz," Jake said softly.

"Me too," Peter agreed. He turned to Jake, and asked, "So what are you doing?"

"Me? Uh, well, I'm goin' back home to coal country to hang with my folks for the summer. Dad's got me something lined up with his company. I'll be bustin' tail all summer so I can earn enough to come back. The college ministry is on pause through the summer, as you can imagine. And since they don't pay all that well, I've got to earn some extra cash. It'll be nice seeing the folks. I don't get a chance to see them often throughout the year with my students and classes and all. And with my mom's health failing, it's always a good to get home."

Peter's eyebrow turned upright with news of Jake's mother. "Did I not tell you about Mom?" Jake asked, noting his surprise.

"No, what's wrong?" Izzy asked, disengaging from her e-mail to engage her friend.

"She's got cancer."

"Cancer?" Peter said. "I'm so sorry. How long has she had it?"

"It was diagnosed a few years ago. Ovarian cancer that they caught too late. Spread last year to her small intestines. They said she'd have three years, maybe. And that was two years ago."

"Wow, I'm so sorry Jake," Izzy said, putting her hand on top of his.

"Yeah, bro. Well, glad you can get home then!" Peter felt a twinge of regret, having not spent much time getting to know his two seminary friends. Here one friend's mother was on the brink of death and the other friend's family had been on the brink of the same. He had learned more in the last seventeen minutes about his two friends than he had learned in the past seven months of their friendship. Peter had always found it difficult to climb out of his own circumstances, his own life, and into the lives of other people. Maybe it was his introversion, maybe his selfishness. Regardless, in that moment he made a silent pact with himself to rectify this next year.

"I should head out," Peter said with a sigh. "Didn't get much sleep last night, and with everything else that's gone on the past month, I'm pretty beat."

"Petey pulled an all-nighter?" Jake asked with amusement. "I haven't done that since, like, college."

"Yeah, well, some of us have been a bit distracted the last month and haven't had much time to study," Peter replied with annoyance.

"Oh, right," Jake said, face falling. "Sorry. But we didn't get to you. What are you doing?"

"Yeah, what about you, darlin'?" Izzy asked.

"Not much really. Definitely don't have the drama you two do," he said. "I've got Sparrows and—"

"Lexi," Jake interrupted, elbowing his friend in the side.

Face reddening, Peter smiled. "And Lexi. And probably trying to process the last year to be honest. A lot has happened. And I don't just mean my brother."

"Like what?" Izzy asked.

"Like my whole reason for coming to seminary. Remember when we introduced ourselves at orientation?"

"Do I!" Jake exclaimed. "I remember you and your '*I wanna reimagine the Christian faith for our modern world*' bit. Sounded like an Amway salesman!"

"VanDyke said the same thing," Peter said standing, eliciting laughter from the three. "Let's just say, I'm not so sure about the reimagining part. Although I'm not really sure about anything anymore..."

Izzy stood and embraced him. "The summer will be good for you, methinks. It'll let you get your head right before school starts up again."

"I hope so. Because my head sure is jacked up!"

Jake stood as well. "You'll get through this, bro. And if not, I'll be right here to kick your butt back into gear."

Peter smiled, realizing the two great friends he had before him. "Thanks, guys. I'm gonna miss you both. You've really been there for me this year. So thanks."

"Well, we're not goin' anywhere!" said Izzy. "And you've got Facebook and e-mail and a cell phone. So don't be a stranger."

"Yeah, if you go dark I'm gonna drive back up to cowtown and smack you around!"

Peter said goodbye until the start of the next school year to two of the best friends he'd ever had.

PETER ARRIVED home to a vacant Cooper Manor. Mom was still at work. Johnny was finishing up his own exams. Dad was interviewing for a seasonal summer position at a lawn care company. He relished the stillness the early afternoon gave him to unwind from an intense day after an intense marathon week toward the end-of-semester finish line.

After making himself a PB&J and grabbing a glass of cold milk, Peter headed up to what had become his home for the past eight months. He couldn't believe his first year of seminary had wound to a close. It was now the beginning of May, one year to the date Peter had decided to return back home. He had made the decision to return to the place he had fled six years prior, vowing never again to return.

"What a year," Peter sighed, setting down his simple meal on a large stack of books next to his bed. He flopped on a pile of clothes his mother must have put on his bed when she vacuumed. He allowed his eyes the luxury of closing shut, and his mind the luxury of drifting off into a short cat nap.

As bone tired as he was, it didn't happen. He couldn't sleep despite how utterly spent he felt. This had been the pattern for several weeks now. Peter would lay awake for hours, drifting in and out of a restless, weary slumber that never made it to REM. Part of it was born out of panic for fear of not finishing his assignments. Part of it was the result of the past crazy eight months, culminating with his brother's death. And part of it was the result of that death.

After resigning himself to the same pattern of restless non-sleep, he turned his head and noticed JT's journal perched on top of his antique roll-top desk.

Peter went to it, having left it alone since his backpacking trip a few weeks ago. He picked it up, his arms feeling heavy from James's weighty words. He brought it to his bed and set it down. He stared at the ceiling, fighting back a well of tears that threatened to leak from his eyes. The sense of responsibility beginning to overtake him, yet again.

"No," he said, wiping his eyes on his sleeve. "This is not my fault. It's those damn ideas' fault!" Peter pounded his bed.

He wiped his eyes again and sighed, understanding it wasn't Prosurgent's fault, either. But the ideas that helped James reimagine his faith, reconstruct his faith after demolishing it, did have consequences. Permanent, lasting consequences for both James and the entire Young family.

"Ideas have consequences," Peter said with a deep sigh. "They sure do."

He tossed JT's journal over to a pile of books sitting at the foot of his bed and got up to retrieve his untouched sandwich and now lukewarm milk.

After witnessing firsthand the consequences that Prosurgent ideas can have on someone's journey, his brother's no less, Peter wondered how he could move forward in his own spiritual quest.

He walked over to his turret window as the sky began to darken from an impending thunderstorm. "I can't keep going down this path of...liberalism!"

Peter caught himself. Liberal.

He chuckled and rolled his eyes at his own characterization of Prosurgent theology, a characterization his parents had made using a label that was akin to atheism.

"So what's the alternative? Fundamentalism?" Peter sneered with a mouthful of sandwich, bread sticking to the roof of his mouth. He continued staring out the window at the world below.

I maybe from there, but I won't go back there!

But then where would he go?

He took a sip of milk. "I'm trapped. I've got nowhere to turn. To the left is liberalism. To the right is fundamentalism."

He sighed deeply and flopped down in his chair. His right temple began to throb under the assault of his anxiety and confusion—from the fear of returning back again.

A light rain began to coat the panes of Peter's bedroom window. Muffled thunder rumbled several miles away. Peter closed his eyes, as much from weariness as it was to pray.

"Lord, I don't know where to turn," he mumbled aloud. "I'm scared. I'm worried about where my life with you is going. It's such a burden—"

His prayer was interrupted by an answer he wasn't expecting:

Peter, My love is enough for you, for your journey.

"Yes, Lord, but here I am training to be a pastor and I don't even know up from down and what's what with you. I'm so confused! Please take away this burden of confusion."

Again, the interruption: *My grace is enough for you, son.*

"But I'm so weak..." he offered with a sigh.

In the next breath Peter had his answer.

Peter, my grace is sufficient for you, for my power is made perfect in your weakness.

Peter's eyes blinked open as he remembered the writings of Paul in 2 Corinthians. "For when I am weak, then I am strong."

I sure don't feel strong! Peter thought as the rain began to strengthen its assault on his window.

Could it be enough for me that God would be strong during my spiritual journey? Peter wondered. *Out of fundamentalism, through liberalism, and beyond?*

Thunder clapped loudly as the storm muscled its way into Peter's afternoon. He opened his eyes suddenly, awakened from his trance. He watched as the branches from the sycamore trees out front began to sway, beating their arms against his window.

So how do I go from here? Where do I turn from here?

Peter paused mid-thought, closing his eyes and letting the inevitable words rise to the surface.

Vintage Christianity.

As ironic and odd-sounding of a term as it was, it did carry a nice ring to it. And wasn't that what he was doing anyway, if he was honest with himself? By rediscovering and retrieving the historic Christian faith, wasn't he returning and going back again? Going vintage?

While he didn't quite know the answer to his questions about his way forward, he had a sneaking suspicion that he'd receive answers in his second year back home.

At least, he prayed he would.

ENJOY A REDISCOVERED FAITH?

A big thanks for joining Peter Daniel Young and friends on their journey to reimagining out how faith connects to their world!

Here's what you can do next:
If you loved the book and have a moment to spare, **a short review is much appreciated.** Nothing fancy, just your honest take. Spreading the word is probably the #1 way you can help authors like me and help others enjoy the story.

Ready to continue Peter's quest to reimagine his faith? Grab the next book in the series in fall 2019. *A Ruined Faith* picks right up where Peter left off in his story.

You can also join another adventure by getting a full-length novel in my religious conspiracy thriller series for free! All you have to do is join the insider group to be notified of specials and new releases by going to this link: www.jabouma.com/faith-reimagined

Continue the journey exploring a faith reimagined with your free course! Details on the next page or at www. faithreimagined.org.

378   ENJOY A REDISCOVERED FAITH?

Continue the journey exploring a faith reimagined with your free course! Details on the next page or at www. faithreimagined.org.

Join Peter Daniel Young's own journey of exploration reimagining faith today.

Discover more at faithreimagined.org

Use discount code **RDF2FREE** *at checkout*

Are you interested in exploring the essence of the Christian faith but don't know where to start?

You're invited to an online learning experience designed for readers of this series to extend the reading experience and offer a way to explore the major elements of Christianity—reimagining your faith along the way.

Get free access to your course at www.faithreimagined.org and continue the journey beyond the book that Peter himself embarked on and continues through the series.

Simply apply the above discount code at checkout when you join the basic course at www.faithreimagined.org/join.

AUTHOR'S NOTE

The story in these pages is a work of fiction. Yet it is more true to
life than I could have imagined on my own as it follows many of
the same contours of the real lives of real people.

Including my own.

You see, this story is loosely based on my own spiritual journey. It follows the major plot points during a season of my life
that followed a personal crisis of faith I experienced fifteen years
ago as a Christian twentysomething. So I wrote the book I wished
I had and my parents had during this season of questioning and
doubt. A book that would help me wade through my questions
and confusion, a book that would offer some insights and direction—all so I could more authentically follow the One who died
and gave himself up for me and passionately join his mission of
rescue and re-creation in my world.

I chose to tell my own spiritual coming of age story through a
fictional lens to hopefully provoke a conversation about faith, life,
and everything in between. It could very well have been a nonfiction memoir-style book, but I hope this way of sharing my own
journey through fiction rang true, and there is resonance with it

for those similarly wrestling with the essence of Christianity and its connection to life.

Much of what Peter experienced I myself experienced. Like him, I grew up in what could be called Christian fundamentalism. While I appreciate the fundamentals of the faith I learned and its deep commitment to the Bible that was instilled in me, I eventually pushed back against it, particularly when it no longer seemed to be able to inform my own faith and ministry. Because like Peter, I was also trained to give answers to questions no one is really asking, like how to get saved and how to get to heaven without much concern for faith's impact on life before life after death.

Unfortunately, this faith experience didn't equip me all that well to engage the world around me in meaningful ways, and it didn't help me answer people's truly visceral questions. So when I couldn't answer my friends' questions about faith and life, the weight and confusion of it all sent me on this journey to reimagine faith for our modern day—launching headlong into a progressive version of evangelicalism that had started asking questions about how the Christian message connects to our modern world, but then began to question the faith itself entirely. Which led to a return to a version of the faith I thought I had left behind.

Similar to Peter's own journey, my own represents a "coming back" to a place I vowed I'd never return—not to fundamentalism, but the fundamentals of the faith. Or as Dr. VanDyke playfully suggested, "Regressive Christianity," and as Peter suggests, "Vintage Christianity." I believe a whole new generation needs to rediscover and retrieve the vintage Christian faith. That's why I wrote this book. To help people realize that progressive Christianity doesn't have to be the only alternative to fundamentalist Christianity. I believe the antidote to both is the vintage faith, or historic Christian orthodoxy as it's more commonly known.

Which brings me to a few aspects to this story that connect to real life. I was fired from ministry in DC (you can read more of that story in *A Reimagined Faith*) and moved back to Grand Rapids to attend Grand Rapids Theological Seminary, served at Fellowship Covenant Church, and realized the need to rediscover and retrieve the vintage Christian faith after having left it in favor of progressive Christianity. Bryan McLaughlin is inspired from a similarly progressive Christian writer named Brian McLaren, whose *A New Kind of Christianity* inspired much of the quoted content in chapters 8, 12, 13, 21, and 23. Same for the quotations from Dale Pagels's book *A Christian Faith Worth Believing* in chapter 8, which was inspired by progressive Christian Doug Pagitt's book *A Christianity Worth Believing*. I also borrowed aspects of the book signing by Trevor Bohls at Barnes & Noble from an actual appearance by Rob Bell during the tour for his similarly titled book *Love Wins*. I wanted to let the content from these actual progressive works inspire these fictional ones in order to offer commentary on their progressive ideas—after all, ideas have consequences.

On the other side of my own dalliance with such progressive thinkers and their ideas, I do believe there is a hopelessness about the kind of Christianity they are promoting. Such progressive Christianity isn't hopeful because it isn't honest—about our rebellion again God, and our sorry state as rebels in need of rescue; about who Jesus is as both very God and very human; about the nature of his work, living the life we could not live and paying our price in our place on the cross to save us from our sins; about the hope of his actual, physical, bodily resurrection from the dead and all that means for our life now and in the future; and about the reality of judgment, that some will be judge outside of Christ alongside others who are judged in him to enjoy life everlasting with God the Father, Son, and Holy Spirit. And those ideas have ultimate consequences—illustrated in the life of JT.

When I set out to write the *Faith Reimagined* series, I made a few assumptions about you, the reader. I'm guessing you are currently or are on the verge of experiencing your own crisis of faith. Or maybe it's not a full-fledged crisis, but you're asking questions you haven't asked before and the creepy, crawly claws of doubt are beginning to prickle the back of your brain. Regardless, you're wondering if the Christianity of your childhood or past still connects to your modern world.

Maybe you're scared or empowered or thrilled or confused or any number of other emotions because of this crisis and period of questioning. And so you've come looking, not so much for answers, but for direction. Maybe you've read some other books looking for that direction—books that have inspired and encouraged you to explore and embrace a new kind of Christianity and to be a new kind of Christian. Maybe you're taken by those ideas or maybe you're skeptical—either way, you've come to this book to get another perspective in your quest to own your faith, maybe for the first time in your life.

Please know that I respect your journey and understand shades of it, and I'm deeply honored you've invited me along for the ride. Because I empathize with that journey, I wanted to write a set of books that offer my own story as a way to guide you along your own path of faith and life, offering what I hope are a few insights along the way. Perhaps the lessons I've learned will help.

I hope the faith journey of Peter Daniel Young is a helpful one, a journey you'll discover is less about him and more about the people he encounters along the way, and the Savior who is big enough to wade alongside us through our sea of questions and carry our boulder-sized doubts upon his shoulders. My hope is that you would learn what Peter begins to learn, and what I myself learned a decade ago: That it's only in going backward that we can truly move forward in our spiritual journey.

The vintage faith represents the core, the essence of what the Church has always believed and how it has always behaved. Another name for it is Nicene Christianity, for it follows the contours of the Nicene Creed and the beliefs which stem from it during the early Church. Regressive or vintage Christianity, then, represents a going backwards. It is not progressive on purpose. Because it's only in going backwards that our generation of Christians will truly move forward in its spiritual journey. That's true for Peter Daniel Young as much as it is for J. A. Bouma. As much as it is for you and your friends, too.

J. A. Bouma believes nobody should have to read bad religious fiction—whether it's cheesy plots with pat answers or misrepresentations of the Christian faith and the Bible. So he wants to do something about it by telling compelling, propulsive stories that thrill as much as inspire, while offering a dose of insight along the way.

Order of Thaddeus Action-Adventure Thriller Series

Holy Shroud • Book 1

The Thirteenth Apostle • Book 2

Hidden Covenant • Book 3

American God • Book 4

Grail of Power • Book 5

Templars Rising • Book 6

Faith Reimagined Spiritual Coming-of-Age Series

A Reimagined Faith • Book 1

A Rediscovered Faith • Book 2

A Ruined Faith • Book 3 (2020)

A Resurrected Faith • Book 4 (Late 2020)

ABOUT THE AUTHOR

J. A. Bouma believes nobody should have to read bad religious fiction--whether its cheesy plots with pat answers or misrepresentations of the Christian faith and the Bible. So he wants to do something about it by telling compelling, propulsive stories that thrill as much as inspire, while offering a dose of insight along the way.

As a former congressional staffer and pastor, and bestselling author of over thirty religious fiction and nonfiction books, he blends a love for ideas and adventure, exploration and discovery, thrill and thought. With graduate degrees in Christian thought and the Bible, and armed with a voracious appetite for most mainstream genres, he tells stories you'll read with abandon and recommend with pride -- exploring the tension of faith and doubt, spirituality and culture, belief and practice, and the gritty drama that is our collective pilgrim story.

When not putting fingers to keyboard, he loves vintage jazz vinyl, a glass of Malbec, and an epic read -- preferably together. He lives in Grand Rapids with his wife, two kiddos, and rambunctious boxer-pug-terrier.

facebook.com/jaboumabooks

twitter.com/bouma

amazon.com/author/jabouma